THE
SPOILED
HEART

ALSO BY SUNJEEV SAHOTA

Ours Are the Streets
The Year of the Runaways
China Room

THE
SPOILED
HEART

SUNJEEV SAHOTA

ALFRED A. KNOPF CANADA

Published in 2024 by Alfred A. Knopf Canada, a division of Penguin Random House Canada
Limited, Toronto, and simultaneously in the United States by Viking, an imprint of Penguin
Random House LLC, New York, and in Great Britain by Harvill Secker,
an imprint of Penguin Random House Ltd., London. Distributed in Canada by
Penguin Random House Canada Limited, Toronto.

www.penguinrandomhouse.ca

Knopf Canada and colophon are registered trademarks.

Library and Archives Canada Cataloguing in Publication

Title: The spoiled heart : a novel / Sunjeev Sahota.
Names: Sahota, Sunjeev, 1981- author.
Identifiers: Canadiana (print) 2023046954X | Canadiana (ebook) 20230469558 | ISBN
9781039010529 (hardcover) | ISBN 9781039010536 (EPUB)
Classification: LCC PR6119.A355 S66 2024 | DDC 823/.92—dc23

This is a work of fiction. Names, characters, places, and incidents either are the product of
the author's imagination or are used fictitiously, and any resemblance to actual persons,
living or dead, businesses, companies, events, or locales is entirely coincidental.

Jacket design: Jaya Miceli
Jacket images: (sky) Airbruh / Shutterstock;
(homes) shokaib ashfaq /EyeEm/ Adobe Stock

Printed in the United States of America

1st Printing

Penguin
Random House
KNOPF CANADA

THE
SPOILED
HEART

1

'Helen Fletcher's returned home?'

Until then, on a call to his baby sister in the spring of 2017, Nayan had no clue what her name was. He'd seen her around a dozen times, maybe more, first her photo – on the phone of that woman from the nursing agency – but most often on those evenings his run coincided with her end-of-day beer, when there she'd be, knee flexed on the busted wooden rail of her porch, in shorn-off denims and a Bud raised to her lips. Hers was the very last house before the unmarked lane shrank to a track rutted by quad bikes, and her nearest neighbour, The Saracen's Head, was a good way back down the hill, a seclusion that dealt his jog past her a tense self-consciousness. Nayan always resolved to say hello, always bottled it. He was out of practice, sure, and also unaccustomed to feeling intimidated: the back of her head against the post, imperious, not giving a shit, and her drive – gravelled, flaunting weeds, too pinched for anything but the smallest hatchback – was far too steep, as if she really was up there on her decrepit throne gazing down her nose at him. He saw her up close about a week before calling his sister, when he was waiting in line at the post office. It was those denims again. Cut-off denims on a cold April morning. The photo must have been from a few years ago, because in the flesh she was older, albeit – and he registered this with a start – still younger than him, and with greying blonde hair hanging loose and jutting cheekbones that gave her entire face a sealed quality. At the counter, she spoke minimally, inaudible to Nayan, collected her gas card and Silk Cuts from Margot, and left, unlit fag in her mouth, wicker shoulder-bag crushed under an armpit.

As if by magic, he saw her five more times that week: twice when he was out running and passed by her porch; in The Head on the Friday night, where he clocked her in her care-worker's uniform; in Aldi the next day, too, grim-facedly studying the back of a Thai green curry kit; and finally: once more in the post office, where Margot caught him watching her leave.

'Looks good out,' he said, putting red-top milk, multi-vitamins and bananas on the counter.

'This is the post office. The shop is over there,' and she pointed to the next counter along. He shoved his items across even as Margot didn't move because the same fucking G-G-G-Granville till served both post office and shop.

'She looked familiar,' Nayan lied.

'Mm-hmm,' Margot said.

'That woman. I can't place her, though. She's new, right? Newish?'

Her mouth a thin rouged seam, Margot plucked the note – she only took cash – from Nayan's fingers.

'I wonder why she looks familiar,' he pressed on.

'Perhaps because she once hit out at the headteacher,' Margot said, in an airy way that intimated she knew all the secrets of this old estate.

'Ah, yes. That must be it. Was it Nether—'

'You'd have long left school by then.' She slapped his change onto the counter, slammed the till shut. 'Your sister might remember her.'

'That so?' Sliding the coins off the counter and into his palm, Nayan said, 'You grow lovelier every day, Margot.'

As he was leaving, he saw her mimicking him in the glass pane of the door. He turned round, curbing his smile when her face froze. 'What's her name again?'

Why did he want her name? What was he going to do with her name? Google it? Certainly, she was an outsider, or she at least projected the aura of an outsider, something he found deeply appealing. Either way, Margot never told him her name, if she even knew it. She seemed altogether too busy stealing a glance at the rose oval of her wristwatch and taking careful note of what he'd bought and what he was wearing, ready to write these details down in a slow neat hand the moment he left, because surely no good could come from this brown man's interest in that white woman, and surely – her mind racing gleefully on – a police officer would be calling in the days and weeks ahead to ask if she could possibly shed any light on who might want to harm the quiet, if unashamedly dressed, woman who lived so remotely? Outside the post office, Nayan spat at the ground, took a steadying breath, and ploughed onwards, to the hardware store for some caulking (leaky bathroom), and then home to call his sister.

'So you do remember her? This Helen Fletcher.'

'Barely. She must've been, what, two years below me.'

That made her thirty-seven, five years younger than him. 'But you know her name.'

'A kid, a *girl*, kicks the shit out of the headteacher? Her name travels.'

He switched ears. 'Merv?'

'Then she left. Broke his nose, I heard.'

'Why?'

'Oh, I dunno. I was away by then. How long she been back?' Sonia asked quickly.

'A few months? She was meant to be Dad's home help, but she turned it down. I can't help wondering why.'

There was a cool silence as Sonia weighed things up: did she need to once again acknowledge Nayan's sacrifice? Because while she lived her zingy lawyer's life with her girlfriend in Chicago, it had been twelve years now that he'd been caring for their ill father alone, a man who obstinately continued to beat whatever odds the doctors threw at him. Speaking of illness . . .

'How's Trump?' Nayan asked, forever the big bro, rescuing his sister from tight corners. 'Gotta be dementia, right?'

But Sonia didn't want rescuing, and looped back, asserting herself. 'They won't tell you? Why she turned it down?'

'Said she wasn't feeling it.' He thought for a moment. 'She left town for punching a teacher? Bit drastic.'

4

'Why you so interested in her?' He loathed, while being half-buzzed by, the teasing lilt of her voice. 'Are you? Interested?'

More than interested. He was rapidly becoming beguiled by this Helen Fletcher. Her direct face, its worries withheld, the challenge with which she set down her beer in the pub, the powerful absence of pleasantries, her refusal of spontaneity; essentially, her willingness to court disapproval meant that for the first time in years, decades, Nayan felt himself captivated, without them having exchanged a word.

He told me all this, their story, several years later, when the country was still wrestling with the pandemic, the talk all of boosters, and I found him occupying a room in a multi-let house in the centre of Chesterfield.

Growing up, though we lived only a mile or so apart, we'd not had much to do with one another. Nayan was six years older than me – I'm closer to Helen's age – and attended Netherthorpe, the former grammar whose Victorian façade still carried weight in the local imagination, when really it was every bit as rough and failing as Springwell, its rival and my concrete block of a school. I'm not saying I didn't know Nayan. There were at most five Asian families in the town back then, all Sikh households, and all, to a man, living above their shops. Sometimes we got together, for Diwali usually, each family taking turns to host. I have jumbled memories of orange, swirly carpets and cord settees that folded out, and of the women, my mother among them, singing hymns and frying crackers in Formica kitchens while, in the front room, great images of gods loured over our fathers and their whiskies. The rest of us would congregate in a kid's bedroom, and I have a clear recollection of one Diwali where I was playing Dynablaster on a second-hand Amiga 500+. I'd have been perhaps eight, joypad in hand and gangling over the monitor because the swivel-chair was taken. All noise was blotted out until a cheer went up behind me, applause that met with my screen death, and I turned round and saw Nayan accept his umpteenth arm-wrestle win. He was fourteen, athletic, the peak of his Steelers cap tilted upwards so his fringe swept across his forehead. He clapped his (older) opponent on the shoulder, handed him back the pound coin, and with that easy smile said, 'I got lucky, man.'

I remember being struck by how cool that was, how magnanimity only furnished his standing among us. Later, we were called into the lounge for final prayers, and since all the rooms were on one level, I stood just inside the bedroom door, keen to bagsy the Amiga. Beneath a photo of a haloed Guru Nanak, an auntie chunni-ed her head and recited. All else was silence. The men stood tottering, holding onto a kid, any kid, for ballast; except, that is, for my dad and Nayan's, who had their arms around one another's shoulders, swaying in place like old chums. Like me, Nayan was near the back, but he didn't see me watching, not at first, and he definitely didn't think anyone spied him tugging the pink jumper of the girl in front. It was Deepti, whom he'd go on to marry and divorce, and the pink jumper was paired

6

with tight white jeans that held the smooth expansion of her hips in a way that did something to my young boy's stomach. Her lightweight chunni was very much an after-thought, balanced over big thin curls lacquered with hairspray, and she didn't turn around at Nayan's behest. She only smiled, twisted her hand behind her back and gave him the finger. He put three Hula Hoops on that finger – there were plates of nibbles on the sideboard – which she brought up to her face and ate behind her hand. Transfixed, I watched them do this twice more, until Nayan caught me looking, winked, and offered the bag of crisps. Before I could shake my head, the auntie's voice cracked at the end of its crescendo and we all folded onto our knees and touched our foreheads to the carpet.

As the Nineties creaked round and I approached my own teens, a couple of the families sold up at a loss and left town, done in by the recession, and the Diwali and Vaisakhi meets began drying up, until they stopped hap-pening altogether. The name Nayan Olak still occasionally got aired in our house – after he won the regional high jump, or when a picture of him appeared in the *Derbyshire Times*, raising funds for former miners suffering with chronic emphysema – and we'd attended his wedding, a speedily organised affair at a community centre with jugs of Five Alive and KP Roasted Peanuts in white paper bowls, all pulled together once some envious, vengeful priest discovered Nayan and Deepti locked in an embrace 'like sucking Velcro'.

I don't remember much about the fire that killed his mother and his child. I was sixteen and struggling, and

7

once I started to get my act together, following a summer in India, I left immediately for university in London and avoided my hometown. Truth be told, Nayan Olak never bothered my mind, not until around two years ago, when I went back to Chesterfield because the only school friend I'd kept in touch with had had his first child and invited me to wet the baby's head.

This was just before the first lockdown, February 2020, and the once busy marketplace was now familiarly sad, with its closing-down sales and boarded-up windows, its Betfreds. Walking the cobbles that cold night, I was once more the cornershop boy, the pedlar's son, whose life felt small and imprisoning, half hung out to dry, all the usual intimations, I guess, when a nearly forty-year-old visits his unhappy past. I arrived outside the bar with a feeling of relief – here was life! – and watched for a while through the large uplit window. People. Laughter. Drinking. I saw my friend, Rory. He was keeping half an eye on the entrance, no doubt mindful of me walking into a busy, small-town bar full of only white people. I've always liked that about Rory, his natural reserves of unshowy empathy. I could see how the evening would begin: I'd walk inside, throwing on a grin, and Rory and I would shake hands homie-style, as we always do, honouring with irony the provincial boys we once were, and would forever be. He'd introduce me to those six others around his table – 'He's a writer,' Rory'll say – and I'd chart them recalibrating their idea of me, and of this evening. There would be wariness, perhaps, because I was an interloper in the group: unknown to them, brown, educated, a writer.

By now I'd lost the voice of my younger self, the Derby-shire teenager with his bare infinitives and rusty vowels. My job was to listen, to observe, question, guess; trying to see what was inside their lives, all lives. Trying on these lives. And I was still watching through the window, my sentimentality like a force holding me in place, when a hand came down on my arm and spun me round. I waited for the blow. I saw a bottle in a pink palm. But the man was smiling, beaming, in fact.

'Boss! I thought it were you. Man, haven't seen you for donkeys. How's tha bin?'

Pallid, skinny, more freckled than not, with an over-eager, manically nodding manner. He was high. I didn't recognise him, thought he meant 'boss' as in 'mate', and fixed him as someone I'd gone to school with maybe, though he looked much younger.

'Finn!' he said, nodding, gesturing wildly at himself.

'Course. Long time. What you been up to?' Did he know me from my wayward days? Was that why I couldn't place him?

He looked over to a woman leaning against the glass, scrolling through her phone. 'Gave me my first job! Got me into the union!' She smiled vacantly. 'Must be what? Fifteen years?'

'At least. But it's good to see you. You take care now.'

'Where you been, though?' he said, semi-blocking me from the door. 'I heard you'd left the union and gone rogue? That you'd gone a bit – I dunno. Strange.'

'Right. Well, it's compli—'

'I didn't believe it. I can't imagine the old place

9

without you repping. You *were* the union for most of us.' He tapped his bottle against my shoulders, one at a time, as if knighting me. 'Nayan Olak *is* the fucking union.'

A real blast from the past; and between raising glasses and buying rounds, whether standing at the urinal or at the roar of the hand-dryer, his name kept on at me like torchlight in my eyes. Nayan Olak. I googled him on the bus back and watched YouTube clips where he demanded financial reparations for everyone whose ancestors were colonised, denounced Americans as murdering Zionists, and called the Manchester Arena bomber the main victim here. There were skits, too, of him explaining to white folk how to speak Punglish, or why bindis 'aren't your ting'.

When I got home to Sheffield, I asked my parents – living with us while their new bungalow was refurbished – if they remembered Nayan, and Mum's eyes widened, such wistful sorrow.

'The nicest boy. What was God thinking?'

'There was a death, right?'

'Two. In a fire. His mother and his little lad. He was, I'm not sure, four, five years old?'

'Jesus. Was it an accident, the fire?'

'They were asleep upstairs. And then he and Deepti divorced.' Mum, lost to her shadow in the kitchen counter, frowned. 'They never caught them. Who did it.'

'I thought I might look him up,' I said.

'Why?' Dad said, stirring tea. 'Leave the family in peace.'

'I'm not bothering them.'

'Make sure you don't. They've been through enough without you asking questions for some fiction novel.'

'Some novelly novel,' I muttered.

'Is his dad still alive?' Mum asked me. 'Pyara. Greasy man. This big, flash-Harry type. Hated running a shop. Thought he was destined for better things.' She cringed, shaking the image away.

'You could lay the same charge at me,' I said, half-smiling. 'Was there ever any suspicion he might have done it? An insurance job gone wrong? If he hated the shop so much, I mean.'

Mum looked at me with horror, disbelief. 'He lost his wife and grandson.'

I showed them Nayan's videos, which seemed to confuse Mum. 'But he always liked goreh. That's not who I remember.' She carried her mug over to the window, where the smoke from one chimney was meeting the call of the next. 'His mother was the same. She was strong. English worse than mine but confident, leading the way. I was at a party that night, can you believe,' Mum said, suddenly angry. 'I was dancing the night Muneet died. I've never forgiven myself.'

'Why are we still talking about this? It's upsetting your mum.'

'Those videos – she'd be turning in her grave,' Mum said.

'If she hadn't been cremated, you mean.'

'Sajjan!' Dad said, appalled, and he turned to Mum, who was still looking out the window, still frowning.

*

11

I wanted to meet him. In his videos he gave off a curdled charisma, was clearly intelligent, and his story seemed interesting. I'd been without an idea for a while; surely there was material here? I created a Facebook account and messaged him, got no reply, and then the pandemic swarmed, lockdowns were announced and the months staggered by as my wife and I tried to work while home-schooling our three children and accommodating my parents, who were trapped with us indefinitely now their renovation had grounded. It wasn't until late summer of the following year that I messaged him again, after a new video of his – 'The Virus Isn't Racist, You Are' – popped up in my feed. This time he replied, said he remembered my family, asked if Dad was still a Derby County fan. That same week, I drove to his address in the centre of Chesterfield and knocked on the door of a red-brick ter-race midway up a hilly avenue off the Sheffield Road. A housemate answered, but before she got a word out Nayan came rushing down the stairs behind her, his gut jiggling under his faded Manics T: 'I got it! He's for me.'

I put on my mask and followed him up to his room, which ran the entire length of the loft and was plenty big enough: double bed, clothes rail, two sofas, coffee table, mini fridge. The quilted green bedspread, diamond-patterned, was ruckled, unmade, and on the bedside table my three novels propped up a kettle that he now flicked on.

'I was looking out the window for you – did you bus?'

'I drove but parking—'

'Hang on.' He opened the dormer window so I could

take off my mask, and then he shut the Velux at the front, cutting out the lorries thundering towards the round-about. 'It's got so much worse lately.'

'It didn't used to be one-way, did it?'

'Christ, how long you been away?'

'I didn't know the Comet had become a Currys. That long.'

He laughed the same sudden laugh I remembered, good looks bursting through creased flesh but also, I couldn't help feeling, made glamorous by the nature of his losses, by the hypnotic allure of the bereaved parent. I couldn't stop staring. Where lay his grief? In his eyes? His head? Did it live submerged in a black pool at the base of his skull disturbed only when he was alone at night? 'I've not read them yet,' he said, nodding at my books, 'but remind me to get you to sign them. How's your latest doing? Not long out, is it?'

'Yeah, it's doing okay, yeah.'

'Reviews been good?'

I had a feeling he'd probably read all my reviews, seen all my interviews. It seemed likely that he prepared impeccably for any encounter. He would also know that I hated talking about my work, a detail I mentioned often enough. 'Yeah, can't complain. But, no, thanks for meet-ing me. For inviting me round. Appreciate it.' I gestured to one of the sofas. 'Mind if I take a pew?'

He said nothing, just kept semi-smirking, and then he went and sat down; with an exaggerated sweep of his arm – 'Please' – he invited me to the seat opposite.

'Thanks. Like I said, I was mistaken for you—'

'Finn! Blind as a bat and always so easily led.' He cocked his head to one side. His socked foot stopped its tapping against the table. 'The place is still full of smackheads.'

'I can believe it.' I looked away. Through the dormer window sat the large grassy roundabout that would take me out of this old town and back to my new city. The kettle, throwing its burbling fit, clicked off. 'But I was interested in the turn your life's taken. From union stalwart to anti-racist activist.'

'Pretty headline. But they're not mutually exclusive.'

'Maybe not. But there's been a change in emphasis. That's clear from your videos.'

His foot restarted its table-tapping, his tongue clacking, a parody of deep contemplation. Already I found him intriguing, even if mildly tiresome. His behaviour – knowing, low-key supercilious – seemed to sanction a brazenness of my own, and I appraised the room, more closely than before. The bed lay midway between the two sloping walls of the roof and I thought I saw rifles underneath it, puncturing the gloom. Peering, I recognised sawn-off ends, wooden poles, placards he'd shunted away just before I'd turned up. Rolled-up posters stood in a tall mess behind the clothes rail, and polystyrene food cartons, smeared with sauce, kept the large bin from closing. There was a sense of things running away with him, or of him trying to catch up.

'I don't like how you talk about us,' he said. 'It's all wrongheaded. You blame our community for everything. For not helping your parents. For hating immigrants. You show us no respect. In your book, even a fucking terrorist has a great white wife.'

'In my book you haven't read.'

'I've read enough. Enough to know all you do is slag us off from your writer's throne.'

'That's not—'

'Sajjan Dhanoa. Local writer. Except there's nothing local about you. Got out to London as quick as you could and never looked back. And now lives within spitting distance, spitting away, building a career out of making us look contemptible.'

'That's not fair,' I said, more firmly this time. I hadn't been expecting this. I'd prepared for a morning of reminiscing, of shared memories that reinforced how brutal this town was, for the clean bones of a story. 'I only want to ask the right questions.'

'You're so basic. If only he could know everything,' he said, in a tone of derision, 'then he'd understand everything, and everything could be forgiven.' He gave me a shrewd look. 'Ask the right questions? The ones that let you bomb the wrong people. All right, Blair.'

'Hey! Now that's below the belt.'

Thankfully, his face broke and he laughed, though for a few seconds there he'd been as still as a waiting grenade. 'Well, I'll have to read you properly and decide for myself. Until then, thanks for popping by. I'm sorry I didn't get round to making tea.'

I didn't protest and watched him in my rear-view mirror, waiting on the doorstep until I'd rounded the corner, the way my parents still do whenever visitors are leaving, even if it's the plumber. I wasn't certain he'd get back in contact, but I felt he would, that our initial meeting was more about him establishing a power play – he was politically adept, after all – so I wasn't surprised when, two weeks later, he WhatsApped: *You shoot pool?*

We became friends, hanging out, playing darts, pub quizzes, shooting pool, the breeze. It turned out he'd left the union he'd loved for over twenty years and was now the Yorkshire and Humberside lead of the Centre for the Abolition of Racism, an umbrella group tasked with coordinating activities between the UK's various anti-racism movements.

'It's so factional,' he said, between dart throws. 'Indians that need a chief, as dicks might say. That's where we come in. In theory.'

His father was still alive, thanks to the ministrations of a blue oxygen tank permanently at his side, and lived in a care facility on the outskirts of town. I asked if he visited him often.

'Not if I can help it.'

'I guess you did your time.'

'Over twelve years waiting on him. Too fucking right I did my time. He can rot alone.'

Through autumn and into winter, as the virus mutated and the nation braced for the Omicron onslaught, we left the pubs and went on weekly long walks through the Peaks, where we climbed great uplands of hawkweed and heather, cotton grass and bilberries, and ate packed lunches sitting on cold crags that evoked a view across the whole of England, its valleys and snaking roads and picture-perfect villages, a church spire fraying the rose-glow horizon. On these walks, he told a little more of his story each time – of Helen, his father, the fire, of a young man called Brandon – and over the months I tried to patch it all together. Sometimes, as I cleared away my lunch and zip-lock bags, he'd shuffle off and stand at the cliff edge, breathing in great lungfuls of air while lapwings darted nearby. At first, and as so often during those early meets, I thought he was being a self-dramatist, that he knew exactly what kind of tragic figure he cut posing there like that, with the long gaze out and the wind in his hair. But then I stopped thinking that.

'Shall we head back?' he'd call.

'Can do. No rush.' The silence up there felt magnificent and bright, giving everything a proper scale, clarity. It brought a comforting sadness. I suspect Nayan felt it, too.

He would nod. 'Yeah, let's wait. We've perhaps another hour of light yet.'

———

Nayan first became aware of Helen when the head of a homecare provider he'd been badgering for months finally turned up on his doorstep – here to, she said, assess their domestic context.

'I'm sorry it's taken so long. Everyone's getting older these days!'

'I feel like I'm on a hundred waiting lists but not moving up any one of them,' Nayan said.

'It's awful, isn't it?'

He showed her – Carole, she reminded him, in her claret suit – through to the living room, where his father sat, grey-stubbled and bald save for the slicked-back wings of hair at the sides. His breathing was rough and his cheeks hung heavy, clutching for dear life the dark red rind of his eyes.

'Hello, Pyara,' Carole said in a voice on its tippy-toes. 'How are you? My, I can see where your son gets his good looks from.'

'That her from the home? Tell her I'm not going into any fucking home.'

'We get this a lot,' Carole said to Nayan in a quick, explaining whisper.

'I just want a day a week to myself,' Nayan said. 'I'm not asking for anything more. Someone to come in and do his meals and check he's not licking the plug sockets.'

'No fucking home!'

Nayan made a face at Carole – ignore him. 'Does that sound doable?'

The way she inhaled, as if she were about to dive into the sea, wasn't promising. She asked for a minute; took out her phone. Nayan waited, and in the quiet he detected the caffeinated undertones in her minty breath, noticed the bars of grey tucked inside her flattened beehive. Mid-fifties? She was swiping through timetables, wincing, shaking her head. Going through the motions, settling into her role.

'It's just us, you see,' Nayan said.

'I do. I really do.'

'My mum died. When we had the shop and flat on the crescent. In the fire.'

Carole looked up, glossed lips parting in surprise. Coffee-stained canines. He imagined the empty flask still in her car, in its cup-holder, beside the breath spray. 'Oh God. I remember that.' She turned to Pyara, then back to Nayan, and he offered a pale smile to dispel any final doubt in her mind: yes, this really was that poor young man who'd lost his son in the blaze.

It wasn't the first time he'd used the fire to tilt things in his favour – only recently he'd invoked Veer's death in a council debate on bereavement leave that until then had been going the wrong way. In the abstract, it seemed a reprehensible thing to do, but in practice, in the act of doing it, it always felt as if he was calling upon his son's help and together they were fighting the system.

Scrolling back up her phone, as if she'd missed some-thing, Carole said, 'We've this new joiner who I'm certain will . . . Here she is . . . Yes!' She flashed her screen at Nayan. 'It looks like she could manage one or two days a week here. She's not very experienced, but we can see how it goes, can't we?'

'That'd be so great. Thank you.'

'She's local, too.'

When three weeks went by without word, he left mes-sages, unreturned. Only once Nayan threatened to protest outside her office – 'You can't treat people like this' – did Carole promptly call him back, apologising for the delay but, and you won't believe this, Niall, but there's still more people getting older every day! Trilling laughter.

'When can your person start?'

'She wasn't free, I'm afraid. But you're slap-bang at the top of my list. Believe me, I want to make this happen for you.'

'But you said she was new. That she had loads of space.'

'She just didn't feel she was the right person for this particular job.'

'She *refused*?'

'I'm confident I'll have someone with you inside the month.'

'Why'd she say no?'

He could hear the clicks of Carole's jaw, imagine the gun-to-head brain-exploding gesture she'd be making for her husband's benefit. *These clients, love, they want the moon on a stick!* 'People are funny things, aren't they?' More trilling laughter.

That was when he started spotting her – Helen Fletcher – everywhere around the estate: on her porch, waiting at traffic lights, buying gas from Margot's, though it was a full two months after Sonia supplied her name that he and Helen spoke for the first time. Late June, and he was out on an early-morning run, lacking sleep and thinking through that afternoon's speech, when he had to detour around the delivery truck blocking the pavement outside her house. He carried on to the road's end, the opening to the fields, but turned round at the sound of her voice, a clear bell of a sound, calm and insistent, devoid of accent.

Standing under the porch at the top of her drive, the broad sky a marvellous blue slate behind her, she was asking the driver, with all due sarcasm, how he'd suggest she get the fridge inside.

'It's just that, Sod's law, my hydraulic lift conked out on me yesterday.'

'Sorry, babes,' the delivery guy said, touching his cap to supplement the apology. 'Brand-new guidelines,' and he drove off, leaving the boxed fridge looking like a tall and ridiculous sentinel on the empty driveway.

She caught Nayan watching, as he hoped she would, so he felt compelled to wave and come forward, his hands flipped back on his waist as he regulated his breathing. He tapped the side of the box, his smile wide and relaxed. Whatever her reason for turning down the job, he would be the bigger man. 'Think between us we could manage it?'

She walked towards him with firm steps, from up in her hips, eyes ahead as if certain her existence meant something. The lower down the drive she came the more the sun, already smarting his back, caught her face, flushing the hollows around her neck.

She nodded up at him. 'The runner speaks.'

'It's been known.'

Sizing up the delivery, she crouched and crept her fingers under the box. 'Get the other end and catch it from tipping.'

Her place was as squat as all the other wood-panelled builds further down the lane: the front door swinging open into a stunted, dark hall, tall stairs directly ahead, the living room to the left full of more wooden things – floorboards, windows, shelving – leading to, through the narrow arch, a poky little kitchen where they deposited the refrigerator. The kitchen was so oppressively small, and the fridge so lumbering, Nayan ducked back under the arch and returned to the living room, where a laptop intermittently whirred on the L-shaped sofa and the floor complained under his spikes. As she joined him, he offered to install the appliance, seeing as they can be a real arse to manoeuvre.

'I've got one, too. Cheap as shit, aren't they.'

Her jeans were worn at the knees, and the grey vest, with its thin straps, showed arms full of sinew and the kind of twitchy muscle that came with manual labour. She was braless, though he was mindful of keeping his eyes on her face. Quiet a moment, she took her sweet time clapping the dust from her hands and she was still inspecting her fingers as she said:

'I was up on the roof taping down tiles yesterday and last month I stripped the bathroom and put in a new one.' She looked at him, then. 'So you know what, I reckon I'll be just fine manoeuvring a cheap-as-shit fridge into place.'

'Oh, course,' he said. 'I'm sorry. That was rude. Of me,' he clarified. 'I was rude.'

She nodded, waited. 'Was there anything else?'

He'd only taken three steps, in the hall already, when he paused. *In for a penny* . . . 'Actually, I wanted to ask you out for a drink? I've seen you around. When I'm running. If you're free.'

There was no shift in her manner, as if he'd only asked if she felt the heat. 'No. I'm good.'

'You might enjoy yourself,' he suggested.

'Teeny bit creepy?' she said, with a flicker of a smile. Was she toying with him? Was he getting somewhere? But he wouldn't push it . . .

'Right. Fair dos.' He made to leave again. 'See you around.'

'You didn't mention your name.'

He smiled. 'You didn't ask.'

'I won't again.'

'Nayan. Nayan Olak.' How eagerly we men proffer ourselves! He waited for her to reciprocate, but now her face changed, now it was filling with expression, with thoughts. She realised who he was, he figured: the guy, with the sister at her school, the one who'd lost his mother and son in the big shop fire all those years ago. There was pity in her face, he felt, which he wanted to drive away. 'And you are?'

'Helen. Fletcher.'

'Do you live alone?' He checked himself. 'I ask that in a totally non-creepy way.'

'With my son,' she said, the voice shorn of its ironic edge, if not its brisk tone.

'How old is he?'

'Eighteen.'

That was a shock. 'Eighteen? You've an adult child?' He didn't know what to say. 'He still asleep?'

'He camped out,' she said, motioning vaguely towards the hills.

'Right, right. That explains – I mean, there's normally a red Micra on the drive, isn't there?' He raised his palm, as if warding off her thoughts. 'I promise you I'm really not a stalker. Just very observant. I've always thought I'm a bit female that way.'

Now he worried he really was coming off all weird, more so when she didn't even smile and avoided his eye. She was fidgeting: hands on hips, in back pockets, hips.

'Is he at college? Working?' Stop talking, Nayan. 'I can see why you need the big fridge. Eat you out of house and home, I bet.'

'He's fine.' Clearing her throat, hands deciding on hips: 'The car's at the garage. He biked. Thanks for your help. I'll let you get on with your run.'

'Oh. Yeah. Sure.' He half-turned, then turned back. 'About that drink?'

'Sorry,' she said. 'I'm not interested,' and she came past Nayan, opened the front door, and he heard it slam before he'd even got off the porch.

The bang-click of the door shutting and locking behind him reverberated in his head through the remainder of his run, and its echo was still there as he showered and dressed, prepared his dad's lunch, and then drove down to the Doubletree Hilton on the Dronfield bypass. Inside, he hung about the rear of the stage feeling sorry for himself, Helen in his mind, and only once the conference room started filling up with coffees and chatter was he able to bring his focus to bear on the meeting ahead. He had a speech to give. It was the quarterly gathering of

Unify, the union he had given his life to, and the Executive Committee had discreetly yet unambiguously signalled that, should he throw his hat into the ring today, they would not only publicly endorse his nomination for General Secretary, but have a word in the ear of anyone minded to stand against him. It's high time, they'd whispered, that Nayan got his chance at the helm.

He came down the stage, buoyed by its creaks of oak, and balanced on the lip of the platform, looking over the milling hundreds. Imagine, he thought. Imagine him leading all these people, and the hundreds of thousands of workers they represented. The prospect awed and frightened him. He fought to ground himself, to not be afraid: he thought of Veér's face. Emotion surged inside him, an uprush of feeling that swept him down the stairs and into the crowd.

'Nayan.' It was a tremendous effort to disentangle this voice from the one inside his head, crowning him in electoral victory, and see Megha standing behind him, asking for a word.

Sleeved laptop in hand, she led him to a quiet corner by the double-doored fire exit, where the ferocity of the heat, concentrated through the glass, compelled them into an oblique angle; to any passing observer it looked as if they were in cahoots.

Megha said, 'I'll be covering the new cameras in my slot.'

'Totally. It's your baby.'

'You look good, by the way. Your skin's practically refulgent.'

'Come again?'

'Look it up.' A moment's pause. 'So! Speech all ready?'

Nayan grinned. 'You're about as subtle as.'

'It's true, then? You're running?' She bumped his arm. 'You'll be a great Gen Sec. The first non-white. Like Obama.'

He took a second to read her tone: was she being ironic? Was he being mocked? No – she was paying him a genuine compliment. 'Well, let's hope I kill a few less Arabs.'

She grimaced, let it go. 'Word is, the committee's backing you. You're a cert.'

'Don't, Megha. I'm having a hard enough job keeping my feet on the ground as it is. It's a long old hill.'

'Then you're lucky you've me marching at your side. Beating the drum.' Her thumbnail was scratching her laptop. 'Have you given any thought to your running mate? Your deputy?'

He rocked back on his brogues, a gentle sway that tried to cushion, to hide from her, his surprise. They were friendly, he liked her a lot, and they'd worked well together on a council initiative, where they'd bonded over the unignorable fact of being the only two browns near the top of the Unify ladder . . .

'It's a great opportunity for a cluster hire,' she continued. 'To show how progressive and inclusive we can really be. We'd be the first movement of the left ever to have two minoritised people leading the charge. I've so many ideas I want to talk to you about.'

. . . But she was too new, and different: how did she

ever think the members would vote for her, with her tailored suits and Charterhouse education, her voice that was full of money? 'I never knew you had these kinds of aspirations. For leadership, I mean.' *When you've only been here five minutes*, he didn't add.

'I want to make a change, Ny. I can't do that by just being the DEI bod. I want to have influence.' She raised her head, and all at once the sun captured precisely one half of her face. 'I know I'm not as dyed in the wool as you, but we've so much common ground. Let's do coffee tomorrow' – reaching for her phone-diary – 'just hear me out.'

Nayan touched her elbow, slowing things down until she calmed, looked. 'Megha, I've asked Lisa-Marie. I've known her for years and – I'm sorry. I had no idea you were interested.'

Oh. She slipped her phone back into her blazer pocket. 'That was quick. When? When did you ask her?'

'Last week,' he said. 'She's supported me from the off and, you know, she's got great contacts. I need you on my team, though. You'd be central to my campaign. I don't want to do this without you.'

'It makes sense, I suppose. A white woman at your side. Makes you more palatable.'

'It's nothing like that. Come on, Megha. She's worked her arse off for us. For years.'

'Unlike me, you mean?'

He allowed the silence to answer for him, then tried eyeballing her, registering all over again just how small she was. 'You okay? We good?'

She nodded, landed a smile through the disappointment.

'You've so much to offer, Megha. You're young. You're talented. I'm in talks about us getting a UBI pilot off the ground. I'd love you to lead that. You're the brains behind this outfit.' Before withdrawing into the crowd, he gave her a chummy side-hug, which fleetingly brought to mind Sonia, his little sister.

Five of them were sitting on stage, at the long table, but because only two of the mics worked, a giant snarling of cables and shrill feedback accompanied their turn-taking. Finally, the microphone arrived with Nayan and after what he knew was a tired yet effective joke on the vagaries of technology – 'about as trustworthy as Nick Clegg' – he told them how pleased he was to have this gathering here in Sheffield, on his patch, especially as, and forgive the pun, folks, it's spines of steel we need right now. 'This government, these employers, still won't meet and they still won't tackle the swingeing cuts, debilitating workloads and entrenched pay inequalities we're all facing. But we won't give up. We can't afford to give up. Despite this government's arrogance, we'll continue to expose how they are lying to the public about the vast scale of the cuts they are forcing through.'

Referring to his notes, he listed the ways in which they were being harmed: a 40 per cent pension cut; pay down a full quarter after nine years of austerity; a twelve-fold increase in diagnoses of work-related depression.

'As the largest alliance of members and workers – across

manufacturing, construction, transport, logistics – we demand that the government and employers act on our concerns. Pension cuts need to be revoked. Unmanageable workloads, deep pay inequalities, dangerous working conditions, unfair casual contracts – these need to be addressed.

'Sadly,' Nayan went on, modulating his voice, 'bosses have time and again failed to show that they care about workers – our lives, our hopes, our needs mean nothing to them. All they want is to exploit our labour. We are asking for so little, and asking it of a government presiding over one of the wealthiest countries in the world, a government happy to give billion-dollar contracts to friends and cronies. But neither the government nor the employers should underestimate our determination to improve the lives of working people. And they certainly should not underestimate my determination.'

He let his eyes settle over the crowd, which seemed to adjust in its seat, as if it realised this was the moment Nayan had been pursuing. If he wore spectacles, he'd have taken them off right about now, relinquishing any mask.

'Friends, the Labour movement, supported by us, has just given Theresa May the biggest bloody nose. As we speak, she's sniffing around the DUP hoping they'll throw her a bone. Now, more than ever, we need a leader who can drive home our advantage.' He crossed his arms on the table. His heart, how thickly it beat. His stomach felt like water. 'I've been this region's champion and voice for six years now and it has been *the* greatest privilege of my working life. I remain as committed as on the day I started, when I came in with my lunchbox and sat through Geoff's *full*-day induction on our six core values. I think Geoff remembered four of them.' Laughter. 'What I want to say is that I'm committed not only to my region, but to you all, wherever in this great but troubled country you've travelled here from. I want to work for you all. To fight for you all. Which is why I've decided to stand for General Secretary of Unify at the elections next spring.'

A whoop went up in the crowd, which encouraged another from the front, until the applause grew to take in most of the hall. Geoff, the new chair of the National Executive Committee – and outgoing General Secretary – reached over, shirt straining around his bulk, and shook Nayan's shoulder. Nayan accepted the room's praise with a smiling shrug, winning in its gaucheness.

'Thank you,' he said. 'There's a long way to go and you'll hear lots more from me in the coming months. I look forward to listening and talking to you all. But I dare say you're sick of my voice by now, so please allow me to leave it here. Thank you.'

They broke for coffee and Nayan hadn't even got off the stage before well-wishers were upon him, digestive biscuit and Styrofoam cup in hand. He spotted Lisa-Marie laughing in the central aisle, and beckoned her outside, where she found him straddling a wall in the car park. A beech offered them shade from the harsh sunlight, though its threat lingered beyond the verge.

'I'm a bit old for these behind-the-bike-shed shenanigans,' she said. 'And you're really not my type.'

'Too brown?'

'Not brown enough.' She grinned. 'I like my jalfrezi spicy.'

'That's fucking bad.'

'Wrong religion?'

'I'm not sure curries have religions, Lise.'

Her navy pantsuit, shiny and uncomfortably new, rustled as she climbed onto the wall beside him. He felt secure with Lisa-Marie, more at home than he had with any woman, even his sister. They'd started on the factory floor at Bristow's Air Con Systems a month apart and risen up the union ranks together. When she was left with four-year-old twins, Buddy and Claudia, Nayan did the school run twice a week until Lisa-Marie quit the factory for the friendlier shifts of a bus driver. In recent years, with the twins off at uni, heading up the region's union membership programme took all her time.

'Congrats. I nearly welled up back there.'

'You taking the piss?'

'Only a little.' She pressed his back. 'You were superb. And you're exactly what we need.'

Inwardly, he winced. An image of his mother floated into his mind, picketing in her salwar kameez, placard thrust up to the sky: Workers United Will Never Be Defeated. She is leading the charge, the chant, and all around and behind her men and women are gathered in support, miners, steel workers, railway technicians. He is there, too, perhaps five years old, on the hip of a green-hatted woman tasked with his care.

'Will you run as my second?' Nayan asked.

'Your deputy?'

'Everyone else said no.'

'The nerve.' Lisa-Marie slid off the wall and gave her face to the sun, eyes closing. Fine gold hairs shone along rosed cheeks. 'I was hoping you'd ask.'

He nodded. He is still thinking of his mother, of her beautiful, rallying face, battle-hardened, even as that seems impossible because she can't have been more than twenty-five at the time. It all gets mixed up and then refracted and distorted by the years until sometimes he isn't sure if what he is feeling, what he thinks, is true or not. Did everyone live with this kind of ambivalence? That holding a position was partly a leap of faith? Most, in his world at least, seemed so certain of themselves. 'You know, Mum was my age when she died. She was forty-two. From now on, I'm always going to be older than her.'

Opening her eyes, turning around, Lisa-Marie said, 'She'd be walking tall as monuments today.'

He nodded again. He supposed she would, though that always felt like pretty cold comfort in the middle of the night. 'I couldn't sleep for nerves,' he said, flexing his fingers: the prominent veins, the flat knuckles. 'And when I came down for some water I saw her hand turning the tap.'

'I know, love,' Lisa-Marie said, waiting a second. 'I've been there. That never ends.'

He exhaled, hard. Nothing ever ends. 'Anyway. You should know that Megha wanted the job. I told her you'd already accepted.'

'Megha wants everything. Because she's always had everything.'

'She wants to make her mark. She's got a lot to prove.'

'Did she throw her toys out the pram? She doesn't strike me as someone used to not getting what she wants.'

There is animosity in Lisa-Marie's voice, the rancour that the grafter, denied entry everywhere, feels for the smooth operator, for the one who is at home in every home because on some level she believes they are all hers. 'She was great, actually. And I doubt she's had it as easy as all that,' Nayan added. 'She's next on, first time on stage, probably shook to hell, so don't go giving her daggers. She's on our side.'

But if Megha was nervous, she didn't at all let it show. In the break, she'd arranged for a lectern to be brought onto the stage, at the far end, which meant Nayan had to turn side-on, lean forward over his arms, and look across everyone else seated at the table to get sight of her as she introduced herself: 'Megha Kamal Sharma' pronounced natively, going on to say how delighted she was to be addressing everyone in her capacity as Unify's first ever Head of Diversity, Equity and Inclusion. She wore her hair up now, skinned back and knotted sleekly at the nape, her centre parting creating an impression of extreme efficiency. Wants to look like a tough cookie, Nayan thought, admiringly, even as he was aware that this admiration was not welcome, was possibly even a sexist projection. Her calves were strong. Did she run, too? Or cycle? He imagined a treadmill in an extended wing of the family house; expensively rubberised dumbbells on a pyramid rack. Her low-heeled black mules were brought together, her backside tucked in, an upright bearing all round, a gymnast who's nailed her landing.

'We'll be paying for these cameras from our wages. Will they be for everyone's protection or just – is it just for minorities?'

The question brought Nayan back to the room. He'd missed her key proposal about installing new cameras on certain bus and rail routes.

'The additional spot cameras will be to the benefit of any staff working at the time,' Megha said, sounding grateful, glad of the opportunity to clarify the point. 'But it's important that as a community of workers we all recognise who amongst us is most vulnerable to assault and attack.' She asked members to turn to the ONS figures in their programme's appendix: assaults on black and minority ethnic staff had quadrupled in the six months since the EU referendum last year. 'A trend that has persisted into this one. Only last week, I was contacted by Hasmig, an Armenian woman working as a retail manager on the East Midlands line – her hijab was pulled off her head by a drunk male passenger, a man who got away with it because of a dearth of evidence, because it wasn't caught on camera. These things are happening, and they're happening with increasing and frightening regularity, and it's important we act against it. Which is why it's vital this motion passes and we start speaking to the rail operators at once.'

34

Nayan kept his head up, his gaze level, as he felt the room's silence bearing down on him. They may not have been staring, probably weren't, but he felt they were, he felt them searching out Nayan's take on all this. And the truth was that he supported the motion, wanted it to pass. Of course he did. Who wouldn't want better protection for workers? But he felt irritated with her presentation of the argument, with its divisiveness and its ignorance of how easily unity can be shattered.

'I'm sensing some resistance,' Megha said, which got a laugh. She had charm in spades. 'Clearly, I need to work on my powers of persuasion. Was it my delivery? My father's always saying I sound uppity.' Another laugh. Her timing was on point, and the crowd were liking this little aside. 'Actual things my father said: why sound clever, darling, when you can just get married?' Megha's relentless smile, broadcasting her enjoyment. 'But come on, folks, leaving my father out of it, let's pass this motion, let's not ignore the trauma – the very real trauma – of our fellow workers just because they're not white.' It was a terrible misjudgement, far too keen a return to business, as if she couldn't be bothered to entertain them any longer, and the room bristled with impatience. Boos went up from the back.

'So we're the racists now?' 'It's not racist to interrogate what you spend our wages on.' 'The same wages that pay you.'

Megha, thrown off balance, wavered, her smile fell and her feet did an anxious little shuffle. And it was the anxious feet that had Nayan grabbing the microphone from Geoff. But the mic shrieked, a protracted sound which quietened the hall and cast Nayan in a quasi-judicial role, about to deliver into the silence his verdict.

'I think we're forgetting that this motion is going to help all of our workers and colleagues. It may have been prompted by the recent rise in attacks on ethnic minorities, as Megha persuasively outlined, but it doesn't stop there. Let's keep in mind that in terms of sheer numbers, most attacks are on our white colleagues. And these cameras will help keep them safe, too. I was looking over the figures last night, and last year there were twelve assaults on white workers for every one on a minority. These cameras will help them. It will help us all.'

'But proportionately, minorities bear the brunt,' Megha said, into her mic but entreating Nayan. 'We need to recognise that and focus our resources there? On those routes?'

Did we? Was she right? Nayan sought out Lisa-Marie, who was gesturing for him to smile: lighten the tone, don't get drawn in. 'Well, proportionately, according to the figures, Mancunians suffer most, and I don't know about you, but my sympathy has its limits.' His own laughter sanctioned further chuckles from the room, and won a thumbs-up from Lisa-Marie.

'The truth is,' Nayan went on, 'the point is, however you slice the stats, whether white or not, one hundred per cent of attacks are on working-class people. That's the crux. Megha and I are as one on that. She's an amazing comrade, I have total faith in her ideas, so let's pass this motion, let's get those cameras in and protect *all* workers. Yes? Yes!'

Applause, reluctant, then spreading, each row coaxing on the one behind. Job done, crisis averted, Nayan smiled at Megha and nodded once, as if to say she was welcome.

The giant grey pipes mazed across the ceiling and Megha stared at one end and tried tracing the shortest possible path to the other side . . . Geoff rubbing Nayan's shoulder, winking at him – such an old boys' club, really. Yes. Old. Nostalgic. Blair this. Comrade that. Still harping on about UBI, about equality – what about *equity*, Nayan? What about autonomy and automation? Liberty and leisure? Decolonisation? Free borders? Representative mutualisation, not old-school state-owned nationalising. She'd so wanted to blow open his mind to new ways of thinking. But he was still stuck on the factory floor, spouting the tired old phrases, the jokes he didn't realise we'd all heard before, lapping up the praise. She doubted his commitment to her agenda. He'd nodded politely enough through last week's roadshow – but when she described the devastation wrought on peasant communities in the global south, he didn't seem at all exercised. As if he couldn't connect things up. Or didn't care . . . Megha flipped over – the pipes vanished – and she curled into a tuck, pushing off the wall, the water slubbing over her body in an elegant wave . . . Nayan would be in power for ten years, at least. Ten years of the same old, same old. The thought was exhausting, depressing. Did it even matter if she won? she mused, her mind very quickly skirting past several difficult questions. As long as her ideas were aired, heard – over time she would gather support. Force a change . . . A final length and then she raised herself out and sat on the rim of the pool, water sucking underneath her hands. When had the place emptied?

She showered – trying not to imagine winning; failing – wrung out her hair, towelled dry and dressed once more in her skirt-suit, without the tights this time, which she'd rolled and stuffed into her pockets. Was it a mad idea? Yes. But exhilarating, too. History-making. Epoch-defining! Not only the first woman leader of the largest union in the country, but the first non-white, too. Deep in thought, she knotted her wet hair into a scrunchie, grabbed her case and left through the foyer.

'Just your signature,' said a voice behind her.

Her autograph? she thought, confused.

'The sign-out sheet?' the boy at the counter clarified, and Megha, blushing a tad, took the pen from him.

At two in the morning, Megha's phone lit up: *How was your speech beti? Mum xx.* For as long as she could recall, her mother had had trouble sleeping, and, tonight, so did Megha, who'd been sitting up in bed for over an hour now, staring out the window. It really did feel as if the night was watching her, awaiting her next move, the planets spinning into view to spur her on. She was on the precipice and could change the course of so much simply by stepping over the threshold of her fear. She thought of her mother, Shreya, and of her scent when Megha would climb into bed beside her. She dialled and immediately Shreya knew her daughter was preoccupied.

'There is something,' Megha said, and she explained the election and this chance to make a stand, make a difference.

'But you're worried people will talk about you, if you oppose this Nayan person?'

'He's a nice enough guy. His heart's in the right place . . . I don't know.'

'I don't think you'd have called me if you didn't know. You always know. You just want me to tell you that you do.'

The phone was on speaker and Megha smiled into it. 'Maybe.'

'Dad is in Dubai all week. But call him. He'll be so happy you're doing this. Running for office.'

'Will he? I thought I was the biggest bleeding-heart disappointment of his life.'

'You said your fair share, too.'

'Don't say we're more alike than we realise. Spare me the daddy issues.'

A pause. 'Are you eating okay? What did you have today?'

'I'm eating fine. I'm thirty-one.'

'I miss you. We'd love to see you soon.' She sounded tired. How Megha loved her mother's soft, slow voice.

'Soon. I just need to . . . get my H-I-T-S together.' An old and private joke.

'Yes. The hits just keep coming.'

———

By the end of the week, a rumour grew that Megha was standing against Nayan. He rang Lisa-Marie, who said she'd heard the same, and then Megha, who didn't answer his call. At nine a.m. on the following Monday he received an email: it was true, she said, she had decided to give it a go. It wasn't that she thought he'd be a bad Gen Sec – she didn't think that – she just had different ideas, priorities, an alternative vision for Unify. An anti-nostalgia one that connected to modern geopolicies: the environment, automation, understanding the trauma of minoritised workers. She wanted a chance to talk about these ideas. To let members see what she was about and what she believed in. *I really hope we can have a good and positive campaign, free of acrimony.*

'What the fuck's she playing at?' Nayan said on the phone to Lisa-Marie.

'She's positioning herself as the change candidate,' Lisa-Marie said, as if she'd just puzzled something out.

'She's a fucking snake.'

'We might not go with that for our campaign slogan. But, come on, as if you've anything to worry about.'

Everyone else agreed: he was going to win, they said. He'd done wonders for the union. Raised its profile tenfold. Increased membership. He was popular, beloved. He'd been Comrade of the Year three years on the trot, for Pete's sake. This Megha what's-her-face doesn't stand a chance; she won't even get the prerequisite nominations to make a formal challenge. 'It's Megha Sharma,' Nayan always corrected them; it felt necessary to do so, despite his hurt, because he knew what it was like to have your name consistently mangled, but also because he too believed he was destined to win, and win easily at that, a confidence that laced the hurt with certain feelings of condolence for his former friend.

On the morning Lisa-Marie rang to tell Nayan that Megha had mustered up the nominations, that 5 per cent of members had signed her ticket, he was on the bypass, driving home from the Sheffield office.

'It's on, then,' Nayan said.

'I'll come round tomorrow and we'll start brainstorming the campaign. I've already told Buddy that he's volunteering for us. Make some bloody use of that marketing degree.'

'Okay.'

'Don't fret,' Lisa-Marie said, hearing the doubt in Nayan's voice. 'People know. They know the years you've put in.'

At the roundabout, he took the exit for home, running the lights, past the few pubs still standing and the trio of shops on the brow of the hill – *The Happy Fryer*, *Margot's Mart*, *Hair and Now*. Descending towards the bus stop opposite Ringwood Park, he muttered a fuck at the UKIP billboard still there from the previous year, for all his many furious threats to the council. And perhaps it was the sight of that board and its message that had him ignoring his turn-off and taking a later left, past my parents' old store on Pine Lane and down the long road, beyond the old gasworks, the old pharmacy (still closed), the old corners he'd spent hours kicking a tennis ball around, and parking up on Exeter Drive, beside the spot where his own parents' small business and home once stood. It wasn't there any

41

longer, of course, the fire took care of that. Now there was a pair of two-bed semis, and the small forecourt he used to fix his Raleigh Lizard on, getting in customers' way, had been split, dug and converted into identically tiny square gardens. How dare she imply that he didn't know what it was like to be attacked for your race? That he didn't understand damage and pain and, seeing as she loved the word so fucking much, trauma? He was understanding it right now, sitting in his blue Civic, eyes prickling. He'd been understanding it for twenty years.

Solidarity, his mother used to proclaim, returning from her shift at the bottleworks and back out again with little Nayan. Find the ground on which you can all stand, beta. They were letter-dropping for Tony Benn, Nayan posting the leaflets while she followed with the umbrella. Together going from house to house. The hem of her sari muddy and sodden with rain, her thick white socks and open-toed sandals. Don't let anyone tell you you're different. Even if they treat you differently. Even if those different things look like they'll help you. They won't. He'd nodded, taken another leaflet, posted another leaflet, ran back under the umbrella. Her glasses had fogged, so she seemed to be eyeless, just a wet face with a wide mouth, the bottom lip fuller. His mouth. The workers in society have to work together, acha? Have to fight together to stand a chance. Have to stay solid. None of this Indians need this, whites this, blacks this. That's them trying to make us fight each other, fight each other over the scraps. Do you understand? We have to be united to crush those holding us down.

Looking back, he doubted she was even saying all this for his benefit. It sounded more like an appeal to the fearless, firebrand girl withering inside her, the one who'd hazily dreamed of leading a revolution, who'd lambasted her government high school so girls could wear shorts, so dalit students didn't eat at a separate table, but who'd also, in the end, given in to her parents' year-long pleas and accepted the offer of marriage to a man from England, a Dev Anand-wannabe judging by the photo, and not just *from* England but born there, too, and therefore surely, she hoped (and how hard she'd hoped, on that flight out of India!), someone too modern to treat her with disdain, to demand that she be only servile.

The visit to his old patch proved a shot in the arm, and by the time Nayan arrived home his sense of betrayal had converted to clear zeal. He felt livid with Megha, with her righteousness and her jibes about nostalgia – as if class struggle was a nostalgic enterprise! She'd destroy Unify. Tear it apart. He wasn't going to let that happen, he wasn't going to let her win, and all evening he could feel this sudden focus in his attitude like an invigorating force pounding through his body. As he boiled the pasta and made the bolognese, everything ran a notch quicker, the blender sounded industrial, whirling his mind towards events and speeches and slogans. He was so fired up that when he put the dish on the coffee table in front of his father it dropped with a clatter, as if the table and his energy had clashed.

'Do you want the telly on?'

'Where's yours?'

'I'll eat in a bit.' He was itching to work, to plan and map out his path to victory, to defeat her. 'Anything else?'

Pyara poked at the meal, and had one trembling forkful before laying down his cutlery. 'Foreign muck.'

'You ate it happily enough last time. And it's healthy. Wholemeal. All good carbs.' This happened now and then. Eventually, he knew, his father would acquiesce. 'You left the taps running upstairs.'

'I was going to have a bath.'

'In the sink?'

'And a shave.'

'Fine. We'll do that later. Together. You can't do it on your own any more. Just wait for me to come home.'

'I don't fucking want to wait for you,' he flashed, kneeing the table away.

Straightening the furniture, Nayan glanced at his phone. Another hour and a half before his father's pills, one each for dementia and incipient Parkinson's. The outbursts now were, praise be, pretty infrequent, two or three a month maybe. He was largely docile, which wasn't at all what the doctors had told Nayan to expect. He'll be violent, they'd said. His frustration will lead to bouts of frightening anger. That hadn't been the case. More often that not, he'd come home and find Pyara seated in the same corner Nayan had left him in that morning. Sometimes he wondered if his father was all out of violence, if his temper had simply run out; he'd used up enough of it in the past.

It was later, as he helped Pyara onto the belt and lowered him into the bath, that the slogan came to mind. *Let's Stay Solid.* His mother's words, resurrected by the

44

unsolid water. They felt right, true to what he believed, and he put it to Lisa-Marie in a meeting room the following morning.

'I love it,' she said. 'It speaks to the history with your mum, which'll move anyone, but also, it tells us about you. You're solid. Trustworthy. You have integrity. Things with integrity are solid, aren't they? Like – a cube?'

'Yeah,' Nayan replied, giving the word a lot of road. 'Quite the PR guru, aren't you?'

Larkily, she flicked the pen she'd been twirling at him, then spotted something on her phone. A circular, from Megha.

Dear Members

Welcome to the first of my regular newsletters. I'm keen that you see how Unify is working for you and driving forward change in your name. With this in mind, these bulletins will outline my main priorities for the months ahead and also be a place where I'll share updates on my inclusivity campaigns. It's an exciting time for us, much is at stake, and I want you to know that I'm here to listen to any problems you have in relation to any DEI matter. Rest assured, I will work tirelessly on your behalf.

The newsletter went on for another page, specifying Megha's main initiatives for the coming autumn before signing off with a simple, cloying, *As ever, your Megha*.

'She means business,' Lisa-Marie said, impressed, and Nayan was already at the whiteboard, filling it with dates, supportive outlets, useful contacts, funding limits, possible marketing collateral. An hour later, vacating the room because another team wanted in, he had a sudden flashback to his last conversation with Megha, at the conference. What *did* that word mean? Irritated that he needed to know, he paused in the corridor and bashed out the letters on his phone: r-e-f- . . .

Where was Helen during all this? Helen Fletcher? Nayan saw her a couple of times, when he was running past her house and into the hills. On the second occasion, he'd seen her son, too. They were washing their hatchback, inside and out, with the boy (tall, shaved head) bent into the boot, vacuuming. Nayan and Helen exchanged looks, no words, and he didn't get much of a view of the boy, but when Nayan pulled the flyer out of his letterbox, he knew at once it was him. *Brandon Fletcher. Hardworking and local. Former cook but will turn my hand to anything.* He was smiling in the photo. He had a perfect rim of white teeth and his mother's candid, brown eyes. *Mowing. Cleaning. Putting up shelves. Give me a chance! Just ask me!* The cheaply printed flyer, the flimsy paper, his 'give me a chance', it all tugged at Nayan, or he was happy to tell himself it did, since he also saw an opportunity to restart an acquaintance with Helen. Did she really think him a creep? The thought pained him. And he thought about her a lot.

Instead of calling the number on the flyer, he determined to first ask Helen's permission, given he'd be hiring her son to do the work she had turned down. Climbing the drive, he hadn't yet pressed the bell when she met him on the porch in her blue home-help uniform, cinched loosely at the waist. She closed the door behind her. Any surprise seemed absorbed into her raised eyebrows.

'Yes?'

He unfolded the ad, by now gridded with creases, the main vertical perfectly bisecting the young man's face. 'I got this through my letterbox. Would you mind if I gave your son some regular work? I mean, do you have any objections to me calling him?' He spoke in a rush, and now a nervy laugh stumbled out of his mouth. 'I wanted to check with you.'

She peered at the flyer, her brow constricted. 'No. No way. He's going back to college.'

'Right. I'm glad I checked.' He nodded at her uniform. 'Seems like it's you that's in the nursing line of work.' He assumed she had no idea that he knew of her refusal to care for his father. 'Maybe I could talk to your agency?'

'My rota's full.'

'It'd be a few hours a few times a week. Just keeping an eye on my dad. I'm busy and need the help – I'm standing to be General Secretary of Unify.' In the moment, he wasn't quite sure if the aim was to awe her or to simply put her in her place.

'It's still full. Good luck with your union.'

'Seriously, what is your problem?'

She turned back to him, all the world's impatience in her face. 'I've got work to get to. My son does not need a job. Thank you for thinking of us. Goodbye.'

The door shut, then immediately reopened, and beside

Helen stood Brandon, in sweats and a plain black top, like a school jumper, sleeves shoved up to his elbows. His sudden appearance, the height, the bristly hair and slight flare of his nose, it all made Nayan expect trouble. But the boy's voice, slow to come, was tentative.

'I heard voices,' he said. Then, finding the flyer still in Nayan's hand, he seemed to spark, come alive. 'You looking for me? Have you got work?'

Nayan nodded, warily, conscious of Helen, who said, 'You're going to college. We've spoken about this.' She snatched the flyer from Nayan. 'When did you do these? How many have you sent out?'

'What's the work?' Brandon said, as if his mother was no more trouble than a pliant branch he could push aside.

Nayan reined in his smile. 'I live with my dad, who's seventy-two. I just need someone to spend maybe two to three hours with him three or four times a week. He's got dementia so he's not all there but he's mostly no trouble. Make him a sandwich, maybe take him for a walk. Or just sit with him.'

'It's only the same as what you do,' Brandon said to his mum. Helen didn't speak, and for once there wasn't any hostility in the silence; if anything, Nayan felt gratified that she was listening to him with hard attention.

'I'm super flexible. And you can bring your homework with you if you want because' – nodding towards Helen – 'going to college isn't a bad idea if you ask me.'

'Just keeping him company, like? I won't have to do any – messier stuff. Toilet and whatnot.'

48

'He's fully toilet trained. I promise you won't ever have to see my dad with his pants down.'

'And – pay?'

Nayan puffed out his cheeks as if to say he'd not given it any thought. 'Tenner an hour? Cash.'

'That's more than my mum earns,' Brandon said, perhaps forgetting himself, and Nayan glanced to the floor, embarrassed.

'Brandon, we'll talk about this later.'

'I can do this, Mum. Let me?' To Nayan: 'I'll take it.'

While Brandon ran upstairs to grab his phone – 'to jot down your address and that' – Nayan turned to Helen with what he hoped was an honest look, one that didn't underplay the difficulties of being a single parent. 'He seems like a great kid.'

'I don't need to be patronised on my doorstep.'

He sighed – what was the point? 'Think what you like.'

She didn't answer, and when Brandon raced back down Helen returned to the living room for her bag and keys, got into her car and reversed off, leaving the two of them on the porch.

'Do you think it's one of life's little jokes?' Nayan said. 'That your mum's in the caring profession?'

Brandon smiled, quietly, and finished typing Nayan's address.

They agreed a Monday start, nodded goodbyes, but when Nayan was halfway down the drive, Brandon called: 'Just one thing.'

'Hmm? Yeah?'

Pushing his hands deep into his pockets, elbows locked, Brandon struggled to say whatever it was he wanted to say. And then he just said it, a small tremor in his throat: 'We're not racists. Me and my mum. We're not. I don't want you to have that impression. Because of how Mum is or anything.'

'Yes,' Nayan said, shocked, impressed, compromised and, somewhere inside, ashamed. He knew he could point out it wasn't for Brandon to decide how far he was a racist, that those verdicts lay with the likes of Nayan. But he couldn't do that. In the same way that, the previous week, he'd never reproved the Zimmer-framed old-timer who'd kept asserting we were *long overdue a coloured leader*. His quivering hand had been on Nayan's shoulder and it would have felt inhuman to correct him even politely, to make apparent that the ground had shifted beneath him, to remind him once more of his obsolescence and death. Brandon wasn't old, or near death, but he looked as genuine, and Nayan felt disarmed. 'I don't think that. I'm sorry you needed to point it out.'

'I just wanted you to know.'

'And now I do.'

Nayan walked away, registering the door locking behind him, and then the sound – though how could he hear, already down the street? – of the boy's quick feet on the narrow, dark stairs.

2

In December 2021, work on my parents' bungalow restarted and I was over there to check how the new roof was progressing: the trusses were in, and the odd joist, but that was about it. No lats, everything open to the souring sky. At this pace, there was little chance of the build completing any time soon – a prognosis I unthinkingly made to my dad.

'We'll be out your hair soon enough,' Dad said.

'I didn't mean it like that. I'm sorry. I'm not thinking straight.' I walked over to a pile of bricks and plaster, an old wall knocked down.

'What's the matter?' Mum asked, coming in from the garden and seeing Dad's face.

'He wants us gone.'

'Of course I don't. Please don't think that. I love you.'

I can't remember the last time I'd said that. Dad suddenly found something of absorbing interest in the floorboards. Mum stepped towards me and held me close.

'What's the matter? You've been – what is it called? – stressed ever since you started meeting that Nayan.'

'That's something he should stop,' Dad said.

Mum pressed again: 'What is it?'

'I don't know.'

'You hated going back to Chesterfield,' she said. 'I always had to beg you to come visit. And now when you need never go there again, you're there all the time. Don't you hate it any more?'

'I don't know, Mum. I really don't know.'

As we walked back round to my house, I asked if they remembered a girl called Helen Fletcher; she lived up by the banking.

'No,' Dad said. 'I don't think so.'

'She beat the head at Netherthorpe,' I said.

'Oh my God,' Mum said. 'What happened to her?'

'She left for London. But she came back for a while. A few years ago. To her old home.'

'And why does this fascinate you?' Dad asked.

Good question. I wasn't sure why, only that there was something off – I felt it early – in Nayan's descriptions of Helen. How he insisted too much on her hardness, on how 'imperious' and 'sealed' she was. I sometimes got the sense that his unconscious was at work, offering me glimpses of a truth he couldn't yet bear to voice.

Chesterfield library was still closed to visitors, so I couldn't get a copy of the newspaper report into Helen's ruckus. Some creative googling, however, popped up the head-teacher's name – Mervyn Hartwhistle BA (Hons), Treasurer of Hope Valley Ramblers – and within the week I was waving at him standing outside his cottage, removing my mask as I left my car and came up the brick path. I had a sudden memory of him powering down the classroom corridor in a green diamond-patterned shirt, like Nayan's bedspread, calling out to students – all of which felt real, even if I'd gone to a different school.

'Thanks for meeting me,' I said, stopping several feet short.

'So what's this research?' I'd noticed this a lot recently, how meeting outside made every encounter feel transient, meant formalities could be discarded.

He had a low, unconfident voice, as if it rose up from his stomach but lost its way around his mouth, and his sandy hair had greyed, lightly. Only when I mentioned Helen, that I was trying to connect with an old friend for a book I was working on, did he remove his mask. His lips were red and startlingly thin.

'You had some sort of altercation?' I said.

'She came at me with a chair. Broke my arm.'

Sonia had said nose. Maybe every pupil remembers it differently. *'It was his nose.' 'His arm.' 'His hip.' 'She shinned him in the bollocks and gave him cancer.'*

'I'm hearing from a few people that she was quite tough.'

He considered me. 'I gave my life to that school. To those kids.'

I nodded, as if to say the matter was never in doubt. 'I'm just keen to know what she was like.'

'She came at me. Broke my arm.'

'You said.'

'Totally out of the blue. She was normally one of the quiet ones. Just kept her head down. And like a volcano she erupted. Screaming and crashing the chair into me. I can still hear the kids laughing.' He looked away, pained. 'They had no idea.'

'I'm sorry. That must have been hard to take.'

'I managed for a couple more years. But I couldn't . . . So then,' he said with a big sigh, 'well, early retirement and a carriage clock, wasn't it?'

'She never gave any explanation?'

'I rather expected you to have one.'

I felt sorry for him, and until then had been surprised he'd not sent me on my way; but, of course, he was hoping I'd come with answers.

'There's always pressure, isn't there?' he said. 'The final year. But we were only at the start.'

Behind him, inside the cottage, the phone rang and a figure crossed the window. His wife, I supposed, which prompted me to ask: 'Helen's home life? She lived with her mum, yeah?'

Mervyn nodded. 'Aye. I believe so. And her mum's boyfriends. A Frank one year, a Perry the next. An unsettled home life, as they say. Usually the case, isn't it? She was on drugs of some sort. The mum.'

'You met her?'

'When she cared to turn up. Which wasn't often.'

'And after that . . . the attack – Helen just left?'

'As far as I know. She just . . . walked away. We did try to reach her.'

'You weren't pressing charges, were you, so why did she—'

'She didn't need anyone pressing charges. She must

54

have had enough going wrong in her life without me adding to it.' He lifted his arm to the white fence; there was a mild palsy in his hand. 'She wasn't in the least academic but I convinced her to stay on. I was teaching her about plants. For this basic GNVQ in something or other. She loved growing things. Sunflowers. Beans. She tended to them so lovingly.' He made a fist and tapped the top of the fence. 'I do hope she's okay, wherever she is.'

———

Over our next several meet-ups, I probed Nayan for what he knew of Helen's life in London. At first he claimed she'd not told him much, but once he started it was apparent he'd gleaned quite a lot. He knew, for instance, that she'd spent some weeks on the streets, until a homelessness task force brought her in and got her on her feet. 'One of New Labour's few half-decent initiatives,' Nayan said, grudgingly. They enrolled her into night school and secured her a job collecting glasses in a local pub, around the corner from her college. The pub was the Queen Adelaide Arms, in Shepherd's Bush, and the landlord a heavy-set guy called Mal Forrester. Fatherly, Nayan said. They got on, Mal and Helen, so when she dropped out of her course and had to leave the charity's accommodation, Helen asked if she could crash in the pub kitchen until she found somewhere else.

'And have you imbibing all my fine wines?' Imbibing was a very Mal word: he was a gifted mimic and loved to exaggerate his Welsh accent. He drove Helen to a tiny maisonette in Ealing, just off the Broadway and three down from a Travelodge. 'I bought this when I first moved to London,' he said, showing her in. 'I own the one down-stairs, too. My pension, they'll be.'

Helen took in the two-hob cooker and slimline dish-washer, the shallow sofa on its short, splayed legs. The bed barely fit its room and, next door, windowless and compacted into no more space than a broom cupboard, was a toilet and shower, no bath. None of that mattered. She'd not lived anywhere that had a dishwasher before, slimline or otherwise.

'It's been empty a week. I'll clean and steam the carpet,' he added, frowning at the stains.

'And my wages will cover the rent?'

'No, they bloody won't. I'm not a charity. I'll give you two months at half-rent until you work it out. I expect you'll have to find a second job.'

And she did. And then a third, too, so by the time the year turned she was, every weekday, up at five to clean the offices of a local enterprise consultancy, and then hotfooting it to the Travelodge, where she joined the housekeeping team, stripping beds as soon as the guests checked out. She'd be done by three, time enough to nip home for a sandwich, one she ate on her way to the pub. Work gave her freedom, gave her money and choices. Gave her mind something to hold on to. At the weekend, with only evening shifts at the pub, she'd stroll through the parks and along the river, avoiding the Lady Di tour-ists and admiring how the winter light crimped the water. On Sunday mornings, she ate jammy toast in bed and played Snake on her mobile, which she'd splashed out for during a spree on Oxford Street.

('Sounds like she was having a ball,' I said. 'Doesn't it just,' Nayan replied. 'When was this again? When did she leave town?' Nayan shrugged: 'Around the time Sonia went to uni. Before the fire.')

She upped her hours at the Adelaide, working mostly behind the bar, a promotion, sliding away to collect glasses when they got tight. One evening a dark-haired man, tall and unkempt, twin shaving rash either side of his throat, offered to lend a hand and between them they grabbed several dozen empties.

'Thanks,' Helen said.

'Any time,' he replied, and returned to his table of friends. A while later he reappeared at the bar with another crate.

'You can stop that,' Helen said. 'That's my job.'

'Won't happen again.' He took his own pint glass and tipped it towards her. 'Another one in there, please?'

Accepting the glass, she drew down the beer. It took a few pumps to get going. She blew the fringe from her eyes. Her forehead felt greasy.

'I saw you here last week,' he said.

'Must have been a treat for you.'

He smiled, said nothing.

'Here you are,' she said, and put the pint onto the drip tray; a golden trophy sparkling.

'My name's Elwood. I shit you not. That is actually

what my hippie mother called me. So you're welcome to be as cruel as you like, I've dealt with a hell of a lot worse.'

Helen watched him rejoin his friends. The accusation of cruelty left a sting and she noticed him more and more as the night ticked on. You couldn't say he was good-looking but he seemed comfortable in his skin, and she liked that. His hair was cut close at the back, flopped romantically at the front, and he was wearing boilerman trousers. She figured he definitely wasn't one of those posho students from Notting Hill.

'Last one,' she said, pulling him another. It was getting on for midnight and he was swaying gently.

'Drinking. It's thirsty work.'

She snorted. 'Try being on this side of the bar.'

'Let me get you one,' he gushed, as if he'd been waiting all night for a way in.

This made her laugh. 'I'll have a glass of wine, seeing as it's my birthday.' She hadn't told anyone this and now, letting the news flutter out into the world in iridescent bubbles, it felt thrilling, waiting to see what adventure this announcement of her birthday might provoke.

'Is it now? Best make it a large glass, I think. And which birthday might we be celebrating? And please don't ask me to guess. It's torturous when women do that.'

'I'm eighteen,' she said, leaning behind for a bottle, pouring her wine.

'Eigh–!' He shouted over to Mal at the far end of the bar. 'Uncle Mal, it's her eighteenth, man. Why you making her work on her eighteenth?'

'Is that why you've got yourself all dolled up like a

slip of tinsel?' Mal said. He was referring to her eyelids and their glittery green, and perhaps also to her hair, curled and kept in check with a silver hairband she'd bought from a stall in Acton.

'Uncle . . . ?' Helen said. Mal had mentioned that his nephew was living with him for a time, a music student, handy with a violin. Suddenly Helen felt herself deceived, indignant too – though this was largely a shield, for the truth was she felt intimidated that this seemingly normal bloke could read sheet music and knew all about Bach.

('Would she have heard of Bach?' I asked. Nayan looked at me askance: 'Let's pretend you didn't say that.' 'I'm trying to understand what she was like. She's quite inscrutable.' 'Try harder.')

'Mal's my dad's younger brother,' Elwood said.

'*Appreciably* younger brother. Young enough to know what's going on in that fetid mind of yours.' Elwood raised his pint to that. 'All week he's been asking me. What's her name? What day's she work? Does she have a boyfriend?' Mal finished significantly.

'She doesn't,' Helen said. 'But that doesn't mean she wants one.'

'I'll take that.' He gulped the final third of his pint and finished her wine for her, too. 'Let's go. You've got' – a fake Regency clock hung above the bar – 'twenty minutes of your birthday before things go pumpkin.'

She fetched her jacket and clutch bag, blew Mal a kiss, and joined Elwood outside. 'Hang on,' she said. 'If Mal's your dad's brother – your name's Elwood Forrester? You're kidding?'

'What chance did I have, Helen, I ask you what chance did I have?' Spoken to the heavens. He spun round, hands in pockets and walking backwards, eyes on her. *Come to me.* 'It gets worse. If you're good I'll tell you my middle name by the end of the night.'

She paused a moment – did she really want to get into this? – and then she hurried to catch up, under the lamp-posts and down the bright, sleek pavements.

Helen was surprised at the glow she felt, two days later, when Elwood strode into the pub. She ceased tidying the pool cues, and watched him lift his violin case to the bar and gaze around for her. He wore a short, collarless military jacket, navy with white stitching and two columns of silver buttons. Was it . . . velvet? She'd never met anyone like him before – so confident and unconventional, so sure of what the world owed him, so far from where she came from.

Controlling her expression, she approached him from behind, dirty wine glasses in her hand. 'Can I get you something?' How large and dazzling was his smile, so much so that the delight came rushing unstoppably back into her face.

Fletcher and Forrester. Rural crimebusters extraordinaire. The joke ran for weeks before even Mal tired of it. Elwood did, however, in the spirit of the joke, get a plaque of their surnames nailed to Helen's front door, which by then had become his front door, too, because less than two months after that first date, he carried his suitcase and violin over from his uncle's. The move made life easier, cheaper, but what enraptured Helen most was hearing him practise in the mornings, his mind submerged in the music, when the entire composition of life rose for a moment and rushed into her with an intensity that was easy to mistake for love. As the final notes left his strings, he'd surface blinking, adjusting once more to the room, the walls, the air. It was a moment she felt lucky to witness.

They split the rent, with Elwood, coming to the end of his post-grad, taking a job delivering pizza, and then also busking on the tube. It was a lot, but they were young and their bodies strong, and climbing into her single bed with him at night, when he couldn't seem to get enough of her, always made Helen's pulse throb, made her eager to finish her shift and head for home.

Naked one night, post-sex and long past twelve, she watched him sitting at the end of the bed, perform-ing some sort of arm exercise. His back was pale and their sheetless mattress had left thick indentations across his shoulders. The dark-brown hair in his pits looked sweaty.

'What you doing?' she asked.

'I came off my bike, as a kid. It plays up sometimes. Makes bowing tricky.'

She stretched out her hand, her fingers, to stroke his back, but he was out of reach. Yes, he was a boy once, on his bike, messing around. Told off, doubtless, for not prac-tising instead.

'You said your dad taught you?' she asked.

'Until I was eight. And then a pro took over.'

'Must be nice. To have parents that give a shit.'

He turned round, smiled, and she smiled, too. Okay, his face said: you win.

The following night, she spoke about her mother for the first time. She didn't say much, only that she was a junkie, had been for all of Helen's life. She used to send Helen out to score.

'I was twelve the first time it happened. When a proper rank scumbag handed me the foil baggie and felt my bum and said I should hurry back soon.'

'I'm so sorry,' Elwood said. 'Did it ever . . . ?'

'Go further?' She shook her head. 'But I could see it in their eyes. Who the fuck puts their daughter in that position?' When Helen got her mobile, she'd called her mum to give her the number. 'And then all day I waited, on my eighteenth, but nothing. Probably why I got lashed with you.'

Elwood enveloped her into his arms. He was so good at giving comfort, so good at knowing when nothing needed to be said, and perhaps these sweet qualities blinded her to everything else. She'd always wonder if there were signs she missed, or chose not to look at too closely. His ingrained assumption that she'd be happy to watch on TV whatever he wanted to. His fury at taxi drivers who failed to stop. When she came home to find him sitting alone in their unlit bedroom, tense because he'd lost out on an audition, was that the moment she should have seen the violence that roiled inside him? Perhaps. But in the course of a day, a week, a month, these things appear small, drowned by the many ordinary, quiet kindnesses: the cup of tea brought to her bed, the ink stain scrubbed out of her favourite dress, the evening text saying he'd bring them a fish supper home.

For Helen to really see Elwood, Nayan said, it took something that more fundamentally and permanently threatened his self-image. It began one warm autumn evening, when she sat on the closed lid of the pub toilet and saw the raging and unmistakably blue line. She fell back against the cistern, knees together and feet cast to the sides. She'd always imagined that one day there would be children, in the same way she knew that one day she would grow old. They'd been impetuous, careless, and part of the surprise, part of the tentative pleasure of that blue line was the realisation that she had, however accidentally, actually made this happen, that this was something she had done and not had done to her. She texted Elwood the news, worried all evening when he didn't reply, and was then relieved to see him walk through their door later that night. He brought a pizza from work, as he sometimes did, and dropped it on the coffee table along with his satchel.

'I thought you'd done a runner,' she said. She offered her hand, expecting him to join her on the sofa, but he seemed not to see her and went to stand at the kitchen counter instead. 'El?'

'It's massive fucking news you've dropped.'

'It is,' she said, feeling chastened, any joy quashed. 'Could it be good news, though?'

'Hard to see how. I want to be playing around the world, Hel. Living in digs. Different cities every week. What hope for that with a bairn to support?' He let out a long sigh – she was making him expel the bright future of his dreams.

'You think we should get rid of it.'

'It's what you want that matters,' he said, in a small voice. 'I just think – you're eighteen. I'm twenty-two. Is this right for either of us? Don't you want to travel? See the world? Babies are meant to be for your thirties, man. When it's all over.'

She clutched one of the cushions and slid it into her stomach. Something to hold on to.

'Don't be like that,' he said.

'I'm thinking. I'm thinking that we've time. Let's sit with the idea for a few days.'

'The longer you wait, the harder it'll be. Best to make these decisions quickly.'

For a moment, she wondered if he'd been here before. 'Sounds like you've already made yours.'

'I'm being honest, Hel. I don't want it.'

They ate their pizza, though he took his slices to the kitchen counter each time rather than sitting beside her. When he returned from crushing the box into the recycling bin, she was worrying at her lower lip, her face off to the side. Her father, whoever he was, never wanted her. Her own mother barely did. Would she visit the same fate on this child?

'You're right,' she said, turning to offer him a pacified

smile. 'It's too soon.' And now, mercifully, he did come to the sofa and take her hand. He kissed it then, her hand, and said thank you, thank you.

Together, they contacted the clinic and on the appointed morning Elwood engulfed her in a huge embrace and said he'd finish early so she wouldn't be too long home alone. She nodded, hugging him back, and an hour later she left too and stood at the bus stop. When the bus eventually came and opened its doors, Helen didn't move.

'You getting on?' the driver bellowed.

As if stunned, she shook her head, once, and hurried home, her footsteps giant in her ears. She stayed in bed, holding her knees close, and when the clinic rang she said she was sorry not to have called but she'd changed her mind. She couldn't quite make sense of it but it had been something to do with waiting at the bus stop. She hadn't wanted to wait for this bus. Neither had she wanted to come to London, or to work three jobs. Or the childhood she got. But she wanted this child. She really did. It felt like it was the first thing she'd got that she desperately, joyfully, fiercely wanted.

She was still in bed when she heard Elwood arrive and then saw him peek around the door before coming in, seeing as she was awake. 'How was it?' he asked. 'Do you just want to sleep? I can crash on the sofa.'

'Thanks,' she said, leaving it at that, because she couldn't face the conversation now. In the morning, he brought her a cuppa – 'a brew', he called it, in some nod to her roots – and she accepted the mug, then joined him in the main room, where he was happily humming around the kitchen.

'So you going to tell me how it was, then?' he said.

'I want to keep it, El.'

Freezing, he gawped, as if to first check whether she was joking, then he closed the cupboard, forgetting all about his cereal. 'Did you even go?'

'It needn't stop you doing what you want, playing all over the world. I'll make it work.'

'But we agreed.'

She stiffened, standing tall, ready to parry whatever argument he'd throw at her. 'I changed my mind. I'm allowed to.'

'And drag me down with you.'

'You can be involved as much or as little as you want.'

'But that's not a choice I should have to make! The absent father or the stuck-at-home dad? You're being so selfish.' Before she could respond, he said: 'Let's be honest, this was just meant to be fun. A couple more months and I'd be off and this'd be done. This was never meant to be permanent, was it?' She stepped abruptly back, away from his words, and whatever was left of those iridescent birthday bubbles burst, the scales fell. 'Oh, come on, Hel.' He rushed up and held her wrists, stroking them. 'What if I went with you? To the clinic?'

'Get lost,' she snapped, shrugging him off. 'Get the fuck lost.'

Turning away, he banged his fist on the kitchen counter and caught the chipped rim of his cereal bowl, sending it

66

smashing to the floor. The shattering unlocked the core of his anger and he took the glass fruit bowl and threw it against the wall. He punched a hole in the cupboard. Pulled down the TV. Broke chair legs. Upturned the sofa. As he went around the room, shouting, destroying, Helen stayed very still and very silent. She'd seen violence before. She knew there was nothing to be done right now and to wait until he was spent. Because it was like watching a vicious dog: her hope of coming out unharmed rested on maintaining control, and then dominating hard. So when Elwood stood in their bedroom doorway with his hands on his knees, panting, Helen took the largest knife from the drawer. 'Come near me and I'll slice your fucking eyes open.' She gave him ten minutes to grab his stuff and go or she'd call the police, just watch if I don't.

'That was Brandon she was pregnant with?' I surmised.

'Indeed it was.'

We were walking along the canal. The day was cold and bright and some kids, bikes laid down, played on the skunk-striped lock up ahead, just as I used to. As we passed the boys, Nayan moved to the towpath's edge, his reflection purling over the water. By now, I'd come to recognise the change in his manner – a certain performed introspection – that indicated he'd finished for the day, that I'd learn no more of his story.

'Got himself into a bit of a pickle, hasn't he? Johnson.'

'This Partygate stuff?'

'Hmm.' Then: 'Your mum likes a party, doesn't she?'

Where was he going now? What did he want to tell

me? I didn't know what to say. He was still bent over the water. 'What's that mean?'

'She was at a party. The night of the fire.' Turning only his head, he looked at me. 'When everyone was coming round afterwards – condolences and that. She said she'd been at a party.' He shrugged, returned to the water. 'It must have stayed with me.'

That evening, Mum was in her salwar kameez, picking basil leaves off a plant, collecting them on a china plate.

'What was the party you were at?' My voice was quiet. 'On the night of the fire.'

It took a moment. 'What's happened? Are you shaking?'

'Just tell me.'

She showed me her palms: there was nothing to tell. 'It was the ladies' sangeet. A pre-wedding thing. In Derby. My second-cousin's something or other.'

'And when was this?'

'The night of the fire. Why, son? What's the matter?'

'But when?'

'It was – let me think. Oh, August? End of August. Yes. The bank holiday. We opened a little late the next day. Then a customer came in and told your dad about the fire.'

'Where was I?'

She made a face. 'Upstairs. Asleep. Being sixteen,' she added, euphemistically. 'Why? What's your friend saying?'

What was he saying? Maybe nothing at all. Maybe I was reading too much into it. Getting too involved. On the morning I was to next meet Nayan, I first climbed up to the pedestrian bridge outside Chesterfield railway station. I looked out. The bent spire. The emptied centre. The desolate car park. The sense of a town betrayed. The waste. If I hated the place so much, why did I live down the road? Why did I keep coming back, time and again?

A spring baby, just, all scrawny and purplish and six weeks premature, Helen named him Brandon. A solid-sounding name, one that would withstand challenges. Bran. Don. The River Don. But it proved a poor augur: feeding was tricky, he didn't latch properly, was colicky, too, and even at eighteen months he screamed if he was ever more than a few metres from Helen's hand. She spent most days attending to him, with the odd afternoon in nursery so she could still clean part time, and every evening she brought him to work, where he'd toddle about the carpeted galley between the pub and the kitchen, until Helen nursed him to sleep for the final hour of her shift. He became known as the pub baby, and Mal adored having him around, pleased as cheese about the boy's Welsh name.

'It wasn't deliberate,' Helen said, spooning the boy his food. 'I thought it was American.'

She cleaned the apple purée from his mouth and forehead, from behind his ear, too, then finally he settled. For a long while she ignored the noise of the bar and looked at him looking at her, with his softly baffled face, this star cradled within the galaxy of Helen's love.

Even once he started at St Raphael's Primary, Helen

brought him to the pub after school because she still had a shift to finish. By then, she only worked nine-while-six; she wanted to devote the evenings to her son.

It was around this time, a long step into the new millennium, Brandon sprawled on the carpet doing his letter formations and Helen chopping vegetables for dinner, that the doorbell rang: through the spyhole, there for the first time since she'd thrown him out, was Elwood. Helen wasn't shocked, not initially. What flooded her body was a combination of relief – it had happened, it was always going to happen – and a feeling of being out of time, as if her mind refused to accept that it was happening in such a prosaic way, while she was halving mushrooms.

'Who is it, Mum?'

'Just the postman, my love.' And she pulled the door only enough to slip outside and onto the landing. He'd aged; no doubt so had she. The lines running between his nose and mouth were more deeply scored. The eyes dimmer, the hair stiff and short. Now, face to face with him, she could feel her heart banging. Now the shock hit her.

'Thanks for answering. I didn't think you would.'

'What do you want?' she hissed, annoyed with herself as she said it. Such a clichéd opener. She wished she'd prepared a profundity – she'd had so many years to think of one! – a withering remark to send him packing, and also, perhaps, to impress him.

'To see you. To see Bran.'

Oh Lord, if she could have pummelled him into the earth right then. 'Are you right in the head? You think you can just turn up and say you want to . . . It'll turn his world upside down. Do you have any idea?'

'I know. I get that. I'm sorry. How have you been?'

'Oh, fuck you.'

He shook his head, exasperated with himself, and shoved his hands into the kangaroo pocket of his hoodie. 'I just heard how I sounded. God, I'm such a dick.'

'You need to go. If you want to see him, there are courts that will sort that out. You've no right to turn up like this.'

He brought a finger to his lips, then said, calmly, 'What if we don't say who I am? Just say I'm an old friend visiting. I just want to see him. Ten minutes, tops.'

'The courts,' she said, chafing against his 'justs', at how naturally he said 'we', as if they were at a dance and she once more on the end of his arm.

'Please, Hel. Ten minutes. I promise. He's my son.'

'He's been your son for seven years. He was your son the last ten times you've been in town and never bothered to see him.'

'I always asked Mal how he was.'

'*Just* fuck off, Elwood.'

'I wasn't ready then. My head was all over the place . . . I'll go as soon as you say. Please, Hel. I'd like a relationship with my son.'

He wasn't going to go. She'd have to cave. And maybe, if she was honest, a small part of her, the part that wanted him to see and feel what he'd missed, wanted to cave, too. 'You don't go near him,' she said. 'You stay in the fucking kitchen.'

He patted down his hair, she saw him gulp, and then he followed her inside and sat on one of two tall bar stools. His eyes didn't quit Brandon, who'd moved to the sofa in the time Helen had been gone. The boy glanced across, took in the stranger, his mother's composure, then turned back to the TV. 'I'm hungry,' he said, as if to the cartoon, to Bagheera.

'Be about fifteen minutes,' Helen said. 'Veggie omelette or waffles?'

'Waffles, please.'

As she set about getting things in the oven – nervy fingers, clashing metal, all kinds of heat crawling up her neck – Elwood whispered, 'Hel. Can I say something to him?'

She paused, finished setting the timer, moved round to the other side of the counter. 'Brandon, sweetpea, it turned out it wasn't the postman but someone I used to know. This is Elwood. He wanted to say hi.'

Elwood waved, sliding off the stool and coming forward. 'Hi, Brandon. It's really nice to meet you. I used to love *The Jungle Book*, too. Is Mowgli still in it?'

'It's Mao-glee,' Brandon said.

Returning to the kitchen, battling tears, Helen watched on while the two finished the cartoon together, Elwood perched like an owl on the brim of the sofa. They had the same colour hair. Identical clefts in their chins. Neither father nor son spoke; neither seemed to need to. When the timer sounded, she took a galvanising breath and said, 'Dinner's ready, love.'

'What about Brandon?' Elwood said, full on grinning.

She didn't flinch. 'I'll show you out.'

Elwood visited every day that week, never staying for longer than half an hour. As he made his goodbyes on the Friday, he paused on the landing and said, 'I've been so fucking stupid. I'm so sorry, Helen.' His eyes were wet. 'I'm in Brighton all weekend – some sessions – but I'd like to come again on Monday. If that's all right?' She assented, then went to the window, waiting for him to emerge onto the street below, whistling probably. But no. He crossed the twilit road; stopped; stared at the pavement. He was breathing deep and slow – she could see the steady lift and fall of his chest. Was he counting? That night she asked Brandon if he'd mind sleeping in the sofa-bed with her and she pulled him close.

On Monday morning, dropping Brandon off at school, she was convinced it'd be a long time before she saw Elwood again. He'd got what he wanted. Seen what he'd sired. Salved any guilt. And now he'd go after the next shiny new thing. She felt relief mainly, and pride: *I've got your number*. But then here he was, six on the dot, xylophone in hand. Surprised, maybe glad to be proved wrong, she allowed the gift, and for the entire visit Elwood instructed Brandon on 'Jingle Bells', 'Love Me Tender' – all on laminated cards that accompanied the instrument.

'I play the violin,' Elwood said.

'Do you really?'

The question lit up Elwood's face. 'Yes. Really.'

'That's marvellous.'

Even Helen laughed, which was perhaps why, when it came time for him to leave, Elwood asked if they might tell Brandon who he was.

'That's for me to decide,' Helen said, but at bedtime the next day she sat Brandon up against the headboard and asked if he still ever thought about his daddy?

'Is Elwood my daddy?' he asked at once, and, oh, how Helen needed to breathe. She felt sick. Had he been holding this hope in his young mind all week?

'Yes, my love, he is. But he might not be able to stay for long so . . . Let's just keep our heads.'

Elwood secured a semi-regular gig in north London, was soon coming round most days, and as the evenings warmed he met them in the park to help Brandon get to grips with his two-wheeled scooter.

Helen watched at a distance. She knew from Mal that he'd been playing all over the shop, minor orchestras, session work, a stint teaching in Edinburgh, always chasing that one major audition. His shoulders seemed slumped; he was diminished, somehow. It's a very heavy world we live in, Helen thought, and as she stepped towards them, Brandon retrieved something from the ground, which Elwood seized and shoved back into his pocket. It was a bottle, Helen saw. Pills.

'Guess what he's been saying?' Elwood said.

'El Hel,' Brandon said, chuffed with himself. 'Or Hellwood.'

'A whole forest of pain,' Helen said, and Elwood raised his eyebrows: was there really any need for that?

Brandon looped in and out of their legs, then scooted off.

Helen said, 'So what's with the pills? Please don't lie. If you're around my son, I need to know.'

'I thought you'd seen.' He jabbed his boot against the ground. 'I get the odd panic attack. But it's under control. It's been a lot less since Bran's been in my life.'

Exiting the park, he handed over the scooter, kissed the boy's cheek; Elwood's bus stop was in the other direction. 'See you soon, buddy. Maybe tomorrow?' he suggested, looking to Helen.

Cutting in, Brandon said, 'Mum. Can' – he thought a moment, a naughty smile developing – 'can Dad bring me home from school tomorrow?'

It was the first time he'd used the word and waves of pride radiated off Elwood. Helen didn't know quite where to look. 'Well, I don't know – he might not be free.'

'I'm free,' Elwood said. 'Of course I'm free.'

'But you've never done it before.'

'I know the school. Will you let me do this? Just text me the details. Please.'

'You sure?'

'I'll be there.'

Once home, wherever Helen went in the flat the image of Elwood kissing Brandon goodbye greeted her. She'd not really thought of it before, but it had been nearly three months now and Elwood hadn't made any attempt to get close. He'd been supremely chaste. When the two of them parted he did no more than nod. He was single, she knew that, and probably she didn't want him thinking of her like that anyway, so why was it rankling? Why was she starting to feel a little jealous of her son? She forced the thought out, only to open the fridge and wonder if she should ask him to stay for dinner tomorrow.

The next day, she was still thinking like this – steak, should she get some in, just in case? – when the school rang to say that Brandon was still in their care; no one had arrived to collect him. She called Elwood, stupidly hoping he might be moments away, got no reply, and then, forgetting her coat, sprinted out of the flat. Brandon sobbed all evening: is it because I called him Dad?

'It is definitely not that. You did nothing wrong, my love.'

She learned the story from Mal: very early that morning, Elwood got a call for a 'once in a lifetime' audition – where, Mal wasn't sure. Paris? Berlin? He cried that he needed to take it, Mal said. To get better. He also took a couple hundred quid off me. I'm positive he said he'd spoken to you about it, but – who knows? – he's depressed, I guess. And embarrassed.

She was sure she couldn't forgive him, and in a way it didn't matter because she never saw Elwood again, Nayan told me. The audition was a dead end, but he hung around in Europe and then somehow wound up in America, on the east coast. Every year, he sent birthday cards with neatly written messages promising a visit to London soon and how he'd then bring Brandon to New York. By the third year, the boy laid these cards and their assurances aside, and set to helping his mum make dinner. One afternoon, when Brandon was twelve and at school, Mal arrived at the flat and handed Helen a box. Inside was Elwood's violin.

'The fool, he did himself in.' Mal explained that his brother, Elwood's father, was flying to Boston to bring his body back. Meanwhile, there was a note some girlfriend found in his apartment and it said that Elwood wanted his first violin to go to his son, and for his son to learn to play. 'So my brother dug it out the loft, dropped it off at the pub and asked me to give it to you. He said he'd have done it himself but, well, he's grieving, isn't he?'

Helen sat for a while after Mal left, then lifted the beautiful instrument out of its box. On the underside was a white sticker: Property of Elwood Phileas Forrester. It took two attempts, but she broke the thing over her knee and deposited it in a bin down the street before Brandon came home from school.

I think I laughed. 'She saw straight through him. I think I'm starting to understand her. Doesn't suffer fools, does she?'

'That she doesn't,' Nayan said. 'Hard as nails. Driest eye in the house. Doesn't care what damage she leaves in her wake.' He gave me a long look, then moved on, up the wooded path towards the car park.

After dropping him off I pulled over, one street away, near the main roundabout out of town. I'd been doing this more often, feeling a reluctance to leave the old place. To leave Nayan and Helen's story. *What damage she leaves in her wake.* Dimly, it chimed with something else I'd heard recently. *She just . . . walked away.* It was the head-teacher. That Mervyn. Who'd also said Helen was *starting* her final year. So, September? But Nayan had said she'd left earlier, before the fire. He'd lied. Or been lied to. The fire was late August, my mum had confirmed that. Did Helen know something? Maybe this was why she'd refused to care for Nayan's father. Rebuffed his advances. I released the handbrake, indicated, and waited to be let in. My eyes on the wing mirror. Cars thrashing past.

I can't deny the thrill I felt. I was no longer sure what story Nayan was telling me.

———

Finished with school, Brandon enrolled on an HND in Food Technology at the College of North West London, and worked evenings and weekends in Mal's kitchen at the Queen Adelaide Arms. He loved cooking, was ardent about it, and though Helen had no clue where this obsession came from, she marvelled that he could still surprise her with these new appetites for life, that even to his mother he remained something of an enigma.

At night, with the pub and restaurant closed, it was now her turn to flick through magazines on the sofa in the pub's galley, waiting for him to finish cleaning down.

'Ready?' he said, bag slung over one shoulder, jutting his chin at her.

Her boy was becoming a man. The deepening voice. The scribbly sideburns he was doggedly trying to encourage.

*

Leon, Mal's head chef, trained in a Winchester restaurant that had won a rosette, but he'd moved back to London to live with his ageing parents, one of whom had since died. He was as broad, pony-tailed and clubbable as Brandon was slim, shaved, reticent, and it seemed to Brandon that Leon enjoyed having someone to command, if only convivially, that to Leon these displays of hierarchy modelled what being a real chef meant. Brandon, for his part, was amenable: he accepted that he was there to learn, even as he knew he fell too naturally into the role of an underling, a facet of his personality he'd have to one day overcome. Also, Leon liked him, this much was obvious.

'You'll be creating dishes for your *own* tables one day,' Leon said, during dinner service on a busy Friday, when Brandon got out five plates of seared salmon all at the same time.

'I'm banking on it.'

Early the next morning, while Brandon sharpened knives against a whetstone, Leon asked him for a chat.

'I'm leaving, Brando,' he said. He was going to head up the kitchens at Ashby Hall. 'It's the private school over in South Ken.' Brandon said he didn't know it. 'It's full of rich kids, but the weekends there are all about fine dining. I'll have to do the school menus as well but ...' He shrugged one shoulder: it was a necessary evil. 'The good news is they've accepted my rider. They've said you can come with me.'

'Come with you?' The confusion evaporated, leaving a warm buzz: some entity he had no knowledge of wanted him; moreover, Leon had insisted on it. 'I'll be working in that school. With you?'

'It's a proper kitchen, kid. And you'll learn so much, cooking at scale as well as the real posh nosh. Best of both worlds. More power to your elbow. More moolah, too.'

'Mal'll throw a fit.'

'And he'll offer you the chance to run this place. It's your call, but you'll still earn and learn more there, I can promise you that.'

Leon told him to sleep on it, to talk it over with his mum, that he didn't need an answer straight away.

When Brandon told his mother about the opportunity a whole week had passed. She didn't upbraid him: he typically kept happy news to himself for a while, as if to first ensure it was true and lasting, and not something that would be snatched back.

'It's a big change, love.'

'I'll have to quit college, too. Long hours.'

'Don't put all your eggs in one basket. You do plenty of hours as it is.'

But Brandon had already decided, and goaded on by his seventeenth birthday, he gave his notice in the presence of his mum, who spent the rest of the afternoon smoothing things over with Mal.

The night before he started at the school, Helen watched Brandon's hands speeding over a Rubik's Cube. Once he cast the puzzle aside, she held his wrists, uncurled his fingers: the side of his thumb, ridged permanently by the peeler; the palm blistered and taped; the grater cuts on his knuckles. The quiet determination and focus, all the qualities that Elwood lacked. She saw much in the son that was a reaction against the father. Closing his hand, Helen said she'd walk him to the bus stop tomorrow.

('She was so nervous for him,' Nayan said. 'She never wanted him to take the job.')

———

In his white apron and a chef's cap that looked like an upturned ramekin, Brandon held open the door for all three students, only the last of whom bothered to say thanks. Even this surprised Brandon. Less than a month in and he was used to occasionally being acknowledged by the staff, but never by students; the previous day, one had crashed straight into him as if he wasn't even there.

'Sozzles,' the student said.

'I was right here,' Brandon replied, piqued.

The student, almost laughing: 'White uniform, white apron, white white. You've got a kind of invisibility vibe going on.'

And he guessed he was invisible to them, with their eyes that only alighted on the aspects of this world they knew best: sunlit quads, ski trips, charity galas, summers in Big Sur. None of that is to say he regretted coming here. Twice a week Leon appointed him head of the school kitchens, fronting the students' three-course meals; and every other Saturday he tied on a fresh white uniform, the school's crest sewn in, and joined Leon to serve the Masters and their guests in the Upper Hall.

'The amount they can put away, it's like the Feast of the fucking Tabernacles,' Leon said one evening, peeling off latex gloves. 'Your veni was okay, but ten seconds longer next time. For the chard.'

They walked out together, along corridors tiled racing green and over the main quad, where moonlight wrapped the columns. At the gated arch, one of the principals was waving off today's guests. We hope you choose Ashby Hall, the principal said, and the families smiled and nodded and said their goodbyes. Once they were dispatched, the principal's smile collapsed; she turned away, near stepping on Leon and Brandon in her haste.

'Oh!'

'Just leaving,' Leon said, touching his white cap. He liked laying it on thick with the higher-ups, and thus managed to both unnerve and reassure them. 'Back in the fray on Monday.'

They passed through the gate and onto the cobbled mews, where the Nigerian family were settling into their chauffeured car. 'There's a lot of black kids here, aren't there?' Brandon said. 'Indian, too.'

'There's a thing, isn't there?' Leon said. 'A quota thing.'

'A quota thing for more rich kids?' Brandon said, and Leon laughed. Leaving the mews, they stood for a moment in a large disc of moonlight, then knocked fists and parted ways.

They couldn't afford the ingredients for Brandon to practise dishes at home, so he spent Sunday mornings with hefty, grease-stained cookbooks he'd borrowed from the library, and in the afternoon, before his mother finished at the pub, he joined a few of the local boys for a kick-about on the common. When the school broke for summer – for which he couldn't quite believe he was still being paid – he went to the common more often and it was around then he saw a girl he liked working the ice-cream van. He didn't know her name, but she wore a denim pinafore, and he saw something kind in her face, in the plainness of her short, mussed, soft-looking black hair, a butterfly clip either side of her temples. Each day, walking down to the green, he promised himself he'd speak to her, say hi, offer to buy her an ice cream, as if he were in one of his mum's 1950s movies, but he choked it, always: he picked up the football and left without a word in her direction; or about to reach the head of the queue, he slid away, blushing fiercely.

'Pathetic,' he muttered.

'What was that?' Helen said, pointing the tub of popcorn his way.

He sulked and tried zoning back into the cop drama. But why were they now in LA? 'I'm going to bed.'

'You going to tell me who you're pining over?'

'Leave it out,' and he carried on to his room, to his cookbooks, until the new school year beckoned, September came gusting into view and the ice-cream girl drove out.

That failed attempt at a summer romance fortified him – yes, *this* was going to be the year he'd make his mark, Brandon assured himself, as the new intake filed in for lunch: he'd be more forthright with his suggestions; he'd enter the London round of Next Gen Chefs; and, generally, he'd take less crap. It was time to be counted, and admitting this, allowing himself to feel that this was merited, filled him with strength, which was why he spoke a little harshly to the new chef who left the lamb in for too long, and when the potwash didn't tidy his workstation. The hardest thing about being a chef, he was learning, was getting his team to care as much as he did.

Service over, he pinned up the next day's lunch menus – headed 'Luncheon' – and was dragging a broom around the refectory floor when Leon found him.

'No issues?' he asked.

'None. How'd the appointment go? How's your mum?'

'Old. No cure for that. The guys say you were like a machine today.' Leon looked pleased. 'Great to see.'

'I want to get on,' Brandon said.

'I can tell. How about we do your halibut confit this Saturday?'

'Turbot. And I want to serve it with smoked lardo.'

'Lardo! Lardo for Brando!' Leon gestured to the tables by the high, bevelled windows. They afforded a view of the quad, and Queen's Tower beyond. 'Once you've cleaned those down, keep them free. Make sure no one sits there. There's a delegation of something coming in half an hour and I've been told to reserve that area.'

'I've still some lamb I could serve,' Brandon said.

'Nah, fuck 'em. I'll do a tuna salad,' Leon said, walking off, giving a thumbs-up. 'Great job, Brando.'

Elated – who knew being commanding was so easy! – Brandon mopped by the windows as if it were the only task that mattered, then returned to the kitchen: had counters been disinfected? Were all knives in their correct slots? Behind him came the clatter and swish of someone opening the door, the squeak of shoes on damp tiles. Leaning through the serving hatch, Brandon saw a girl – in a senior's blue blazer – take a seat at the table by the high windows and proceed to pull out her laptop. There were only ten minutes until the delegation arrived.

'Excuse me,' Brandon called. 'Can you sit somewhere else? That area's reserved.' Met with silence, he felt further slighted when she sank down in her chair, as if someone like him had no business even being in her eyeline. 'Hey! Excuse me? You're not allowed there!' Again, nothing, so this time he walked round, adamant that he did not have to put up with being treated like this, by these rude, rich kids. He stopped mere feet from her and said, in a voice just short of angry, 'I said you're not allowed here.'

She slid her braids behind her ear and took out her AirPods, and with something like belligerence, or was it fear, stared up into Brandon's determined glare. 'I'm not allowed here?'

'No. You're not.' His hands closed into fists with the effort to stand his ground, to fight a voice whispering that this was dangerous territory. But he hadn't done anything wrong. He would not back down. She should. And she did. Before Brandon could say anything else, she hooked up her bag, clutched her laptop to her chest and hurried off, looking behind her as she shouldered through the door, as though retaining his face, or worried he might follow.

*

That night, when he replayed the incident, he felt proud that he'd backed himself and not let her walk over him. Though, truthfully, he spent more time recalling her Air-Pods, which were a new thing and seemed to Brandon some brand of technological magic. He googled how much they cost, let out a 'Fuck me', and carried on scrolling. Perhaps he could ask for a raise, Brandon thought, seeing as he was being so assertive these days, and had half a mind to put it to Leon in the morning. In the morning, however, Leon WhatsApped to say that Brandon shouldn't come into work, that there was some sensitive stuff that needed sorting out. *What stuff?* he asked, but got no reply, either to his message or to his call not ten seconds later.

'You'll be late,' Helen said, coming out of the shower.

'I've called in sick. Not feeling great,' he added, which was only a partial lie: his stomach did seem to have been turned over. It was the word Leon had used – sensitive. It must be to do with the girl yesterday. He was restive all morning and when his phone rang at lunchtime he near enough pounced on it. It was the school's Head of HR, Felicity – Flick – O'Rourke. She confirmed a formal complaint had been made. That he'd committed an act of emotional race-based violence, of racism, against one of their students. Brandon dropped to the sofa, his forehead in his hand. His heart railed against his ribs.

'But I never said anything! I just asked her to leave.'

'I understand you had to keep that area clear. But how did you ask her? Were you abusive?'

'No! I was annoyed, I think – there was a misunder—I didn't know she had earphones in. But I never said

86

anything racist,' he repeated, keen that she understand this fact, which in Brandon's mind was surely enough to exonerate him.

'Things are never as clear cut as that. Did her race play a part in your decision to ask her to leave, in the way you did?'

'No!' Though did it? he wondered, bewildered, thoughts wriggling away. Then, with decisiveness: 'No. It didn't. And she didn't look abused or anything. She looked angry.'

'Abuse takes many forms, we can all agree on that, can't we?' He nodded, though of course she couldn't see him. 'Brandon,' she said, with a little more warmth. 'It's a delicate situation. I'm sorry, but I'm going to have to sign you off for the rest of this week while we investigate.'

As soon as the call ended his googling began and he rapidly uncovered the girl's Facebook page. She was a diplomat's daughter from Richmond; her profile picture showed her paragliding. She'd written a long post about her abuse at his hands. 'Two hours ago,' it began, 'I was just sitting there looking up presents for my brother's twenty-first, when this angry, red-faced white man came right up to me and told me to get out, that I wasn't allowed to sit there, that I didn't belong in that place.' The piece described him as one of the cooks and that his hands were ready in fists and his eyes bulging he was so out-of-his-mind with hatred at the site of a Black girl calmly getting on with her life. 'Are we not even safe in our schools?' She called upon the leaders and principals to listen to Black voices, to believe Black voices when they say they are treated with violence every day of their lives. The post had garnered, was still garnering – live and in front of him the numbers ticked up – thousands of shares, likes and comments, and before he'd finished reading this first post, a second materialised. Everything was happening so fast, speeding to the shocked pace of his heart. 'Update! He called me angry! I've been told he said I behaved angrily. This is what happens, people. They pull out the Angry Black Woman trope. They make it the Black Woman's fault. I was not angry at the time – I'm fucking raging now – but at the time, Mr Brandon Fletcher, I was scared. I was frightened. I was genuinely fearful that you were going to follow me and do to me what is done to Black Women all over the world since time began. Just *this year*, I've had my bag searched because this woman said I looked 'suspicious'. I've had some white guy make monkey noises at me on the bus. And I won't take it anymore. I've had ENOUGH. So, *Brandon*, don't you dare say I deserved your rage. Don't. You. Fucking. DARE.' Seeing his name like that, so baldly, so basically, stripped of every decent thought he'd ever had about himself, triggered an internal convulsion, and he staggered to the toilet to be sick.

Later, standing at the long slit in the curtains, he watched his mother stopped by the man who'd been outside all evening, ringing the bell; then Brandon heard her feet on the stairs, her key in the door.

'Love, what's happened?' she said. 'Are you okay? What's that reporter want?'

He gazed at her, astonished that, despite all this, she remained his mother. Still in her coat, she gathered him into her arms, and the touch brought out more tears than he knew his body could contain, so many tears that they altered his breath.

'Easy now,' Helen said, and led him to the sofa. 'You're having a panic attack. Breathe with me.'

Slowly, he explained everything as he understood it, and after he showed her the bearpit online, Helen held him again, more strongly now, pressing his face into her neck as though she might hide him there. Before her own tears could fall, and with an effort verging on violence, she broke the embrace.

'Are you absolutely certain you didn't say anything racist, Brandon? Even without meaning to? Be honest with me.'

He raised his face to the ceiling, and Helen feared some terrible confession was coming; instead, he shook his head. 'No. I keep going over it. I told her to leave. Angrily, maybe, but not . . . not in the way she's saying. I promise you, Mum, I didn't say anything racist.'

She called Leon, several times; he responded with a single text: *The School have told me not to be in touch with Brandon. I'm sorry.*

'At least the reporter's gone,' Helen said, from the window.

Neither of them could sleep that night, and at around two a.m. Helen came into Brandon's room, where he lay in bed, his face a green oracle in the glow of his phone.

'Put it away. Stop reading their nonsense. It'll mess with your head.'

In the morning, she couldn't stomach breakfast, nor could he, and the toast went into the bin untouched.

'There was a girl I liked over the summer,' Brandon started, faintly. 'I never spoke to her and I didn't think she'd noticed me but it turns out she did.'

There was a note in his voice that made it impossible for Helen to talk.

'She saw the posts and said that she recognised me and that I used to hang around the common ogling her. She said that even then I looked like a creep.'

'She's reimagining things,' Helen managed. 'Ignore it.'

'I did want to talk to her. But I kept losing my nerve. Maybe it was creepy.'

'Don't. Keep your spine, Brandon. A boy tries to inno-cently approach a girl he finds pretty and we call that creepy now? I'll be sure to remember that.'

'But maybe I *am* creepy?'

'Oh, no, love. Don't.' She held his head and brought it down to her shoulder. 'Please don't let them do this to you.'

She called Flick O'Rourke, the Head of HR, demand-ing a meeting for that very day, and not until Helen threatened to talk to the reporter did Flick consent. 'I've time over lunch. One o'clock. But I insist you come alone, for your son's sake.'

Helen had never been to South Kensington before, let alone to this parodically expensive school that spread out from a mews. She gave her name to the ancient grey-suit at the arch, who spent an age finding her on his iPad, scrolling with excruciating hesitancy, as if any wrong move might trip an alarm. Inside, the quad was near empty – a few students sitting on steps, phones out – but all was noise indoors. She heard the chanting at once – 'Kick him out! Kick him out!' – and, as if entranced, walked towards it, along a high-ceilinged corridor and through a set of double doors that led to a gallery, a mezzanine floor looking down onto a large hall. Below her, tens, perhaps even a hundred students were shouting as one, stamping their feet. 'Kick him out! Kick him out!' They brandished home-made boards, many showing a red no-entry sign painted over an enlarged photo of Brandon. Leading the protest, on the stage, was Brandon's accuser, impassioned, bespectacled, a jade bracelet sliding up and down her thrusting arm. Helen recognised in that instant that there was no beating this for her little boy. Not because their words were buttressed by wealth and power, but because it wasn't about words at all. Looking at the girl, the woman, she was all conviction. Amid the ardency of that truth, her boy's pleas were about as audible as a robin's heartbeat. Helpless, Helen shut her broken-zipped coat around herself and returned to the lobby, from where, a full fifteen minutes later, Flick O'Rourke collected her.

'How is Brandon?' Flick asked, half-sitting on the corner of her desk, motioning Helen to the visitor's chair.

She was youngish and recklessly tall, with sharp lips that seemed of a piece with her pointy lapels, her geometric haircut. Helen wished she'd just go and sit behind her desk like normal folk, instead of trying to be friendly. 'Not well. We've had people at our door.'

'I'm sorry to hear that.'

'You lot abandoning him isn't helping. I'm here to ask you to please sort it out. He's not done anything wrong. It was a misunderstanding. Any idiot can see that.'

'Well, even idiots have to investigate, I'm afraid.'

'And how long will that take?'

Flick raised her shoulders and smiled, though it was a smile that expressed weariness more than anything else. 'I know it's difficult. But it's a serious charge.'

'Have you found any evidence that he did something racist?'

'No,' Flick said carefully, 'but that doesn't mean we can discount that racism was present.'

'That sounds insane,' Helen said. 'You can find no evidence for racism, but you won't discount that it was racism? Is that what you're saying? So what would make you discount it?'

Flick brought her hands together under her chin, a contemplative pose. 'It's been brought to our attention that Brandon had recently voiced an opinion on the number of students of colour here at Ashby Hall. An opinion that could be characterised as negative.'

Helen felt wrong-footed. 'What's that mean? What did he say?'

'His comments were to the effect that there were many students of colour.'

'Well, that's just a fact, isn't it?' Helen said, rallying.

Flick looked pained, as if she hated having to spell it

out. 'The implication being that there are too many students of colour here. That they should not be made so welcome. Some might say Brandon's pattern of behaviour is damning.'

'This is insane!' Helen said again. 'You're just seeing what you want to see!'

Flick reached out, as if to comfort, but her hand didn't quite touch Helen's shoulder, and instead spent some seconds stroking the air around her coat.

A video of the school protests had been uploaded onto Facebook and Brandon was watching it on repeat when Helen strode into his room and slapped the phone out of his hand.

'It's doing you no good!' she said, caving to her own despair. 'Stop it now.'

But he couldn't keep the images from gnawing at his mind: the hatred in their eyes, the snarl of the crowd – or was he projecting onto them his own anger? They were so many, and so decided, so educated. Maybe he had said and done things to deserve this treatment. It all confused and anguished him to such a pitch that, five days later, it was almost a relief to receive the letter terminating his employment. The letter contended that he'd not behaved in accordance with the school's values and had brought Ashby Hall into disrepute, and this was advanced with due reference to the applicable clauses in his contract that furnished the school with the right to administer whatever reasonable, proportionate and swift action it deemed necessary in such circumstances. Given he was yet to complete a full year in their employ, it went on, they were only obliged to give one week's statutory notice, offered here as a period of gardening leave. Felicity O'Rourke's name was printed at the foot of the thick, creamy paper, though it was pp'd in a different looping hand indecipherable to Brandon, which felt like a pointed insult.

'Good riddance,' Helen said, refolding the letter and pinching her fingers along the crease. 'We can move on now. I'll speak to Mal.'

Silent, Brandon was sitting on the sofa, his face to the TV, reminding Helen of the afternoon Elwood entered the seven-year-old boy's life.

Mal pretended to withhold his affection – 'I won't let you take advantage of my good nature again, I'll tell you that for nothing' – but, really, he loved the boy and was overjoyed to have Brandon back in the pub kitchen. In any case, Mal said to Helen, the lad didn't need or want his pity; he wanted to get on with rebuilding his life, make no mistake. He worked seven days every week, and Helen rearranged her shifts so that mother and son could arrive and depart together. 'He doesn't need a chaperone, either,' Mal commented, but Helen insisted: she feared him spending too much time alone, on his phone, going over and over his final days at the school. Brandon, of course, knew what his mum was doing, with her uncharacteristic chatter on the bus, the unbidden pressings of his hand. He didn't mind. He liked it. It didn't stop him thinking about what had happened. But he still liked it. It reminded him that he had worth, which was the thing that had been most eroded. He became so accustomed to the eight-thirty commute together, that he registered a pang when Helen said one morning that she wouldn't be going in.

'You feeling all right?' Brandon asked.

'I got off the phone earlier. My mum's died.' She'd never called her 'Nana' or 'Gran', never asked him to, either, and he'd never met her, all of which explained his initial muddle: had her mum called to tell her this? It was the police, Helen explained. Natural causes, they said, which sounded like a morbid joke.

By lunchtime, she was in Chesterfield for the first time in nearly twenty years. It hadn't seemed to have changed: the spire, twisted as if trying to peer behind itself; the allotments and washing lines off the railways; the station's dual platform like a trench. The same damp foreboding. She took a taxi to the hospital, where her mother lay in her own room, the sheet taut to her neck. The nurse said they were waiting to move her 'downstairs' – they just needed the forms – and that she'd been in for over a week struggling to breathe. And then her sodium levels fell through the floor. 'Her brain scan showed up two recent, minor strokes. Were you aware?' When the nurse left, Helen didn't sit down. She stood over her dead mother, who was sixty-two but looked eighty, her face ravaged by heroin. Her hair was like straw and hacked at the ends. She must have started bleaching it, since Helen only remembered a chestnut brown. Her lips were very pale, almost not there, like candyfloss, but her hands were big and present, bearish at her sides. There really is something animal about a dead body, as if some elemental regression takes place at the moment of death. If her mother's corpse were to suddenly awake, Helen felt sure it would be growling.

Returning to reception, she overheard the nurse say to a flabbergasted colleague: 'Not a single word. Driest eye in the house. Her own mother.'

'Where are these forms?'

'Oh!' the nurse exclaimed, scurrying behind the desk. 'Yes. Of course.' And she slid across three documents, which Helen signed without reading. 'And here's a bereavement pack,' the nurse went on. 'It's got some numbers that might help you through this time and details of what happens next. There are some local funeral directors in there, too.' Helen left the pack on the counter and as the lift doors closed she saw the nurse and her friend swap silent, significant looks.

She didn't weep until one week later, when a solicitor wrote to say that her late mother's property now belonged to her. She'd had time on the train up to Chesterfield to steel herself, but not with the letter, and the grief it trailed ambushed her – grief, not for her mother, but for the mother she wasn't able to be, for the mother who always buttoned her cardigan in an effort to look respectable, who'd braved her daughter's nativity knowing none of the parents would sit beside her.

Once probate was completed, Helen rang a Chester-field estate agent who called her back after viewing the house.

'It needs a suite of modernisation, put it that way.'

'What's it worth?'

'Thirty K, twenty-five if you want a quick sale.'

'I want a quick sale. I want it out of my life.'

And it might have been, if not for one hectic pub lunch-time near Christmas, when they were all rushing to keep up. Helen was front of house, serving meals, chivvying along four temps, relishing it despite the clamour and pressure. She'd risen that morning in happy spirits, wallowing in a lovely dream which she forgot the instant she woke, like a rainbow evaporating; the bright feeling it engendered stayed with her, and it was still there in her smile, in her confident sway from kitchen to tables, dishes held high in her hands.

'Two amber puddings,' she said. 'Enjoy.' Noting table five were nearly done – and, more subliminally, how the winter sun made a cornfield of the bar – she backed into the kitchen. 'Those ambers are going down a treat,' she said.

'Good,' was all Brandon managed, stirring a copper pan hard, with all of his elbow. 'Behind,' he muttered, to a newbie coming past. 'Unless you want food to go flying, always say behind.'

'These the beef for the end booth?' Helen said.

She carried the plates out, forgetting the gravy boats. 'I'll be right back,' she said, but here was Brandon with the missing items.

'Sorry about that,' he said to the couple.

'I'd forget my head,' said Helen.

As Brandon turned to go, a male at their only round table stood up. 'You. You're the Ashby cook,' he said, so loudly diners peered over their booths. He belonged to a group of six, all men, not more than eighteen, and dressed erratically – ponchos, Stetsons, medallions – signalling the kind of old wealth that exempted them from convention. Another stood up, addressing the patrons with show-stopping confidence: 'He was sacked from my school for telling a black girl she doesn't belong in England. Do you think his boss knows he's employed a massive racist?'

Brandon hadn't moved, hadn't felt able to, the shock bolted him to the ground, and then Mal was beside him, telling him to get in the kitchen.

'Are you the landlord? Can you explain to us why someone reprimanded, sacked, for his racism is working in your establishment?'

'I'll decide who works in my establishment if it's all the same to you, you plummy-voiced cunt.'

'Who you calling plummy-voiced?'

'I want you all out. Now.'

'Standing up for this loser racist isn't the win you think it is.'

Brandon was shaking so hard, his very mind rattling to escape, that he didn't see his mother charging forward until she'd already punched the guy. 'Get fucking lost,' Helen seethed. She swiped the phone from a third friend recording everything and brought her heel down on it. 'Get the fuck lost.'

She and Brandon spent that evening in silence. Will he ever be left in peace? she wondered, and felt an answer of sorts arrive the next morning, when Mal rang to say it'd be better if they took the week off. He had some idiots causing a fuss outside. Wait while it dies down.

'It's happening again,' Brandon said softly, and slumped back to his room, where Helen found him a few hours later staring at a brown bottle of barbiturates. How long has he had these? Since the school? She sat at his side on the red-grey duvet, the sandwich she'd made for him on her lap.

'Care to explain?'

'Leave off. I'm not going to do anything stupid.'

'Glad to hear it,' and she eased the bottle from his hand, and held him while he wept. 'I'm cancelling that house sale. We're moving,' she said, surprising even herself, as if the decision had been made only by its utterance.

'That poor kid,' I said.

Nayan didn't say anything. The parchment enclosing his lunch rustled in the breeze. We were sitting at a table in Longshaw. Deer nearby. The boggy smell of cowpats.

'Remind me, when did she leave town again? The first time, I mean.'

He remained silent, then picked up his lavishly buttered brioche and took a deep bite. The wind snatched the parchment. Startled the deer.

'Cool your jets,' he said, mouth full of food.

3

Even in his lunch hour, Nayan pulled on his running gear and up and over the monumental grey hills he went, the gaping concrete waves that the city surfed; his calves burning up to Weston Park and the children's hospital, through Ponderosa, then freewheeling down to Kelham, darting in and out of the students, freshly arrived, and back up again into Parkwood Springs, where he stopped on a mound and surveyed the city, the multicoloured flats and Edwardian villas gripping on to the hillsides lest they fall into the shoppers' bowl below. Running through the city was different to running in the Peaks, and that difference was Veer. Alone on the heaths, all that wild green and open weather, all those cycles of feeling, the atmospheric circular gesturing towards pain – he felt so close to his son. Here, climbing through the city, gasping, his mind shredded to rags, it was as exhilarating as sex, as if he and this place really were made for each other. Checking his heartbeat, the time, Nayan turned away from the view and started hard for the return leg. Meanwhile . . .

*

'What's this meant to be?' said Pyara, his neck extending over the meal.

'Cheese on toast,' Brandon said, and filled a glass with water from the jug. 'A bit jazzed up, maybe. Give it a go.'

'But what's the muck on it?'

'I can add more chilli if you like.'

Brandon switched to *Bargain Hunt*, which, over a month into the job, he knew helped Pyara finish his food, and then moved to the armchair and his phone. Two messages: his mother, telling him to clear his camping gear out of the front room, and a form text from Ashby Hall (*Revision Tips!*) whose notifications he was still to unsubscribe from, as if even now he harboured hope for an acknowledge-ment they'd got it all wrong. He seemed not quite able to accept that any such acknowledgement would arrive irre-spective of whether he was on their mailing list. It was like pressing on a sore, the way he kept returning to these things, and he swiped up to an archived message, a link to a statement by the Dean of Ashby Hall confirming that the member of staff involved in the recent incident was no longer in their employment. In the smug voice of the school's management, the statement went on to outline the steps the school was taking to ensure this never happened again, which included 'working with a BAME-centred recruitment company to conduct a root-and-branch over-haul of our hiring practices. This will take several weeks, such is the size of the task, but we're pleased to today share that progress is already being made. All our staff have sub-scribed to a privilege walk, and next Saturday, Toby Lassiter, an outstanding British-Jamaican chef to the stars, will be joining us as we deliver meals dedicated to Caribbean cuisine and history and display on the canteen walls real-life stories of Britain's hand in the slave trade. We're also delighted to let you know that we have a new recruit to the Ashby kitchen family. Please welcome Chand Chawla. Chand, who is from North London but boarded in Brighton, is taking a brief break from what sounds like an unforgettable gap year of travelling to help us . . .' Brandon had to stop reading.

After washing the dishes, he coaxed Pyara out for a short walk, and they hadn't been back long when Nayan came through the door trailing a further blast of cool air. Despite an overloaded rucksack and arms full of papers, he was full of bonhomie as he unburdened and collapsed onto the settee, hands behind his head.

'Finally brought down capitalism?' Pyara said, with a shaky smirk.

'New goals, Dad. Not bringing it down – using it against itself.' He leaned forward, radiating purpose. 'I've been with the district council all afternoon and they've finally agreed to commission a report into a citywide UBI pilot.' Then, because Brandon looked nonplussed: 'How've things been here? Did you eat your lunch, Dad?'

'Polished it all off, didn't you?' Brandon said, Pyara's attention suddenly lost to the wall. 'There was some béchamel left over,' Brandon continued, 'so I made a cauliflower thing and put it in the fridge in case you fancy it later. Plenty for two.'

'Wow,' said Nayan. 'Thank you. You said you were a cook, weren't you?'

'Once upon a time,' Brandon said, as if he was five times his actual age. Nayan was reminded of the mock-up Lisa-Marie urged on him outside the lifts, when he'd been dashing off to meet the council. He jiggled the leaflet free from the paper pile.

'I could do with a fresh set of eyes on this. Young eyes.' Really, he just wanted his great slogan praised. 'The election I'm running for, yeah? This is our headline messaging.'

'Let's Stay Solid?' Brandon said.

'Solid as in solidarity. Sticking together to make real change happen.'

'Right.'

'Why? What's the matter?' The boy was looking doubtful.

'Nothing. I just think – solid to me means, you know, solids. Like – poo.'

'Poo?'

'But that's just me.'

'So you're reading it as "Let's Stay Shit"?'

'No! Just . . . Well, yeah, I guess I am. Sorry.'

Nayan flopped back against the settee. Beside him, his dad was chuckling, though whether at this or at something entirely other wasn't clear. 'Fuck,' Nayan said. 'Thought we'd nailed it.'

'Let's Stay Together?' Brandon suggested.

But Nayan could feel himself losing faith with the

whole angle of it, the slogan retreating from his mind and leaving him dazed and empty-headed, as if in some strange sympathy with his father. 'Hmm, maybe. Like that crappy remain campaign.'

'Sounds a bit like a broken marriage, too.'

Snapping out of it, standing up with a sigh, Nayan said, 'Not your problem. He's been okay, then, you said?'

'Fine, yeah,' Brandon replied, getting to his feet, too. 'We went for a little walk while it was still light out. And I put the receipt for the food by the cooker. I had to shop at Margot's,' he added, in an ominous voice.

'Jeepers. Twenty questions.'

'At least. She even offered me a paper round. Said the fresh air would help clear any smells off my clothes.'

'She's such a racist.'

Flinching internally, Brandon took his jacket from the newel post in the hall. Nayan settled up, giving the lad a bit extra for all the food help.

Brandon was back on Thursday that week, which was when, saying goodbye and putting the car into gear, the idea for the Diwali night came to Nayan. Perhaps seeing the boy-cook again stirred up thoughts of *food* and (Let's Stay) *togetherness* and ('while it was still') *light*, so that by the time Nayan reached the office he was convinced an evening celebrating Diwali, where all parties were invited, would get his message across better than any mere slogan.

'Sounds a bit forced,' Lisa-Marie said.

'Is the annual Christmas do forced?' Nayan countered.

'I hate the Christmas do.'

'And you can hate this, too. I'm only asking if you think it'll help my campaign.'

They were in the boardroom with five others, everyone sitting on the same side of the oval table, and Megha now walked in and took a chair opposite, as if arriving before a panel. Since announcing her candidature, Nayan had seen her around the office, even held the door open for her once, but – what with the summer break – this was the first time they'd been in the same room, and with other people, with an audience, which lent events a frisson.

'Morning, Megha,' said Nayan.

She took a beat, smiled. 'How are you?'

'Just dandy.'

'Good. And thank you,' she continued, not fazed by the onlookers, 'for being so professional about . . . well, everything.'

Nayan happily accepted the public flattery, understanding it as a ploy to remain in his good books, and decided then and there to invite her to the Diwali event.

The session over, Richard caught up with Nayan and Lisa-Marie in the corridor. He was the Health and Safety lead, in the union since his teens and a contemporary of Nayan's, with dark, determinedly receding hair pruned close to the skull.

'You off to Swinton right now, Ny? Can't cadge a lift to the steelworks, could I?'

'But you drove here,' Lisa-Marie said. 'I saw you parking up. Badly.'

He held up his wrist, which was in a cast: a squash injury, he'd explained in the meeting. 'Here's fine. But doesn't look great, the health-and-safety dude rocking up in his car like this. I'll get enough grief as it is. I keep getting asked if I tripped over a filing cabinet.'

'Sure thing,' Nayan said. Then, to Lisa-Marie: 'Diwali. Let's do it, yeah?'

'Do I have to wear a sari?' Lisa-Marie said, walking off down the corridor. 'I wouldn't want to offend.'

'There's a line, Lise,' Nayan called. 'A fucking line.'

In the car, Richard asked after Nayan's dad and Nayan after Richard's youngest, who had started secondary school that year. How was it going?

'Good, yeah. Annie seems to have managed the transition well enough. You got any weekend plans?' Nayan was used to this, the discomfort men felt when speaking to him about their own children, the hairpin swerve towards safer, blander territory. It was a loss on top of the loss: he missed knowing he was a person who made others feel comfortable.

Hitting the dual carriageway, Meadowhall rising like a glass ogre on their right, Richard asked, 'What was that about Diwali? Isn't that Megha's brief?'

'A campaign event, for me. To bring everyone together. You're coming, by the way.'

'Love me a tealight. But she will drag it onto her agenda. You do know that? Did you see it back there? The prevailing what-now? And she was straight on at me with the asthma rates, wanting the numbers split every which way. Do we even have any Jain members? Christ on a fucking bike,' he added, which made Nayan laugh. 'It's no joke,' Richard said, raising his elbow onto the windowsill, awkward with the cast. 'She's so far up herself. Telling you, mate, you're in for a right old ding-dong.' Then, after what seemed like a reflective pause: 'She gives nothing away, does she?'

'I imagine she's – can I drop you at the golf club end? – I imagine she's built an armour around herself. Can't blame her, really. With people going round saying she's up herself.'

'Point taken. I'm just saying be ready to roll up your sleeves.'

'As long as I've got your vote, mate.'

'You'll win, no probs. You're about everyone, you don't care about colour' – then hastily, because Nayan had begun to protest – 'you know what I mean. You know it's not everything. You know that most of the workers being failed in this country are white.'

'Starting to sound like you care about colour as much as she does,' Nayan said, making light, but Richard was not in the mood. Reaching them through the trees, the sun repeatedly shuttered across his face.

Nayan veered right at Parkgate, found a bay behind a flatbed truck, and Richard clambered out, waving adios with his broken wrist. Once his friend rounded the corner, out of sight, Nayan yanked down his visor. He should have set straight off for Swinton, but couldn't bring himself to. Richard's words. Hurtling him back to adolescence, when his (white) schoolfriends' parents would seemingly congratulate him on not being like the others. You're just like one of us, they'd say, as he helped them with their welfare forms. He'd sit with his mother on those evenings, eating the roti she made for him. He never told her what the parents had said, of the confusing blend of pleasure and injury, of being both co-opted and made to feel traitorous. He didn't need to. He watched her hands instead. Mornings in the shop, afternoon on the production line, and now here, flipping rotis straight on the flame, rotating pans between hobs. No care for a tea towel. Her fingertips ironed flat from years of heat. Sitting in his car, he remembered those hands. Hands that taught him how to hold a spoon. Assured himself that if he was at odds with 'the prevailing cultural discourse', this didn't mean he was wrong. How could solidarity ever be wrong? Still, as he drove away he spotted one of the Tories' 'Go Home' vans parked in a lay-by and felt compelled to wind down his window and spit, if only to once more prove – to himself, to the Meghas and Richards of this world – that he was no fucking traitor.

Nayan arrived home via the gurdwara in Attercliffe, hiring it for the evening after Diwali. He liked it: the space, the canteen, the garden at the rear for fireworks, the lack of expense. Apologising for being late, he escorted Brandon to the front door.

'A quick word?' Nayan said. 'I could maybe do with your services. I'm holding a Diwali event in a couple of weeks – do you fancy doing the food? Be about a hundred, I should reckon.'

'A hundred quid?' Brandon said, sounding eager.

'A hundred *guests*. God, I'll pay you more than that. It's hard labour, cooking. Burns your hands.' He let Brandon have the details. 'It has to be all veggie, though. Even if you're using stock, use the veg one. And no alcohol at all, not in the food, not anywhere.'

'No sweat. I used to have to make halal versions of everything – but I know this is different,' he immediately added. 'Is it all Indian dishes you'll be wanting?'

'A mixture. That's kind of the whole point. And you're fine doing it all yourself?' Nayan asked, suddenly having his own doubts, the way you do when about to close a deal.

'I'll do a great job, I promise.'

In Brandon's mind, he was already there, spearheading a live kitchen, shouting for service. Smiling a little, Nayan looked down and noticed Brandon was wearing old black dressy shoes with tiny perforations at the toe-box. Something about this threatened to move him stupidly, foolishly. 'Usually never see you without your trainers.'

'Hmm? Oh, they split. I'll get some new ones after this job,' he said, with a laugh.

'Yeah, yeah, deffo. In fact, I should give you an advance.'

'You don't have to,' Brandon said, seeming to sense Nayan's pity.

'I can't go round talking about workers' rights and hold wages from you, now, can I?' He pulled out his phone and transferred half of the money across. 'Now you can't go round badmouthing me.' Brandon nodded and extended his hand, since a formal gesture felt necessary. 'One last thing,' Nayan said. 'Buffets are always messy. So I thought we'd have people serving the food. Would you happen to know—'

'Do you mean Mum?'

He hadn't meant Helen, or anyone specific but . . .

'Well, now you mention it – I mean, if you think she'd be interested. Be good to keep it in the family, wouldn't it?'

'She practically used to run a restaurant.'

'Is it? That's a stroke of luck – to have someone with that kind of expertise.' He made an iffy motion with his hand. 'Not sure she likes me much, though.'

'Yeah, but she loves me, so maybe I should ask.'

'Sounds like a plan,' Nayan said, with a quick wink.

Helen declined – 'She's not really a party person,' Brandon said, in a tone of apology – and Nayan accepted this, albeit sourly, and on the rainy evening, days later, when he and Helen crossed paths in the doorway of Margot's, Nayan only nodded; it was Helen who spoke:

'I just want to say thank you for giving Brandon a chance. He's made up.'

'Happy to. I'm sorry you can't make it.'

'I'm busy.'

'Of course.'

But with less than a week to go, Nayan was still struggling to find anyone, risking the whole shebang, so Brandon pressed his mother again. Unhappily, she agreed, and now here was Nayan once more ringing her bell, feeling nervous as the door opened.

'He's camping,' she said, by way of hello. 'You can try his phone.' Gone was the modest thaw in the shop, as if she'd had time to deliberate, think better of it.

'He said, yeah. I might try and join him one day. Not camped' – his smile faltered – 'well, for years.' She stared, waiting. Before he'd knocked, he heard the Hoover going and behind her it stood ready to be roused again. 'It was you I wanted, actually. I thought we could quickly go over the evening.' And he told her that it would only be three or four hours, that she wouldn't have to do anything other than help serve the food – he'd stay back and do the clearing and washing-up himself if needs be – and he'd gladly pay her extra. 'It's an evening out of your thrilling social life, after all,' he couldn't refrain from adding, capitulating to a low misery at her refusal to even invite him inside. His mother used to say, admiringly, that goreh never felt the need to be suffocatingly hospitable; but this was simply rude.

'How much extra?' she said.

'Fifty.'

'A hundred.'

'I could just cancel it,' he said. Two can play at this game.

They agreed an eighty-quid uplift and Nayan offered to pick her up – she said she'd make her own way there.

'It's through Darnall way. Just off Lovetot Road.' Though why was he telling her this? Brandon would let her know. 'For the record, I wouldn't have cancelled it. It'd break the poor kid.'

(I wanted to press Nayan on this: 'What did she say?' 'Not much. She seemed pretty shaken.' 'Why would she be shaken?' 'Beats me,' he replied, in a cold voice.)

Nayan continued: 'I guess he must get it from you, his love of food. He said you worked in a restaurant. Pretty much kept it on the rails as Brandon tells it.'

She was silent a moment, then pulled open the door, holding it flat against the wall. 'Do you want some water?'

He waited in the front room and as she returned from the kitchen with a full glass, he offered his condolences at her mother's death.

'Brandon mentioned it. I don't think I ever knew her.'

'She kept to herself.'

'He said, yeah. Did you know my sister? Sonia. She was a couple years above you.'

'Not really.'

'She's a lawyer now. In Chicago. Legged it as soon as she could.'

'Good for her.'

Nayan sipped his water. Why invite him inside if she was going to be so standoffish? 'I hope I'm not overstepping the mark, but I really admire what you did. Leaving to make a whole new life. At that age. Takes guts. Real guts.'

'Maybe,' she said, and wrenching her eyes from his face, she unplugged the Hoover, crouching to coil the lead. He watched her fast hands, the sensuous mouth, her figure. Once she'd rolled the Hoover aside, he looked away and tried to concentrate on the photos of Brandon cluttering the windowsill.

'He's a super lad,' he said, pushed to say something more wholesome than his thoughts.

'He's had it tough.'

Was this her bridge to a little more familiarity? 'To be honest, he's not really said why you came back after all this time. He just said he was having some issues at work. I hope he was all right?'

'We got through it.'

'Was he a member of a union? That's what they're there for. To stand up for him – to help him.'

'No one helped him.'

'What was it, if you don't mind me asking?'

'You don't want to know.'

'I wouldn't have asked if I didn't. I care about him.'

She thought a while, a hand to the back of her neck. She seemed to say nothing without long consideration. 'You best take a seat.'

'You sure? I'm full of sweat. Still not showered off my run.'

'I have an eighteen-year-old. You're fine.'

From the kitchen arch, her arms and ankles crossed, she told him about the school, its grounds and blazers and Latin classes, and how Brandon had been there for less than six months when the incident occurred. The girl had her earphones in. All he asked was for her to move tables. Nothing at all racist had been said – 'it was all in her head'.

'They even admitted there was no evidence for racism, but they said that racism might still have been present. So they fired him. Just like that.'

Nayan listened without comment, appalled for Brandon and, suddenly aware of his own skin, moved that she'd shared this with him; perhaps it explained, too, her refusal to care for his father, to put her family in another situation where they might be similarly accused.

'They destroyed his confidence. They ruined his life, his dream. I was watching him crumble. He tried ending it all.' She paused – maybe she was misremembering, or if not that, allowing small embellishments to the whole sorry saga, turning the screw on Nayan's pity. 'I just wanted him out of there. So we came here.'

'I'm so sorry,' Nayan said. 'And angry. So fucking angry. Even though they found no evidence, they said . . . ? That's some next-level chilling Orwellian shit right there.' Then: 'How is he coping now? Does he ever talk about it?'

'He's better. He still loves cooking. There's not much chance of making that into a career round here but he's getting on with things.'

'He really is a super lad. If Veer was around and turned out half as good, I'd be a very proud father.'

As if prodded, she popped forwards, took the empty glass from his hands and spent many moments at the sink with her back to him, so many that he began to wonder if she was okay. When she did finally turn around, she said, 'I've never mentioned how . . . I'm very sorry about your little boy. And your mum. I'm very sorry.'

('She said that?' 'She did.')

He felt the thrill of surprise, as much for the sense that she was warming towards him as for this voicing of his losses. 'Thank you. Yes. He would have been twenty-four now. Which is nigh-on impossible to get your head around.'

'I think you were married? Did it end because of . . . what happened?'

'The weight of it was too much. We broke.'

'And how is your ex-wife? Did she have any more children?'

'A girl. After we split – well, even before it really – she

114

got a job in Birmingham and moved. Away from here. She met someone and their daughter – she must be ten now,' Nayan said.

'She was a teacher?'

'Yeah. Yep,' he said, impressed by how much Helen remembered. 'In infants. But she quit. Understandably.' He sat up straight and met her gaze; he wouldn't be maudlin. 'She's some sort of NHS bod now. Doing well. We get together once a year,' he went on. 'Without the new bloke,' he added, with a laugh. She was still staring at him, a steady look – he felt compelled to explain. 'On Veer's birthday. I think it helps us both.'

The door-lock rattled and in walked Brandon, hunched under his massive green camping holdall, from which hung a tripod stove and a small orange beach bucket.

'Nayan,' he said, freeing himself from the bag-straps, letting it all schlump to the floor. He looked to his mum, then back to Nayan. 'Is everything okay?'

'It is now,' Nayan said, 'though your mum drives a hard bargain.' He told them a friend from work had roped her twins into giving a hand, too. 'So full steam ahead for Friday.'

'I picked these blackberries,' Brandon said, putting the bucket on the table. 'Don't often get them this late. I was thinking some small tarts, maybe.'

Nayan got to his feet, ready to leave. 'That's your department, chef. But I was saying to your mum' – Helen looked on as Nayan felt a renewed surge of affection for the boy – 'I might join you camping one day. What you reckon? We could get the bikes out as well.'

'You and me?' Brandon said. 'I'd be up for that.'

'I'll find someone to keep an eye on my dad for the night and we'll sort it.'

'Mum'll do that, won't you?'

'I can't,' Helen said, with quiet alarm.

'Your mum's got enough on,' Nayan said. 'I'll sort it,' and he thanked Helen for the water and clapped Brandon's shoulder as he left the house and semi-jogged down the steep drive, enormously pleased with how his morning had gone.

———

The sun had set early and by the time Nayan steered through the gates the gurdwara's orange flag flamed against the dark. He was anxious, keen for things to go well – his pulse had been sickeningly fast all day – and now inside, he vaulted up the stairs, paid cursory respects to the holy book, then raced back down to the canteen, where Brandon was at work.

'All okay?' Nayan asked. 'Everything on track? Do you need anything?'

'Someone sounds twitchy,' Brandon said.

'But have you got everything?'

'It's all good. Everything's ready to go in the fridge or the oven.' He was kneading what looked like a mash-up of butter and flour – a beurre manié, he explained, to thicken one of the sauces. Nayan listened, watched the lad work, the absorption on his face. He deserved more than this, more than a one-off gig in a back-street temple. 'I'm not sure everyone's happy to see me here,' Brandon went on, meaning the two women at the rear of the kitchen, making urgent, clanking work at the concrete sink.

'Sat sri akal, aunty. It's good to see you. How's your health?' Nayan enquired, in Punjabi.

'Save it. We'll be gone in a mo. But I'm not happy. This is a temple not a disco. That new treasurer of ours has a lot to answer for.'

'Ji, ji.'

'What did she say?' Brandon asked. 'Do they want me out?'

'She wants the recipe. When's your mum getting here?'

But it was Lisa-Marie who arrived first, arms linked with her twins, Claudia and Buddy. 'Do we cover our heads?' Lisa-Marie asked.

'Only if you're going upstairs. And you can keep your shoes on in here.'

'This your big election push?' Buddy said, hi-fiving Nayan.

'My subtle election push,' Nayan replied.

'But I brought my megaphone,' Claudia said. Her habitual irony gave way to delight: the blackberry tarts, the pastries trayed on the long metal tables. 'Oh my days, did you make these yourself?' she asked.

Brandon, who'd been quiet around Lisa-Marie and the twins, only nodded, he didn't even look up; Claudia swivelled to Nayan, flicking her eyebrows to ask what that guy's problem was. Nayan couldn't be sure, and hoped – and hoped dearly – that it was nothing more than Brandon's shyness, and not some self-silencing fear of offending Claudia.

'This is Brandon,' Nayan announced. 'As well as taking care of my dad most days – no mean feat – he's also a wizard in the kitchen. He's the boss this evening, no question.'

Together, they transferred the food to fridges and ovens, poured juice into jugs, hung a sign for the cloakroom. Midway through this operation, Helen appeared in white shirt and black trousers.

'The only one dressed for the part,' Nayan said, so happy to see her, grinning propulsively.

'So I see,' she replied, indifferent.

Outside was a garden, more width than depth, in the centre of which Nayan set up a firepit he'd fetched from his Civic. He got a neat flame going using lighter fluid, kindling the licks into a small crown of blue. He stood there watching it; above, the night a dingy sparkle. When he returned indoors, rubbing his hands for warmth, two things happened simultaneously: the first guests arrived, raw with cold, and Helen lit the final dia lamp, a light for every recess that lined the longest wall.

An hour in and Nayan felt pleased, relieved it all seemed to be going well. He'd never had any doubt, of course. The room was full, but not rammed, and the guests, even the ones often at loggerheads – the Corbynistas, the former Blairites – were interacting amicably. He could rely on Lisa-Marie, busy cornering the floaters, talking up their campaign, to spot any acrimony a mile off. On the food front, Helen, Claudia and Buddy were doing a fine job

118

with the canapés, god love 'em, and there was Richard, his wrist now in a rubber flexi-cast, animatedly wagging his finger, either denying a misdemeanour or trying to excuse it. Moments earlier, much later than everyone else, Megha had arrived, too, in a plain wine-coloured sari. He should bite the bullet and say hello, so he cut a diagonal across the room, touching his pocket as much for reassurance as to check his hastily written little speech was still there.

'I thought you couldn't make it,' he said. 'A friend's thirtieth?'

She'd seen him approaching, her smile on. 'I managed to rejig my diary.'

'You managed to rejig your friend's birthday? Did she say she'd turn thirty next year? Can we all do that?'

'There'll be other birthdays,' she said, and swiftly changed the topic. 'Thank you for inviting me. It's large of you. Considering.'

He brushed aside any allusion to their rivalry. 'Though I can't help feeling you've come to see what the enemy's up to.'

'Are *you* the enemy?'

'Nah, definitely not. We're all friends here. It's just the union celebrating Diwali.' She nodded, twice, and suddenly, distressingly, the wind came out of their sails and they were stranded in the doldrums of their conversation. Laboured smiles. Downcast glances. At last, Nayan found an oar. 'You look lovely,' he said, and discovered that he meant it.

'Thank you. I don't often get the chance to dress up.'

'Only at weddings, isn't it?'

She said, heartfully, 'Is it true? That we're all friends here?'

'Course.'

'Really?'

'Megha! Come on – we're a family. More than friends. And like all families we make it work, despite the occasional dispute, right?' He wanted to leave – this was already too heavy – but he didn't want to abandon her, or risk her feeling abandoned. He didn't want to be the bad guy. 'Do you see your family much? They're London way?'

'No,' she said, with false brightness, her smile working too hard. 'That's all gone. I'm the blackest of sheep.'

He didn't know how to react; fortunately, she seemed keen to move beyond this small, personal revelation.

'I just wish you'd asked me to be involved. I am still the DEI lead. Electoral bid notwithstanding.'

'But didn't you say you wanted us all to take a lead on diversity?'

She gave a gracious little bow of her head: touché. 'You're a paragon.'

'I'm just a worker who left school at sixteen,' he replied, unsure if he were being insulted or not, a doubt that, when it came to Megha, he could never quite lay to rest. But Megha only nodded, accepting the barb, and he rallied to cover up his rudeness. How was the campaign going?

'We're having lots of meetings and writing newsletters. It's slowly picking up.'

'I like what you said about educating the union on worldwide resistance movements. What did you call it?'

'Decolonising.'

'Yeah. That's good. I might nick that,' he said, and they both forced a laugh. 'I don't know about you, but I didn't appreciate what a juggernaut this'd all be. Marketing, campaigning, fundraising, canvassing. God, the canvassing. Begging-bowl stuff. It's embarrassing.'

'I like that side of it,' Megha said, as Claudia swung by with a tray of bright, carroty roundels.

'Can I tempt you?' Claudia said, all singsong, and left when Nayan and Megha chose one apiece.

'The food's amazing,' Megha said, wiping her mouth with the back of her hand, a rough gesture that charmed Nayan. People were so full of these tiny surprises!

'Brandon's crazy good.' Should he share Brandon's history, his treatment at the hands of that school? 'He's like me. Or I was him. A working-class kid, trying to get on.'

'Aren't we all? Trying to get on.' Perhaps she was annoyed. Anyway, he wouldn't tell her; she wouldn't, maybe couldn't, understand. 'It's just a shame that the only black people here are the ones serving the food.'

'They're friends,' Nayan said. 'And, in case you need reminding, so are we. You and me.'

'Then, as your friend, can I tell you that given it's a Diwali event, it's very disappointing you opted for a white chef.'

'Do you ever take a day off?'

'From highlighting inequities?' she said, amused, as if she had Nayan on the ropes.

121

He let out a patient sigh. 'Claudia and Buddy, the ones serving the food, are kids I've known since they were born. They offered their help.'

'Regardless. Optics matter.'

'Give me a break – they're Lise's twins.'

She blinked for several seconds, as though refiling Lisa-Marie, whom until this point she'd largely written off as unreconstructed, secretly prejudiced. 'You know, I knew she was a single parent, but not . . .'

'But not what?' He watched her squirm, enjoying it for longer than was necessary. Now who was on the ropes? 'Lisa-Marie's husband was called Peter. He was a joiner, his family were from St Lucia, and he met Lisa-Marie on holiday in Cyprus when they were eighteen. He died of an aneurysm on his way to pick the twins up from nursery.'

Megha was gearing up to respond, when a loud clinking sounded and there was Lisa-Marie herself, standing on a chair with a glass and a teaspoon. The crowd quietened until only a low murmur remained, the faint hum of the strip lighting overhead. 'Before I fall off this thing and crack my pelvis, I just want to thank you all for coming. We don't get together often enough – who is the social sec anyway? – but it's great to see so many comrades in one place. Just to say, if anyone wants to donate, or donate again, to mine and Nayan's campaign, then just be in touch. And I promise I won't mention that again tonight. So Happy Diwali, fuck the Tories, and I'll hand over to Nayan to say a few words.'

Amid the applause, Nayan spun back to Megha and considered assuaging the guilt on her face – but no, she could suffer awhile. He only nodded; and she, who wasn't clapping, looked relieved as he left her side to tunnel through the crowd.

'Well,' he started, placing one foot on the chair before thinking better of it. 'Actually, maybe not. I've had a few too many of those delicious pastry things. So let's hear it for the amazing Brandon!' There were chef's kisses and more applause as Nayan singled the boy out, smiling through his crimsoning face.

'Give us a wave, chef!' Richard called, videoing away on his phone. Nayan had asked him to record the speech; footage that could go out with one of their campaign circulars. With a little retraction of his neck, like a tortoise, Brandon withdrew into the kitchen.

'Camera-shy, isn't he,' Nayan said, delving into his pocket. 'You'll be glad to know I'm not going to say much, but, Lise, can we keep the swearing to a minimum, please? It's a temple, not the navvies' – ('Sorry, boss!') – 'but, yes' – and here he began reading – 'to echo what Lisa-Marie said: thank you all for coming. I thought it was important for us to come together in one place, in solidarity. And what better time to do that than at Diwali, a festival about light, about seeing the truth. Because too often we forget to notice that we're all on the same team, that we all want a better deal for working people. For *all* working people.' He paused. 'Let's remember that and stay together. Let's not let anyone try to divide us. There are those among us who would create splits, based on our background, our gender, even our race.' He seemed not to recognise the line and felt almost surprised to be seeing it, to be reading it out. It was something he'd written when he thought Megha wasn't going to be here and then forgotten, or at the very least not fully apprehended how bald an accusation it would sound when spoken aloud. Sweat invaded his armpits and he could sense one or two turning round, to eye Megha, no doubt. 'These are not modern socialists,' he resumed, speeding up now, 'and they do not have Unify's best interests at heart.' His eyes leapt down the page, willing the end. 'So let's stay together, always, while keeping the socialist fire in our bellies alive.' Wan applause. 'Speaking of fires, I invite you all outside for the fireworks and to celebrate Diwali properly.'

There was a solitary cheer from Lisa-Marie, and as he refolded the speech he knew it had been a damp squib, far from the vitalising address he'd imagined, and when he dared to look up into the crowd, he saw Megha holding her shoulders as though shielding her body from attack.

He caught up with her in the foyer, buttoning her long, camel coat with quick and angry twists of her fingers.

'I'm sorry. That wasn't meant to be aimed at you, I was trying to speak more generally' – he gestured to some place out there, beyond the glass doors – 'but, yeah. The wrong words at the wrong time. I'm truly sorry.'

'You talk about not being divisive,' she said levelly, though the hurt was apparent. 'But that's exactly what you did. You won't *listen* to anything I have to say – I mean *really* listen,' she repeated, cutting across Nayan's attempt to interject. 'You just harp on with this sentimental view of the working class and anything that even looks like it might challenge that, you dismiss.'

'Stay, Megha. Please. We've not even done the fire-works yet.'

'I can't.'

'You can't? Oh, come on.'

She exhaled, making obvious her annoyance. 'I work early on Saturday mornings. In my local foodbank,' she added pointedly. 'You look surprised. Does that not fit with your idea of me? That I do my bit? For the white working class?'

'I've said sorry.'

'Oh, just toddle back and make hay with your friends – your *family* – seeing as they love you so much. I hope for your sake they never turn on you.'

'Why are you being so stubborn?' he said, confounded, provoked by her 'they'. 'Has something happened? You're acting crazy.'

'What do you even think you are?' she cried, with real pain. 'Some sort of brown, working-class maverick?'

'Maybe that's the difference between us.'

She eyed him straight. 'It's a fine line, Nayan, between a maverick and a full-blown narcissist.'

'You know what, I'll tell you what the *real* difference is between us, Megha, if you'll fucking forgive me for mansplaining –'

'Oh, fuck off, you jerk.'

'– it's that I know that there's no such thing as the *white* working class. It doesn't exist. Shouldn't exist. There is only *the working class*. Your kind of politics' – he didn't real-ise that he'd taken a step towards her, that his shoulders had expanded and she was bending away from him – 'this identity swizz you get off on,' Nayan continued loudly, 'has cost them their dignity, their pride, their sense of self-worth.'

'You don't know what—'

'*Your* kind of politics has forced that phrase on them and left them behind as backward, racist fuckwits.'

'I'm going. You need to move aside.'

'You need to hear this.' She tried to go; he wanted her to stay.

'What are you doing? Get away from me!'

'You're the one pushing!'

By degrees, they disengaged, and he watched her cross the forecourt: the hem of her sari fussing below the long coat reminded him of his mother's walk, though that was all they had in common, he lamented, already heading back into the canteen and out to the garden, where guests were assembling around the fire.

Buddy, all skinny arms and agile feet, let off the rockets, and there were the usual appreciative noises when sudden chandeliers rained up the sky, through the peaty autumn air. Nayan looked on desultorily, the argument still batting around his mind; and when Richard nudged his elbow and nodded towards the few lads who'd sneaked in alcohol, Nayan simply shrugged.

'I've told them not to take it indoors,' Richard said.

'Good. Thanks.'

'You squared things off with Megha?'

'Not sure.'

'You both looked a bit . . . fraught.' Did Richard see?

Did Nayan care? 'We needed that speech, Ny. Put her in her place.'

Nayan frowned, as if he'd been praised for taking a shit. 'I wasn't aiming for that.' Had he gone too far? Did she look scared? What if she went to the committee?

'She looks at me with total contempt,' Richard said.

'Bit of a stretch.'

'She won't let people just get on. Making everything a black–white issue.'

The darkness, the old, tedious lines of this conversation, the thought that probably Richard had made use of the alcohol, too – it all depressed Nayan further, and it wasn't until guests began searching for their coats, shouting goodbye, and he shuffled into the kitchen, did his mood lighten. Because Claudia and Buddy were laughing, and sharing that laughter with Brandon.

'Ny, man, what were you thinking?' Claudia said. 'Let's Stay Shit?'

'It's got potential,' Buddy mused. *'For losing,'* and he and Brandon touched fists.

'Your mum seemed to like it.'

'Life pro tip number one,' Claudia said, flourishing a miniature wooden skewer, 'don't take presentation advice from a woman with a mullet.'

Helen entered, empty trays in both arms, and froze: her son joking with Claudia. She dropped the trays by the sinks, untied her apron. 'Brandon, let's go.'

'What?' he said, still smiling. 'There's the clean-down to do.'

Helen looked to Nayan, who wanted to be left alone for a while anyway, to clear his head; he insisted he'd do the rest. 'Honestly. You've all had a long day. Just go. Especially you, Brandon. But, hey – this was something else. Everyone was complimenting the food—'

'Like you wouldn't believe,' chimed Claudia. 'Give me your number. I'm always seeing cheffy jobs on the uni noticeboards. You'd be interested, right?'

So the guests all left, as, one by one, did Helen, Brandon, Lisa-Marie, Claudia, Buddy – only Nayan remained. Stepping into the kitchen, he clapped his hands in self-motivation and began with the metal pots stacked in the trough, using the pipe to hose them down, then scouring with wire wool. The hobs took longer – the hot plates needed soaking – and then he tore bin liners from a roll dumped on the windowsill and cleared all the cups and skewers, the bottles of beer littering the garden, and compressed the bags into the giant roadside bins. He wet a few dishcloths, found an aerosol with which to polish the steel tables, a disinfectant and mop, and filled the first of what would be several buckets of water. Three hours after he began, he stood by the exit, in his jacket, car keys in hand. The kitchen shutters were down, the floor shone, the tables gleamed. It all looked impossibly new. No, he thought: it all was possible. He lingered a while, reluctant to leave, then switched off the lights and silenced their buzzing hum.

4

There aren't many Lisa-Marie Watkinsons in Chester-field. She lived in a pebble-dashed semi on a small corner-plot two miles from my and Nayan's old estate. Pallets of green tomatoes lay outside the gate. *Please take. Free.* A wireless buzzer for a doorbell. Inside, birthday banners smiled across the bay window's pelmet, in the living room.

'My son turned twenty-five,' Lisa-Marie explained.

Buddy, I thought. Photos of him and Claudia on the wall. And of their father – Peter, wasn't it? 'What's he do?' I asked. 'Your son.'

'Not much. Temping. His sister's off doing her PhD. At Manchester. Wouldn't think they were twins.' Then: 'I'd ask you to take a seat but there doesn't seem any point. You said five minutes.'

'Yes. Thanks. I appreciate—'

'How is he?'

'Nayan? He's okay. Quite cynical, I'd say. I'm enjoying reconnecting with him. I'm just not always sure what he's telling me. He seems a bit lost.'

She was how Nayan had described: a round face; marble-black eyes, now fixed on me. I'd imagined her with bigger hair, all volume up top, but it was straighter, with only a single dying fall of a wave. 'What's he telling you?'

'About the election.'

'What a shitshow that was.'

'I'm gathering.'

She looked to the wall, to the photos of Peter: cycling hard up a hill; in another, a little Buddy on his shoulders. 'He left us, then. After the election, he wanted nothing to do with us. Ignored my calls. Refused to let us in the house. I google him sometimes,' she continued, 'and I don't recognise the man. I can't believe the language he uses. He's changed so much.'

My chance: 'Was there something else going on, do you think?'

'What?' she said. 'Like what?'

'I don't know. Anything in his personal life?'

She looked perplexed. 'His dad getting worse didn't help matters.'

'His dementia worsened?'

'Usually the way, isn't it?'

This didn't interest me; I'd have to just ask: 'What did you make of Helen?'

Lisa-Marie tugged down her jumper, displeased. 'They went out for a while until she jumped town. Deserted him, at a guess. My daughter was seeing her son. Are you just out for gossip?'

'No. Truly. I just want to get to the bottom of who Nayan is.'

'Who he is?'

'I mean – why'd he change?'

She didn't look convinced. 'He was devastated and . . . just walked away from us all. Even Buddy went round, offering to help with Perry and that. But Nayan wouldn't open the door.'

And now it was me who was perplexed. 'Who's Perry?' I asked.

'Perry. Ny's dad.'

'Of course,' I said. Nayan had never called Pyara Perry. But I'd heard that name before. The headteacher, on Helen's mother. *A Frank one year, a Perry the next.*

'You okay?'

'Yes,' I said. 'Yes. That makes sense.'

Neither had Nayan ever told me that Helen's mother was involved with his dad. Maybe he didn't know. Maybe it wasn't the same Perry? This needn't be a big thing. Except that I felt it was, that there was so much Nayan was concealing from me, that I needed to uncover for myself.

'Will you tell the daft bugger I miss him?' Lisa-Marie said. 'Tell him he's always welcome here. Always.'

Leaving Lisa-Marie's semi, shutting the gate, I saw a figure standing at her upstairs window. Sizeably muscled, an expansive chest. Buddy? It took me a scant minute to work out what he was doing, to discern the iron weights, lifted time and again in upright rows. I raised my hand, waited; still looking at me, he didn't pause.

In the New Year, I travelled down to London, to Shepherd's Bush and to the bar of the Queen Adelaide Arms. Helen wasn't there. I didn't expect her to be. I don't know what I expected but I needed to see the place, to feel it, and had been nursing my beer for some time when the landlord asked if he could get me another. I grinned – here was Mal! – which clearly confused him. Broader in the face than I'd pictured, he was grey now, and he really was on the short side.

'I'm good, thanks.'

'Good, good. It's just it's been brought to my attention that you keep eyeing my staff. Is there something I need to be worried about? We take staff security very seriously in here, you know,' and his squiggly eyebrows gestured to the CCTV.

'Oh, gosh. No. No, I mean, *no*. I was only seeing if I recognised anyone here.' I came out with it: 'I'm from Chesterfield, in Derbyshire. I used to live near Helen Fletcher and hoped you might know where she was.'

He nodded up. 'What you want with her?'

'I'm writing a story about our estate and wanted to see what she remembers. That's all. I'm a writer,' I added.

He looked dubious – 'Helen's not been here getting on for six years' – and far from furnishing information, filling gaps, he kept pumping me for answers: did I know how she was? When had I last seen her? What was Brandon doing?

'I really don't know anything.'

'Sometimes I worry myself sick thinking about those two.'

'She had some tough knocks. I remember her mum,' I lied. 'A mess. Don't blame her for getting out.'

'She'd never have gone back. But there was . . . some trouble for the lad.'

'Sounds like you knew her well.'

'Gave her a place to live.' Then: 'So she's not in Chesterfield any more. When did she leave this time? Why?'

'She only stopped a year, as far as I can make out.' My thumb stroked my pint glass, as if I were urging myself on. 'Can you tell me anything about her time here? Maybe we can piece together what happened to her?' There was a flicker of reluctance, and I worried that I'd gone too soon – but he was too loquacious to hold out. He invited me to an oak-panelled corner booth, all pink felt seats and hexagonal beermats. It felt disorienting, almost magical, to be sitting opposite him, that someone I'd heard so much about was suddenly made flesh. But, of course, I knew only a small part of him, of any of these people, the part that could be held and beaten like metal into some kind of form.

Frustratingly, he told me little I didn't already know: her mum was a user, Elwood a fool who'd killed himself, Brandon's time at the school. It all checked out with Nayan's version.

'Did she mention anyone called Perry? Or Pyara?'

'Perry, yeah. Indian bloke,' he said, throwing me the quickest of glances. 'Her mother's ex. Nasty piece of work. Why? She's not with him?' he exclaimed, deplored.

'No. She's not.' The pub was filling with a lunchtime crowd, with punters expressing relief: how good it was to be doing this again, unmasked. I thought of Brandon in the kitchen; Helen front of house. 'She's lucky she found you,' I said. 'Really landed on her feet. A job, a flat, shopping sprees on Oxford Street,' I added, recalling Nayan's irritation.

Mal seemed to take offence on her behalf. 'It took me an age to build her confidence. She was a wreck. Afraid. Distraught. Every night a new nightmare. Broken. Probably why she latched onto that fool so sharpish. She wanted rescuing.'

More here that Nayan had not told me; maybe Helen had not told him.

'She wasn't a charity case, either. So don't go thinking that. She paid me a year's rent up front. From the start.'

It was the most surprising thing he'd said. 'Where did she get this money from?' But now perhaps he feared he'd said too much, because he was rolling back off the table, away from me. 'It'd be good to know anything,' I said hastily. 'It might help her. And Brandon. And you want to help them, right? Tell me what made her run away from Chesterfield.'

'I've a pub to run.' He stepped out of the booth. 'Can I get you anything else?'

'Was it a fire?'

At this, he looked agitated, even spooked, his eyes roaming me: who was I?

'Mal, what did she tell you about the fire?'

'How do you know my name? Who are you?'

'I'm not the police. But they can be here,' I said. An empty threat.

'Get out. I want you to leave.'

'Next time I *will* come with the police.'

Mal held the wooden frame of the booth, looked away. When he did speak his voice was calm. 'She never said anything. Only that she didn't know anyone was inside. She didn't mean to hurt anyone.' He closed his eyes. 'I cared for her as if she were my own.'

Afraid. Distraught. Broken. I thought of Helen stripping beds in the Travelodge, pulling pints in the pub, riding the bus with Brandon. How did she stare down the hours, the days? When every today trailed this yesterday as well? I remembered her in the doorway listening to Nayan insist that he'd never have cancelled the party, not on Brandon. I remembered her folding her arms, shaken. Then in the kitchen, trying to turn around and face him. *I've never mentioned how – I'm very sorry about your little boy. And your mum. I'm very sorry.* She'd had to say the words. She had to know what it would feel like to say them. Perhaps it would help. And also – because she'd noticed this the last time he was at her door – the more they spoke the further she felt from her crime. That was why she'd told him Brandon's story. So he'd know they had suffered, too. That she hadn't got off scot-free.

———

Nayan was waiting on the street as I pulled up. He got in, trenta-sized coffee in hand, and picked up from where he'd left off before I'd even shunted into gear. For me, though, focusing on what he was telling me required such effort, my mind all the time wheeling: did he know? Does he know?

Every Friday, Lisa-Marie emailed him the polling report on the members' voting intentions. The results consistently put Nayan so far ahead that as they rolled into December they took a kind of easy confidence into their advertising campaign. Lisa-Marie sent him mock-ups of the ads and asked which colour combo he favoured. *I've no clue. You choose*, he WhatsApped back. The images were all the same: his smiling headshot, the strapline 'Vote Nayan Olak: the Worker's Worker'. A cheap taunt, but as Buddy advised, it established 'clear blue water' between him and Megha, it 'resonated'. *Claudia says the blue background*, Lisa-Marie wrote. *Like you're an angel coming down from heaven.* She added an angel emoji and Nayan responded with a double thumbs-up. *Keep losing reception but dad ok?* he asked. *Fine. Bud's got him all night. Don't worry. Have fun.* Nayan sent a heart and a picture of a tankard. *Owe you 1. More than 1!!* she replied, and appended a string of red wine glasses. *Claudia says hi to Bran and tell him to reply to her msg.* One last thumbs-up and he pocketed the phone and resumed pitching the tent, securing the last pole through the top slips and attaching the canopy just as Brandon emerged over the hillock, without the bikes. He must have caught the lock-up before it closed.

'You made it, then,' Nayan said.

'This place is something else. I want to do that trail

along the river and up into those massive hills there. Can we do that in the morning? Before we head home?'

'We can ride up to Thor's Cave. It's over that way – I reckon you'd like it.'

Really, Nayan would have preferred to go home, where it was snug and dry, and even be there right now instead of out here on a near-empty campsite in Tissington, with the frost underfoot and his nose streaming. He'd tried to suggest they wait while spring, but since Diwali Brandon had kept asking, and looked overjoyed when Nayan finally agreed.

'My phone's trying to tell me there's a pub thataway,' Nayan said, eyeing a brambly drop at the rear of the site, and once there, in the pub, he made straight for the log-burner, all the while removing his gloves and scarf, sliding his woollen hat into the pouch of his windcheater.

'That's better,' he said. 'What you having?'

The pub wasn't even half full and they took the pedestal table close by; but the burner drove them into a booth, under a grimy window with a square trim of condensation, and then forced them to strip to their Ts. After a day spent in layers, disrobing down to T-shirts carried an intimation of nakedness, of being vulnerable.

'You've been round here before, you were saying,' Brandon said.

'Think so. Years ago. The walks are nice. Gives you time to think, doesn't it.'

'But you've never camped?'

'Not camped for donkeys'.' The last time he'd been in a tent was with Veer, when the boy was three and on his first – and only – camping trip. It had been in a field outside Buxton, near a petting zoo they'd visited the following morning. 'No time, is there,' Nayan said, and sipped his beer. 'How's Claudia? Seen much of her since the party?'

'Not really.'

'She's a top girl. Smart, clever. Got her head screwed on. You could do a lot worse and not much better.' Then: 'Don't want to speak out of turn, but . . . Has your mum told you to stay clear? Because of – she told me what happened.'

'I know. She told me.' Brandon turned to the window, was met by his reflection, and as if in response, withdrew his hands from the table and into his lap. 'It's got dark.'

'Happens every night.'

Nodding, Brandon said, 'She's just worried for me. What mums do, isn't it? I do like Claudia. Do you think she likes me?' He asked the question with such incredulity, as though only now had the thought occurred to him, after Claudia's numerous texts, her frank flirtation. It made Nayan smile: even the small amount of self-regard required to believe Claudia fancied him sat beyond Brandon's grasp.

Mid-afternoon, the next day, and Nayan was back at Brandon's, the two of them carting the gear out of the boot and lining it up the stairs. Helen, in her blue tunic, eavesdropped from behind the kitchen archway. They weren't saying much, certainly nothing interesting, but what words were exchanged flowed easily, happily, lightly, between them. There were times during the move here, when Brandon had barely spoken for days, that she'd thought he'd never let anyone else into his life. Hearing them now, Helen felt a pressure inside her chest, an intensity in answer to Nayan's voice, not Brandon's. It wasn't romantic. Of that she was certain. But it was a pressure that filled her with gratitude. Whenever she overheard Nayan, she was reminded not so much of what she had done to him, but that he had survived it, which perhaps, somehow, in some less degraded universe, meant that she wasn't beyond forgiveness, that even redemption might lie around the long corner. She'd had this paradoxical sensation – that the closer she got to him, the lighter her guilt – whenever they'd interacted, and the feeling deepened each time. How alive he'd seemed at the Diwali party! Laughing with the revellers, teasing his many friends and well-wishers, teasing her once, too, when she came by with a tray of some chilled beetroot things and he'd said they weren't quite as cold as the look in her eyes. She'd walked away half-convinced she hadn't committed any crime at all, that his joshing was surely proof of that. And this was a potent, seductive feeling, a lie of a feeling, yes, but one she hadn't known just how much she craved.

The front door shut and Helen swooped into the room, making a show of looking for her work bag.

'Mum. Didn't know you were in.'

'The car's outside, isn't it?' she said, finding her bag underneath her coat. In a tizz, she hooked the bag onto her shoulder. She'd meant to put her coat on first, but her heart was going hard and she didn't want to look at Nayan. She really didn't.

'Work?' Brandon asked.

'I'll be back to put the dinner on. Or you can do it. And shift your stuff off the stairs.'

'Sure,' Brandon said, dismayed at the rudeness, throwing Nayan a look of apology.

'He knows how to ride a bike, doesn't he,' Nayan said. 'I had a job keeping up.'

And now she faced him – she thought she'd worked up the strength, but she was wrong, because to face him was a glorious calamity, the awful absolution of his smile shining down on her. 'I'm glad you had a good time,' she said, quietly shaking.

'We're doing it again,' Brandon said. 'When it's warmer. I think Nayan found it a bit cold.'

'Even the icicles had icicles.'

'There were no icicles,' Brandon said, so droll.

Smiling feebly, Helen draped her coat across her arm. 'I'm going to be late.'

'Let me move my car,' Nayan said, since it was blocking her in. 'And then I should go, too. See how the old man's getting on.'

Closing the front door, they walked down the drive together, until Helen stopped beside her Micra and hunted for her keys. Nayan felt compelled to stop, too. 'Look, I wasn't going to ask – I don't want to be a twat – but if you ever change your mind about that drink, that'd be really lovely.'

'Because I might enjoy myself,' she said.

He cringed. 'I really did say that, didn't I? I'm sorry. But I promise I've completely revolutionised my patter since then. I'm like a new man.'

'Perhaps the problem is having a patter in the first place.'

'Right again,' he said, nodded a goodbye and carried on, towards his Civic.

The further he moved from her, the more frantically her stomach lurched, her body staging an insurrection, hungering for the very thing she was letting walk away: that stirring sensation which only seemed to exist in his presence, a feeling that was no less than the possibility of forgiveness.

'But let me be clear,' she said, as he rounded the boot of his car and turned to her. 'I'm not going for a drink around here.'

One morning, I drove to Helen's house. The tiny drive, the steep incline – it was all weeded over. The wooden porch flaked paint. A firm push swung the front door open and inside, too, everything was as Nayan related: the nothing hall, stairs straight ahead, the living room with the fiddly arch into the kitchen. I could see them pivoting the fridge through it. What was new, what was more recent, were the streaming cobwebs, the thick dust and stale, winter smell. The absence of furniture. No one had lived here for a while. I climbed the stairs, seeing shapes in the maroon carpet. Helen's feet? Brandon's? The landing was crabbed, low, and light stained the wall, seeping in via a cracked window above the toilet door. I knew at once the way to Helen's bedroom. I knew this house so well. I applied my hand to her door and pushed it open, and her bed edged into view.

———

Perched on his own bed, showered and fighting damp feet into socks, Nayan could hear Buddy downstairs, loudly, repeatedly, asking Pyara what he wanted to watch on the telly, and Pyara spitting back profanities. He was in one of his scrappy moods and it'd be a tough evening for the lad – whom Nayan called upon more, now Brandon was so taken with Claudia. Standing, Nayan appraised himself in the mirror – windowpane shirt; sleeves squared and uncuffed to show strong forearms; black jeans: did he look a bit try-hard? No, he looked fine, and whistled a tune down the stairs, grabbing his jacket from the white globe of the banister.

'Look out,' Buddy said. 'Man's getting his brown suede jacket action on.'

'If he's any trouble, just give me a bell.'

'Tsk. We're old friends, ain't we, Perry? Though he did just say to me that "blacks don't work".'

'I'm sorry, Bud,' Nayan said. 'But do you have any weed?'

Laughing, Buddy pointed: 'Back to you: Mum told me to find out who's the lucky lady?'

'No one she knows,' Nayan said, which was more or less true. Lisa-Marie hadn't met Helen, other than perhaps briefly at the Diwali thing. And, regardless, Helen wanted it kept quiet. He'd not questioned why, but she preferred privacy, and there was Brandon to consider, he supposed. From the cupboard under the stairs, he dug out his ancient brogues, frowns of deeply scored leather across each shoe. 'Thanks again, Bud,' he said, lacing them up. 'Claudia and Brandon gone camping, I hear. Didn't fancy it?'

'With Clau's friends, yeah. Her politics crowd,' he added, miming a yawn. 'And I need the money. Living in skintsville ain't no fun.'

'Anything in the offing?'

'Nah, brah.'

In recent weeks, they'd all noticed Buddy's newly American diction, that he was scrabbling around for a way to be that might hold some currency in the world. Nayan knew from Lisa-Marie how hard he was finding even getting an interview, that she worried it was filling him with a sense of failure. Now, Buddy shrugged, as if to shake off the burden of dejection. The dejection remained, though: in his eyes, his hunched bearing. It wasn't long ago that he used to stand with his shoulders rolled back. How quickly the world had made its feelings about him known. On his way out, Nayan kissed the side of Buddy's head.

He was still thinking of Buddy as he retrieved cash from the ATM outside Margot's Mart, and then waited for Helen in the bus shelter opposite. She said she'd drive, which he assumed meant she wouldn't be drinking much, if at all, and this disappointed him a little. He'd hoped alcohol might bring down her guard, smooth her edges, but when she turned up in her red Micra, any disappointment was overridden by a teenage buzzing all across his skin, and any last thoughts of poor Buddy were left on the side of the road, in the coming drizzle.

He was right about the drinking. Nayan suggested they get a taxi back and pick up her car tomorrow, but she said no, to both the taxi and the ordering of a bottle, and she opted for a small glass of white, retained for much of the evening.

'I don't know the first thing about wine,' Nayan said, returning from the bar with his second pale ale. 'Thought I'd best stick with this.'

'Is it too bourgeois for you?'

'You just don't get much of it, do you? One glug and it's gone. Call me a philistine, but I like to get my money's worth.' He tapped his pint with a fingernail. 'Not that I drink much of this hoppy stuff, either. But it's a special occasion.' She said nothing, only raised her eyebrows a fraction. Her knees were crossed under the table, and she still wore her pleather jacket, though they'd been in the pub some forty-five minutes now. Their window over-looked a broad expanse of dark countryside, hills whose murky outlines protested a futility Nayan was not giving in to. 'I don't know if you know,' he ploughed on, 'but I let Brandon drink, that time we went camping. Nothing heavy. I made him stop at two.'

'He's old enough,' she said, with a downturned mouth.

'An old head on young shoulders,' Nayan replied, feeling absurd the second the words left his mouth, but, boy, this was hard work. He sounded like one of those pub bores, full of dull, stale talk. Getting his money's worth? He never spoke like that. It had started in the car, where he'd had to make all the conversational running: how had her day gone, how long did she think the rain might last; at one desperate point he'd said she looked refulgent. 'And he's gone camping again! Just doesn't like being at home, that boy. Always on his bike.'

'She drove this time. His bike's playing up.'

'Claudia? I think she's teaching him to drive. Have you heard? And he's teaching her to cook. Isn't that funny?'

There was another silence, a longer one, and this time Nayan didn't rush to puncture it. He was making a fool of himself. If she didn't want to be here, then fine. If she was only here to get him off her back, then that was fine, too. He wouldn't pursue it any further. These thoughts came quickly, in the time it took the waiter to stop by and Nayan to confirm that, no, they wouldn't be eating tonight. As the waiter left, Nayan felt himself relaxing, and where moments earlier there had been blather and strain, there was a decision: he wanted her to know how he felt. He wanted any choice she made about him to be reached in the knowledge of how deep his admiration ran.

'Look, we can go if you want. You're clearly not enjoying this. But can I first tell you how I feel about you? Would it make you feel too awkward if I did that? I'll get a taxi back by myself, I don't mind. Can I have your permission to speak?' Her hands were still, as was she; she gave a small nod. 'It's probably no surprise that I like you. You're so strong. The way you walked away from here, the way you brought up Brandon alone. He told me about his dad and he said you never made him feel as if he missed out. All that blows my mind. You're a great mother. That's

145

huge.' He could feel the heat in his cheeks, but it was too late to stop now. 'But we're grown-ups. And I'm sorry if you felt coerced into coming out tonight. It can end here. It's fine. I promise there'll be no awkwardness. No grudges. No anything. Let's never mention this again.'

Helen said not a word, and Nayan took some time finishing what was left of his pint. He'd done all he could, and because of that whatever happened next didn't matter. He still desired her, but he felt freed from the ache of wanting her, and the relief of this, a kind of vertigo, was a while in subsiding.

They walked out of the pub, crossing the wet, glistening tarmac, and the only sound on the journey back was the rubbery squeak of the single wiper. He said nothing when she failed to take his turning and drove on past the parade of shops, down the fall of the main road and left towards her house. She parked up, toggling off the headlights, and he followed her inside and waited at the door once she carried on into the room and, at last, removed her jacket. She took a glass of water at the sink, a tall glass, and he saw the wave in her throat as the water slid down, and the way she let the empty glass dangle at her side, the rim of it gripped only by her fingertips. He was held by her. He could not remove his eyes from her, standing there, looking out the window above the sink, the glass surely, any second now, about to slip from her hand and shatter. Everything seemed charged, and she turned round, stepping straight towards him. She took his hand and led him up the stairs, up the maroon carpet, past the toilet with its cracked window, and asked if he'd mind waiting out here until she sorted herself out. So he leaned against the landing rail and watched her door shut while, inside, she drew the curtains and sat on the bed and faced the covered window. She edged her thumb under one of the straps of her top and shed it down her shoulder, as if she'd never done this before, as if she was learning how to undress all over again. How to be new again. Her shoulder bare, she looked behind her, to me, exploring the room, with its old, ripped stickers on the wardrobe, its chequered lampshade, bought for nothing at a boot sale, the kitelike pattern of plaster cracks behind the radiator, which is just another thing that reminds me of the quilted bedspread in Nayan's loft flat. Or does she not? Where am I placing my attention? Is she instead at the wall with a pillow to her stomach, doubled-over, wondering if this pain will ever go away, waiting to see if I can locate in all this her reason for bringing Nayan to her room. If I can provide her with an answer for her actions. A secret wish to be discovered after all these years of hiding? Will giving her body to him make her feel purged, reborn? Is that what she hopes? Does she, on some tortured level, feel she owes him this? Is that why you're doing this, Helen? She doesn't quite move from the bed, doesn't quite step away from the wall, but she raises her face to the ceiling, lengthening her throat as if offering it to the blade. It is all these things, perhaps, as well as something bigger and simpler. It is taking a chance. It is staking your life on the hope that something less painful lies on the other side of the door, which is what she's gambling on as she stands aside, avoiding Nayan's eye as he crosses into the room.

From Helen's house, I drove to the shop where I grew up. I didn't go inside. I didn't get out of my car. It had been redecorated – new paint, new signage in the window. The Sri Lankan buyers had spent some money. The building was still the building, though. The street still the street. Grubby semis. Sad gardens. The rusting, iron chest that housed the overnight newspaper returns was still there, too, at the side of the shop. I used to stand on it as a kid, launch off, see how far I could jump.

Restarting the car, eager to leave, I was soon at the main road when a quicksilver flash of a boy ran out in front of me. I braked hard and saw a purple shirt and a sparkly paper bag as he dissolved into the park opposite. Shaking, still watching for the boy, I let the moment calm, recede, and then carried on my way.

5

A period of time passed in which Nayan and I couldn't meet – work was busy, he said, the pandemic had necessitated a lot of rethinking – but that isn't to say I didn't see him. One darkening afternoon, I walked to Millhouses Park convinced he would be there. So would Deepti. It was Veer's birthday, the day of their January ritual, when Deepti travelled up from Birmingham and they'd spend some time together in the park.

I waited by the basketball courts, behind wire mesh. I wasn't intending to spy, but the moment I saw two figures crossing the grass, spying was what it felt like. They were coated, hatted, shoulders narrowed against the wind – that's all I could make out. I didn't dare get closer. The park wasn't busy; I'd easily be recognised. They sat by the lake and after a while Deepti rose and I watched her walk around the water, my palms clammy because I thought she'd seen me, was coming to confront me. But, no. She settled on one of the benches, right there, not far from where I stood. I could walk past her and she wouldn't know. I moved off, my impatient heart a step ahead. Her hair was tied roughly. Snow-white strands among the black. Her face communicated no expression at all.

'Are you all right?' I asked, pausing.

She seemed surprised, annoyed, though more at herself, as if she'd hoped to do a better job of guarding her grief. 'I'm fine. Thank you.'

I nodded, walked on, along the path and out of the park, leaving the two of them alone.

———

Nayan cut the engine and waited in the warmth of his car until Deepti arrived. He was still undecided on whether to tell her about Helen: it felt faintly comical to say he had a girlfriend, at his age. The sheared turf spread out on his right, ending at the basketball courts, beyond which lay the boating lake. A single jogger in a triathlon suit was doing circuits, rounding the courts, the lake, the kids' playground, coming back up along the stream and towards the car park. Nayan had half-heartedly suggested an indoor venue – 'on account of the frost' – but Deepti sent a gif of a wrinkled man in long johns, which made him smile.

Her car swung through the gate and he realised that, actually, he was anxious – how long had his thumb been tapping the steering wheel? The anxiety wasn't to do with meeting his ex-wife again, one year on. He simply feared the days afterwards, all that sad leftover thinking. Getting out of their cars, they didn't embrace, they never embraced, because this wasn't a social thing, it always felt more formal than that, and they walked to the lake (the jogger panting past them) asking how the other was, if work was going well. Strained chat, as it often was to begin with. Unlike Nayan, she'd had the foresight to bring a blanket, a fleecy Mondrian, and she folded this once and laid it on the grass mound overlooking the lake.

It's called the boating lake, but it's not one, not really, not even by our country's meagre standards. It's a large pond that, in the hotter months, is aswarm with paddle boats. They'd – Nayan and Deepti – come here twenty – no, now twenty-one – years ago, to Millhouses Park, a winding drive from their home, an excursion to mark Veer's fourth birthday. The boy liked boats and Nayan had spoken to the council the previous week, who'd agreed that, for no more than an hour, one paddle boat could be taken out of winter storage. Sitting on Deepti's blanket, Nayan suddenly remembered the council man greeting them at the lake that day. His green, cable-knit jumper. The many befuddling pockets of his combats. The way he'd asked Veer which colour boat he'd like. A picture-book example of a park ranger.

'I guess this is what's meant by bracing weather,' Deepti said, sitting down, too. She was shivering.

'Biting weather,' he said.

'Bitter weather.'

'Brisk?' Nayan offered, and she smiled, a little. Her legs, in their wool-lined boots, were set aside underneath her, her gloved hands in her lap and an old, knitted hat, one Nayan recognised, was stretched low over her ears. In profile, she could be mistaken for being haughty, with her ski-slope nose and raised chin, and people were always misreading her reserve, her habit of reflection, for high-mindedness. In the beginning, even Nayan's mother imagined Deepti had airs, that she looked down on folk from that 'stupido' long neck of hers. A neck that, Nayan noticed, was starting to crêpe. As if following his thoughts, she adjusted her scarf and popped up the collar of her coat. He was reminded of the afternoon she lay in a sunbeam on his bedroom floor, her neck exposed as she pushed up onto her elbows and announced that they should marry. I say that it reminded him, but truth be told it's the memory Nayan always recalls: both sixteen, a Sunday in March when his parents were away, the shop closed, and he'd sneaked her upstairs and into his box room. When she announces the idea, she is enjoying the sunlight, which tints her hair, drapes her skin, as if, in fact, she is not luxuriating in the light at all, but wearing it.

'And how's Usman?' Nayan asked, staring out over the lake. The still water had the cold, dark look of leather. In the minutes taken to walk here from the car, daylight had all but gone.

'He's working hard on his surgeon exams. Too hard. I'm worried about him.'

'*I'm* worried about him.'

'Be nice,' she cautioned, not entirely solemnly.

'Last year you said you were talking about more children. I felt like you were prepping me.'

'I'm forty-two. I'm not having more children.'

'Is he no longer capable?'

He didn't know why he indulged in these ugly competitive swipes: they'd separated, and Deepti had been in Birmingham for three years before Usman arrived on the scene. Dismayed, wondering why she bothered, she pressed Nayan's wrist and said she was going for her walk. He remained on the blanket, hugging his knees, face down, and when he glanced up some time later Deepti had arrived at the other side of the lake. There are three iron benches on that stretch, each held in a cone of light, as if the benches had been positioned there precisely so they'd be lit by the arterial road beyond. Deepti sat on the very lip of the middle seat, one hand on the armrest and her head tipped low at the neck, as if in submission to her grief. Without the bench, it'd be like she was curtseying.

———

Nayan and Deepti married in the same year as that sunlit afternoon in Nayan's tiny bedroom, when Deepti had first suggested it. They'd not intended to wed quite so soon – Deepti wanted to prioritise her teacher training – but when a priest drove by the local leisure centre one evening and spied them 'mouth-kissing, so much mouth-kissing', her entire extended family turned up at Nayan's house and insisted a date be set. Within two months, the ceremony took place; Deepti moved in with Nayan, his parents, and his sister, Sonia; and then, in 1993, when they were just eighteen, Veer was born, ten days late. He kept them busy, and they chose to wait before having a second: Deepti had finally begun a part-time degree in primary education, Nayan had been promoted to assistant team leader at the Bristow's factory, and they were both keen to buy their own place.

'It's a mistake,' Nayan's mother, Muneet, declaimed.

'Whatever happened to living together? To sharing food and breaking bread? The communal life? You're not that English yet, are you?'

'We won't be far,' Nayan said. He felt bad, especially as Sonia would leave home, too, the moment her university offer came in. 'But at least you'll get your room back,' he contended, because his mum and dad hadn't shared a bed for years. 'It's not the best fold-out settee in the world.'

'Have I complained? Once? I love having you all here.'

'And you'll be over all the time.'

'Just try and stop me. Is all this Deepti's idea?' His mum was at the stove, frying aubergines, and he came up and held her from behind. 'Stupido,' she said, lifting her bangled arm to stroke his head.

Nayan registered for extra shifts at the air-con factory, Deepti walked to her campus and back, saving the bus fare, and in time, and not long after that birthday on the boating lake, when they'd celebrated Veer turning four, they were handed the keys to a three-bed terrace on the other side of the estate, close to both sets of grandparents. They were trying for their second child by then, so this house was what they needed, Nayan said.

Muneet, as it happened, did come over all the time. Regularly, Nayan drove them to his straight from work; or if their shifts didn't coincide, he'd pick her up on his way home and she'd be with them for the evening. It was understood that this was so she might spend a few hours with her grandson and give Deepti a break, but also, Nayan knew, she needed the time away from his dad.

'I wish you'd sleep here sometimes,' Nayan often said, as he prepared to drive her back.

Muneet always deflected: 'And I wish for world peace and the waist of a twenty-year-old. What can you do?'

On one Friday in August, though, when Nayan stopped by at the shop, he was adamant that his mother would be staying overnight. It was his and Deepti's anniversary, and they were hoping to go drinking in Sheffield after a meal in an Italian restaurant. They wouldn't be back until late.

'But who'll open the shop in the morning?' Muneet asked.

'Can't Dad do it?'

She made a screwy face, as if to say that would be the day. 'You know he goes out.'

That his dad 'went out' most weekend nights had been a feature of Nayan's life. Relatives, friends, fellow shop-owners, they all commented on it. *Likes going out, doesn't he, your dad? Goes out a lot, huh?* He knew what they were getting at. It was no secret among the community that his dad was a pubber and a drinker, that he slept with women who weren't his wife. Once, years earlier, Nayan had challenged this behaviour, accused his dad of being a nasty husband, of making his mum's life hell. That he made her work all mornings in the shop, then she was on afters at the factory, then waiting on him at night. Apologise to her, he'd demanded, with all the tearful rage of a fifteen-year-old. Pyara had listened, then said, quietly, 'She doesn't have to work at that bottle place. That's her choice.' He was louder at night, when Nayan and Sonia heard him shouting, blaming Muneet for poisoning the children against him.

'I'll ask,' Nayan said, and indignation propelled him down the stairs and into the shop, where his dad was sitting on a button stool behind the cash register, bagging up a customer's shopping. He was already in his fake, red Ralph Lauren shirt, tucked into starched straight-cut jeans. A big-buckled belt and square gold watch. Tan, pointy shoes. His hair was gelled and combed into glossy rivulets that showed no real sign of the baldness to come. As soon as the shop closed at eight, he'd snatch up his jacket and go. Nayan waited for the customer to leave.

'Dad, can you open up tomorrow? Mum's going to stay at ours.' He tried to be nonchalant, as though he were only asking him to pass the salt. But then why the damp under his arms as if he were that fifteen-year-old again?

Pyara arched one eyebrow, not so much considering the question as wondering why his son felt it was a reasonable one to ask. 'I've been in here all evening. I'm not opening up as well.'

'It's just it's our anniversary and we'll be late back. It'll be easier if Mum just kips over with Veer. I'll drop her off at around eight? It's just an hour or so in the morning.'

'Why doesn't Veer stay here? I'll take him to the park tomorrow.'

'He's got swimming. It's not practical. Come on, Dad.'

'Nope,' Pyara said, with a sigh. 'I've folk expecting me. I don't know when I'll be back.'

Nayan heard his mum's angry feet on the stairs – she

must have been listening over the banister – and then her voice, before she'd even entered the shop: 'Why? Which whore's bed are you defiling tonight?'

'Mum, please,' Nayan said. 'Let me talk.'

'You should be ashamed,' Muneet said. 'You've grand-children now.'

'Look, I don't care,' Pyara said, infuriatingly calm. 'She can open up at eight if she wants. It's not the end of the fucking world if the papers don't go out. But I'm out all night.'

'Why you no fucking care?' Muneet said, in a switch to English.

'Why you no fucking care?' Pyara mimicked, mocking his wife's accent, which seemed to chasten her. 'My friend's on his way back to pick me up. You do whatever the fuck you want.'

Nayan had heard the fights so often, had listened with horror as his father hissed that he'd never wanted to get married, not to a village idiot from India, that his family had twisted his arm. And he'd not wanted this shop either. Why would he? Why would anyone? Forced into marriage, into dropping out of college, he had no other way of making ends meet. This day-in, day-out arse-licking that ought to be beneath any man with a bit of dignity. There was a time when Nayan and Sonia had spent the entire evening comforting their mother because she'd asked him why, even if all that was true, did he have to go around sleeping with other women when he had a wife at home? He'd opened the till, filched fifty quid and said, quietly: 'They know how to . . . laugh.'

157

How cruel, the kindness shown in avoiding the word he wanted to use.

Muneet returned upstairs to collect her overnight things, and then she and Nayan left via the shop without acknowledging Pyara's breezy goodbye. She didn't say much in the car at first, and Nayan felt a sharp desire to simply drive, drive his mother away, with him, the two of them alone in the world. So often over the years he'd fantasised this: he and Muneet leaving it all behind. He patted her arm, rubbing life back into her, but she removed his hand. She hated being pitied. Only when they passed a faded Labour poster did she find her voice, telling Nayan all the reasons why this Blair looked to her like a shifty fraud. The signs were there in the election, she said, gesturing towards the windscreen, as though the votes had been counted on the bonnet.

At the house, Deepti met them in the hallway, gave Muneet a hug – 'Love the top, Mum' – and bounded up the stairs to get ready, shouting ringingly back, 'He says he's still hungry!'

Veer, in shorts and a T-shirt printed with palm trees, was on the sofa, watching some cartoon Muneet didn't recognise.

'Vee, Biji's here,' Nayan said, but Veer didn't look away from the screen. He always took some inspiring; sitting beside him, Muneet tapped his knee.

'Don't,' Veer said.

'I'm sorry,' Muneet said. 'Can I have a hello-hug, please?'

'Hug your biji, Vee.'

158

'Maybe later.'

'Maybe *now*.'

'Stop it, Nayan. It doesn't matter,' Muneet said.

'*Veer*.' Something of the pain and rage at his father still endured, there in Nayan's impatience. Muneet, because she was his mother, recognised this and reached up to squeeze his fingers, and it was as if she'd pressed the anger out of him.

'Can I have cereal?' Veer asked.

'I'll make you some eggs,' Muneet said.

'He's just had dinner, Mum. He's not even hungry. He's just delaying bedtime.'

'Is that true, young man? Are you playing games?'

Jutting out his bottom lip, Veer showed his palms and shrugged. He'd had a big haircut recently. It had hung past his shoulders, but now the fringe was a neat, snippy line above thick brows, and the hair at the nape came to a curving, wispy comma. Secretly, Muneet had been upset – she'd hoped Veer might one day sport a turban like Udham Singh – but she'd come to love his new hair's silky touch, the soft shape of his skull, the tidy whorls of his ears, no longer hidden. And not just that: she could register more cleanly the colours of his face, which she sat there silently itemising. The pinkish edge to his nostrils, the darker brown of his forehead, the lilac blush that swept the large domes that were his eyelids.

Nayan made Weetabix with warm milk, hoping it might usher sleep, but then Veer insisted that Nayan, and only Nayan, feed him, which forced Deepti to call the restaurant and delay their table by half an hour.

'Can you eat a bit quicker, Vee?' Nayan said. 'I'm going to switch the telly off at this rate.'

Muneet made a full half-turn of her knees towards Deepti, who was sitting on the armchair, her new mauve handbag – Nayan's anniversary gift – at her side. She'd straightened her hair, a vanity Muneet didn't particularly care for, and had paired a silver-green, sweetheart-bust tunic with black jeans gemmed all along the outer seams. Far from perfect – can't cook Indian – but all in all, she was a good wife to her son.

'Beta, can I take Veer home to sleep?' Muneet asked.

'What?' Nayan said, before Deepti could reply. 'Why? I'll drop you in the morning.'

'No, no. It won't work,' Muneet said, and reeled off several names that Nayan did, eventually, recognise: Reg, Stewart, Mary, Owen. 'They'll all be waiting for me.' She explained to Deepti: 'Sometimes they even help a little with the newspapers. They're very kind. I feel bad here' – she touched her stomach – 'knowing they'll be waiting and I won't be there.'

'It's just Veer might not settle, Mum,' Deepti said. 'Though I guess he is old enough now. I don't know,' she went on, looking to Nayan. 'What do you think?'

'Are you worried about Dad? I don't think he minds opening up late. So long as he's not the one doing it.'

'But think how happy he'll be when Veer wakes him up in the morning.'

Silence, and Muneet looked guiltily into her lap, caught out. Watching her, Nayan felt a keen and upsetting pity: still thinking of the small ways in which she

160

might please her husband, if only to compensate for the ways in which she didn't.

Taking a breath, Muneet tried Veer. 'Sausages for breakfast at Biji House?'

His eyes grew, his thumb went up. And how well his Punjabi was coming on!

'But you work so hard already,' Deepti said, 'without having Veer to manage.'

'You don't have to do this,' Nayan added.

'Just leave him with me all morning,' Muneet said. 'He likes sitting on the counter helping me. You two wake up late, have a nice breakfast, a good time. You look beautiful,' she added to Deepti, in English. 'Go and enjoy.'

'What do you think?' Deepti asked Nayan again.

A joint lie-in. A cosy breakfast. The thought of it was a balm. And if tonight went okay, Veer could sleep over more often. Maybe make it a weekly thing. A weekly lie-in. Christ, how nice that would be. And so what if it pleases his dad? At least he'll be in a good mood. 'Let's give it a go. It clearly means a lot to Mum.'

Nayan hurried Veer into pyjamas, Deepti folded clothes into his rucksack, and they all drove to the shop. By now, it was closed, his father gone, and Nayan had to carry Veer inside and up the stairs because he'd refused his slippers.

'Behave for Biji, yeah?' Nayan said.

'Yes,' Veer replied crossly. 'I just said!' He really was an irascible little boy. Rude, even. It already had Nayan and Deepti worried, that what might pass for cute now would be intolerable in a few years.

Muneet emerged from the kitchen, blowing on a microwaved bowl of over-sweetened semiyan – Veer had mumbled the order in the back of the car.

'After he's gone!' Veer exclaimed.

'Oh, he won't say anything. You eat.'

Muneet was right. Nayan lacked the energy to protest, let alone scold. 'I'll be round by ten thirty. His swimming's at eleven. Can you just make sure he's had his breakfast early? Don't want him being sick in the pool again.' He embraced his mother and kissed the top of Veer's head, then walked back to the car, where Deepti was retouching her lipstick in the wing mirror, a reminder that Nayan still hadn't replaced the broken visor.

The restaurant, with its red-and-white tablecloths and Italian-flag bunting, was a family-run affair in the centre of Chesterfield. From their table Nayan could see both the crooked spire and the snooker club beyond it.

'It's all for Dad,' he said, as their dishes were served. Lasagne for him, gnocchi for her. 'That's the real reason.'

Deepti waited until the parmesan had been proffered, sprinkled, withdrawn.

'Mum does care about her customers,' she said. 'But, yeah, Dad's an arsehole. No arguments.'

'I wish I could drive her away. I wish she'd left him. Years ago. Disappeared with me and Sonia and raised us alone.'

Taking an experimental bite of her gnocchi, Deepti nodded that it was good.

'She nearly did,' Nayan said, and Deepti looked up from her plate, for this was news. 'She had her suitcase packed and ready. Ours, too. But then she didn't. She got scared. She was so scared.'

'Fuck. I never knew. When was this? How old were you? What did Dad even say?'

Nayan shook his head, as if she'd misunderstood, and stabbed his fork into his dish. 'Ten, twelve. *He* wasn't there.' Then, still jabbing his fork around, ripping up the pasta sheets: 'By the time he got home, she'd already unpacked and was getting the dinner on. As if nothing had happened. Just being Mum again.'

Softly saying his name, Deepti extended her arm over the tablecloth and stroked Nayan's hand.

She reminded him that it was their anniversary and they made an effort to touch on happier matters, until it wasn't an effort at all, and they were laughing at the things they'd done behind their parents' backs: the time Nayan hid in her dad's shed, behind his birdbath collection; the school falconry trip they'd both bunked off from, only to get drenched in the rain. They ordered another bottle of wine, shared a tiramisu, and were talking about Veer and how starting school next month would alter their routines, when the bill arrived.

Around three in the morning, key finding the front door, Nayan patted the wall until a light came on. They'd washed up in a nightclub and were tired rather than drunk, though they'd drunk a lot, and Deepti had fallen asleep in the taxi home.

'Too old for this,' she said, dragging herself up the stairs, hand over hand on the banister.

He gave her a playful little boost. 'Don't make me carry you.'

She dropped gratefully onto their bed, and he shucked her heels off her feet and set them side by side against the wardrobe. 'I need a piss,' he said, and she grunted an acknowledgement, muffled by the pillow.

He'd expected her to be fast on by the time he returned, in vest and boxers, but she was more awake than when he'd left her, and had switched into her usual oversized white T-shirt.

'How you feeling?' he asked, sliding in beside her. Then: 'Shit, I've got to go get the car first thing.' He'd forgotten about that – that he'd have to fetch the car from town before Veer's swimming lesson. 'Bang goes my lie-in.'

She rolled towards him, and they'd been kissing only a short while when the bedside phone rang.

'What the hell?' Nayan said.

'Maybe it's Veer,' Deepti said, the worry jumping at once into her throat.

It was Sonia, calling from her university digs, and Nayan relaxed, because she'd probably had a bit to drink, too, and just now realised it was her brother's wedding anniversary.

'What's up, Sone? Everything okay?'

But Sonia was frantic, asking where he'd been, that Dad was trying to get hold of him. 'There's a fire. At the shop. The shop's on fire, Ny! Get down there!'

There were two of him: the Nayan that was already running through the streets to save Veer, and the real one, somehow still here, snatching on clothes, trainers, shouting to Deepti that he didn't fucking know if Veer was all right. As he sprinted out and down the road, she was hammering on the neighbours' doors, begging a ride. But he couldn't hear her. All he could hear was the pounding, of his feet, his heart, of his great hurtling fear.

He didn't stop, not once, and when onlookers in dressing gowns got in his way, he pushed them aside, kept going, his eyes scanning everywhere: the firefighters, the ambulance, the cordon, and then, lifting his gaze, the black smoke, and the flames, both crowning the roof and running around it like a demented orange train.

Nayan raced under the tape, to the ambulance crew, refusing to acknowledge the searing heat on his face. 'Where's everyone?' he cried, to the paramedic, but then saw his dad inside the van and felt relief, because if he was safe then surely Veer and Mum were, too. 'Where's Veer, Dad? Where's Mum?'

Still in his pubbing clothes, his face murky, coughing but otherwise apparently fine, Pyara looked at Nayan uncomprehendingly. 'They're at yours. You took them.'

'No!' He whirled back round to the fire. 'Where are they?' he bellowed.

'Are there more in the building?' the paramedic asked.

'My son! My mum!' He had to shout over the bangs of the blaze. The thudding wallow of wood expanding, snapping.

The paramedic, an older man with a frothy beard and

165

a composed manner, brought Nayan to the firefighters, one of whom asked him where he thought his son and mother were.

'Her bedroom's at the back. On that side,' he said, pointing. 'Why haven't you got them out yet? Where are they? I want to go in.' But the paramedic steered Nayan away, and over his shoulder Nayan saw the firefighters regroup, hook on their breathing apparatus.

He waited by the ambulance. He was praying, pleading, hitting his head with his fists as though this was all happening inside his mind, as though it was his mind that needed putting out. When the paramedics rushed for their bags and hurried forward with the stretchers, he followed. 'Are they all right?' Nayan asked, but they said they didn't know yet, that they'd only been told to get ready. More minutes passed, until Veer and Muneet were carried out and laid on the beds. She was still in her top, the grey turtleneck Deepti had liked, and her hair and face were sooty. But there were no burns. None on Veer either. Which was a good sign, wasn't it?

'Are they all right?' Nayan asked again, but the paramedics requested space, sir, please. To let them do their job. They had their machines out, their defibrillators, cables, too, and all of it impeded, stopped Nayan getting close. Behind him, the two firefighters were taking off their jackets. They looked despondent. One was crying.

Days later, reading the initial police medical report, Nayan would learn that the fire had been started deliberately, by a lit cigarette thrown through the letterbox of the shop door. It caught hold of some flyers, some cardboard, and proceeded to spread up the stairs. In his mind, Nayan imagined a huge, blind, gnashing animal, ravenous, hunting its prey. Muneet Kaur Olak (42), the report said, was found in her bedroom, blocking the door. Her grandson, Veer Singh Olak (4), was in the room, too, but crouched under the window. Both were unresponsive. Paramedics on site determined death by smoke inhalation, most likely from carbon monoxide poisoning, which put their lungs under excessive stress and triggered a heart attack. Smoke, the doctor will say, gently leading Nayan through the report. Everyone thinks it does the lungs in, which is true. But it spoils the heart so mercilessly.

For now, the paramedic stepped away from Veer. He had his big hand on Nayan's shoulder and he was saying how sorry he was. His words sounded tiny, far away. Once more, every noise outside of Nayan was fading. Even Deepti's screams he registered only dimly. What he heard above all else, falling to his knees, was his son's face. He could actually hear his face. Its stillness was saying that I'm not happy, Daddy. Its silence demanded to know what was going on. With only the pads of his fingertips, and with awful delicacy, Nayan touched the face, the cheeks, the eyes. He whispered that he was a really good boy and that he loved him very much.

There's little else to say, other than to briefly outline the slow collapse of Nayan's marriage. Slow, because there was no great, long-forestalled confrontation when they parted. There was no conversation at all, in fact, dramatic or otherwise. Guilt did them both in over time, a gradual, piecemeal fraying. Nayan started attending more out-of-town union conferences, paying to stay at the hotel a day or two longer than was required. When he came home, he'd find a note on the fridge explaining that she'd be at her mother's for a few days, maybe a week, and that there were meals in the freezer for him and Dad, who was now living with them. Month on month, the hotel stays increased, the maternal visits lengthened, until neither expected the other to be at home, and if they were, they ate separately, in different rooms, with Nayan listening out for Deepti, to hear their bedroom door shut before he fell asleep in front of the television. It all felt inexorable. More so, because they couldn't look at one another any more, as though in the other's face resided their own culpability. Her wardrobe began to empty, and then one morning she mentioned applying for a teaching role in Birmingham, where her massi lived. When he talks about it now, when he talked about it with me, Nayan chokes on the sadness of it all, but back then he felt relief, as he's sure Deepti did, too. By the time she left, it had been eighteen months without Veer, and they didn't see each other again until the following winter, when she suggested they meet up on Veer's birthday. In the same message, she proposed the park. He didn't reply for days.

———

Up ahead, Deepti was no longer on the spotlit park bench, and Nayan couldn't see her anywhere, but then there she was, beside a big old tree, her hand on its bark. Old thing, he imagined her thinking, feeling. You'll still be here long after me and my pain are gone. There was solace in that thought. Nayan rose from the blanket, the frosted grass crackling free, and wandered over to the basketball nets. He'd lost sight of Veer here once, soon after they'd moved into the new house. His sleeping had regressed and Nayan, on a mission to build the boy's confidence, brought him to the park. We shouldn't smother him so much, he'd said to Deepti. They'd not been playing long when Veer said he really needed to go pee and tried to drag Nayan with him. No, Nayan had said. You're a big boy. You can go yourself, and he'd let his hand slip out of Veer's and continued shooting hoops while the boy powered angrily out of the gate and stood peeing behind a line of rosebushes. Nayan could see his head, his eyes down, but then the ball ricocheted off the ring and he rallied to retrieve it. When he turned round Veer wasn't there. The ball under his arm, Nayan exited the court, calling Veer's name. No sign. Soon, he was freaking out, and it took a full ten minutes before some footy boys found Veer, crouched behind the café, hiding. So next time come with me, Veer yelled into Nayan's face, whose relief was rapidly morphing to anger.

Deepti joined him at the nets, a hand on his hand, and they walked back to the blanket together.

'How's the election going? I occasionally google you,' she said when he looked surprised. 'Find out what you're up to.'

'It'll start ramping up now, for the next couple of months or so. It's going okay.'

'They'd be mad not to elect you.'

'Yet people do do mad things. Hello, Theresa May.'

Arriving at the blanket, they stayed on their feet, hands buried in coat pockets. 'How's Dad?'

'Same. Well, worse. He forgets stuff, then gets thrashy. But Buddy – Lisa's boy? – he's started helping. And there's a kid called Brandon lends a hand, too.'

'Round-the-clock care.'

'He's a chef, really. Brandon. A good one. I'm trying to find him a job.'

'Kind of you,' she said, betraying a slight confusion.

'Well – I'm seeing his mother.' 'Seeing' felt like the right word, encompassing the months he kept sighting her on his runs as well as the intimacies since their date the previous month, when in bed he'd gaze at her gazing at him and wonder what accounted for the troubled look on her face.

Deepti's lips parted, and spread to a broad, warm smile. She knew, he guessed, that for him to tell her, the woman must mean something quite special. 'Oh, Nayan – I could cry.'

'It's early days. Let's just see,' he finished, closing off any further discussion. He turned back to the lake, where an evening mist had rolled in, a frail stage above the water. 'I've never been to a play since Veer.'

'He set a high bar,' Deepti replied smoothly, because she'd learned to navigate the swerves of his conversation. 'Wasn't he a bush?'

'Those branches. Kept knocking that girl's crown off.'

She laughed, a hand to her mouth, and they began folding the blanket away.

*

Sitting in his car, he watched the gold flashes of Deepti's indicator, the final sight of her face as she gained speed and fussily adjusted the rear-view mirror; an old habit he'd all but forgotten. He remained where he was, key in the ignition but not twisted. The rush from meeting her was already leaking away, and he drove home on sad roads, couldn't sleep, and before dawn was out running in the hills, up steep rocky trails, stones sliding underfoot, and down into the valleys, carving a path through these feelings. He could see the air. Touch the light. Hear his face. Sense made no sense. He gave no thought to the direction he ran in. He didn't care. It was only vital that he not be still, that he try to free himself. But from what? His grief? The past? From me? Keep running to the end. Make it to the finish and the pain would be no more. Is that what the election was, Nayan? Did you think that waiting at the line would be your boy, waving a flag, finally happy? Sunrise glimmered behind a quiet hill, a pale blue melody heard across the dales, like waking up in a hymn. Far away, deer, small and black, and now here they all were, wild-eyed and teeth-bared, stampeding past him in a violent roar of noise.

For the next few days Nayan worked late: contracts, employee tribunals, reviewing the UBI pilot, and, in the evenings, ordering salads into the office while he and Lisa-Marie made e-drops and vlogs for the campaign. Work straightened him out and driving into the office on the fourth day, a Friday, he texted Helen, and then arrived at her house that evening with a six-pack of beer in one hand, a takeaway in the other.

'Sorry I've not been in touch,' he said, snapping free two cans and tidying the rest in the fridge.

'It's fine. You explained. I understand.'

'I'm always a bit like this around this time of year. But I shouldn't go quiet on—'

With some urgency, she clapped her hand over his mouth. 'Really, it's fine. Let's not talk about it.'

Her legs across his lap, they drank their beers, Nayan chatting about his day, about Brandon, out with Claudia, and the campaign, too, which was going well, and they had another two cans with their chow mein before Nayan began nuzzling Helen's neck.

In the morning, light slanted in, too weak to do anything other than slide off the duvet in waxen stripes. Nayan had been sitting up for a while, content, silently marvelling – it was still enough of a novelty that Helen lay asleep beside him. He touched her hair, which smelled of cheap apple shampoo. Her bottom lip hung loose and slewed to one side, offset by her hands, her beautiful hands, pressed together under her cheek. Taking care not to disturb her, he headed downstairs to make tea; the kettle must've woken her, though, because as he returned she was pushing a hand through her hair, shaking out the night's dreams.

'Thanks,' she said. 'I've not had tea brought to me in bed since' – she rowed back from Elwood – 'I can't remember when.'

'Not even on Mother's Day?' Nayan rushed under the

duvet with his own mug. 'The boy's a cook. You should be getting the full breakfast works.'

Helen held her mug in both hands and leaned forward, away from the headboard. Her back was long and curving and lightly freckled, the shoulder blades sharp. He placed the meat of his palm between her shoulders and started kneading, one-handedly, and she smiled and murmured and swept her hair to one side so it didn't get in his way.

'Plans for today?' he asked.

'A woman in Brim. Meds, dinner. Just making sure she's comfy.'

'Fancy popping into mine on your way and letting Buddy know I'll be over by noon?'

She didn't quite bridle; a contraction of the muscles in her neck was all he felt. 'You going somewhere?' she asked.

'I thought I might take a look at Brandon's bike. You said the gears have gone?'

'They have.'

'I've got some tools in the car.' Helen said nothing. 'So will you? Just let them know?'

'Can't you phone?' she said.

'I mean, yeah, I could' – his massaging hand halted, then resumed – 'I thought you might just check they're okay. In your expert opinion.'

'I'll be tight for time,' she said.

'No worries,' he replied. So: still reluctant to get too deep into his home life, which he told himself he understood. Did he? She had Brandon to think about. Her job was secure. No need to risk rocking the boat. His thumb began working either side of her spine. 'You know, it'd save me a small fortune if we hung out at mine once in a while. Finding a dad-sitter's an expensive business, even if he's pretty harmless these days. But no rush.'

The tea finished, she set the mug aside, swiped up her packet of cigarettes. 'Were there days when he wasn't pretty harmless?'

'Course,' Nayan replied. 'Though no one's bad all the way down. He loved Veer. Could spend hours playing with him. Did.'

'What about your mum?'

Nayan looked into his mug, put it next to hers. He'd never play down what his mother put up with. 'Different story. He treated her like shit. Flaunted his affairs. He'd come home smelling of them. He didn't respect her at all.'

'Did he hate her?'

'Yeah. Or he hated himself, his life.' Nayan gave a faint, low, exasperated growl. 'Isn't that usually why we treat others like shit? Jealousy, bitterness, self-hatred. It's why the so-called centrists hate us so much. They know they sold out and we didn't.'

But Helen wasn't interested in this line of thought; she wanted to go back. 'You still chose to take care of him? You still let him live with you?'

'Yeah.'

She relit an unfinished Silk Cut and nodded up: *Go on.*

'Nothing. It just didn't sit well with me. Someone else looking after him.'

'A cultural thing.'

'A thing thing,' he said, sighed, and in the same breath he drew her close, her breast in his hand. He loved how soft it was, the tissue loosening beneath skin; his fingers left imprints. 'Can I ask you something? It's important.' She waited, nodded warily. 'What chance a blow job?'

She burst with laughter, they both did, and she stretched out on top of him, unfurling and lengthening and planting her elbows hard on his chest, digging them in, even harder. He felt certain she was going to extinguish the cigarette on him, and she seemed to know this electric, erotic fear was in his mind as she blew the smoke sidelong and crushed the filter into a terracotta saucer by his head.

'Am I your first efnik?' he asked, in a voice of slightly puckish defiance, because as much as he enjoyed her shows of dominance, he wanted to assert some control of his own, to remind her that he, too, had cards to play. 'You only went with your own kind before?'

'Looking for bragging rights?' she said.

Gripping her armpits, he hoisted her up and towards him, so she straddled his stomach.

'Bit wobbly,' she said, smiling down at him. 'Not been running for a while?'

'I'm still carrying a little holiday weight right now,' he answered, in his most nasal all-American.

'Dad-bod alert,' she teased – her smile lingered a fraction longer, like a still point before the fall. She covered her face.

'Don't sweat it,' Nayan said.

He didn't hear her exhale, only saw the swift collapse of her ribs. She climbed off him. 'I should get ready.'

Closing his eyes, he listened to the quick flick and slap of knickers being pulled on, the dull clink of wooden coat hangers, a fleetness on the stairs. He gave her a few minutes, then went down to the kitchen, where she seemed to have been waiting.

'I can handle not always saying the right thing. I just wish . . .' She looked about, at anywhere but him.

'What do you wish?' he asked.

Her mouth moved, struggling, wordless. He circled his arms around her and she rested her weight against his chest, yielding more readily than she'd done before. The morning sun, rallying, crawled warmth over their naked, overlapping feet.

'I wish I could do something,' she said. 'I wish I could take this pain away.'

Humbled, gratified, he took her to mean only his pain, and laid his cheek on top of her head.

Helen left in her uniform and for the rest of the morning Nayan commandeered the drive, repairing Brandon's mountain bike. The gears wouldn't shift, or if they did, they kept skipping. He adjusted the barrel towards the spokes, tightening the spaces between the cogs; when that didn't work, he turned his attention to the derailleur. It looked aligned well enough, balanced with the chain and that cable pod thingy. But what were these two screws meant to be doing? He freed them one at a time, certain he'd solved the problem, but then the derailleur clanged off, the chain slackened, and bits of bike were rolling away across the ground. Shit and fuck, he seethed, scrambling for the parts. He went indoors for water, returned armed with YouTube videos, and over the next hours reassembled the back end of the bike and fixed the trouble with the gears. Apparently, or so some Canadian in a pink velour headband assured him, the problem had lain with the B-tension screw and the cycle's cable indexing.

Jubilant, Nayan biked up and down the lane, pulling wheelies cumbersomely, like a horse rearing. He was so taken with his success he didn't see Claudia park up in her Beetle and Brandon jump out the passenger side.

'It's fixed!' Brandon exclaimed.

'You're back!' Nayan pedalled over. 'Good as new.'

'*You* fixed it?'

'It was no bother. I had the morning free,' Nayan said, made self-conscious by Brandon's disbelief, which highlighted his own generosity in an uncomfortable way. Should he not have repaired it? Was it too much? Helen said he'd been grinning from ear to ear when she told him, over Christmas, that she and Nayan were seeing how things went. Nayan didn't want to ruin that, but suddenly, acutely, felt sure he had, that Brandon now saw in him a pitiable, bereaved father scouting round for a replacement. Embarrassed, Nayan looked away, down the road, as if his heart were hanging on the bare elm tree.

Claudia perched against the hood of her car. 'That was just *the* nicest thing to do,' she said.

'How are the lessons going?' Nayan asked quickly. 'Clau?'

'He's ready. I'm putting him in for his test.'

Brandon moved towards Nayan. 'Thank you.'

The quiet feeling with which Brandon thanked him – it was still whirring around Nayan's mind as he arrived home and asked Buddy how the night had gone.

'He woke up, looking for the toilet in the kitchen. Tell you what,' he continued, reaching down to prise on his Converse, 'Bran's spoiled him. He gave bare cut-eye to my beans on toast. Like, wouldn't eat it until I got out the herbs and shit.'

'Dad's a food snob.'

'Proper cut-eye.' Shoes on, Buddy stood upright. 'He's extra, for sure. Bran. Made a full-on roast at ours last week and, no joke, it popped my mind. He made a red wine reduction?' Buddy said, amazed and waiting for Nayan to be amazed.

'He's talented,' was all Nayan said, aware of feeling like the proud parent, and aware of the risks of that, too: he had to protect himself. 'Any joy on the work front?' he asked, as a distraction.

'It is what it is, man,' Buddy said. He lacked his sister's ability to bluff, and though he'd attempted indifference, the smile came too late to hide just how demoralised, how unmanned, he felt.

'Hang in there,' Nayan said. 'Something'll come good. Meantime, do you want to help me out with Dad a bit more? Extra cash?'

'Sure,' Buddy said; then, wagging a finger, 'But tell him not to slam my food, yeah? I take *exception*.'

Buddy gone, Nayan checked on Pyara: asleep on the settee, legs spread, head thrown back to the wall; every snore tapering to a frail whistle. Seizing the blanket from the armrest, Nayan pressed it around his father, then went to the window. The street was quiet. Buddy and the quiet ache on his face, and Veer; the grown son, and the not. He moved to the photograph hanging above the gas fire. In it, unaware of the camera, Veer was delighting in a bathtub of bubbles, all white peaks, like meringue. Muneet crouched on the tiled floor beside him. Chin on her fist, she was unsmiling, serious, as if monitoring Veer's fun. Veer and Muneet: a study in contrasts. Nayan had no recollection of taking the photo when he found it, underneath a pile of political biographies, a year on from their deaths. After getting it enlarged, he'd made the grey mount himself, along with the solid, beechwood frame.

'Where's laddo?' Pyara asked.

Nayan didn't look away from the photo. 'He's just gone.'

'The cook,' Pyara said, all impatience.

'His name's Brandon. He'll be here on Monday for a few hours while I'm at the office. I've decided to split your care between the two of them.' More than once, Nayan had considered disclosing his relationship with Brandon's mother. But why should he? He wouldn't register it, would soon forget if he did. Or, worse, start pestering Brandon with questions. He'd not considered that Brandon might have already told him.

'Been with his mum, have you? Getting your end wet?'

'Her name's Helen, Dad.' He could never decide if Veer was three in the shot or two?

'Helen is it?'

'Yes.'

'Who's Helen?'

'Brandon's mum, Dad.'

'His name wasn't Brandon,' Pyara said, suddenly vehement.

Nayan turned his whole body around to face his father, who was staring past Nayan and at the photo. 'No, Dad. That's Mum and Veer. Your grandson.'

'No! Don't! Look! You don't look!'

Nayan said, 'It's okay. I'm not looking at it.'

'You shouldn't have let them go back!'

'Okay,' Nayan said.

'He was my boy!' Pyara said, his face trembling. 'My little boy.'

Nayan gathered the blanket Pyara had kicked to the floor and billowed it once more across his lap.

Losing his wife and grandson, in the way that he did, had been too heavy a blow, everyone said, when Pyara was diagnosed with early onset dementia, and then Parkinson's to boot. It would, they said, floor even the strongest of men.

In the year after the fire, Pyara succumbed to violent episodes: Nayan arrived home to be confronted with him screaming, repeatedly knifing his own bed; Deepti found him in the small, now-unused garden, punching the brick wall, blood raw over his knuckles. They lost count of the number of times Pyara told the same relatives that the

police were racist, that they weren't investigating anything and didn't care if whoever killed his family got off
unpunished. He repeats so much, the family told Nayan,
and after only a few minutes! It's his way of coping,
Nayan assured them. But then he made an appointment
with their GP, after Pyara yelled at a blonde schoolgirl in
the town centre, demanding to know what she'd done
with his family.

('Why a schoolgirl?' I asked. It'd felt like an odd emphasis
from Nayan: the *blonde* schoolgirl. 'Search me. He was
going gaga.' I still didn't know if he knew the truth about
Helen.)

That night, in bed, Nayan received an email from one of
the many local restaurants he'd approached with images
of Brandon's Diwali platters. It was from a Carl Evans,
who said he'd been in the same running club as Nayan.
Did Nayan remember him? (He didn't.) But, yes, Carl
said, they were happy to meet this Brandon Fletcher, with
a view to a trial period in their kitchen. Nayan sat up, did
a little fist pump, started forwarding the mail to Brandon –
then stopped. In person. Yes. He wanted to see the joy on
the boy's face. Leaving the phone aside, switching off the
lamp, he sank back down into the bed, alone, and the
burst of happiness he'd just felt gave way to despond-
ency, and he lay there feeling suddenly sorry for himself,
thinking of Brandon together with Buddy's family, and
all of them enjoying their roast, speaking over one another,
laughing. Would he ever have that? Perhaps it wouldn't

be long before Helen joined their dinners, and maybe then they might think to ask him, too?

With a grunt and a jerk of his head – he was being pathetic – he steered his mind towards the election. Megha had been quiet over the holidays. And into the New Year. Nothing had come of their argument at Diwali. A cool civility in the office had been maintained. Accepted defeat, hasn't she, Lisa-Marie said. Maybe. Probably. And then the two strands of thought – the family meals and the election – touched and sparked in his mind and he imagined what Megha would say about Brandon cooking fancy food for Buddy's family. Some inane comment, for sure, about white people always thinking black folk need civilising. She was so wrongheaded – *she* was pitiable, not him – and something of that feeling, of feeling sorry for her as a way of not feeling sorry for himself, carried over into the office on Monday morning, when he perched on the corner of Lisa-Marie's desk.

'Enjoy your roast last week?'

She'd been mumbling a song, and now broke off to give an exaggerated shiver of happiness. 'I hope Claudia keeps hold of him. I'll see out my days in cutlery heaven.'

'Culinary. *Cul* – Jesus wept. It's coming to something when I'm the cultured one.'

'Don't you have some ads to smirk for?'

'I was thinking . . .' He flicked his eyebrows towards the rear of the office, where Megha was holed up now-adays. Only the crown of her head was visible. She appeared to be reading something on her desk, a Biro tapping her temple, now making a change, an edit. 'The numbers don't look good for her,' Nayan said.

'They're the worst,' Lisa-Marie said, rocking back against her chair. 'I hate to say this but maybe you should have a word.'

'No, I agree. Been thinking the same.' He foresaw the morning after the election, Megha isolated, humiliated. 'No. I'll give her a ladder to climb down. She's right that Unify's not always been on the front foot on race. It's true enough. And now she's asking for support for workers who aren't – who identify as –'

'Non-binary.'

'Yeah. I'm not against any of that. It just sounds humane.'

Lisa-Marie's lips were closed, yet her smile stretched into her cheeks. 'You're a good man, Nayan Olak.'

'Shh,' he whispered, finger to his mouth. 'Our secret.'

Nayan was grateful that Pyara had already taken to his bed when he arrived home, so he could think about how best to approach Megha. Which concession to suggest? Which post might he offer her?

'He was exhausted,' Brandon said, as Nayan showed the lad out.

'It's his age. Always dozing off.'

'It's just' – Brandon hesitated a second – 'on his way up he went into the spare room and knocked a few things. He broke one of the animals on the windowsill.'

'Ah.' Then: 'I'll take a look. Thanks for letting me know.'

'I left it on the window. I didn't want you to think I did it.'

'No, no.' Nodding a goodbye, Nayan made to shut the door.

'I'm guessing it was your son's room.'

'Got it in one,' Nayan said, needing the boy gone, and, finally, shutting the door.

To work, he said out loud, and with a large breath he returned to the front room and unfolded his laptop.

An hour passed. Two. Three. Vaguely, perhaps not even altogether consciously, he was aware of avoiding the trip upstairs. And, anyway, he was flying through his paperwork. He'd already written up three comprehensive recommendations for financial support and, for the other four members, typed up Further Information Requests, minutely, supportively, detailing the 'missing particulars' and linking each incomplete section to the relevant guidance note – notes that he'd once spent weeks formulating to help workers lay out their case in the most trenchant and persuasive manner. He submitted all these reviews via the online portal, went to make himself a coffee, and was reading through the next allegation when his phone buzzed. A WhatsApp from Lisa-Marie. *Have you read Megha's newsletter? We might need to rethink.* He smiled. What had Megha done this time? In her last member communication, she'd accused Nayan of being stuck in the union mentality of the Eighties. He whizzed down his unread emails and opened it. Up flashed a new, studio headshot of Megha, with only her face turned towards the camera. She had a candid gaze, as though she really were communing with you, and beneath it ran her slogan: *A Bold and New Direction.* Then: *Read my latest newsletter for my ideas for change and why General Secretary Candidate Nayan Olak thinks white people don't exist.* Nayan skimmed over the sinister, side-eye image of him, and began.

Last October, Nayan Olak hosted a Diwali party at the Sheffield gurdwara to which he invited various key union figures and local members. I felt it was an odd party for a supposedly progressive union to endorse, where the food was high-end and the serving staff Black – but I attended in the spirit of collegiality. Late on during the party, Olak told me how much he favoured my proposals to decolonise the union (see overleaf), which gratified me. When it came time for me to leave – I work every Saturday morning in a foodbank – he tried to get me to stay, rather insistently. We spoke for a little longer and I mentioned that the majority of the users of the foodbank were members of the white working class. Here, Olak said something that surprised me. I quote verbatim: 'The difference between us, Megha, is that I know that the white working class doesn't exist.' He went on to say that not only do white working-class people not exist, but that they shouldn't exist either. I was confused, and my confusion only grew when Olak seemed to change tack and suggested that he did think the white working class existed but that they had been 'left behind as backward, racist fuckwits'. Please forgive the language; I feel it's important to accurately convey what was said. What did Nayan Olak mean by this? That is a question for him to answer. And he should be permitted the chance to defend himself. Of course, given the trauma he has suffered in the past, we should all understand why he might harbour some resentment towards white people. But such ideas should never be held by anyone hoping to lead our alliance. Unify needs a leader they can trust, someone who is honest; someone who doesn't on the one hand say that the white working class shouldn't exist, that they are 'racist fuckwits', but on the other hand claims to be about solidarity and peaceful co-existence.

We are a union made of many races. Race exists. White people, Brown people, Black people: all should be recognised and allowed to live full, unhindered and dignified lives. We should acknowledge that it's in our differences that our wonder lies: that's how we'll learn and become better people, by which I mean how we'll become fairer people better able to challenge unfair practices. That's how we'll grow.

As ever, Megha

In the time he'd taken to read the piece, his phone had pinged maybe a dozen times. He read down the green banners, catching the first few words but not sliding into the messages proper: *Pack of lies how can she get away . . . What is she on . . . Do I not exist Nayan or am . . . So sorry you're going through . . . You got some explaining to . . . WTAF? Is it true or . . .*

Quietly, he closed the laptop and placed his phone at the far end of the sofa; notifications still pinging as he ascended the stairs to Veer's old room. It had altered a great deal in the last twenty years, been redecorated twice. Veer's wallpaper had been stripped. The walls were now an essential white, like the ceiling. The lampshade, the clock, his clothes and toys, all had been boxed and delivered to a charity shop. That's where he still imagined them, not in landfill somewhere. Veer's single bed, too, had been repainted, white, like the walls. He'd been such a fastidious sleeper. At attention, arms locked at his side. Not a sound from his lips. The number of times he'd felt compelled to check! Ear to mouth, hand on stomach. And then Nayan would simply watch. He only ever stayed a short bitter-sweet minute, because watching, with all those intimations, is hard, acutely so, with a sleeper like Veer. An austere sleeper. And now this room, too, had become a clean, austere square, with its clean, austere atmosphere. The only sign that it had once belonged to a young boy was the plastic deer on the windowsill. They'd missed it during the packing and when Nayan found it weeks later he left it on the window, expecting he'd get round to throwing it away later. But it stayed and the years passed and now the animal's head had detached from its body. Nayan picked up the severed parts and left them on the newel post at the top of the landing, a reminder to take them downstairs in time for the bin men.

Richard, the next morning, was the least calm person in Nayan's living room. Where Nayan and Lisa-Marie sat on the sofa discussing how best to counter Megha's news-letter, Richard was on his feet, pacing. His eyes kept expanding, as if in response to some throb in his brain.

'Rewind a sec. Are you actually admitting to saying that fucking shit?'

'We've been through this, Richard,' Lisa-Marie said. 'We need to move on.'

'I never said that about people being racist,' Nayan said patiently, though he'd made this point several times now. 'I said that's what they're perceived as. That's the narrative allowed to take root. By the right, mainly. But also, indirectly, by the so-called left. By Megha's left. This isn't controversial. She twisted my words. I'm happy to clarify that in my next comm.'

'And the crap about white people not existing?' Richard pressed. 'Am I wearing a fucking invisibility cloak here?'

'I don't know if her misunderstanding was deliberate or not.' Refusing to be goaded, Nayan persisted with his measured tone, very aware of Richard's florid neck, his glower. 'But when I say that the term "white working class" shouldn't exist, I do mean that. Class should not be raced. It's not a cultural categorisation. It's a social and economic one.'

'Now you're sounding like a fucking textbook.'

'Mate! These are things we have to think about.' He paused, wondering how best to explain. 'I guess I mean that we only talk about the "white working class" because the working class have been left with no other way to talk about themselves. Labour doesn't give a shit. Unions have lost power. All that's left is this language of – of representational politics. Identity politics. That's all I'm saying, Richard. And I'm happy to clarify that, too.'

'I'm not a fucking kid, Ny. Don't talk to me like one.'

'Then listen to what I'm saying.'

'What, listen to you telling me that I shouldn't exist? That blacks can exist. Browns can exist. The fucking Jedi can exist, but not me? Not my parents? Because you think they're racists and fuckwits? And at the same time you're in cahoots with her about de-fucking-colonising or some shit?' Richard was grandstanding now, his arms wide, as if all had been revealed. 'I *knew* you and her looked all pally at the conference last year. Thought you had it all stitched up between you? But now she's broken ranks and sold you down the river? *That's* what's happened!'

'You're out of your mind, Rich. None of that makes the slightest sense.'

Richard took a step towards Nayan, who was still on the sofa. 'My dad didn't give his life to the pits, didn't die because of them, so someone like you could say he shouldn't've ever existed.'

'Someone like me?'

'Fuck you.'

'I think you need to dial it the fuck down, pet,' Lisa-Marie said.

But Richard made for the hallway, the door, and though Nayan was braced to hear it slam, it didn't, and they watched him cross the window, straightening out his lapels with a flap of the blazer.

'He's got a strong voice among the membership,' Lisa-Marie said, her frown holding a worry.

'He'll calm down.'

'I'm not so sure. And plenty have been saying similar things. Messaging and that.'

'I'll issue that clarifying statement,' Nayan said, a little blithely. 'People know me, Lise. They're not going to be taken in by some toff who's never done a day's graft in her life.'

Sitting forward, Lisa-Marie reached for Nayan's hand. 'I think you may well ride this one out. But what about the next time? And the one after that? She ain't going to stop. So!' she burst on, releasing his hand. 'We should take it seriously. Stay one step ahead. I've been thinking.'

'Always a worry.'

'And seeing as Megha's trying to make everyone think you secretly hate white people, I reckon our best way of knocking that on the head is Helen.'

It took Nayan a moment to latch on to what she meant, and he found the idea so extreme he laughed. 'You want her to be my consort?'

'Hear me out. I don't mean in any obvious way. Just have her beside you at the next rally. A photo. Make it clear you're an item. The odd smooch for the camera.'

'Please! She'd never agree. I wouldn't want her to. "Look, some of my best friends are white! Even my lover!"' He shook his head. 'No.'

There came a clatter from the room above their heads and Nayan left to tidy the bag of coat hangers Pyara had emptied across the floor. When he returned, Lisa-Marie resumed as if there'd be no interruption at all.

'It wasn't beneath the Obamas.'

'I'm not taking my cues from a fucking neoliberal shill.'

'Think about it,' she said, knocking her shoulder against his. 'It's just about having Helen around so people can see she's with you. It's not like I'm saying you need to make some grand pronouncement about your undying love, am I?'

Nayan wouldn't agree to make Helen part of the campaign, and he didn't issue a clarifying statement either. After the initial outcry, the disgusted messages died down; his poll numbers had dipped, sure, yet they still far outshone his rival's. Told you it'd all blow over, he said to Lisa-Marie. Richard remained intransigent, ignoring Nayan's texts, taking sideswipes at him during a panel event, but he was an outlier as far as Nayan was concerned, a friend who felt deceived and thus wasn't thinking straight. In time he'd come round, too. We just need to keep our eyes on the prize, Lise. Rise above.

'When they go low . . .'

'Don't fucking dare,' Lisa-Marie warned.

Neither did he confront Megha about what she'd written. Far from it. He smiled a hello when they crossed on the walk into work. He deferred to her opinion in meetings. Because he'd point-blank refused to acknowledge the accusations, let alone take them seriously, he felt that very few others had either, and so nothing changed for him, not really. 'I played a blinder, if you ask me.' If anything, he wondered if Megha had ended up only harming herself, because he'd started to sense a certain attitude in the room when she walked in, and on more than one occasion her evening goodbye had gone unanswered.

'Is she getting a hard time?' Nayan asked. 'Because of what she wrote.'

Lisa-Marie minimised her screen, sighed. 'It's a rotten business, this. I really hate it sometimes.'

He took no pleasure in seeing Megha suffer but that didn't mean he was still going to offer a hand. That chance had gone. Maybe after the election the two of them could sit down over a drink, but for now, things were on track. He'd just left a meeting where the Executive Committee had agreed to his terms for the final leadership debate, and he was arriving at Helen's with wine to celebrate Brandon clearing his driving test.

'You didn't have to bring two bottles,' Helen said, setting them in the centre of the table.

'It's been a shit-ton heavy week,' Nayan replied. 'And it's one bottle for passing his test. And another for my own surprise for him.'

'Oh? What's that, then?'

'Wait and see,' and he gave her arm a rub. 'Thanks for asking me over.'

For a long time they kissed against the countertop, tongue thickly arousing tongue, until Helen remembered the chicken in the oven. Nayan called for Brandon and Claudia, who came down, hair mussed, effortfully casual.

'Smells great,' Brandon said, far too emphatically.

'Just sit down,' Helen replied.

It was a squeeze around the small table, but pouring wine for everyone, Nayan led a toast to Brandon's success, then asked Claudia how her masters was going.

'Good, good. I'm taking a module on the demise of social democratic parties. Right up your alley.'

'Did you get that essay done?' Helen asked drily. 'The one you needed Brandon to stay over and help you with.'

'He was *deeply* insightful,' Claudia said, grinning at Brandon, who blushed hard into his plate.

Nayan loved this quality of Claudia's, her talent for insolence, her lack of embarrassment. She was so different from Buddy: her twin, full of bluster but ultimately deferential and easy to railroad. Brandon, too. Oftentimes, Nayan wished these boys had some of Claudia's fearlessness.

Nayan got in before Helen could respond: 'We've the final debate coming up in a few weeks. They've just agreed the format.' He set down his fork. 'So I'll speak and then I can ask someone else – any member, even juniors – to speak, too. About why they support me, why they think I'll be a great General Secretary, et cetera. A kind of character reference.'

'Who you thinking of?' Claudia asked, steadying him with her gaze. 'And don't say Mum.'

'You're still in the youth wing, right?'

Clapping hands, she cried, 'I knew it. As soon as you started talking I knew you'd ask me.'

'You'll be great,' Brandon said.

'Of course I will.'

'I meant Nayan?'

'And I can use the whole experience for my diss.'

'You won't want for confidence,' Helen said.

'It's very canny of you, Mr Ny-An,' Claudia continued, twirling a finger near his face. 'Getting a black woman to speak on your behalf when what's-her-face's on the other side.'

'Can't get nothing past you.'

'Are you,' she said, mock-outraged, 'playing identity politics?'

'Well, if you can't beat them . . . But, no, seriously.' He sat upright and, under his chin, made a steeple of his fingers. 'I can't think of anyone in the world I'd more like to be standing up there speaking about me. The way you and your brother have turned out, after losing your dad so young. I haven't forgotten all the paper rounds and summer jobs you did to help your mum. All the things you went without. You're a credit. I'd be very proud if you did it, Claudia.'

A waiting silence – then high, breaking laughter. The table was struck; forks aimed at Nayan. 'Oh my God,' said Claudia.

'Too earnest?' Nayan asked.

'Even for you,' Helen said.

Then, Brandon asked, 'Can I be there?'

'I suppose Claudia will need your deep insight, hmm?' Helen couldn't resist saying. 'More wine?'

'You can be there,' Nayan said, 'if you're not working, that is.'

Confused, because keeping an eye on Pyara wasn't work exactly, Brandon said, 'Maybe Buddy could stay with your dad?'

'He will, yeah. I've already asked him. But *you'll* have to ask the head chef at Parl and Cam if they're happy for you to be out of the kitchen for a few hours.'

Now Brandon looked even more confused, scanning round from face to face. Only when he felt Claudia excitedly grab his wrist did he allow himself to comprehend.

Softly, Brandon said, 'But Pam Gascoigne's an amazing chef.'

Nayan explained that he'd spoken to Carl, who managed the staff end of things, and he'd said they'd be well up for meeting Brandon. To try him out. 'I'll text you his number,' Nayan said, already on his phone. A ping sounded from Brandon's pocket. 'They're expecting you on Monday.'

The table waited for a reaction. Brandon was staring at his lap, stunned by the good fortune that had landed in it. 'I don't know what to say,' he said, very faintly.

Nayan reached across and shook Brandon's shoulder, which suddenly seemed no more than a pointy little bump of bone. He was about to affirm that Brandon didn't have to say anything at all, when he saw Brandon's brow flinch. He felt crowded. He didn't want to be touched, not yet, he didn't want his feelings to be forced into the air, to be pounced upon. He wanted to hold them close for a while first. Everything was provisional and could be ground to dust at any moment. Understanding this, Nayan removed his hand – 'More wine, yes!' he said – and pushed his glass across the tablecloth and towards Helen, who still held the bottle.

Around eleven o'clock, after a chocolate dessert, Helen drove Nayan home. She'd not felt she had much of a choice when he asked for the lift, seeing as she'd only had the one glass. All the way, she repeated how tired she was, and yawned genuinely, as though her body, too, was laying the ground for a quick getaway.

She crunched up the handbrake.

'Thanks again,' she said. 'It's the kind of chance he's dreamed of.'

'Come inside,' Nayan said. 'Thank me properly?'

'I shouldn't leave them alone for too long.'

'They'll be fine.'

'I really am tired,' she said, but without conviction, because since Nayan's terrace came into view her eyes hadn't left its dark, light-rimmed windows. She wanted to know how he lived. She wanted to know if she could face it, if her tangled feelings for Nayan were making any kind of difference. A mineral, dangerous force drew her towards the building.

'I'd like you to come inside. And Dad'll be long asleep. The new pills, they're fucking awesome,' he added, kissing the side of her mouth as he stretched for the driver's door and opened it for her.

Buddy was waiting inside the hall, his shadow vaulting up the stairs, fleeing the kitchen glare. He confirmed that Pyara was asleep, had been for hours, and then he left for a mate's flat in the next street.

'Welcome,' Nayan said, flicking on the front-room light and quickly dimming it, as though the room had shot open its eyes only to half-close them again. 'Sorry about the mess,' he said, because he'd earlier put washing to dry on the radiator, across the backs of chairs. 'Do you want a coffee?' He tried to make his voice sound easy, as if this wasn't the first time he'd invited to his house a woman he cared about. There'd not been anyone serious since his divorce. The handful of women he'd slept with in the last twenty years had been at union conferences far from Sheffield, and those liaisons hadn't ever travelled beyond the threshold of the hotel lobby.

Helen stepped around the room, pausing occasionally as though paintings hung on the empty walls. He watched her stop at the only photo, as if she'd been homing in on it, the one of Veer and Muneet and the bath-time bubbles. Neither Nayan nor Helen spoke. She didn't resist, either. She seemed to be mirroring Muneet's look of unbending concentration; forcing herself to memorise this image, the way Muneet had been storing up the particular thrill of her grandson in a foamy bath. After some time, Helen bowed her head, withdrew, and reached for a large white bedsheet stretched over the settee and the armchair. Nayan took up the other end. They billowed the sheet, folded it lengthways, straightened and shook it again so the material waved and thudded, and only then did they step towards one another, pressing the sheet in half until their foreheads came together and their fingers touched at the corners. Helen, closing her hands around Nayan's, said: 'You're a good man.'

His brow still against hers, he shook his head. 'I took them back. Because I wanted a night without him. So I drove them back and they died.'

She kissed him, hard, to stop him from talking, and she didn't stop until his passivity gave way and it was clear his mind was now on her, on this. She pulled him down onto the settee, away from the photo, and cast the folded sheet, squashed between them, to the floor.

He was working from home the next day, so he messaged Helen to say he'd be round to pick his car up later, that there was no rush. *Also: when did you leave?* He'd fallen asleep on the sofa, her in his arms, but at around three a.m. he broke glancingly through the surface of his dream and may have registered a door closing. When he woke properly a few hours later, he pushed his face into the cushion, convinced he could still smell her trace. He wondered whether to furnish the text with a kiss or a heart, his thumb hovering over the keypad. Kiss, heart, both? Lord above, since when did he start worrying about nonsense like this! Anyway, *she* never added emojis or kisses. Her messages, when she bothered to send them, were terse, as curt as her cheekbones. She wasn't demonstrative. It was one of the things he loved about her.

Late in the afternoon, Pyara walked, fed and settled in front of the TV ('Just stick me on a lead,' he'd grumbled), Nayan laced up his runners and jogged out to the edge of the Peaks. He ran through the evening sun soaking through the green-hilled universe, towards that tantalising seam where earth met sky. He felt alive.

Brandon wore black trousers and a grey, collarless shirt. He was nervous: the moment he got in the car and thanked Nayan for the lift, he sprinted back inside for his cookery notebook, and then again for his wallet.

'Sure you've got everything now?' Nayan said. 'Take a minute. Have a think.'

The NCP car park was thronged, and Nayan spiralled up to the top storey before bagging a space. Together they awaited the elevator, then walked round the corner to the restaurant. He hadn't intended on accompanying the boy, but Brandon was still jittery, and Nayan didn't have it in him to simply offload the lad onto the pavement. It brought to mind a cub shivering at the mouth of a cave. Nayan wondered if he was starting to love him.

'It's natural to be nervous,' he said, as they reached the restaurant's polished, black door. 'But remember they'd be lucky to have a talent like you working here.'

Brandon nodded, exhaled, nodded again, this time at Nayan, and with an attempt at confidence.

They were let inside by Carl, who greeted Nayan and Brandon with extravagant hugs and preceded them through the small, carefully styled space – heavy wooden benches and tables; slate-grey cone uplights hanging from the ceiling at uneven intervals. The spare, white typography on the lemon walls was trickily visible and vanished when the sun razored in. 'We're excited to meet you, Brandon,' Carl said, over his shoulder. He pushed through swinging double doors, into the kitchen, and Nayan watched Brandon's face of guarded awe; the reticence and the desire. As far as Nayan could tell, the kitchen was even bigger than the restaurant, and all chrome, with a vast central island flanked by complicated arrangements of cabinets, drawers, shelves. A woman approached, tired-eyed and grim-lipped, in chef's whites, her red hair cut choppily short – wiping her hands on a towel.

'Pam,' she said, though it might have been 'palm' such was the firm, directive way in which she spoke, her arm extended. 'Brandon?'

'Yes. Hi.' Then, so eagerly: 'Thanks for giving me a chance.'

Feeling altogether out of place, Nayan told Brandon to give him a bell when he needed picking up, and all day, in meetings and even as he delivered his presentation to the committee, Brandon was there in Nayan's mind: how was he getting on? Had nerves got the better of him? Was he struggling? Was he happy? It was this fear that had him accelerating hard once the shutter lifted, speeding out of the car park to reach the boy. But Nayan needn't have worried. Look at him, leaning all casual outside the restaurant, beaming into his phone. Messaging Claudia, probably.

At first, Brandon chatted breezily, incessantly, about the role and the kitchen and how brilliant Pam was, even Carl's nice, in his funny way, but as they came off the dual carriageway and crossed the roundabout into Chesterfield, he quietened. 'I'm going to be working till gone midnight some days,' he said. 'And I've got enough to put down for my own car.' He paused, his brow twitching as though configuring his thoughts into their best possible expression.

'That's good, yeah?' Nayan said.

'Will you come with me to choose one? A car?' he asked.

'Of course,' Nayan said, letting out a laugh. 'Was that it? Daft sod.'

Brandon said nothing for a time, not until they were on the main road and heading past the chippy, the mart, the hairdresser. 'You're doing all the things I always thought I'd have to do by myself.' He looked harder out the window. They arrived at his house. 'I don't feel on my own any more. I wish I could make it so you didn't either.'

Nayan held it together while they said their silent good-byes, and once Brandon was through the front door, Nayan drew away, fighting tears, refusing to let them fall. It wasn't that he'd never cried since Veer's funeral; there were occasions when the grief, mixed with his own guilt, took him under. But these occasions always came in the dark and private night, as if his tears didn't deserve a full airing and had to be kept under the floorboards, like the dirty magazines he once used to steal from his parents' shop.

('*Did* you love him?' 'I doubt it.' 'So was he ever not sweet? Not good? Don't you think you make him sound quite idealised?' Nayan said nothing, kept walking.)

———

On his lunch break, Nayan hunched over his desk scrolling through the 'some ideas!' Brandon had WhatsApped him. Golfs, Citroens, Clios. *I like the Astra maybe?* Brandon wrote. *Will be pricey to insure*, Nayan replied. *I'll take a look and see you later.* Nayan altered the search parameters – honestly, the boy hadn't even considered mileage, let alone CO_2 emissions – and then bookmarked and messaged back a handful of 'more sensible ideas' on sale nearby. At four thirty, laptop jiggled into rucksack, he waved to Lisa-Marie – she didn't see him: she was on the phone arguing with a lawyer, palm flat against her forehead. Leaving her to it, Nayan made for the lift, and it belled cheerfully open just as Richard came up the stairs.

'Rich,' Nayan said, letting the lift depart empty. 'What brings you to our floor?' But Richard was not ready for geniality. 'Mate, can we talk?' Nayan asked.

Without even a backward glance, Richard heaved open the door, strode off. Saddened, Nayan pressed the bridge of his nose between fingers. 'So stupido,' he muttered, and summoned the lift again, except this time, as it obediently returned, he heard his name. He recognised Megha's voice before looking round, and felt an intense flare of annoyance, a concentrated sharpening of his more formless sorrow over Richard.

'Can I have a word?' she asked. 'Please?'

'I've an appointment,' he said, with finality, and it was broadly true: he was meeting Brandon at the car dealership.

'Five minutes. Please?'

They repaired to a table in the smallest meeting room, a glass-fronted cube that faced the office floor. Out there, desks were being tidied, mugs washed; an evening of family life ahead.

Turning away, to Megha, Nayan asked, 'So. How are things?'

He saw that she looked wrung out, her eyes heavy, her skin dull and flaking around her mouth. She tried to smile. 'Not good, to be honest. I'm being treated quite appallingly by my own workplace. Ironic, huh?'

'I'm sorry to hear that,' Nayan said diplomatically. 'Appallingly in what way?'

'I'm being ignored and excluded. Ostracised by colleagues. I've been snubbed – left out of social gatherings. People stop talking when I enter a room.'

'If you feel comfortable doing so, I'd recommend you speak to your line manager. Or you can go directly to HR. There's an established protocol for dealing with such matters.' If she was hoping for sympathy, she wasn't going to get it.

'I'm a pariah. It's making me ill.'

'If you feel this is impacting negatively on your mental health, there is also a helpline. The number's on the intranet. Or you can, of course, speak to your GP.' The power lay with him and he wanted to wield it cold: as if only now, sitting face to face with her, was it clear just how much damage she had tried to inflict.

'They call me a liar,' Megha said, watching keenly for his reaction.

'That's something you can discuss with HR.'

'You know I only spoke the truth.'

He wasn't going to be drawn in. He wasn't going to explain himself to her. 'I've got to go,' he said, rising.

'No!' she exclaimed, and the urgency halted him. 'They listen to you. Can you please just tell them I'm not making it up? That I'm not out to defame you or anything? They were your words. Just explain yourself to them. I'll then happily fall into line over this. I won't push it again.'

He leaned over the chair, his knuckles to the table. 'You twisted my words. You tried to make me out to be some two-faced slippery piece of shit. But they know me,' he said, pointing to the glass, 'they know I'm with them, that I've always been with them, and they also know a scheming little Judas when they see one.' The anger was there, low, measured. 'You thought they'd fall for your truth-twisting. You were wrong. You thought they were thick. You were wrong. You underestimated their intelligence. It's what the rich have always done.' He swung on his rucksack.

'And that's it?' Megha said, standing up too. 'You're going to stay silent and let them make my life hell. Abuse me. Bully me. Is that the dirty campaign you're running?'

'You dragged my dead son into it,' he flashed. His jaw was trembling it was clenched so hard. 'And *you* accuse *me* of playing dirty?'

She looked contrite, ashamed, and folded her arms across her chest. 'I do regret that. I'm sorry. I guess – it's no excuse – but I've heard you mention him – and your mother – in speeches, when you want to win people over, so . . . I suppose I thought it was a legitimate connection to make. But it wasn't. It was callous and heartless. I'm sorry. I'm really sorry.'

She was being sincere – he could see that – and he nodded, relented, and straightening up, he tugged at his lapels, as if tidying his anger back inside his jacket. 'This election's doing strange things to us. Thank you for apologising.'

She nodded, too. She was near tears.

'You're an unbelievable fighter, Megha. My mother

would love that about you. Believe it or not, *I* love that about you. You're a role model.'

'I'm really sorry,' she said again. 'I can't believe I mentioned your son.'

'It's done. You don't need to keep saying sorry.' A look at his watch: 'But I do need to go.'

'So will you do something?' she asked.

He waited a few moments, as if the truth needed clear space around it. 'Maybe some people feel aggrieved that you parachuted straight onto the SLT on a diversity ticket, that you should have started from the ground up. Like me, like Lisa-Marie, like Richard, like pretty much everyone else. But it's not too late. I mean that. You can still admit that you've a lot to learn and want to start on the shop floor. Be a rep. Speak to workers. All kinds of workers. Actually listen to their problems.'

'That's all I do,' she said, with extreme tightness. 'Every. Single. Day.'

'You listen to the problems you want to hear.'

She gave a startled shake of her head, not able to believe what she was hearing. 'Would your mother be happy to see you standing by while a woman of colour was being hated on like this?'

'If being liked is so important to you, then build that trust from the ground floor. Like I'm saying.'

'I'm not concerned about being liked. I just don't want to be abused.'

'You're not concerned – Right.' His eyes contracted, as if at a bright darkness in her face. 'Yes. I see now.'

'What's that supposed to mean?'

'Your little routines on stage. Bossing it in meetings. Your newsletters. You don't want comrades, do you?'

'What?'

'Let alone friends. You want an audience.'

'That's not true,' she said. 'That's the most ridic—'

'And please don't presume to know what my mother would think. She'd admire your spirit. But she'd run a mile from your politics. She'd hate your constant eroding of genuine solidarity.'

'She'd be ashamed of you,' Megha said, whispered, really – because by then no one but me was around to hear it: Nayan had walked out of the room, and she was watching him, at last, enter the lift.

———

'It sounds like it all got incredibly charged and heated.'

'I don't think either of us covered ourselves in glory,' Megha said, looking beyond me as if into a long-ago past. 'Like he said, the election did weird things to us. At a cost to our better selves, I guess.'

She was up from London for a two-day conference and had agreed to meet in the Sheffield office. I'd been visualising a sharp face, all resolute angles; in reality, the cheeks were softer and the jaw rounder, the eyes gently sloping. Her hair was well cut, like her calico smock, like the ferozi chunni she wore for a scarf, and she looked pregnant, though I couldn't ask; feeling some loyalty to Nayan, I didn't want to ask, either. Her voice, though, was precisely, disconcertingly, how I'd anticipated: sheathed in velvet, as if the words themselves adored being spoken by her.

'It was a phenomenally testing time.'

'You must have been surprised to beat him? The odds-on favourite?'

'He pulled out. Surely he's told you that?'

'Not yet. We've not got to that yet. But' – I looked at her – 'I read the write-ups online. What really happened?'

'I'll leave that to Nayan. It sounds like he's on a truth-telling mission. I wouldn't want to step on his shoes.'

'Toes,' I said. 'You walk in someone's shoes.'

Eyes on me, she sank back a little, pleased this encounter promised more than she'd allowed for. We were on chairs, wire creations both, around a squat table; the bottle of sparkling water unopened. 'How is he?' she asked. 'He's doing great work with CAR. I got him that gig, you know. And he's really taken to it. He's come good, hasn't he?'

'He seems passionate about it.' Then: 'Nayan said so much about you – I just wanted to meet you for myself.'

'For something you're writing?'

Through the glass, across the office floor, was a very small meeting room. 'Is that where you argued? Can you tell me about what you did afterwards? You must have, understandably, been very hurt.'

Arriving home, Megha double-locked the door and fell back against it, laptop case in hand. As if in a fug, she padded into the front room: the carpet taped together from mismatched offcuts; the worn seat of her armchair; the rubbish heater. She felt an unhappiness at base, in her belly, a solid ball of misery that rolled around inside. She pulled her hair out of its ponytail and felt around her skull for the smooth, blank disc of skin. The size of a two-pound coin, she'd noticed the hairless patch over a week ago. Entirely stress-related, the GP had said. No shit, Megha thought. She wanted her mum. Dropping the case, she went to her phone, her photos: she and her mother in a souk; now in a tea-house; at a Bharatanatyam concert. Nayan wasn't the only one who drew strength from their mother, and Megha ratcheted through more photos until she came to the one of her bruised wrist. She moved to the armchair, the image still in her palm. Would anyone believe her? Would it only make her life worse? She hadn't even wanted to go to the Diwali party. Not when her parents were coming up, visiting her in Sheffield for the first time since she'd left them so abruptly.

'So no friend's thirtieth?'

'No,' Megha said.

'So why go? To the Diwali thing – if you didn't want to?'

She poured herself a water, fizz hissing up the glass. 'This is something you're writing for publication?'

'Or just for me, really.' I tried to laugh it off. 'It's all become quite personal.'

She seemed intrigued by this. 'Personal how?'

'We're from the same town, Nayan and me. Maybe that's all I mean.'

'The town forged you. It's in you?'

'Maybe.'

'Then break away,' she said, with a flick of her hand, as though dismissing someone from the room.

'Is that what you did?'

*

All afternoon, Megha prepared a biryani, then followed a YouTube tutorial on how to wear a sari. She was thinking croissants for breakfast – hoping her parents might stay – when the doorbell rang.

Hugs, Diwali wishes, coats – each making an effort and Megha getting drinks as her dad, Dinesh, said: 'Shall I just leave the car on the road, then?'

'Yes, Dad. I've not got off-street parking just yet.' She brought juice. 'Why aren't you sitting? Take a chair each. I've got this,' she added, meaning a stool.

'How's the election?' asked her mother, Shreya, still standing. Her kameez was ankle-length, plain, the jewels reserved for a decorously brocaded dupatta. 'We're incredibly proud.'

'Are you?' She didn't mean it to sound so much of an accusation. 'It's early days. I need to build support.'

'I want us to go out and celebrate,' Dinesh said, his smile forced. 'Not every day your daughter stands for office.'

Unlike her mother, he'd kept on his shoes, Megha noticed.

'We're staying here,' Shreya said. 'Meghloo's cooked.'

How long had it been since she'd heard that? 'I'd love it so much if you stayed. I promise you, Dad, your car'll be fine. Can I take your jacket?'

He stepped away from the window, into the room, taking in the small corner of mould on the ceiling, the cold. 'Megha—'

'Don't say anything. Please. Let's just have a nice meal. I just want to be with people who care about me. It's been so long.'

Shreya accompanied Megha down the hall, but there wasn't really space in the kitchen for two, so she hovered at the doorway while Megha dished up and passed her the plates. They ate on their laps, Dinesh scraping his fork through the rice. Still in his suit jacket, chessboard tie slipped inside, between the buttons of his shirt. Every inch the property magnate, the commercial developer, the non-dom. Not his fault, Megha reminded herself. Her dad was an economic migrant. In a racist society. Continually passed over for promotion. What choice did he have except to strike out hard and alone?

'Let me take your jacket,' Megha tried again. 'Relax.'

'I'll freeze,' he replied. 'Your mum's toes are turning blue.'

'Don't be so dramebaaz,' Shreya said, crossing her ankles. 'I'm fine, beti.'

'I'll put the heater on. I want you to be comfortable.'

But the loud clatter of the fan-heater seemed only to spur Dinesh's irritation, and he brought his heel down on it, twice, until the blasted thing switched off.

'Dinesh,' Shreya warned.

'What are you playing at?' he said. 'If you lose this election, and you will, are you just going to carry on living here? In this crap-tip?'

'Dinesh!'

'It's fine, Mum. I don't need him to believe in me.' She looked at him. 'I have enough belief in myself.'

'You're a megalomaniac.'

'Ha! You would know.'

His plate in one hand, Dinesh pointed at the ground

with the other. 'What exactly are you trying to prove here? Do you feel guilty? For growing up with money? Is that it? It can't all be a reaction against me.'

'She's always cared, you know that,' Shreya said. 'More than her sisters ever have. All those marches she went on. Those vigils. Always helping the poor. Even when they poked fun.'

Dinesh set the food on the floor, exhaled. 'Just come home. There's nothing for you here. Only losing. The polls don't lie.'

'I'm trying to make a difference,' Megha said, in a conciliatory tone, to help him understand. 'I want to change people's lives, change society, lead from the front. I know this all seems really maverick to you, but it's who I am.'

'It's a fine line, between a maverick and a full-blown narcissist.'

Megha shrank from his cold tone as much as from his words. When it came to his youngest daughter, Dinesh was like a malevolent doctor: he knew where she bruised.

Megha didn't finish the rest of her meal and her parents left soon after, not an hour into their stay. She put the heater back on, for company if nothing else, then unplugged it, drew on her coat and googled the address of the gurdwara.

'All in all, it had been a horrendous evening,' Megha told me: her parents' aborted visit, Nayan's speech, their subsequent quarrel. She'd lost her self-control, which aggrieved her. Not that this excused for one moment Nayan's behaviour. And now, when she'd gone pleading to him for help, he'd refused. She whisked the photo, the image of her wrist, back into the app, opened her laptop, then a blank new document. The more she wrote, the better she felt. Yes: it felt good to not be supine, passively accepting the blows. She still didn't know whether she'd send this latest newsletter. Would it do any good? He had everyone wrapped around his finger. Apart from Richard? At the lift, had she imagined it or have Richard and Nayan fallen out? Midsentence, she looked up from the screen, wondering how she might fashion to her advantage any hostility between them, and she was still thinking it through when the letterbox rattled. She edged into the hallway. Hello? There was mail on the floor, glossy junk. Plus, a package. A bomb, she thought, weirdly calm. But, no, it was a card, a birthday card. One of those personalised photo collages. She'd forgotten. But her parents hadn't. Standing in the silent hallway, she held the card to her chest.

———

It was getting late, this was their fourth car lot of the evening, the second Peugeot they'd test driven, and still Nayan refused to waver. Sighing, Lincoln, their fifty-something sales adviser, said he'd speak to his manager, and toiled up the steps and into the brick cabin.

'I think it's a good price,' Brandon said. 'And it drives well. And – and this is important – I'm really, really tired.'

'That's what they're relying on. That you'll back down. Give in. Just leave it to me.'

When Lincoln reappeared, he held on to the stair rail as if recovering from the fight he'd just put up. He raised his wiry blond eyebrows apologetically: *I gave it everything, lads. I laid it on the line!* 'She won't let me. I'm sorry. Half a tank is the best we can do.'

'A full tank, mats, and the drive-away insurance is on you.'

'I wish I could. I want to. Believe me, no one wants this more than me. But no dice. To be fair, we have already taken nearly a third off the price.'

'Because you'd overpriced it in the first place,' Nayan said, reaching into his back pocket. 'We can go over your competitors' prices again?'

'No,' Lincoln said hastily. 'That was very thorough. It'll live long in my memory. But, like I say, I'm sorry.'

Nayan tutted in sympathy and said in that case they'd have to leave it there. 'Thanks for your time this evening, Lincoln,' he finished and turned to go, forcing a reluctant Brandon round too.

'Keep walking,' Nayan said.

'Are you sure? I'm ready to buy it.'

'Have you seen anyone else while we've been here? They need the deal.'

Sure enough, Lincoln called them back, and asked for a moment so he could check if there was anything else they might do.

The deal struck, they drove home, to Brandon's, where he told his mum and Claudia that he'd be picking up his Peugeot tomorrow, that Nayan hadn't stopped chipping away at the price even once they'd agreed to the tank and mats: he'd got a bit more off because the handbook wasn't exactly the right one and then more because the – V5C, was it? – would need restamping.

'That franchise makes a tonne,' Nayan said, pleased with himself. 'And big man Lincoln drives a Jag.'

'He looked exhausted,' Brandon said.

'Look at you,' Claudia said. 'New car, new job. Going up in the world.'

'Old girlfriend, though,' Brandon replied, a nod to their three-year gap.

Helen, Nayan noticed, had been leaning against the kitchen arch this entire time, listening, observing. Unlike Nayan, she never allowed herself the pleasure of basking in her son's happiness.

'It'll save you being a taxi,' Nayan said to Helen.

She came forward, placed her arms around his neck, and kissed him; his lips, his cheek, his ear.

'Whoa,' he said. She was smiling. He'd never seen her quite like this before. 'Tired and emotional?' he asked.

Maybe, her face said. 'Stay for dinner?'

How he wanted that! But there was no one with Pyara. 'Can't. I've got some calls to make.'

'Okay,' she said, or rather mouthed.

'And you two,' Nayan said, turning round, anticipating derision – but they didn't seem to care, or even to have noticed, and what a warm, giant sensation it was, to not have his presence in the house remarked upon, to be let into a world where him kissing Helen was now an everyday sort of thing. 'Well, behave. And get that car taxed first thing.'

'Before you go,' Claudia said. 'About my speech. How, say, theoretical can I go? Can I bring in a bit of Frantz

Fanon? Maybe throw in a quick recap of the Haitian Revolution?'

'As long as it makes me look good,' Nayan said, snapping into his jacket, 'you can say what you want.'

Nayan didn't, in actual fact, have any calls to make. He just hadn't wanted to admit that he needed to get home and bath his dad, not just then, when she was being so loving. He wanted to leave her picturing him fighting for the masses, not cleaning around the shrivelled spigot of his dad's dick.

'I was by myself for too long,' Pyara said, sitting on the end of his bed.

Nayan was helping him with his trackies, jiggling the lining up one wettish leg at a time. 'It wasn't that long,' he said.

'Were you with your piece? Busy fucking? Is she good at fucking?'

Crouching, Nayan yanked his father's drawstring with such indignation that Pyara struck him across the side of the head, so hard they both unbalanced and fell to the floor. Nayan took a moment, swallowing again and again, submerging his anger, then eased out from under his father and cradled him back up and onto the bed.

'What happened?' Pyara said, fearfully. 'How did I fall?'

'You're fine. You just need to sleep.' Nayan passed him his pills, a tumbler of water. For a while now, Pyara had insisted all his drinks come in a frosted tumbler; he gave no reason, though Nayan suspected this was his pubbing, whisky past emitting a faint signal from beneath the detritus of his mind.

'You're bleeding, lad,' Pyara said. 'How you gone and done that?'

'I fell,' Nayan said, accepting the empty tumbler. 'Lights off now.'

The cut by his temple was wire-thin yet persistent; it wouldn't be staunched. He searched the kitchen drawer for Steri-Strips, certain he still had them from when he'd slit his knee out running and the nurse let him take the rest of the packet home. He looked upstairs, too, in the bathroom cabinet, and in the cupboard under the sink, and then he checked all three places again, confident that this time the packet would be there, in plain sight, and incredulous when it wasn't. Giving up, sweaty by now and tissue still pressed to the wound, he made for the lounge, where his phone was lit up – a concertinaed ladder of green notifications. *Jesus Ny she's got you by the short and curlies . . . I'm revolted . . . You've lost my vote . . . She's not making *this* up is she . . .* Don't react, he told himself, and perhaps spoke it out loud – it's just the usual suspects, the ones that have never liked you; she's done this before. It felt vital that he go through the messages systematically, one by one and in the order they'd arrived, as a way of flagging to himself that he was calm, but when two, then three, referenced an assault, and he the perpetrator, his composure ran to panic. He needed the settee, lowered onto it gingerly, as if it was this act of sitting down that risked exploding his reputation. A message from Lisa-Marie: *Check your inbox and try not to worry. Let's talk first thing and thrash out a plan.*

'Do we want a duplicitous, violent man as our new leader?' That was the title of Megha's email, and it had been cascaded to Unify_MemDistList_Intl_All – the entire global membership. He read on, the tissue on the floor, blood trickling past his ear.

In my most recent newsletter I articulated several of the contradictions and hypocrisies in both Nayan Olak's personality and his political position. To briefly recap, my main observations were twofold: 1) though Olak argues against a polity that centres identitarian concerns, be they gender, sexuality or, especially, race, the serving staff – chosen by him – working at his Diwali party were Black. It's clear that Olak, on some level, does centre race, and it's also clear which jobs Olak thinks Black people are fit for; 2) my even larger point was that Olak styles himself as an evangelist for the working class, and yet he said to me that the white working class didn't exist and that they'd been left behind as backward, racist fuckwits.

The last newsletter also spoke of how Olak tried to keep me at the Diwali party 'rather insistently'. That wasn't entirely truthful. Perhaps I wanted to spare his blushes, but we were in the lobby of the temple as I was making clear my desire to leave the party, and when he realised that I wasn't going to stay just because he wanted me to, Nayan Olak became not just insistent, but aggressive. All women will recognise the dark look that overtakes a man when a woman refuses to submit. Olak had that look as he stepped towards me, cornering me, making it hard for me to see around him.

When I tried to get away, he assaulted me. So hard he left a bruise. Only when I shouted did he finally back off, no doubt fearful someone might see him unmasked. I don't want to imagine what might have happened had we not been in such a public arena. But I do want to be clear: Olak assaulted me.

It was made abundantly clear to me after my last newsletter that not everyone believes me. I have been shunned by colleagues. I have received vicious hate mail. I have been called a liar, a scab, a c**t, and been told my election campaign is the 'Blair Bitch Project', which might be funny if it wasn't for the violent misogyny of it all. I am not a liar. I have never resorted to untruths. When I get things wrong, I admit them and apologise. I should not have used Nayan Olak's past trauma against him in my last newsletter. It was a callous thing to do. I have apologised privately and in-person to Nayan and I apologise here again, publicly and wholeheartedly – on that front, he has my every sympathy. I repeat: I do not like liars and it pains me deeply to be thought of as one.

My final point is that when I asked and begged Nayan Olak to condemn the abuse I was, and am still, being subjected to, he refused. Why won't Olak condemn my abusers? I guess the question is why would he? His brand works and he clearly has very ardent fans. He's done a great job of manufacturing a Teflon persona. And no doubt he feels as if the hand of history is upon him, that he can do anything, be as hypocritical, abusive and aggressive as he likes, and that he'll still walk this election and become our first non-white leader. And perhaps he will. But I couldn't live with myself if I didn't do everything I could to expose his duplicity and violence, to

show you all the man behind the mask. If he still ends up as
our General Secretary, leading our great union, then at least
now we'll only have ourselves to blame.

Standing up, he screamed at his phone, at her lies.
What assault? They'd argued. That was all. And she's
going on about a bruise? He'd never laid a hand on her.
His blood was hammering around his body; the rage felt
total. *It's all lies!* he texted to Lisa-Marie. He didn't know
what to do. And then he did. He sat back down, seized
his laptop, and pressed 'Reply All': These are lies, he
wrote. You were angry about my speech at the gurdwara
and we argued heatedly about that but it's completely
wrong to say I assaulted you. This is a fabrication. Retract
your accusation at once or I'll be speaking to my lawyers
in the morning. He waited, staring at his screen, not
moving from the sofa. WhatsApps, texts, emails – all kept
crowding in with a mocking whoosh. A few pledged their
continued support, most were vituperative: . . . *sick in the*
head . . . fuck off you bully . . .

Then another email from Megha, again addressed to
everyone:

I'm sharing an image of my wrist following my interaction
with Olak at the temple – date-stamped photo below. I had no
plans to share this – it gives me no pleasure and I very much
hoped I wouldn't have to – but it's become clear to me that
this is the only way people will see I'm telling the truth. Since
my last mail I've already received several messages of hate,
from people calling me a liar. So look at the photo. You can
decide for yourselves.

This was it, was it? She'd resorted to lying in a last-ditch bid to wrest the election from him. Knowing she was bound to lose, all she had left to throw at him was defamation and faking injuries.

The messages, the abuse, continued. He turned his phone off. He wanted it all to go away. But now the silence sounded worse, bigger, as if it hid some beast lying in wait.

For a long time he sat there: help, memory, help. He could remember his anger in the gurdwara and the sense of having overstepped the mark. But he'd not hurt her. Of that he was adamant. She really was lying. He let out an agonised cry and kicked as if at a cage. His heart kept coming like a crashing tug. His fingertips covered in watery blood. The blood confused him. He touched the side of his head, his cut; more blood came off his fingers. He stood, and felt suddenly woozy and slack and groped for the doorframe. Slow breaths, he told himself. Slow in, slow out. But instead of air, the entire room was being expelled, shrinking away from him as his eyes flickered, closed, and he fell first onto the settee, and then rolled to the floor.

By the time Lisa-Marie arrived with Buddy the next morning, Nayan had already woken to an email from Geoff Carswell – his boss and de facto returning officer. He wanted to meet, he said, to discuss the concerns raised by Megha Sharma's recent communication.

'You going down to London?' Lisa-Marie asked.

'He's coming up tomorrow.'

'Wow. Not often he gets off his backside.'

'I guess he feels it's important.' They'd been waiting for a pause in the traffic, and now crossed into Ringwood Park, where the ground was mulchy and every other tree dotted with lilac buds: spring, coming round again. 'We've always got on well enough. And he came up to the conference last year.'

'He got on with you when he was certain he was backing a winner.'

Nayan halted. 'Meaning?'

'Meaning let's wait while we get this week's polls in. Scarswell's a shifty fucker. He just wants to check which way the wind's blowing. He's probably meeting her as well.'

They climbed the shallow, gravelly steps to the lake, past a purple-shirted boy nibbling birthday cake on a bench, and continued along the lakeside path. The water held the wet slate of the sky, and large spotty carp were questing beneath its surface.

Nayan had come to by midnight, his body jammed between the sofa and the coffee table. He lay dazed, figuring out what had happened, then at once remembered, like a thunderclap in his mind. In the bathroom, he scrubbed away the blood, which had stemmed by now, and applied strips to the cut. Returning downstairs, he tapped on the photo of her wrist. It showed a dark purple bruise, an elongated oval yellowing at the edges. The date stamp. He threw his phone aside. How could she be doing this to him? He hadn't realised he was shaking, until his body convulsed and he stumbled to the sink to retch, emptily.

'What'd you do to yourself?' Lisa-Marie asked, looping her arm in his.

'Hmm? Oh, nothing. A cut. Dad was playing up.' He kicked a stone, watched it go plopping into the lake. 'So can I get publicity maestro Lisa-Marie's official take on it all? How do I get past it?'

'It was a panicky letter,' Lisa-Marie said, as if she'd been waiting to be asked. 'I'm amazed she didn't say it was my kids helping at the party. Friends. Only that it was "Black serving staff". No mention of Helen either. She's got that talent for manipulative omission.'

'Manipulative all right.'

'I also think she's angry, alone, scared. It's not easy being a woman in our world, Nayan. Trying to be heard. Taken seriously. She's fighting with everything she's got. Her back's against the wall.'

'Not all women would resort to these tactics, Lise. These lies. You wouldn't.' Then: 'That photo. I didn't do it. We argued. But I didn't attack her. That photo's not real.'

'You were riled.'

'But I'm not a monster.'

She sighed resignedly. 'You're going to issue a statement. Refute the accusation, sympathise, lance the boil, move on. Hopefully, we've enough support to ride it out.'

'So she gets away with it? No, no way. I'm getting onto my lawyer.'

'The worst thing would be if this drags on. It's you who'll be ruined, even if she is lying. My inbox is heavy with anger, Ny. And it's not just the usual handwringers.'

'What do you mean *if* she's lying?'

Lisa-Marie stopped, was silent a while. Then: 'Step outside of . . . all this for a second, all this . . . *rhetoric*. She might not be herself right now, but are you? Are you still you? I don't want to lose the best friend I've ever had.'

'But she *is* lying, Lise,' Nayan said. 'Why is no one believing me? I never attacked her. Of course I didn't. And she knows that. But that's the lie she's happy to put out there. Why? Because she's losing? So that means she can destroy a man's reputation?'

Her eyes slid away from his face, as though he wasn't quite getting it. He'd never seen that in her before, this hesitation to support one another come what may. Unnerved, he gestured for them to resume walking.

'I used to come home this way after school,' he said, feeling suddenly nostalgic for the known past. His tie clipped short, his white shirt untucked, he and Sonia would break through the field, take off from the swings; the trudge up to their estate, arguing all the way.

'Chin up,' Lisa-Marie said. 'It's all contained to Unify – chances are it'll die a death and that'll be the end of it. It can't get out. Promise me: no lawyers.'

'It's typical private-school, entitled shit,' Nayan said. 'Thinks she can behave as slyly, as terribly as she wants, say whatever crap with complete impunity, knowing she'll get away with it.'

'Aye. It gets on my tits.'

Nayan grinned. 'Gets my dander up.'

'Oh, I love that word.'

They laughed – they could always make each other laugh – and turning for home, still smiling, Lisa-Marie peered over her shoulder. She was half-anticipating flowers, hyacinths, for she'd sensed a flash of purple at the edge of her vision. But there was nothing there.

('You found the Steri-Strips, then?' I said. 'Turned out they were in the drawer after all,' and he flung a peanut into the air, caught it with a crunch.)

The next day, Nayan shaved and dressed with deliberate, prolonged movements to counter the waves of anxiety speeding through him. Before he knew it, he was at the office. The receptionist greeted him as merrily as ever – his heart leapt in thanks! – but once out of the lift and on his floor, all eyes glanced up from their desks, fastening onto him, seeking something they had previously missed. He felt sick. Deep breath. Keep walking. And somehow he got to his desk, hauled out his laptop – how heavy it was – and hung his jacket on the back of the chair. Only as he sat down did he suffer a view across the floor: Megha was there, eyes on her screen, but now turning to accept a mug from a desk-colleague. The colleague simpered, squeezing Megha's shoulder in apparent sympathy. When they looked over, Nayan averted his attention, to his own screen, which was taking years to boot up.

At eleven thirty, his e-calendar gave a little musical flourish – *meeting with Geoff Carswell* – but Geoff's secretary had already been in touch to push it back by half an hour. Grabbing his jacket, Nayan decided to get some air. It was better than staying at his desk with everyone's gaze tiptoeing around him. And it wasn't as if he was getting any work done: three hours and all he'd accomplished was last week's timesheet and a mandatory CBT; for much of the morning he'd been deleting the enraged emails that kept sweeping into his campaign inbox.

Outside, at the rear of the building, he lay on the low wall separating the path from the grass verge; hands behind his head, jacket slung across his stomach, discerning shapes in the bronze-tipped clouds like he used to as a kid. A woman's profile. A paw. He was thinking that once through this meeting with Geoff, he'd write that note Lisa-Marie suggested, publicly, and draw a line under it all.

'Tough day?'

Nayan shifted his eyes across: Richard's face, a cloud passing behind it. He sat up and drew his feet in to make space, though Richard remained standing. 'It'll pass,' Nayan said, still half with the clouds. 'Sooner or later.'

'Everything does.'

'Yep. None of us are getting out of here alive.'

Richard smiled, did sit down. 'That picture . . .'s not good.'

'She's lying.'

'Oh?' He sounded surprised. 'That's your defence?'

'We argued. End of. She's making it out to be something it wasn't. Faking a picture's a new low, I'll give her that.'

'You're passionate. People get that.'

'Maybe.' Then: 'I'm meeting Scarswell.'

'Yeah, I heard he's in town.' Richard, who'd been

rubbing his thumbs together, brought his hands to rest. 'Listen. I wanted you to hear it from me and it's not got anything to do with the picture, but Megha's asked me to run with her, on a joint ticket, as co-leaders.'

Nayan felt an urge to laugh. 'Jesus. She must be desperate – no offence. You're not, are you?' But it was clear that Richard was. Nayan swung his feet onto the ground. 'Rich! But you're totally different. Politically. You don't believe in anything she stands for.'

'Maybe,' Richard said, swaying his head, weighing things up. 'But it turns out we're not too far apart on the big picture stuff.'

'She's not a socialist. Like you are, last I checked. She's a liberal. An identitarian. How big picture you going?'

'I can see the way the *world's* going.' He met Nayan's disbelieving look. 'Has already gone. I'm white working class. I'm going to own that. I'm going to fight for my people. I'm not going to let them be looked down on any more.'

'Can you hear yourself? *I'm* your people, Rich. We worked on the same fucking factory floors together.'

Ignoring this, Richard said, 'We had a long talk, Megha and me, and we both agree that different identities have different needs. Initiatives to help black and brown workers, *and also* for white workers. We're on the same page.'

'For now. Because she needs the votes you'll bring in.'

'She's added it to her charter. That pledge thing she came up with.' He went to his phone, read: ' "The culture and humanity of workers of all races, whether White,

226

Black or Brown, should be praised and protected equally."
That's good enough for me. For now.'

'Am I full-scale tripping? Are you actually saying this?'

Jumping off the wall, Richard drove his hands into his pockets. 'Word of advice? Be honest about the picture. Stand down. Don't make things worse for yourself.'

'What? So you and her can carve us all up? It's not a big step from there to separate buses.'

The sun escaped from behind a cloud; Richard squinted. 'We've all got identities, mate. Not just you lot.'

Cruelly dubbed Scarswell on account of his lifelong affliction – a pitted, acne-scarred face – Geoff Carswell was a big bull of a man, in his sixties, whose ample stomach meant there was always a healthy measure between his desk and his chair. His bouffant hair was a pristine white, ditto his eyebrows, but his neat beard remained dramatically, non-chemically black, an incongruity that blocked Nayan from ever quite making sense of the guy. It also subtly encouraged the widespread notion that Geoff Carswell wasn't someone to be taken at face value. He nodded at Nayan to continue.

'I'm not denying I got angry. Or that we argued. We were discussing our different approaches to questions of identity and things got heated. But I didn't lay a hand on her. I definitely didn't physically assault her.'

'Are you saying she's lying?'

'I'm saying she's confused,' Nayan said, mindful of the tone Lisa-Marie wanted him to strike. 'I'm sure she believes what she's saying, but that bruise did not come from me.'

'Well, that picture's all we've got to go on.'

'We could go on the truth,' Nayan said. 'We could go on the fact that she wants to turn Unify into her pet race project.'

Geoff leaned back in his chair, all that leather creaking, his arms flat on the support rests. His face really was big, and craggy. A former Eighties union god. For real? 'Look, I don't really care about the ins and outs of your disagreement. My priority here is to protect our union from disrepute. And plenty of members – oh yes, plenty of *our* members – are asking me what we're going to do about this. Some are even asking how we can employ someone like you, let alone have you as our potential leader – that black staff at your party debacle?'

'They're friends. Lisa-Marie's kids. I've known them for ever. There was also Helen, who's—'

Geoff waved the explanation away; it was too complicated. He wanted straightforward solutions, in that he wanted problems to straightforwardly disappear. He rotated his monitor towards Nayan. 'These are all emails about you. I had to create a subfolder.'

'I get them, too,' Nayan said. 'I ended up putting a redirect on my phone.'

'It's all patriarchy and white supremacy,' Geoff said, looking at Nayan with pained confusion. 'I'm not sure how but ... And now I'll have to address this at the debate, from the off.'

'I'm more than happy to issue a statement of sympathy.

Publicly. I'm sure Megha will understand and we can move on to discuss what really matters.'

'Got more than you bargained for with her, didn't you?' Geoff said, to his own rumbling laughter.

Nayan eked out a smile. 'She's a fighter all right.'

'Still think you've this in the bag?'

'I'm doing my best. Nothing's in the bag.'

Geoff moved his mouth around, pondering, then lurched decisively forward, hands together and pointed at Nayan. 'You've still my support.'

'Thank you, Geoff. That really means a lot. Coming from you,' he added, because Geoff was someone who liked to know his largesse was appreciated, that his clout still carried.

'She's not one of us, Ny. She's not put in the hard yards like you have. So apologise, grovel if you have to, and then get back out there. Call her out on her wealth. Call it obscene. Call *her* obscene. Repulsive. A shark.'

'I'll win this without resorting to slurs,' Nayan said, staring his boss down.

Geoff sat back; then, taking up his pen, under his breath: 'Bad habit of yours, making me feel like a worm.'

Leaving Geoff's office, feeling sullied all over, Nayan longed for a shower. He went straight to Lisa-Marie, and she held his arm; it was trembling.

'How you bearing up?' she asked.

'I met Scarswell.'

'Ah. Enough to rattle anyone.'

'He's still behind me. But Richard's backing her. They're standing together.'

'Right,' Lisa-Marie said; then, in exasperation: 'He's hurting. She's hurting. You're hurting.'

'I need to get that statement out pronto.'

'Take a step back first. Let's think about how we're going to pitch it.'

'I don't want to think. I don't want to pitch it,' Nayan said. He put his head in his hands. 'I just want to tell everyone she's lying.'

Alone in the boardroom, he drafted his statement, and finished up with a lengthy email that spoke of how much he admired Megha, how happy he'd been when she'd accepted his invitation to the Diwali party, but how sad he was that they'd argued on the night. He absolutely wasn't responsible for the bruise to her wrist – he had no record of violence anywhere in his life – but he deeply regretted that they *both* lost their temper. Politics was a cut-throat business, tempers did flare, but everyone at Unify had a duty to be aware of how their anger – even if justified – could be felt by others. The statement went on for a little longer, emphasising that he'd always deplored bullying and abuse of any kind, that his life's work had been focused on fighting for workers and against bully- ing employers; he closed the email by hoping he and Megha could work together in the future to stamp out this kind of behaviour and improve the lives of all work- ing people. Pressing send, he sighed, feeling suddenly lighter; not so much because he thought the matter was dispatched, but because he felt he was once more in con- trol, once more setting the parameters of the debate. So bolstered did he feel, that when he saw Megha coming up the stairs, he hurried to catch her.

'Megha,' he said. 'A word.'

She almost did a double-take, then collected herself. 'And what can I do for you?'

'You can take back your false accusation. But failing that, I just wanted to say I'm sorry.' He could feel his chest widening; again, he was being the bigger man. 'For our argument at the gurdwara. I've just this minute issued a statement and sent it to all members. And I made clear that I support you, that you should not be bullied.'

'Unless it's by you.'

'I didn't touch you.'

'You left a raging bruise.'

'You know, I've still a mind to get the lawyers involved. Quit these lies. Stop framing an innocent man just to win an election.'

She turned a touch, standing square on, and enunciated very clearly. 'For the avoidance of doubt, you're not standing down?'

'Of course I'm fucking not.'

'Right.' The 't' came swinging up hard, all rip and intent. 'So you can threaten, abuse and assault a woman, lie about it, stand aside when that woman is vilified, refuse to call off the dogs, and then, when forced kicking and screaming into making a statement, send out an email denying you did anything wrong and think that's the end of it? That you don't even have to stand down? Is that the world men like you live in?'

'I'm not standing down because of one argument.

Because you banged your arm and think I did it. You don't get to come in here and shit all over what I've worked all my life for.'

Taking a second, she tried a different, softer approach. 'Nayan, please. Stand down. You made a mistake. Learn from it. But please stand down. I really don't want to keep fighting you like this. I think you're a good man. You just made a mistake. Stand down.'

(*You're a good man*. First Lisa-Marie, then Helen, now Megha. For what it's worth, I don't think Nayan was aware of how often he'd put these words in the mouths of these women. And on this I sought neither Lisa's nor Megha's corroboration. I didn't want them to deny ever saying it. Like Nayan, I wanted to believe that it might be true. 'Sounds like she wasn't accepting your statement,' I said. 'It was infuriating.' 'What was?')

It was infuriating how she spoke as though she were the wise, elder statesman dispensing advice to the feckless newcomer. 'Just stand down,' she said again, bewildered that he failed to see the simplicity of the solution.

Nayan didn't have a chance to reply: her desk-colleague (tea-bringer, shoulder-squeezer) had appeared, an extremely lean, balding guy with a rat-a-tat delivery. He held two green binders in his arms. 'Everything okay, Megha?'

'We're just talking, Max,' Nayan said. 'Of course everything's okay. Jog the fuck on.'

'No offence, Nayan, but I'm asking Megha.'

'You on some rescue mission? She's fine. Can't you see she's fine?'

'Let her speak for herself.'

'It's fine, Max,' Megha said sadly. 'He's not leaving me with any choice.'

Nayan watched her drift back to her desk, each slow step conveying thought, flip up her screen and start reading. Her head, and not just her eyes, moved from left to right and back again. She was reading his statement, without doubt. Returning to his own desk, he awaited her next salvo, her fuming riposte – but none came. An hour passed. Two. Colleagues glanced over, cagily. Someone in Digital Affairs exited the lift, looked across, looked away. He didn't understand. Then Lisa-Marie came.

'What's going on, Lise?'

'I'm sorry, Ny. She's put it all online. The picture, the emails. Everything.'

'She's fucking what? Can we delete it?' But he knew they couldn't.

His heart beating in an awful way, he logged on with Unify's handle and saw just how much the world now hated him:

@WeUnify Why the fuck is an abuser in your company?

@WeUnify He can't even say 'I'm sorry'

@WeUnify Nowhere near good enough. Racist misogynists like #OlakMustGo

@WeUnify The picture doesn't lie, you do, again and again #mangotcaught #misogynyintheunions

@WeUnify That's not an apology. That's damage limita-
tion #OlakMustGo

@WeUnify When someone shows you who they are,
believe them the first time. RIPower Queen Maya

@WeUnify NO NO NO! Stop trying to save your
white-adjacent skin. Have some shame

@WeUnify Fixed it for you: 'I resign'

@WeUnify You abused a woman of colour. Now you're
calling her a liar. Do the right thing and resign

@WeUnify I bet Olak eats roti with a knife and fork
LMFAO

@WeUnify I can't see a simple I'm sorry? Am I missing
something?

@WeUnify Oh for a world where we're NOT abused by
men like you!! #OlakMustGo

@WeUnify #OlakMustGo

@WeUnify Even I (a man) can see that this 'apology' is
nothing but gaslighting and trolling

@WeUnify Why is it only women who have to resign?
The guy assaulted her and is lying about it

@WeUnify I wrote a paper on Foucault and the political
saliency of South-Asian male violence. A thread 1/n

@WeUnify #getthefuckerout

@WeUnify #OlakMustGo

@WeUnify I'm a #unify member and this guy's always
been chippy. If he stays, I'm out #OlakMustGo

@WeUnify #OlakMustGo

@WeUnify It's important you stop centring yourself.
How you feel doesn't matter. Just GO

@WeUnify How can Megha ever feel safe working any-
    where near you?? Do Better #WeWhiteify
@WeUnify OMFG He can't even bring himself to say
    sorry to Megha. You're trying to DEVASTATE her
@WeUnify #OlakMustGo
@WeUnify He looks rapey, no?
@WeUnify #OlakMustGo
@WeUnify #OlakMustGo

He banged shut the laptop, jerked back from his desk as if he'd glimpsed live gargoyles in the abyss. What was that? What was that in there? He looked to the window. Out there. His whole body was quivering. He felt cold, palpitating all over. From somewhere started the industrial hiss and shunt of a photocopier, soundtracking the mute fact of his mind's entire apparatus coming undone. 'Lise—'

'Just go home. Get home. You shouldn't be here.'

'Yes. I'll just . . .' he said in a small voice and staggered to his feet, to the lift, the whole office glaring. He needed to be outside. To think. But it was hopeless. He couldn't order his thoughts. They careened about his head, refusing to settle and make sense. Not even the sky made sense. Nor the ground. It was all spinning. Or he was spinning. The centre of him untethered. A passer-by asked if he was all right, and the look Nayan levelled at her must have been so stranded, so full of distress, because she quickly put back in her earplugs and paced on. He needed Helen. She didn't answer, was probably at work, so he walked the hard eight miles to Chesterfield, through fields and along towpaths, perhaps hoping if in some unrecorded way this act might count as penance.

At her house, he waited by the porch, going mad reading the rage online, unable to stop himself from reading it. Kids biked past, short-sleeved, school jumpers knotted around waists. He watched them and was only saved from tears by Helen pulling up, letting him in. She listened hard, his words tumbling out in a terrible rush; he showed her the reaction whipped up. 'I feel like I'm being destroyed. I don't know what to do.'

She hadn't interrupted once, and now clasped him tight. Quietly, as though waiting for sufficient seconds to pass, she said, 'Don't mention this to Brandon. He's still fragile. I don't want this to bring back memories.'

It turned out, though, that Brandon already knew – he'd stopped at Claudia's on his way home, where a distraught Lisa-Marie told him everything. He burst into the front room, saw Nayan at the kitchen table. 'What's happening? They're trying to kill you!'

'Calm down,' Helen said, going to him. 'No one's killing anyone.'

'It's happening again.'

'I'm fine,' Nayan said. 'I'll be fine. We'll get through this.'

The boy fumbled for his phone, brandished it. 'Have you read what they're saying? Abuser. Rapist. Sicko. They don't want you to live.'

'Brandon, please!' Helen said. 'Here – sit down. You'll make yourself ill again.'

'I don't want them to do anything to him!'

'They won't,' Nayan said, rising from the table. Brandon surged forward and his hold was so strong Nayan fought to steady himself. 'Come on,' Nayan said, rubbing the kid's back. 'This'll all blow over in a day or two.'

'Come and stay here. You and your dad. They won't get you here.'

'You're not going to lose me,' Nayan said, and felt Helen join their embrace. What strength, what love Nayan felt in those moments as Helen found his hand: more love than he'd ever dared hope he might feel again.

'Just come and stay here,' Brandon said again.

'You're not thinking straight,' Helen said. 'Of course they can't stay here.'

'You're not going to lose me,' Nayan told him again.

Tenderly, Nayan sat the boy down, and when Brandon said he was hungry, Nayan cooked an omelette, glad of the task and the focus it required. As he watched Brandon eat, one bite on top of another, barely chewing at all, Lisa-Marie rang to say the latest polls were in and for the first time he was behind Megha. 'And this is before everything today. And before Richard goes public with his support. We'll take another hit then.'

'I'll bring it back at the debate,' Nayan said. 'I will. They'll come back once I make my arguments. She ain't going to win by lying. I won't let her.'

On this, Lisa-Marie remained silent. 'How are you? I'm so worried.'

'I have to win, Lise. Everything, my ma, my life, Veer – it's all this.'

'There'll be other elections. Maybe now's not the time—'

'No, Lise. No.'

A despairing pause. 'Okay. But don't come into the office until I say. Lie low. We're expecting demos outside. No one would want you to suffer that.'

'I need to get my stuff. My car.'

'Leave it. I'll get it.'

'My wallet. Cards. House keys. Oh God.'

'I'll bring them. Tomorrow. Just stay clear of the office.'

'Why is this happening to me?' he asked in an anguished growl, and stopped just short of putting his fist through the window.

To take the call, he'd retreated to a corner of the living room. Turning around now, pocketing the phone, he met Brandon standing in the kitchen arch. 'What are they doing?' Brandon demanded.

'It was only Lise. Giving me the latest polls. Not as bad as we thought,' he added, mustering a smile.

'You're going back to the office. I heard.'

'Just to get my stuff.'

'But they'll be there.' He shook his head, all vehemence. 'You can't go by yourself. I won't let you.'

'Can't Lisa-Marie get your stuff?' Helen asked.

'She can't drive two cars. I'll go at dawn. As soon as security can let me in.'

'We'll go together,' Brandon said.

'No!' Helen said. 'No way. You are not getting mixed up in all this again.'

'No one needs to come. I'll be fine,' Nayan said.

'I'm coming,' Brandon said, as if that was the final word.

'I'll go,' Helen said, and gave Brandon a stare that was pure warning. 'You don't go near any of this trouble. Do you understand?'

Leaving Helen's, Nayan messaged Buddy and asked him to put the door on the latch – *forgot my keys at work*. He walked a very long way home, yes, all along his old streets, with their thin, rippling shadows, their lengthening days. It was that nostalgia again – he'd felt it so much since everything first kicked off; finding shelter in a past when he was so manifestly the good boy, when he'd look up from his schoolwork and watch his mother at the window, the sun on her face. What was she thinking? Was she disappointed at how her life had panned out? He felt glum that his mother might not be happy, that he wasn't enough. He could still remember the fierce urge he felt to take her hand and lead her away. You okay, Ma? he said, and he must have left his chair, for he has a clear memory of standing beside her at the window, of how cold her hand was in his own. She'd smiled. 'Oh, Ma,' he began now, crossing a green, his heart a mess, unable to finish the thought.

That night, Nayan sat in the silent semi-dark of his front room, where an orange streetlight broke through the curtain and speckled the bath-time photo above the gas fire. The quiet permitted contemplation for the first time that day and he didn't move from the old armchair for hours, forcing his thoughts into straight lines, checking his phone occasionally – *How many more WoC has he done this to? . . .*

He'll make Megha relive the racist trauma over and over again until she gives in . . . The entitlement is maddening . . . This is internalised racism in action, out in the wild #OlakMustGo . . . Just resign muthafucka! . . . Change can only start with his resignation . . . Probably a blessing his son died. Imagine having him for a dad?? . . .

Hands on top of his head, thinking hard, Nayan remembered being on the picket lines with his friends, and how they jeered and shouted at the men who crossed into the mines. Calling them all sorts of names. Scab. Rat. Traitor. Once, Nayan landed a rock between a scab's shoulders and the man – face hunkered into his black woollen council jacket – hadn't even dared to turn around. Those men were never forgiven. Their beers were spat in. Their families ostracised. Their children bullied. To this day, I hear people referred to as the offspring of a scab. *His granddad was the same. Scabby shit.* As if betrayal was an original sin that could never be atoned for. No amount of apology would ever be enough. The sin, the gathering around the heretic, the stoning, the whole sorry religious tapestry. Were we simply back there? So did that now make me the scab? Nayan thought. *#IbetOlak loves white women wearing bindis . . . #IbetOlak doesn't use a lota #dirtybum . . . #IbetOlak only does missionary #vanillasex . . . #IbetOlak asks his mum for a cup of 'chai tea' LOL . . . #IbetOlak thinks he can't be racist . . .*

But we were fighting for people's livelihoods! he assured himself. For social transformation! For root-and-branch economic change. Not about bindis and chai fucking tea.

'I'm not going to let them win,' he said to Helen the

following morning, on the drive into the office. 'I'm going to keep on fighting.'

'They don't deserve you,' Helen said. 'But . . . I don't know.'

'You're worried about Brandon.' He placed his hand across hers on the gearstick. 'Me too.'

'He barely slept last night.'

'Makes two of us.'

He felt his stomach lift as the office loomed, its concrete made harsher overnight. There was no one there, Nayan saw with relief, no one protesting. The glass entrance shone greenly. 'I'll be straight out. Then just drive me to the car park. By A&E.'

'I'll wait here.'

This time, as he entered the building, the receptionist looked the other way, suddenly organising papers. 'Hello,' Nayan said, and she nodded, once, her head still averted. Up on his floor, there were a few early risers – none of them responded to his good morning, none of them wanted to be *seen* responding to his good morning. One woman, a senior in legal, gave a sad smile and seemed eager to say something, how sorry she was, perhaps, for what was happening. But she didn't, and Nayan carried on past. Megha wasn't in yet, thank God; there was just lean Max, looking incredulous to see him. Nayan gave an ironic wave, then arrived at his own desk, which was as he'd left it: the rucksack agape, the laptop on powersave, pen uncapped and coffee only half drunk. He unplugged his devices and began packing them away, tipping open drawers as he hunted for his keys.

'What are you doing?'

Nayan looked up. It was Max, in very short sleeves despite the morning chill. 'Aren't you cold, buddy?'

'It's set to warm up la—What're you doing?'

'Doing? I'm getting my things.'

'You're leaving?' Max asked, sounding suspicious and hopeful. 'Have you stood down?'

'Bet you'd love that, wouldn't you?' He found his keys. Shouldered up his rucksack. 'I'm working from home for a few days. Back soon. Try not to miss me.'

'I'm sure it must be difficult, what you're going through,' Max said, stepping into Nayan's path. 'It's hard for us all to come to terms with what's happened.'

'And what *has* happened? Tell me, Max. We argued, she lied. Isn't that it?'

There was a spontaneous splutter of a laugh, as if Nayan had said something patently absurd. 'Look at the evidence. Even before this, you tried to organise a pile-on with that Diwali speech of yours. And then you refused to help her when she came *begging* to you. You've had it in for Megha ever since she said she was standing against you. And then you not only violated her, you're lying about it. It's unbelievable.'

'Wow. Jeez. Did lil ol' me do all that? All by myself? I deserve a fucking statue.' He made to get past; Max blocked him again.

'Your arrogance is breathtaking. Can't you even bring yourself to acknowledge the pain you've caused? Come on, Nayan. You're better than' – he waved his hand up and down, as though it were Nayan's clothes that appalled him – 'whatever this persona is.'

'What are you getting out of this, Max? And why aren't you letting me go?'

'I'm an ally. I'm sure you find that word hilarious. I'm sure you find ideas like patriarchy and white supremacy all just so much liberal distraction, but they mean something very real. Even if *you* can't believe it. Read the books. Look at the facts.'

'What I can't believe is that I'm being lectured on about racism by a skinny, blond, white dude who carries oat milk with him everywhere.'

'But if that's what I'm doing that should be fine by your lights. Because you don't think race matters, right?'

'No problem with you being white. It's the oat milk.'

'I'm really happy to send some books your way,' Max continued, undeterred. 'Real testimonies and analyses about how power differentials work in society. Can I do that?'

'This conversation is wild,' Nayan said, and this time he did get past, but only after tussling Max aside. 'What the fuck, man!' Nayan exclaimed. 'What's your problem?' Max, though, was tapping into his phone and Nayan realised he had to get out of the office. He hurtled down the stairs and past reception, coming to an abrupt stop at the exit. Protestors – five, six, seven of them. Student-types. Placards: *Olak Must Go*. They were chanting it, too, in unison, each of the four syllables carrying weight, the final one shouted loudest of all. O-Lak Must *GO!* O-Lak Must *GO!* He couldn't see Helen, and when he stepped outside the demonstrators closed around him. O-Lak Must *GO!* O-Lak Must *GO!* They wouldn't let him through. He was aware of phones, of things being recorded. Head down, he tried to force an exit. The heel of a palm crashed into his face. Blood down his nose. 'Try hitting a man next time,' someone said. Another spat in Nayan's eye. 'Let me through!' Nayan said, and seeing a gap develop, he ran for it and to Helen across the road.

Too shaken to drive, Nayan left his car to be collected another day, and in silence Helen drove him back to hers. 'I'll cancel my calls,' she said, unlocking the front door, but he persuaded her to go, said he'd be okay, and, in all honesty, she looked relieved to be going.

'She's stressing about me,' Brandon said.

'I'm scared to look at my phone. To go into work. My heart was racing the whole time I was there. And that's my *work*. My *life*. My *home*. The place I know better than my own house. And I was scared of it. Like it was the last place in the world I should be.'

'You're still shaking. Shall I get you a blanket?'

After a quiet minute, Nayan said, as if remembering, 'Shouldn't you be at work?'

'I can stay.'

'Get,' Nayan said, pointing to the door. 'That's not on.'

'They'll manage.'

'I said get.'

He heard Brandon reverse out his Peugeot and nose down the hill, P plates flapping tightly. What's going to become of me? Nayan wondered.

Vid showing Olak trying to sneak away unseen . . . This abuser must have nowhere to hide #OlakMustGo . . . Clearly he

thinks he can get away with this . . . He has a white gf surprise
surprise . . . Dawn raid! Well done to all who caught the creep
out! . . . Unify are you seeing how one of your employees vio-
lently attacks protestors?? . . .

Phone in hand, Nayan fell to his knees in the middle
of the room. 'The bastards!' he screamed. At intervals
throughout the morning he screamed again, often through
tears, and afterwards he felt purged, hollowed, as if a
path had been cleared and at the end of it stood Megha.
She was the one he needed to speak to, who they might
listen to. Helen, home between care visits, was sceptical.

'The genie's out the bottle. I doubt she could do anything. Hasn't she actually done enough? She threw you to
the lions.'

'I have to try,' Nayan said. He slid his arm around her
waist, kissed her behind the ear, where the sheen of her
blonde hair was at its greyest. Her arms, he noticed, were
listless. 'Everything okay?'

'Not really,' she said, pressing away from him.

'Is it Brandon? You still worried about him?'

'I'm always worried about him.' Then: 'He's become
very attached to you. For obvious reasons.'

'And me to him. For equally obvious reasons.'

She met his eye. She always met your eye when she
had no intention of yielding. 'While this is all going on, it
would be better if he didn't see so much of you.'

'You mean if you didn't see so much of me.'

'Same thing. He's my priority, Nayan. Surely you
understand?'

'So things get tough for me and you want to bail?'

'I'm not bailing. I care for you.'

They were still working through this – did she not know how much he needed her? How will Brandon feel? – when Buddy, who'd pretty much taken over Pyara's care, called to say that someone had sprayed his front door.

'I didn't see who,' Buddy vented, ten minutes later, as Nayan got out the car. Helen remained in the driver's seat, staring straight ahead. 'I only saw it when I put the bin out,' Buddy continued. 'Wankers, man. Have you any paint?'

Nayan stared at the word – ABUSER – daubed in a drippy white diagonal, the R squashed up into the corner, running out of room. Is that what he was? Behind Nayan, Helen drove off, wheels spitting gravel.

'What's her problem?' Buddy said.

Nayan touched the front door, the word. The noon light, glazing the letters, splashed yellow over the window, where his father stood vaguely in splendour. He'd always thought it was him that the accusation applied to. 'I do have some paint,' Nayan confirmed, very calmly, and went to fetch it.

That evening, he was standing guard at the window when Deepti phoned. He'd nearly missed her call; he was letting everything go to voicemail – there'd been too many threats, and some local reporters had got hold of his number – but he spied her name just in time and moved to the kitchen, away from his father.

'Hey,' he said.

'Nayan,' she said, and simply hearing her voice was a salve, the sound of an old friend come to prop him up.

One of her periodic googling sessions had alerted her to what was happening; she'd only gone online in the first place to see how his campaign was getting on. 'Did you really hit her? I can't believe it.'

He spent a full, mystifying hour unravelling it all to her – how had so much happened? In not even a year? The conference where he announced his candidature, when Megha asked to run as his deputy, her background and their ideological differences, the speech at the temple, his 'white working class' comments, his anger and refusal to criticise her detractors, and now this whole shitshow. 'Someone sprayed my front door today.'

'Have you told the police?'

'I thought I might go see her. Megha. See if she'll do something, you know? Now the boot's on the other foot. But maybe that's not a great idea.'

'I'm sure that boot'll find a way onto your backside.'

'It already has,' Nayan said, smiling. 'My backside's bearing a pretty strong imprint of her boot right now.'

'Well, she's doing what I never managed.'

He leaned against the lip of the worktop. How good it felt to speak to her, to feel known, undiminished. Uneasily, it occurred to him that these might be the same needs driving Megha.

'How's your woman friend? I saw that video. Calm as horses, ain't she?'

'Helen. She's tough. Tough as they get. Her boy's the softie.'

'She's got a boy? I think you said.'

'Brandon. He's been in pieces about it.'

Deepti didn't need to speak for Nayan to feel the sadness on the line. During the silence, which wasn't in any way uncomfortable, Nayan noticed that Buddy had mopped the floor. Arcs swept across the olive lino. As a teen, Nayan would sit on the chest freezer of their shop, feet dangling, the blue of his trainers reflected in his mother's mopping. She'd mop, nudge the bucket along with her foot: mop, nudge; mop, nudge.

Nayan pushed off the kitchen counter. 'I've got to see this through, Dips. I can't stand down.'

'Can't? Or won't?'

He thought of Veer, waving a flag, flowers. It made no sense. Win or not, he would still be gone; except that the boy had been with him every step of the way. Nayan couldn't abandon him now. He could see him at the end. So, yes, win or not, he would still be gone. But less gone. That was how little sense it made; and how much.

'I can't, Dips.'

'Then go and speak to her. To Megha. She must be hurting, too. No one sets out to destroy someone else unless they're suffering as well. Have you even tried understanding her?'

'Not especially,' he said, though he wasn't really listening. Veer was running in from the hallway, onto the mopped floor. *Careful!* Nayan wanted to say. 'I guess she's just doing whatever she can. To win.'

'Not even you, Nayan Olak, are stupid enough to believe that's all there is to it.'

Veer rushed under the table. *I'm not under the table! Don't look under the table. Promise you won't. Promise!*

248

'So will you go and see her?'

'I promise.'

'Good. You must. Olak must go,' Deepti said. 'Rhodes must fall,' she added, though neither could quite summon the laugh Deepti intended.

It didn't take Lisa-Marie long to WhatsApp him Megha's address, which she'd wheedled from a new starter in HR: *Please don't do anything rash. Try and listen to her.* Too stubborn to ask Helen, Nayan got a taxi to his Honda Civic, stranded in the city car park for three days now, and then drove north, through the centre and into the sketchier parts of town. Graffitied shopfronts. Boarded-up terraces. A languishing air. The sun had been in and out all afternoon, pleasantly enough, but now, in this worn-grey place, the earlier weather seemed nothing more than a giant con. Heeding the Satnav, Nayan was led to an estate of bleak semis fronted by collapsing fences, by weedy, overgrown verges. Discarded crisp packets spangled silver in the grass. He braked at the avenue's end, outside the final pair of houses. Megha's place, on the left, was a rarity: the handkerchief garden mowed, the fence repaired, the glass in the door intact. Mattresses stacked her neighbour's yard, a sordid pile of them, broken chairs and toys, too, all set to be fly-tipped, and it was this collection Nayan was eyeballing as he lifted the latch and walked down Megha's path.

'You got a problem?' the neighbour said, emerging from behind the mattresses, startling Nayan.

He was around thirty, leather-jacketed, instances of psoriasis on his hands. Nayan wished he'd not worn his work shirt and trousers, his black shoes like a tax inspector. 'I'm just visiting a . . . colleague.' He couldn't bring himself to say friend, but colleague was all kinds of wrong.

'Colleague, you say? Well, ain't that pretty. Come on, then, what's she do?'

'Keeps to herself, does she?'

'I asked what she did.'

'We work for Unify. The union. To help workers.'

'Right,' he said. 'Not the council, then? Cos if you say owt, about any of this' – meaning the fly-tipping – 'I've got your plate. Won't be hard to find you. Bruck that curry face a yours.'

'I'm not the council. And threaten me again and I'll lamp you into next week. Fucking get me?'

The man sneered, and though he didn't quite back off, he seemed content to leave it there. Nayan pressed the doorbell, waited. He could still feel the neighbour staring. Imagine living next to this shit. Every day.

'Why don't you fuck off?' Nayan said.

'Got a council house before any a my mates, she did,' the neighbour said. 'Can't get a job cos a you lot. We'll rise up sooner or later, you know. Give you all a fucking lesson.'

Ignoring him – he'd heard it all before – Nayan gave the bell another go, then peered through the window and saw Megha folded into an armchair with her back to him. She was reading a book open on her lap, thumb and finger primed to turn the page. The way she bent over the text, eyes bearing down, forehead tight – she read with her whole body; every sinew was directed towards the book. Tentatively, Nayan knocked on the glass, then waved,

250

and the shimmer of light must have alerted her, for she spun round. After a moment of shock, she set the book to one side, her surprise with it, unplugged her earbuds and rose to let him in.

'I see you've met my neighbour,' she said, shutting the door.

'He seems nice.'

'At least his music's stopped.'

Ah, Nayan thought – the earplugs.

They were in a short hallway with the tiny front room to their left and an even tinier-looking kitchen at its end. Midway, low-ceilinged stairs wound steeply up to the first floor. The steps were so thin Nayan could only imagine Megha climbing them on the balls of her feet. There was a picture on the wall, beside Nayan's head, which disoriented him briefly, because it was a print of a woman reading as privately, as intently, as Megha had been; albeit the woman in the picture seemed to be reading a letter, not a book, and she was half-sitting on a cushioned ledge in some landing from a hundred years ago. It was a very still picture, externally, as if all the thinking, thrusting life, the life worth anything, exulted in the privacy of the young woman's mind.

She showed Nayan through to the front room, where alcoves beside the fireplace housed Megha's many books. On the back of her armchair draped a thick blanket, and there were two smaller, upholstered chairs, mismatched, at an angle to the larger one. Her laptop was open on the floor. There was no TV.

'No point heating up all the rooms,' she said.

251

He realised she meant the fan-heater, which he hadn't noticed. The room seemed not to accept that it was spring. The window was deeply recessed, shying away from the light; a chill persisted. 'No, no. I'm the same,' he said. 'Constant battle with my dad – he wants it on all the time. It's something we should have a proper policy on,' he added, not quite sure what he was saying. Did she really live here? Like this?

'I saw what happened at the office.' She gestured to his nose. 'No lasting damage?'

'None,' he said, refusing to be embarrassed.

'I'm sorry you're having such a hard time.'

'I find that hard to believe. Wasn't it you who started this all?'

She retreated to her armchair, pensively, bringing one socked foot under her thigh. Her woollen shirt, green-on-black, was tucked into black Levi's, her hair scrunched back. Huge wire hoops hung from her ears. She indicated one of the seats opposite, which he took, without comfort – the chair was low, his knees near his face, almost blocking her from view. He hunched forward instead, on the rim of the seat, and let his knees fall either side. Suddenly, he felt made to look like a supplicant come before his god.

'I suppose I mean I'm sorry you've brought this on yourself.'

'You've *lied*. To ruin me. You've lied, Megha.' Then, recalling Lisa-Marie's injunction to listen: 'Maybe you remember things differently. It was a messy time. We were both arguing, angry. Maybe you believe I did grab you. Do you think that's possible?'

'This is called gaslighting. You know exactly what you did to me.'

'You wouldn't've let me through the front door if you thought I'd hit you. Doesn't that give you pause?'

'You're right,' she said, nodding. 'You didn't hit me. You were simply violent and abusive, physically. And that's all I've said. I've been very careful about that.'

This, and her poise, was too much. 'I was not violent! You went public for one reason only. To beat me. To win this election.'

'Damn right, I did. You're not fit for office. People should know who they're voting for. I went public because you won't stand down. You've had every opportunity to come clean, but you can't let go. Then you lied, you called me a liar. You refused to help me. You've had so many escape routes,' she said, throwing her hands into the air, inviting Nayan to see all his missed chances raining down. 'So many, Nayan. Instead, you tried to set the mob onto me with your speech. What choice did I have? I'm not massively proud of what I've done but – again – what choice did I have?'

'Even if all that's true – it's not, but say it is – it's going mental out there. They want blood. I've been attacked. I've had my property attacked. My girlfriend's son won't leave the house' – a perfectly human exaggeration – 'my life's being destroyed in front of my eyes.'

'Then stand down. Resign. That's all people want. I'll fully support you back into the fold. But a violent misogynist should not be standing for—'

'I'm not a—' He regrouped: 'Look, we should be

talking about the issues, right? Not . . . not this. Just make this go away. Tell your supporters to back off. Let's have the debates that matter.'

She looked off to the side, to the wall, the cords of her neck visible. She blinked away a tear. 'I pleaded with you to do the same.'

'You did. You did. I know that. And I'm very, very sorry for not helping you. I was angry. And wrong. I'm asking you – begging you – to try and put that aside. To help me in the way I should have helped you.'

In a balletic movement, she unfolded her legs from under her and fished beneath the armchair. A ring-binder was brought out, flipped open, pushed across. 'After your speech at the temple, I started getting threats. By email, stuck to my car, even posted here, through my letterbox. And then more abuse after my newsletters. I've only kept the most colourful ones.'

Nayan paged through the file, each threat slid into its own plastic pocket: . . . *stop trying to split the union fucking Jew-loving bitch . . . fucking fake ass socialist . . . Leave Nayan alone you cock-sucking cunt . . . Smash your posh head in half if I see you in our office again . . . We all know you live alone . . .*

'I've never said a word. I didn't dare. No one would believe me. No one would believe Megha. They'd say I made them up. Like you're saying I made the photo up. Because I'm just a troublemaker, aren't I? The rich, posh girl playing at politics. Only interested in her own ascent. I don't have any humanity. Humanity's for people like Nayan, the class crusader. Good old Nayan.'

He closed the folder. 'I'm sorry. That's horrific. Go to the police. I'll go with you—'

'I couldn't believe it. When I told everyone, that first time, what you said, I couldn't believe it was me they turned on. They called me a liar to my face. Someone sang "True Blue" at me as I stood in the café queue. While everyone laughed.' Megha laughed now, too, but miserably. 'No one's supported me. Ever. Not at home. Not here. But *you*' – swiping at her wet cheeks – 'how they rallied round. How they defended you.'

'They know me. One newsletter from you wasn't going to change anything.'

'They couldn't even entertain the idea that you might be at fault. Oh no. Not you. Not their Nayan. Not one of their own. They just came straight for the brown woman outsider instead.'

'Is that what this is? We had a fiery argument, I should have helped you – my mistake – but you now whip up a massive storm that's destroying me, and all because of your self-pity? Because no one lets you feel like you belong? Because no one let you into their gang? Is that really what this is? Cos it sounds pretty pathetic from where I'm sitting.'

'I gave up everything!' Megha seethed, with a grotesque stretch of her mouth. 'I deserve to feel good! I deserve to be respected! Look where I'm living! Look! I turned my back on everything! I don't deserve to still feel guilty!' She shook her head, almost snorted. 'None of it counted. None of it mattered. But at least now everyone can see some of what I put up with. And who you are. I deserve this win, Nayan. No one's given up more for it than me.'

'This is wrong, Megha. What's happening to me is wrong. You can make it stop. Please make it stop before things get worse. I feel like I'm dying.'

'If it's so intolerable just stand down. I keep telling you. It's all in your power.'

'This is everything to me.' He could hear the despair in his own voice. 'I can't stand down.'

'Of course you can stand down. It's the right thing to do.'

He thought of Veer. Again and again, he thought of Veer. 'Megha. Please understand. Megha, please. My life.'

Geoff Carswell issued a statement in his capacity as leader of the Executive Committee, calling for calm, promising 'lessons would be learned' but as no official complaint had been lodged the democratic process should not be stymied, the leaders' debate would go ahead. The loud insinuation was that, for all the vitriol, Megha was blustering and had failed to provide any real evidence to support her allegation. There was uproar: protests amplified outside the office; online, there were calls for members to cancel their fees, for Unify to be investigated, for staff to not go into the office until Nayan was sacked. Every day he received mail threatening him, mocking him. He had messages of strength, too, but not only did these shows of solidarity misread his stance, they came from figures so far to the right of him that their support only made him feel lonelier, more isolated, as if he really was toxic. He had no choice, he said to Lisa-Marie, but to put his faith in the following day's debate.

'It'll get things back onto what our actual policy differences are. Back onto what matters.'

'You keep saying that,' Lisa-Marie said. 'But what if what matters to you isn't what matters to them?'

'My speech'll light the place up with your name,' Claudia said from the breakfast bar, where she was spearing strawberries onto her fork. Nayan had read her speech, been touched by it, too, though the monochrome portrait, if he was frank, depressed him; the way it spoke of 'weekend trips to the Abbeydale Industrial Hamlet, to the National Coal Mining Museum, Nayan all the time teaching me and my brother about class struggle and the means of production, the sick legacy of Thatcher and Blair's moral bankruptcy'. ('I only wonder if it's a tad on the nose,' Nayan had offered in the spirit of cautious feedback.)

'You're the ace up my sleeve,' Nayan now said.

'I'll wipe the smile off her face.' Claudia slid off the stool, to the sink.

'Dishwasher, please,' Lisa-Marie said, and with an affected slump of her shoulders, Claudia plodded round with her plate.

'How's Brandon?' Nayan asked, trying to keep his tone breezy.

'Working. And when he's not he's practising dishes. Luckily for him I've got my dissertation to keep me occupied.'

'He was round here Tuesday just gone,' Lisa-Marie said. 'Making chicken in a bag.'

'Chicken sous vide,' Claudia corrected her, on her way out the room and up the stairs. They heard her door shut and music start.

'Has he not been in touch?' Lisa-Marie asked, her voice changing, as though at last they could speak properly, without restriction.

'He's busy, ain't he. You heard.'

'And you've not been round?'

'Not while all this is going on.' He shrugged, with effort. 'It's probably good for him to keep away. Not see too much of what's happening up close.'

Lisa-Marie hmm-ed, nodded. They were at opposite ends of the armless sofa, in her knocked-through kitchen-living area. Before the wall was demolished, this room had housed Peter's workbench and lathe. It used to drive her mad that he stored it all indoors; but she kept the room for a decade after he died.

'And how is Helen?' she asked.

'Okay, I think. Petrified Brandon'll get caught up in all this – after last time. So, yeah – giving him space means we're having some space. Understandable. I'd be the same.'

She pressed his hand. 'Give it time. For now, just concentrate on tomorrow.'

At home, Nayan made dinner, which he and Pyara ate in the front room. He tried to engage his father ('Did you like the walk with Buddy?' 'Shall we put a movie on?')

but Pyara was having an off day, not taking anything in. There'd been more of these off days recently, when he'd sit there looking utterly forlorn, frightened by his surroundings. He'd stare at the ceiling, his neck stretching as if his mind was in a river cave, dark water rising. He should get him to the doctor, Nayan thought tiredly, tramping upstairs for Pyara's pills. Maybe see about increasing his dosage. He returned via the kitchen to find his father standing at the window, curtain thrown open.

'Your pills, Dad,' Nayan said. 'Then let's get you sorted.' Pyara didn't move. 'Come on. I've got work to do. Important day tomorrow – so much prep still.'

'Who is it?' Pyara said, in his shaky voice.

Putting the pills and water down, Nayan joined him at the window, where the night was so close and TV lights glowed the blinds of the houses opposite. He couldn't see anyone. 'Was somebody there, Dad? Did you see something?' His baseball bat was in his room, by his bed. It always was now. Should he get it? Had one of those trolls decided to come for him? His hand went to his pocket, his phone. He considered calling the police. 'Tell me, Dad. What did you see?'

'Who was she?' Pyara asked. His eyes darted about, wide with fear.

'You saw a woman? Now? You saw a woman outside our house just now?'

Pyara shook his head, several times: *You're not listening*. 'Not now. Not today. But I knew her. When she was younger.'

'Are you thinking of Mum?' Nayan asked, and relief

259

washed through him. It was just his dad, lost in the memory swirl. 'Do you miss her?' He hoped he did, that somewhere in his mind, in those half-glimpsed rabbit-holes of thought, he missed his loyal, clever wife enough to feel ashamed. 'What do you remember? Can you tell me?'

But it was clear from the disappointed fall of Pyara's face, the slow release of his shoulders, that the past had given him the slip, that whichever thread his father had been clutching at had escaped, the memory unspooled into the night.

'Have your meds. Then bed,' and Nayan guided him away from the window.

He sat at the kitchen table going over his notes, beefing up his points until gone two a.m., a cramming teenager all over again – still, Nayan woke very early the next morning, before sun-up. He stood in the gloom of the landing, a hand on the painted white rail, where yesterday's towel hung. In his mind, the day wouldn't start proper, wouldn't have to be accepted, until he descended the stairs, and he wanted to put that moment off for just a while longer, to abide in the withdrawal of his dreams. Because he knew, he surely did, that the game was up, that there were so few now at his side. Is that what life is? he wondered, folding the towel into a neat square and setting it down; a slow and inexorable thinning until the intensity of isolation is all that's left, when the birds have sung the dawn away and you're standing alone at the top of the stairs with your unattended heart. As the hour turned, pale light, the colour of an eggshell's interior, encroached on the hall below, and Nayan, gripping the banister hard, knew it was time.

A little before lunch, Buddy arrived and Nayan brought in sandwiches on a tiered tray.

'Special day sarnies?' Buddy said, taking two white-bread triangles and passing one to Pyara. 'You nervous?'

'A bit,' Nayan replied.

'Just give them what for.'

'I'll do my best.'

'Clau's buzzing. Thinks it's her time to shine. She's even got her uni crowd invited.' He took another sandwich from the tray. 'Thinks she's Glenda . . . I don't know. Mum said it. You not hungry?'

'Jackson. No, can't face it.'

'Nerves, innit.' Then: 'I'll make myself a tea, shall I? Want one, P?'

The sooner Nayan made a move, the sooner he got his body moving, the better he might conquer this foul dread. So he showered, quickly, and shucked off from the coat hanger the black suit he'd ironed and hooked onto his bedroom door late the previous night. Down in the hall, he stamped into his shoes, seized his rucksack. Blood heaving around his heart, his stomach.

'Wish me luck,' he said, feeling so much like he had on his first day at school.

From the sofa, Buddy raised his fist in salute. 'Knock 'em dead, star.' Then, pointing, for Pyara was at the window again: 'Who's the big fella waiting for? Been standing there for time.'

'He's missing Mum. Thinks she'll walk down the street any minute.'

Buddy nodded, all thoughtful, perhaps because he'd been there. 'Speech all set?'

'I'm going full class warrior on their ass.' But something about this was misjudged and Buddy's face changed, the bright smile inverting. 'Bud? What's up?'

'Nothing.' He was stroking his palms together, slowly, wiping the moment away. 'Go. Don't wanna be late.' His tone was insincere.

'You'll find a job.'

'Yeah. No thanks to you.'

'What?'

'Allow it, man.' But it was Buddy who couldn't let it go. 'How long you known me? But it's Brandon you help get a job?'

Nayan, taking a further step into the room, balked. He would never intentionally . . . 'He's been through a lot, Bud. I know you have, too,' he was quick to add. 'I'm with you as well.'

'I get it,' Buddy said, after a beat. He spoke without bitterness, and with the kind of calm resolve that his mother knew was the real difference between her children. 'I get what you and Clau say. I get it. I *agree*. But' – he thought again – 'you say you're with me. But do you *see* me? Is that going to change? That's not about money or hate, is it? Will people start actually *seeing* me? Start paying attention? No matter my class, no matter my colour?' His hand was at his chest. 'I just want people to *see* me.'

Crouching, Nayan held Buddy's face. 'I definitely see you, Bud.'

'Right. I guess that's that, then.'

'We'll talk about this more later, yeah?'

'You better go.'

'Later, yeah?'

'*Yes*. Now *go*.'

Buddy heard the front door shut. Rousing himself to his feet, if only to temporarily walk away from his sadness, he sidled up to Pyara and watched Nayan get into his car, fling his rucksack onto the passenger seat, turn the engine. 'Big day for old Ny,' Buddy said. 'Let's hope they treat him nicely.'

Seeing the car disappear drove its own clearing through Pyara's mind, his past, and now he was daylight-bound, sprinting cleanly into the sparkling present. 'The woman. The one who was driving.' He tapped the window with his fingernail, commanding Buddy to see what Pyara so manifestly could. 'The woman driving.'

'Which woman you dreaming about now, P? Did your old lady drive a car?'

'You were here. Door paint. And she drove away. Like that.'

Thinking, thinking, then Buddy clicked his fingers. 'Helen? Nayan's girl. That was – last week?'

'Yes, yes. She was a girl. A young girl. I remember her.'

'Now you're just confusing me. How about we go for a walk?' He peered up into the grey-blue sky. 'Seems good for it.'

'Helen,' Pyara said. 'Helen. Helen.'

'You never met her?' Buddy asked. 'Has Ny been keeping her from you?'

'Show me her picture,' Pyara demanded, and he was already pawing at Buddy's pocket, at his nothing hips.

'Easy, man,' Buddy said. 'I don't have no picture of her. Why would I have a picture of your son's girl-friend?' But then he remembered – 'Wait up . . .' – and he streamed through his video-roll, hunting for the pro-test outside Unify's office. 'He got it taken off YouTube but I got a copy . . . What you so interested in her for again? You got designs, P? Does she remind you of some-one when you were younger? I bet that's it, am I right?' He found the clip, squared his phone across the flat of his palm, pressed play. The recording wobbled everywhere, sky, floor, someone's chin; now Nayan, bloody-nosed, hastening into the car, and finally a direct shot of Helen, focused, speeding away before Nayan closed the door.

'Again,' Pyara said, and this time Buddy paused on Helen's face, handed the phone over.

'Knock yourself out. I need a slash. And then we're walking, aight? Some exercise!'

When Buddy returned, still adjusting his cargo pants by minute degrees, Pyara seemed not to have moved: he was on his feet, angled away from the window, head bent over the frozen image on Buddy's screen.

'Done? Can a brother have his phone?' And Pyara passed it back, meek as he watched the clip vanish into a rear pocket. 'Shoes on. Let's go.'

'Helen,' Pyara whispered, allowing himself to be led into the hall, where Buddy helped him with his loafers.

'I don't know her well myself,' Buddy said, 'but she seems legit. Always happy to offer a lift. Her son and Claudia – my sister? – they're a thing. You know Brandon, right?'

'Helen. She was young.'

Buddy laughed. 'Everyone's young to you. Now – you need some air,' and Buddy held open his coat, zipped it for him, then took a firm, reassuring grip of Pyara's shaking hand.

Nayan had time, there was no rush, for all the clamour in his mind, so he drove on past the debate venue and to the gravelled car ports of Millhouses Park. He sat in his Civic, feeling ashamed at the thought of Buddy, then reading the latest on what a monster Nayan Olak was, how today's conference would be a site of protest against abusers like him. He set his phone to silent and walked to the lake, where four T-shirted juniors raced their motorised boats. It must be half-term, Nayan thought, continuing past the basketball nets and to the playground. The day was cool and blue, if not quite cold, the coming warmth detectable in the glistering slide, the pale shadow of the seesaw. A pregnant mother pushed her daughter on the swing. An elderly man panted alongside his scootering grandson.

Unable to resist – he needed to know what people were saying – he took out his phone. A message from Helen: *Good luck*. He stroked the screen with his thumb, as if it were that lovely soft part of her cheek. Why leave me when I need you most? *I miss you*, he wrote back. *I miss you too*, she responded. He stared at the screen. *Helen is typing . . .* Would she suggest he come round? *Helen is typing . . .* That she was sorry? He waited; but no message materialised, and Helen was no longer typing, or even online. Still, it was something, and Nayan felt buoyed. Up ahead, the man was encouraging his grandson to the top of the slide. The boy wibbled, scared, and seemed set to give up. Silently willed on by Nayan, he found his mettle and came smoothly down, into his grandfather's waiting arms. 'Great job!' Nayan called – but when the pregnant woman looked over he moved on, around the playground and back past the lake and the courts. He was hurrying. A man like him, he realised, had no business being alone in a park like this.

By the time he arrived at the Doubletree Hilton, the air had thickened to a slow spring mizzle, and the wind, too, turned pitchy. None of that deterred the protestors, milled outside the hotel with placards and Thermos flasks. Geoff had already messaged Nayan to park round the back, use the rear doors – *We don't want a spectacle, do we?* – and Nayan was driving that way when he saw Megha. She was with Richard. He held an umbrella high, shielding them both down the hotel's box-hedged path. Megha, in belted black coat, collar up, black heels, too, stopped to chat with the protestors, laughing with them, before ducking into the building, traitorous butler Richard in tow. Jabbingly, Nayan accelerated, roaring the engine and feeling like some slug as he hid his car behind the huge, overflowing kitchen bins.

He wasn't familiar with this flank of the hotel and took a while finding his way to reception, and from there to the main conference hall, where chairs were stationed in rows that allowed for a wide central aisle, and up on the stage, as last time, the table and microphones. A lectern stood off to the side, all but in the wings, and at the rear of the stage hung a white screen. He spotted Geoff, talking at Megha, who listened with a deliberate attitude of patience; Richard, too, working the room, drumming up support, not that many were in yet. The doors were still to open.

Nayan's phone buzzed once. *Helen.* He swiped in. A simple *x*.

'I'm glad you're smiling.' It was Lisa-Marie. 'Thought you'd forgotten how.'

'Me too.'

'Look at her. I've never seen her so engrossed.' Megha? he thought, in a muddle. But no: Claudia, on the end of the second row, speech in hand, muttering to herself. Now and then she troubled to revise a word, decide against a conjunction. 'She's got your back.'

'One hundred per cent.' Then: 'Seen the latest polls?'

'There's only one poll that matters.'

'That bad, huh?'

She started straightening his tie, his collar, more to settle her own nerves, he felt, and he decided to wait until the session was over before mentioning Buddy. 'Be yourself,' Lisa-Marie said. 'Thirty years of service has to count for something.'

He held her hand where it was still fussing with his

tie. 'Don't fret, Lise. Whatever happens, I'll be fine. I really will.'

'But you deserve to win,' she said, and her face was a breath away from crumpling.

'It'll be done soon,' he said, as a large group came clattering into the hall. They had the swagger of youth, all black eyeliner, trailing immortality. Claudia yelped, straight up prancing to them.

'Her pals?' Nayan asked.

'From uni,' Lisa-Marie supplied.

Peeling her friends towards Nayan, Claudia announced, 'My politics class. They're under strict orders to cheer you on. And maybe heckle your opponent?' she added, looking at the group for affirmation and in threat.

Most of them were eyeing the refreshments at the back, except for one young man, who said, 'It'll be interesting to see what you have to say.' His head rose elegantly from the wide sloppy neck of his blue sweater.

Claudia frowned. 'You mean hear. Not see. And I don't remember inviting you, Sean.'

'And yet here I am. Working to live my life like any other man.'

She turned to Nayan, shaking her head free of this Sean boy. 'All set?'

'As I'll ever be.'

'Don't *worry*. It'll be awesome. Oh, FYI, I sent word round to Mum's contacts in Bradford, Leicester, Leeds. So fingers crossed we get a good showing of non-white reps. Give it a rest,' she continued, speaking over Nayan, 'have you seen your numbers? We need all the help we can get.

No harm in having some working-class brown faces in the audience, cheering you on. In fact, play on that,' she instructed, as if she were giving a team-talk. 'Get them on side. I will be. You know I've got this being live-streamed, right?'

Nayan breathed out – how long had he been holding it in? – as Claudia led her friends away, towards Geoff, who watched them advance with some alarm. 'What was that?' Nayan said, and Lisa-Marie shrugged, replied, 'The future, by all accounts.'

On the hour, the doors opened, voices multiplied, feet filled the room. Reps from all over the country – from Glasgow to Truro – funnelled inside, shoulder to shoulder, then roamed freely through the hall like particles given air. Geoff motioned Nayan to the stage, and on the steps up he passed Megha. He'd seen this coming, had prepared to deliver a single, curt nod, but she stayed him with a hand: 'It's good to see you.'

'I had to skulk in through the back,' Nayan said, the humiliation of it rising within him once more. 'While you were laughing with everyone out front.'

'I wasn't laughing. I was offering them my umbrella. Nothing more. Believe me, no one's laughing. None of this is funny.'

'But some of us are definitely finding it less funny than others, yeah?'

Geoff settled in at the centre of the table, shuffled himself comfortable. On either side of him sat Claudia and Richard, and then Nayan and Megha bookended the panel. Not for the first time today, Nayan tried to exchange a friendly look with Richard, but he wasn't interested, had kept avoiding him.

'Big crowd,' Claudia said, and took a slow, contented breath, as if she'd already ascended to the mountaintop, where the air was so much sweeter.

Was Nayan imagining it, or was it really that as soon as members took their seats, they sought him out? Absorbed, as though he were an exhibit of monstrous intrigue? The woman with the sapphire brooch, the pony-tail in a shiny suit, the two machinists hugging the aisle, all averted their faces when Nayan met their gaze. What's more, Nayan realised, with a kind of horror, he recog-nised their looks: they were the same curious, embarrassed glances he'd got from friends twenty years ago, when he'd stepped out of the crematorium and waited for the smoke. His thoughts swarmed; they were escaping his mind and dripping into his hands. He held onto the table's edge, squeezing hard with thumb and forefinger, and when he next felt able to raise his head, Geoff was already speaking: 'And I can't tell you how wonderful it is to be back here in Sheffield, not yet a year from when we all last assembled, when nominations began, and hosted once more by this august venue that continues to inspire us with its support,' he added, as though they were sitting in the Parthenon and not a two-star over-nighter off the Dronfield bypass.

He went on, cataloguing the union's achievements thus far and its priorities for the balance of the year. Then, with a change of tone, propounding a more sombre note, he folded his arms on the table.

'Of course, it would be remiss of me not to acknowledge that this has also been a time in which a lot of soul-searching has been taking place in our organisation. There's been much and much-needed discussion about who we are and who we want to be. As I've made clear in various communications, it's a conversation I fully support. We do need to be more open, more welcoming, more aware of our institutional and personal biases, more aware, too, of our less conscious biases. As an amateur, though I like to think knowledgeable, horticulturalist, I can tell you that diverse, thriving gardens are the ones which flourish best, are the ones with the combined strength to withstand inclement weather and grow year on year. And this is because each flower, each plant, each hedgerow, no matter its *roots*, no matter which part of the earth it originally sprouted from, supports every other flower, every other plant, and every other hedgerow. The British peonies share water with the' – he glanced down to his notes – 'the African impala lilies, and the impala lilies are shaded by the Indian kikar, and the kikar in turn is protected by the Japanese bamboo. What I'm trying to say is that a diverse, thriving garden is what our alliance needs to become, a place where everyone shares water with everyone else and everyone speaks up for everyone else. Because, as many have said, silence really is violence. We must all speak up against injustice. That is at the heart of our union. Though, of course, while always remaining mindful that ... that' – patting his arm for reassurance, Geoff went to his notes again, cleared the itch from his throat – 'that by speaking out we're – you're? – we're ... that we're not centring our own voices and thereby ... centring out ... other voices ... from the centre. Anyway,' he continued, with palpable relief, 'as chair of the National Executive Committee, I'm incredibly happy to be chairing this afternoon's discussion between our two candidates standing for the election of General Secretary of Unify, Megha Sharma on my – oh dear! – far right, and, of course, Nayan Olak. For those that don't know, Nayan has been a member of Unify for over twenty years, joining when he started on the factory floor at Bristow's Air Con Systems, but has been a campaigner and canvasser for us since he was but a boy, when he pounded the streets alongside his late mother, Muneet Olak, one of our very first non-white members, and who I know is much missed and much remembered.' Geoff allowed himself a respectful pause. 'Nayan continued to work at Bristow's as he rose to senior union rep, helping to treble our membership in the North-East Derbyshire and South Yorkshire region. However, in the mid-Noughties, I'm glad to say that I finally managed to twist his arm to leave the production line and get behind a desk, as a manager in the disputes team, and then as Head of Workplace Disciplinary Actions. In that role, Nayan has achieved remarkable success, rewriting the rulebook, literally, and last I looked, a favourable outcome for the worker had been registered in over ninety-five per cent of the unfair dismissal claims that he has taken the lead on. Two years ago, Nayan joined the Unify Board, and serves the union in this additional capacity with a huge amount of dedication, flair and authority. As

a member of the working class, he's long been a forthright defender of working-class rights, and of workers'
rights. It's good to have you here, Nayan.' They exchanged
nods. 'Now, turning to Megha Sharma. Megha has been
our Head of Diversity, Equity and Inclusion for little over
a year, and is doing sterling work in that arena.'

A deliberate, brutal silence; an anxious laugh from the
audience. Megha, despite the open, outward set of her
face, was shaken, Nayan saw: the two rapid blinks, the
ever-fiercer smile.

'As to the running order, each candidate is permitted
to nominate an advocate of their candidature, who will
give to the members, both to those here with us in person
today and to the many thousands joining us via the magic
of technology, a statement in support of their candidate.
So supporting Nayan we have Miss Claudia Watkinson.'
Claudia bowed her head as if in her mind the audience
were cheering. 'Claudia is from our junior wing – Unify
The Youth – and is currently undertaking an MA in Politics at the University of Sheffield. Also with us, in Megha's
corner, so to speak, is Richard Allen, no doubt best known
to many of you as Unify's Head of Workplace Health and
Safety. Welcome to you both. To you all.'

There was low applause, a mix of hands and thighs,
and the panel nodded, Nayan nodded. He turned round
to the screen, which showed the five of them on stage
and, along the bottom, the sundry heads of those in the
front row: bobbed brunette; a pink tonsure; long black;
capped. Nervous all over again, Nayan went to cross his
legs at the knees, to gather himself up a little, but the table

didn't quite allow it and he succeeded only in knocking his complimentary bottle of water. 'Shit,' he mumbled, saving the bottle before it fell – the word caught on the microphone and he looked into the audience, something he'd avoided until now. The hall was packed, not a seat empty as far as he could see; some were forced to stand, even sit on the floor – indeed, a ten-strong faction of tram operators, late to arrive, had set themselves up in the aisle, cross-legged on their blanket of coats. Reclining, Nayan tried to capture the whole of the assembly in one panorama, and he still couldn't be certain: were they staring at him when he wasn't looking? Ready to record every move, twist every utterance and throw it to the webbed masses to gorge on? Was that hatred in their eyes? He snatched at the bottle, tried to sip, couldn't. His heart surged. Claudia took the water from him and handed it back with the top unscrewed. 'Get it together,' she whispered. But would that now be up for commentary, too? Was it already doing the rounds? *Olak demands black girl open his water for him #misogynist #modernslavery #OlakMustGo.* How fucking paranoid was he?

'We'll begin with me asking some questions of both our candidates and then we'll have the supporting statements from their advocates. There will certainly be time for questions from members at the end so please do have them ready, and that goes for both the members here in the hall and the ones watching the live-stream, who can use the chat function to submit any comments. Right,' – Geoff turned to Nayan –'Nayan, if we can start with some words from you on what your main priorities as Gen Sec would be? Yes?'

To look into the audience again would be lethal, would wipe clean his mind until not an idea remained, so Nayan zeroed in on Geoff and recalled the numbered yellow index cards he'd compiled the previous night. He knew there were four points he wanted to make, each one growing on the last, though he couldn't quite recollect them all. 'For me, one of our biggest challenges is ensuring employers and governments uphold the integrity of employee pension schemes. It's not the sexiest subject, granted, but when you've paid in good faith, and for all your life, into the employer's pension pot, and when the employer has invested that fund to line their own coffers, and, at times, raided it to pay their execs huge bonuses, then the very least workers deserve is to be given a fair and equitable annuity that allows them to retire with dignity. Too many retiring workers are relying on foodbanks, while execs work out new ways to evade paying tax. So, as General Secretary, I'd lobby for a robust pension guarantee fund that actually works, one that employers would legally have to participate in and contribute to. Without boring everyone with the details, employers would pay an annual premium into the fund. Where the employee plan is currently underfunded, the employer would pay an additional premium. The more underfunded the plan, the higher the premium. The point is that the fund, underwritten by the government, would be available to workers if their pension benefits, and their retirement, are under threat. That would be my first priority. Secondly, I've been working with several councils, nationally, on a universal basic income pilot. I'd want to continue and expand that work. There have been plenty of studies that show a universal basic income reduces income inequality and empowers workers to hold bosses to account. I'd also lobby to cap exec pay to no more than five times the lowest earner and insist wages are pegged to inflation – again, it's about reducing economic inequality and giving workers a voice. And, bluntly, we need to stop letting those at the top cream off ever more outrageous salaries while workers are expected to get by on a pittance. That's my third point.' The fourth point, too, mercifully, now landed in his head. 'Lastly, as General Secretary of the biggest union in the country, and the biggest donor to the Labour Party, I'd lobby to have more working-class voices in parliament. There aren't even five MPs, across the house, who have a working-class background. There are plenty of career politicians, plenty of special advisers turned politicians, but practically no one who understands what life is like for ordinary workers in this country. We've had all-women shortlists in the past and the Tories deliver all-private-school shortlists without any effort at all. I'd lobby hard for all-working-class shortlists. We need our people in the room. We need our voices heard. But here's the kicker, here's the big picture: we should only want those voices who believe in and want to bring about worker ownership of firms. Those voices who will argue for bringing proper democracy into our workplaces and not leave power with dictatorial bosses.' He thought of his mother's hands. 'We need to start ripping power from the hands of the bosses and placing it into the hardworking, labouring hands of workers.'

With this, Nayan got the applause he'd hoped for, and feeling as if this afternoon might go all right, he rested his ankle on his knee and relaxed back into his seat.

'Megha, is that something you could get behind?' Geoff asked. 'Lobbying for all-working-class shortlists to get more working-class people into parliament?'

'Well, those shortlists sound like a Trojan horse to cull union voices Nayan Olak disagrees with, and he should be honest about that. But perhaps I could also be given the opportunity to first outline what my priorities would be if I was elected—'

'If you could answer my question, please,' Geoff said, with a late, feigned smile. 'Do you favour all-working-class shortlists?'

Megha took a moment, fixing on some spot in the distance. In a supremely even tone, she said, 'It's already clear that I'm not going to be given a fair crack at this today, which is disappointing if unsurprising, but mostly really quite upsetting. But I'm aware this afternoon is the only chance I'll be given to have *my* voice properly heard so I guess I have no choice but to play along with your game, Geoff.'

'I assure you, these debates aren't games, or if they are they are governed by rules which I know very well and am following to the letter. In any event,' he went on, chuckling, encouraging everyone else to do the same, 'isn't it customary to wait for the game to start before getting your excuses in?'

'To answer your question,' Megha said, once the

audience had quit tittering, 'I believe if we're going to make a difference to the lives of marginalised communities then we absolutely need their voices in our institutions. Including in our parliament. I wonder why, though, we're not first getting our own house in order. As you know, because I've said this frequently enough, fewer than five per cent of our members are non-white, even fewer identify as LGBTQ, and well under a quarter are women. These would be my priorities, Geoff, because as you laboured to articulate, we're stronger when we have a multiplicity of backgrounds, when differing experiences can be brought to bear on our decision-making. Like Nayan Olak, I won't go into detail – it's all in my manifesto – but I have several initiatives in mind to make us a more welcoming home. That is not at all to say that the concerns of working-class white members are not important to me. Far from it. It's because I recognise the central importance of difference that I, more than anyone, more than Nayan Olak, am able to see that our white members have specific needs that should not be ignored, that cannot be expected to be captured by one-size-fits-all initiatives or, worse, by claiming that race does not matter. This is why Richard and I felt it was so important that we come together and present a united leadership front, with each of us representing the notions of cultural difference that, harnessed properly, will elevate Unify. We need to reject the universalist pieties that say "all lives matter", that we're all the same – because we're not: some of us have far more privilege than others, have far more of a voice than others. So while *I* lead on initiatives that specifically target the needs of non-white and other minority workers, Richard will be the lead and point of contact for white working-class members, ensuring their concerns are heard and given equal weight.' She paused, sipped – leisurely, controlled – resumed. 'To give a practical example: one of our main priorities is around decolonising the union and part of this involves looking at how the unions haven't always in the past been hospitable to all people. And we need to understand this, not brush it under the carpet. We need some education that black and brown people at one time weren't allowed to be fully unionised, recognised members and the harm this caused. The jobs and income that were denied to these workers as a result. We absolutely need to apologise for this. And make financial reparations where possible. Build bridges, you know? And then I'd take that message out to the communities, to non-white workers, showing them how we're changing, learning, and asking them to join us. At the same time, Richard will be leading on a project on white working-class revolts, like the Jarrow Marches, say, another example of when the unions didn't support those in need, and we'd learn from that and take that message out, too. Everyone taking their union history out to their separate communities and bringing in more members. What could be fairer? And then, of course, we would also ensure that those members' voices are heard by the Board by monitoring who is being selected to become reps, senior reps, et cetera – we need appropriate representation throughout the decision-making framework of this organisation. If suddenly ten per cent of our members are non-white, then so should be the make up of the senior reps, right? Again, what could be fairer? What could be more respectful? Ninety per cent would still be white, of course,' she added, levelling an ironic smile at Richard. 'No takeover yet.'

There was some laughter, patchy applause, though much of it cautious.

'Apologies?' Nayan said. 'Reparations? We used to say, "Don't cry, organise". But Megha Sharma is only interested in organising in order *to* cry.'

'Which only confirms how outdated you are,' Megha said. 'I'm about respecting and celebrating *all* working-class lives. Abolishing *all* classism.'

The coinage grated, yet striving to understand, Nayan said, 'But celebrate what, Megha? Being poor? Being good at scratting around the back of the sofa for a quid to put in the meter? I really can't fathom why you think class is just another identity. It's not. Because it's not a lack of *respect* the working class suffer from. It's a lack of money. Of means.'

'And it won't have escaped anyone's attention,' Geoff said, keen to make this point, 'that the leadership contest is between two non-white candidates. This would have been unimaginable just ten years ago. Perhaps some progress is being made? Would you not allow that at least?'

'I can see how it may appear so,' Megha said carefully. 'But I've already given the membership stats. And, frankly, it's deeply racist to suggest that people of colour should be satisfied because two of us are up here duking it out. You wouldn't expect white people to be similarly grateful. Not all non-white people are the same, Geoff. We don't all have the same brain. I can't be expected to speak for all people of colour.'

'I was talking about an indicator of progress not—'

'The fact is we're so far from looking like what the country *actually* looks like. And it's precisely for that reason that I'm standing, that I felt compelled and forced to stand, to alter what we as an organisation look like. Nayan Olak certainly isn't going to do that. Given that he doesn't believe in race, I'm not even sure if he'd be happy being categorised as a non-white. You'd have to ask him. He's more a neutral shade, perhaps. Off-white, you might say.'

More laughter; fuller laughter.

'My problem,' Nayan said, determined not to bite, 'with the kind of diversity schemes you advocate is that the non-white people best placed to take advantage of these initiatives are those that enjoy a lot of class advantage already. They've been to the best schools, have the best contacts. Perhaps not unlike yourself. It's extraordinary that barely two years into your post you're standing for election. It's extraordinary you got your post so easily in the first place. Can you imagine someone without your colossal privileges doing all that?'

'I'd been a supporter for many years before I started working for Unify,' Megha said. 'You'll have to do better than that if you want to malign me.'

'No doubt. But my point stands.' He could see the words he would next say laid out on his kitchen table, across those numbered cards; written in his hand, all capitals, underlined in red. He felt immense relief at the opportunity to unroll all those pre-prepared sentences. 'It's true that I'm against diversity schemes, against DEI surveillance, against race-based corporatism. Why? Because representation is not the answer. A politics of aspiration devised by elites in order to create more diverse elites is not the answer. The better world does not consist of the richest among us being in the correct racial, gender, class proportions. And the poorest being made up of the right number of whites, blacks, browns, women, gays, working class. That's not *better*. That's the same old socially conservative world, but with a colour chart. The *better* world is one in which the rich do not exist. Where no one is poor. I'm here in front of you asking that a distinction be made between discrimination and exploitation. By all means, let's fight discrimination against non-whites, against every minority group, but let's not for a moment kid ourselves that this will make the slightest bit of difference to the system of exploitation that ruins the lives of so many. You know, friends, there's a reason why corporates are falling over themselves to have women, gays, people of colour on their boards – but remain reluctant to ask the socialists.' A knowing laugh rippled through the audience. 'Megha is our Head of DEI. But when the bailiffs are at the door, inclusivity will not help you. When your mother is sick, equity will not bring a doctor. And if your children are starving, then what should you do? We know what my opponent would say: Let them eat diversity.' He didn't look across to Megha, not even as approving murmurs suffused the room; he had to keep going. 'Megha Sharma's policies are anti-solidaristic. They don't work. Despite her claims, policies like hers do not help the non-white working class, or the non-white poor. The people that benefit from these schemes are those whose pockets are already pretty fat with social and cultural capital, because they're the ones who are best placed to take advantage of these initiatives. There was a not-isolated case a few months back – you may have seen it – where a British Asian man got a paid-up spot on a prestigious journalism course via the BBC's inclusivity drive. He was the son of a billionaire. It's a curious kind of diversity, don't you think, that serves to undermine questions of economic inequality? And all this while my friend's son, an amazing, hardworking, *black working-class* young man, can't even get his foot in the door. Who worked as a waiter at my Diwali party to earn a crust. Who's this minute caring for my father. Whom no one *sees*. I should say that I know plenty of *white* working-class folk who also can't get their foot in the door. Has it escaped Megha Sharma's attention that the vast majority of the poor people in this country are, in fact, white? White supremacy and white privilege doesn't seem to have served them very well. Or, as I say, is it only the proportions that matter to Megha Sharma? It appears she's fine with the poor being poor as long as they're in their correct racial percentages.'

Here Nayan raised his hand, a star, and pointed to each fingertip in turn:

'Meaningful employment, good housing, a decent education for their kids, a feeling that they have a stake in this country, and the opportunity to live lives full of choice and dignity – it seems clear to me, if not to Megha Sharma, that these are the things that working-class people of all races desire – let me repeat that: of all races. And these desires have *nothing* to do with race. And we'll only win these things if we organise and fight for them together.' He paused. 'A good friend of mine said to me recently: *We've all got identities. Not just you lot.* He's a white friend. I still consider him a friend. And he's right, in a way. If non-whites will insist on using their identity as a political vehicle, then white people will, too. Especially if they've been left with no other way to think about the problems they face. If the fake left, the liberal left that Megha Sharma is so in thrall to, is no longer concerned about social and economic change; if the unions, weakened already, now forget why they exist; if every social justice issue must be seen through a lens of race. Then, yes, we've all only got our identities, we've all got our race, and we leave the space open for the racist right – who *love* diversity politics, by the way – to step in and poison the minds of those white working-class people that have, yes, been left behind. What Megha Sharma is proposing, with the best of intentions no doubt, is more separation, more division. Her vision is one of inclusionary neoliberalism. It is pro-capitalism, anti-socialist. She's playing straight into the hands of the far right. She is, true to form, the far right's useful idiot. At the risk of being accused of propagating universalist pieties, it is, actually, a return to a politics based around solidarity and universalism that will save us. A return to our principles. A return to our values. A return to our actual lived lives! We need bare-knuckled class politics! Not – resoundingly, emphatically, vehemently – not Megha K. Sharma!'

He hadn't quite built up to the end he'd rehearsed, and neither had he accompanied each closing adverb with a strike of the table, as he'd imagined doing. It didn't matter: the applause unbottled at once. Some were on their feet – on their chairs! – cheering, egged on by Lisa-Marie. Hands above their heads, clapping hard and fast and loud. The noise of it all! As if the very air in the room was being made to dance! Claudia shook a winning fist under the table. 'You nailed it,' she said. Nodding, Nayan puffed out his cheeks and looked into the audience. Now he could face them. Now he felt cleansed, yes, the applause felt like a cleansing, as if they were washing him of the mud thrown these last few weeks. How many of them there were. Surely among all these faces, one would belong to Brandon? All he'd had were a sequence of encouraging emojis, probably sent amid a frenetic kitchen. Then he saw him. Alone at the very back. Proffering Nayan hyacinths. Happy. Wondrously happy. Entranced, Nayan waved, delicately. Wondered if he'd be cold in just that scrappy T-shirt of his. But then the applause petered out, taking his little boy with it, and so bewitched had Nayan been he failed to spot the audience member step into the aisle and approach the standing mic.

'Quick comment, if I may?' the young man said, his voice screechy with feedback until he took a tiny pace backwards. Only when Claudia bridled did Nayan recognise him: her uninvited classmate. 'What you said is all well and good and of course ideally we'd all live together in some happy-clappy way, but the key difference between you two, as it appears to me, is that you want a colour-blind society, where race doesn't matter – that's a kinda mantra for you – but you' – he motioned to Megha – 'actually recognise that race is a reality that affects, and has always affected, and in fact harmed, non-white people. And that it will continue to do so unless we address race specifically. Not pretend it isn't even a thing. At a most basic level, if I go into any city or town in this country there's a good chance I will be stopped and searched. A white working-class man won't be. When I go to the US, I genuinely fear for my life whenever a cop's near. That I'll find *his* knee on *my* neck. A white guy doesn't have that fear. These are real things. Wake up, man.'

'I'll fucking kill him,' Claudia muttered, which distracted Nayan and allowed Megha a run.

'Precisely,' she said. 'We can all whoop and cheer at the utopia Nayan Olak envisions, but while we do it is brown women, not white, who are having their hijabs ripped off, that are being spat at. It isn't white women but women of colour who are dying in childbirth at far higher rates. It is black boys who are going to prison, who are getting much longer sentences than white boys for committing exactly the same crimes. A class-based analysis is good in theory, but it doesn't tackle the very real biases in our institutions and workplaces, and it certainly won't face up to the – again very real – structural and systemic racism whose eradication our union can lead on, if we, to put it plainly, have the cojones to do that. I'd argue that *you're* the reckless one' – gesturing expansively at Nayan, but without in any way looking at him – 'for throwing people of colour under the bus, for sacrificing us on the altar of your universalism, and not even recognising that the civil rights movement achieved what it did precisely through a politics based around identity.'

Megha frowned. Evidently, she'd wanted to end on a fatter, more stirring note. Geoff jumped in, addressing the young man still in the aisle: 'Questions really should be for the end. For now, let's move on to—'

'Can I just say?' Nayan said, leaning into the mic, repressing a smile at Megha's failure to land a blow. 'I'm not saying racism doesn't matter. It matters very much. I have the scars to prove it. I'm saying that race – and not racism, but race – only matters if we make it matter, it only has the power we decide to give to it. And I think we'd be better off reducing the power we give to an idea that has given me the scars I now bear.'

Perhaps Nayan looked infuriatingly smug as he withdrew, still savouring his speech's success, because the young man whipped the mic off its stand. 'It's not whether *we* think it matters or *you* think it matters! Society – everyone out there – *they* think it matters. They *insist* it matters. They're the ones who see a black man walking down the road and judge him because of it. They're the ones who don't give the black man a job or a place to rent or the benefit of the fucking doubt. They're the ones who see race. And that's why we have to see it, too. Don't you get that? Get out of your ivory tower, fool. Come down and spend some time with those of us living this life every day on the streets.'

'*Thank* you,' Geoff said. 'If you've quite finished, perhaps you can retake your seat and we can proceed with the advocating statements?' The young man, impressively unperturbed by the few boos aimed his way, simply sat on the floor, alongside the tram drivers.

'He's a dick,' Claudia said. 'He's the same in class. As if he's ever *not* been able to pay his rent.'

'Just concentrate on your speech,' Nayan advised, which was all he had time to say, because Geoff was inviting Claudia to the lectern.

She rose in a quick, surprised, upright way, as if programmed by a button; too quick, really, because she seemed unprepared for this new vantage, and held her chair for support. Her insides felt altered, made soft and so porous that the nerves, circling for the last hour, stormed gleefully in, chasing away all that bravado. You got this, she told herself, and walked to the lectern, her trainers making no sound, which only exaggerated the anticipation. She breathed. Her mum, out there in the big hall, pressed her lips together in an understanding smile. *Take your time, love.* Bringing her trembling hands to the lectern, either side of her speech, Claudia began.

'I've known Nayan . . .' Her voice sounded small, blocked. She coughed, looked for water though there wasn't any nearby, restarted. 'I've known Nayan my whole life. When my father, a great Unify man himself, died and my mum couldn't afford childcare it was Nayan who dropped us off at school, Nayan who cooked our tea. While he sizzled sausages in the pan, me and my brother would listen to him telling us about some of the great working-class heroes of the past. About Aneurin Bevan and Hannah Mitchell, about Cesar Chavez and William Cuffay. Nayan knew how to keep us kids on the edge of our seats as we waited to hear whether Cuffay would be caught before he set fire to Queen Victoria's petticoats. I don't know about you, but I for one was on Cuffay's side. Still am. So was Nayan, of course. And he got so wrapped up in these famous tales of working-class heroism that he'd forget all about the sausages. I can still smell them burning.' Soft laughter; a fillip to her confidence. 'What I'm trying to say is that Nayan, as much as anyone or anything in the world, is responsible for my political education. It's because of him that I know that the challenges, the obstacles and, yes, the racism I experience isn't solved by bandying about with people simply because they share the same heritage as me, or because we have similar levels of melanin. The challenges I and many non-white people in this country face are the challenges that working-class people have been facing throughout history.'

'Haven't we already heard all this?'

It was her classmate, Sean, calling up from the aisle. Claudia looked to her mum, then to Nayan, who nodded a half-inch, intimating that she continue, that she was doing really well.

Swallowing, she scanned to her place in the speech. 'It was Nayan who, when I was in my teens and being belligerent and snotty and loud – I know, hard to believe, isn't it?' – they liked that little joke, too – 'brought my attention to the thinker Frantz Fanon. Fanon was—'

'Please, Claudia! Spare us the history lesson! Fanon? Seriously?'

'Young man,' Geoff said, 'I've a mind to ask you to leave the hall.'

'How can you stand there and spout this crap? As a black woman?' There was an earnestness in his delivery, a genuine confusion which married with the silence of the hall and gave Claudia the certain impression the question was coming not just from him, but from all the world's misguided. And Claudia, who more than anything loved clarifying people's confusion for them, felt a constitutional compulsion to respond.

'The problem with you, Sean, is you don't listen. Because if you did, you'd know that it's exactly that phrase, that *formulation* – "As a black woman" – that betrays your poor intellectual grasp of the situation. I don't think anything "as a black woman". Being black and being a woman informs me but – and listen up, kiddo – it is not the lens through which I view every last thing. Heard of Claudia Jones? I was named after her. Black activist *but* first and foremost – and despite everyone's attempt to hide this – fighter for the Communist Party. *She* got it. She got it when Fanon said,' and in a move that reminded Nayan uncomfortably of Margaret Thatcher, Claudia's eyes shone as she lifted her gaze from Sean and to the audience at large, ' "I cannot disassociate myself from the future that is proposed for my brother. Every one of my acts commits me *as a man*. Every one of my silences, every one of my cowardices reveals me *as a man*." He is identifying, correctly, that the pain of one oppressed group is the pain of every other oppressed group. That's the hard truth,' she looked back to Sean, with contempt, '*bruv*.'

Now, the child so roundly dispatched, she was raring to return to her speech. She still had over a century of ground to cover, from Toussaint L'Ouverture, via C. L. R. James, to the League of Revolutionary Struggle, from the Chartists' alliance with Indian mutineers all the way to Jayaben Desai, and that was before she even got to the two-page conclusion where she'd make the case that Nayan, and Nayan's politics, sat squarely in this radical tradition of lasting social transformation brought about by transracial, working-class solidarity. But the idiot Sean spoke again, and he didn't just speak – to Claudia's astonishment, he was standing up, addressing the audience. He was ruining everything. He was muscling in, taking over, just like he did in class.

'*She*, and Nayan Olak, presumably, forget that Stephen Lawrence was a *black* man. He was murdered for being a *black* man. In the states, the police murdered Eric Garner because he was a *black* man. They murdered Michael Brown because he was a *black* man. Do you even know, *Claudia*, that black people aren't even fifteen per cent of the US population but make up a quarter of all police homicides? Do you know that? Do you even know that when you're murdered for the colour of your skin, *Claudia*, that is a normalising fear? That it tells every black man that they should be scared for their lives? That it stops black people being free? Cos it does. It enslaves us all over again. It enslaves me. The trauma of our people comes rushing back. Do you not know how trauma works? Because *as a black man*, I know that I could be the next man shot by the po-leece. No white guy is enslaved by that fear. So you – and your Nayan Olak – can't just lump black and white together, as if all oppressions are equal. Keep your racist equivalences to yourself. You try to do that in class and you're doing it now. And it's hideous and embarrassing that you just don't get it.'

'*I* don't get it? *I* don't?' She was shouting. 'Do you want to hear some facts, Sean? Do ya?'

Nayan half-climbed out of his seat. He needed to steal Claudia's attention, tell her to not engage, to sit down and back the hell off. This was being live-streamed, for crying out loud. Nayan entreated Lisa-Marie, who'd raised her hands as if to push Claudia back. Claudia, however, wasn't at all looking their way, not at Nayan, not at her mother.

'It's you. It's blacks like you that are the real problem.'

'Wow! Wow, people! She says black people are to blame for their own persecution! Does Nayan Olak think this, too?'

'Claudia,' Nayan said, into the mic, and she appeared to register this, marginally, but she wouldn't be stopped. She was the pudgy thirteen-year-old again, blocking the mayor's exit from the school car park, demanding the mace-bearing kids be paid. She'd harangued the mayor then, and now, too, her finger was levelled, thrusting.

'Blacks like you, yeah. Understand this: Stephen Lawrence was a *working-class*, black man. Murdered by a gang of white racists who were also *working-class* men. How do

292

you not even know that in every corner of this country, the chances are that the victim of violent crime, the perpetrator of violent crime, everyone, whether black, white, whatever, will be from a poor, deprived, *working-class* area. Does that not, for even a *scintilla* of a second, make that little brain of yours think that inequality, that *poverty*, might be a ginormous factor here?' She leaned over the lectern. 'You keep mentioning the States. So shall we take a look there? Eric Garner was a *working-class*, black man. Michael Brown was a *working-class*, black man. But wanna bring this bang up-to-date, Sean? Let's take a look at last year, hmm? Because Alton Sterling was a *working-class*, black man. Philando Castile was a *working-class*, black man. Terence Crutcher was a *working-class*, black man. So you know what,' she said, her voice seeping sarcasm, 'I don't think you really need to worry about walking around New *Yoik*. Go for it. Knock yourself out. You'll be *just* fine. Shall I tell you why? Cos you went to *A FUCK-ING PREP SCHOOL IN BANBURY!*'

The laughter was immediate, raucous; the applause wild and uninterrupted. Chairs were rocked. Feet drummed. Straightening up, Claudia experienced the acclaim as heat in her face, her smile was shining so hard, and, defeated, sheepish, Sean sank to the floor, drowning in the tram drivers' ridicule.

'Great stuff.' It was Nayan. Mesmerised by her triumph, Claudia had not noticed him vacating his seat. 'Leave it here.'

'What?' she said. The applause hadn't finished. 'I've still – over two pages to go. They love me!'

'End on a high, Clau. You won't top this. Just go. Please.' She did, reluctantly, the applause following her back to the table. Relieved – how nearly had she spiralled – Nayan found himself alone at the lectern, facing an audience who expected him to speak. 'Thanks, Claudia. She speaks a lot of sense, doesn't she?'

'YEAH!' said the audience, still euphoric. The strength of this reaction shocked Nayan. He hadn't foreseen it. But now he had it, he craved more.

'Workers first, yeah?'

'YEAH!'

'Elites out, yeah?'

'YEAH!'

'Because this is what happens,' Nayan said, gesturing to the aisle, where probably that Sean boy still was. 'When non-whites enter elite spaces they turn their backs on making real change. It becomes all about using their race only to further their own elite, privileged lives while giving cover to the actual racism going on in the world, that actually affects poor people, that requires more change than that which can be brought about by squawking over who can say namaste or wear dreads, that requires change that doesn't fetishise and police language and etiquette in a way that is absolutely designed to humiliate and exclude the working class – of *all* races – to exclude precisely those of us who the elite know would actually challenge their shameful, elite lives.'

Further applause, equally full but more considered, which Nayan took as his cue to leave. Before he quit the stand, Megha spoke: 'Love an audience, don't you,

Nayan? But no one's said anything about the policing of language, so a little less of the dog-whistle grandstanding, please.' She sounded calm, disturbingly so, to Nayan's ear. 'But we can, once more, talk about basic respect. For instance, respecting places of worship enough to not allow alcohol to be consumed within their walls.'

Nayan looked to Richard, whose eyes were on the table, the members, anywhere but at Nayan.

'Was alcohol consumed at your Diwali party, a party that took place in a Sikh gurdwara?'

'It was done without my knowledge.'

'Are we expected to believe that?'

'It's the truth. Maybe you can ask your co-candidate to confirm. He seemed more than a little acquainted with any alcohol that night.'

'Perhaps you'd also had a drop? Maybe that's why you can't remember assaulting me.'

'If you insist on continuing with these lies, we must stop here and involve our lawyers. This is reprehensible. Fight this election with integrity if you can.'

She didn't respond. Instead, she reached for her phone.

'Megha?' Geoff enquired.

After a moment, Megha said, 'I'm going to cut into the live-stream to show you all something.'

Nayan twisted round to the screen, which had frozen, then to Richard, who finally looked at his old friend. Shame was writ large on Richard's face; he was besieged by a dire need to explain, helpless with it. The screen revived. It was – the gurdwara, the canteen. The party. The chatter of people talking.

'You won't be able to hear what's being said,' Megha intoned. 'But if I could draw your attention to the upper right corner.'

Everyone's attention was duly drawn. Was that him? Yes. It was him. Talking to Megha. Arguing. She was scowling, quarrelling. He – Nayan winced, his heart thrashed – he was bearing down on her. It looked ugly. She tried to push him aside. He nearly lost his footing. He grabbed her hand. Her wrist. She struggled. He didn't let go. Let go of her wrist, he said to video-Nayan. But he didn't. Let go of her fucking wrist. The screen paused. His hand hard around her wrist. Her face in pain. But that couldn't be him, he thought. This wasn't who he was. But it was him. It was him.

6

When Nayan came to my house one recent morning, I should've guessed something was afoot: it was the only time he'd insisted on picking me up; said he wanted to see my parents on the day of their move. I loaded a bag, filled my water bottle; Mum went through the hugs; Dad rubbed Nayan's back.

'I'm so happy you two have become friends,' Mum said.

'Isn't it?' Nayan said.

I glanced over.

'Yes. So, where are you off to today?' Mum persevered, a little cowed.

'Some trail,' Nayan said.

'Monsal,' I said. 'By Hassop.'

Nayan shrugged, a quick flick of his shoulders that said he didn't care. 'I'm just driving.' Then: 'Big move, eh? Excited? You must be excited.'

'It'll be nice,' Mum said.

'It's taken a while,' Dad added.

'Yeah, a real long while.'

His tone was strange at the best of times, but more so

today. Mum, perhaps wishing to address matters, took his hand. 'I think about your son and your mother a lot. She was a great woman.'

'Wasn't she, though? The bestest. Such a shame about who she married.'

'Well' – Mum took her hand back; he hadn't reacted to it at all – 'maybe he's getting his punishment now. His poor health.'

'Do you think it works like that? It might have been better if she'd just left him, don't you think? If she hadn't been scared off from leaving him?'

As if slapped, Mum looked away. I wriggled on my backpack – 'Let's go,' – and Nayan pressed his hands together in farewell, a gesture more sardonic than sincere, and wished my parents a happy move.

In the car, we didn't speak and only the radio – Capital – played. *He* wasn't there, Nayan had said, to Deepti in the restaurant. But really to me. Pyara wasn't there, frightening his mother into staying, into not leaving. But someone else was. Misery came over me. 'Why didn't you tell me that it was my mum? Who convinced your mum not to leave your dad.'

'You wanted the whole story. That's what you said. So shall we do that? Shall I tell you?'

———

The end of June, the election over, and the sun at last had broken through, was blazing. Outside Sheffield Station, kids thrilled at the fountain as bright light travelled along its curving steel wall of running water, like white noise on an old TV. For a while now, Nayan had been walking through the city, without destination, hands in his jacket pockets. He wasn't, per se, avoiding the office; he simply wanted to exist a little in a place that was neither home nor work, where he wasn't and didn't have to be Nayan Olak. He'd even left his phone at home, something he did more and more often – this did mean he had no idea what time it was. He scanned about for a clock, a clock-tower maybe, and failing, sighing, supposed he had better make his way in. Perhaps he had been avoiding the office after all.

Two weeks on from the debate, there were no longer any protests outside the building, and the new guard unlocked the glass door and nodded once as he let Nayan in. He took the stairs, slowly. He wasn't sure if in all the years he'd worked here, rushing up the stairwell from one battle to the next, he'd ever paused to notice the particular sea-green shade of the steps. There was no one on his floor, an emptiness he encountered as a reprieve, and at his desk he unzipped his rucksack and packed away the wood-framed triptych of photographs, the very small pile of leaving cards left on his chair. In his drawer were several souvenirs, bits and bobs from work trips. He'd thought he'd want to keep them, but no, he shut the drawer and locked it with the trinkets still inside. All he did want was a final look around the place. Would he miss it? He wasn't sure. Walk out, he said to himself. But he stayed put, the chair tidied under his desk. Soon, he heard voices – Megha strode in, then Richard.

'Nayan,' she said.

Well, he thought, best to just make a good fist of this.

Leave with what dignity he could. He walked over. 'You're keen,' he said – and remembered to smile. 'Week-end working.'

'There's a lot to do,' she said.

Nayan nodded, kept smiling.

'How are you?' Richard said. 'You not going to reply to my messages?'

'I will, I will. You're on the list.'

Richard took a pace towards him. 'I wasn't intention-ally recording, you know. It was just . . .'

'Lucky?' Nayan said. 'It's done, Rich. Don't sweat it.'

Geoff called off the meeting once the video went out, and days of death threats against Nayan followed. By then, he'd already stood down from contesting the elec-tion. Less than a week later, when colleagues staged a walkout, Geoff called Nayan and told him to resign both his post and his membership.

Megha gestured to the laptop in Nayan's hand; his lanyard, too, dangling from his fingers. 'I'm sorry it came to this. You've given so much to this place.' She touched his arm. 'I know we've not always seen eye to eye, but I do respect you a huge amount. If there's ever anything I can do . . .'

'Oh, hey, I'll be fine. Things change. We move on.'

'Nah, mate,' Richard said, 'you'll be missed. You've been this place's beating heart.'

Hearts get spoiled – a cheap thought formed before Nayan could stop his mind from forming it. He gave an enormous smile to mask, to stay, the emotion coursing up his body. He nodded once at them both, handed in his laptop and lanyard at reception, and was ready to add his signature to the sign-out sheet when the guard said it wasn't needed.

Until this moment of exiting the office, he wasn't sure he'd ever quite accepted they'd be prepared to see him leave. Was that a measure of his arrogance? he wondered. Had a part of him been convinced that someone, at the eleventh hour, was certain to lunge forward and confess this was all a massive prank, that of course they'd never let him go? Not Nayan Olak, union man and boy, indefatigable defender of the working people. All was silent as he walked away from the office. Up in the sky, contrails crossed. The sun spread through white gassy clouds and tainted them gold. He got as far as the Botanical Gardens before realising he couldn't go home, not right now, not yet. It would just be him and his dad and the desolation of this was too much. He turned up towards Sharrow and was soon peering through the window of Parl and Cam. There he was, in his blue-and-white striped apron, chatting animatedly to the head chef. Pam something, was it? They'd not spoken for a while, he and Brandon, and Nayan had no intention of intruding now, ruining the boy's day. Seeing him was enough. Already Nayan felt better for it, and he stepped out from under the awning, back into the sun, and was sloping off down the hill when he heard Brandon calling to him.

'Where you going?' the boy said, jogging. 'Come in.'

'No, no. You're busy. You're closed. I was just passing.'

Brandon nodded, not really believing him. 'How are you? I've tried calling a few times. I came by, too – the other day. No one answered.'

'Sorry. I was . . .' What? Busy? No. He'd been keeping his distance, respecting Helen's wishes, as hard as it was. The way the sun fell in coins down Brandon's apron. Veer might have been a cook, too. Nayan screwed his eyes shut, crushing the thought, opened them. 'How's Claudia?'

'Same. Angry at how it all went.' He smiled, a little. 'You know how she is. It's you we're all worried about.' Even your mother? Nayan wanted to ask, because Helen still refused to let him come round until it all blew over. Brandon intuited the question: 'I don't know what's wrong with Mum. I said to her again you should come stay with us for a bit. You and your dad . . .' Shaking his head. 'She worries too much about me.' He looked over his shoulder, to the restaurant.

'I'm keeping you. You should go.'

'I've just got the clean-down for dinner. Stay. Have a meal on me.'

'Dad – he's on his own. But you can come round later? If you like? If you've time, that is.' Stuff Helen. The boy wanted to see him, too.

All evening Nayan felt agitated, checking the time; he checked it again as he settled Pyara, when there was a quiet double-tap on the front door.

'I didn't want to wake the old man,' Brandon said, coming through, sliding out of his trainers.

They carried on to the kitchen, where Nayan boiled the kettle and Brandon set about washing the dishes. 'I'll do them later,' Nayan said, embarrassed he'd let the plates pile up so.

'It takes me back,' Brandon said. 'I think I might even

like it. Do you think I could be one of those OCD clean freaks?'

'The place *was* always spotless when you babysat Dad.'

'Wasn't it? To think, I cook *and* clean. World's best catch.'

How his confidence had swelled! Smiling, Nayan set the teas on the counter and watched Brandon dry his hands on the cloth hanging off the oven. 'Work all good?' Nayan asked.

'It's okay. Nothing special. Work's work.'

'You don't have to be tactful,' Nayan said. 'Not that that was, especially. But I was thinking. We never did that second trip into the Peaks. How about it? We could go for longer this time. Not exactly rushed off my feet, am I? Bike up past Derwent, maybe.'

Brandon crossed his arms, holding the mug up against his shoulder. 'Sure thing.' Did he sound doubtful? 'Maybe in August, when it's quieter? Things are getting pretty busy now. I don't think Pam'll give me the time off.'

'Okay,' Nayan said. Two months? 'August's good.'

'I do want to, though.'

Had Nayan sounded sorry for himself? 'Course! It'll be better then. Less chance of getting rained on.'

They sipped their teas, in unison. 'What's going on with you and Mum? She won't tell me anything.'

'All this just threw us off course.' He sighed; his tea rippled. 'It'll come good.'

'She thinks you might go away. Start again. And that I wouldn't cope.'

'I've no plans to go anywhere.'

Brandon nodded. 'Don't get me wrong. I'd be dead sad. But' – he was choosing his words with care – 'if going away for a while is the best thing for you, if it's going to help you get over this, you should do it. I mean, it worked for me, right?'

It was hard for Nayan, in his oversensitive state, not to hear this as rejection, as ingratitude. This boy wouldn't have the life he had, his job, a girlfriend, confidence, if it wasn't for him. And now here he was, on the day Nayan had lost everything, telling him to go away and leave him alone. He didn't want to have to deal with this old man's pain, have him turning up at his restaurant, asking him over at all hours, planning weekend trips, not when his own life was so on the up. That's how Nayan saw it and he was surprised how wounded he felt, how fiercely he wanted Brandon out of the house.

'You may have hit on something. Maybe I do need to up sticks.' He necked the rest of his tea and brought the mug down on the counter, hard. 'I should call it a night. Been a long day.'

Brandon – was that relief in his face? – set aside his unfinished drink and they headed into the hallway. 'Do what's best for you. Don't worry about anyone else.'

'Careful, son,' Nayan said, in a tone so upbeat it may have contained menace. 'Don't go sounding like a Tory.'

Brandon laughed, a tad nervously – shoes on, he slipped past Nayan and out the door. 'Rest up, man. I'll see you soon.'

Nayan turned the lock and stood there with his hand

still on it. First went his mother, and Veer. Then Deepti. And now there was no work, no Helen, no Brandon. Truly, he was a careless man. Had anyone ever lost so much, so swiftly?

Passing the front room, he saw Pyara, holding aside the curtains with both hands.

'I thought you were in bed?' He joined his father; bathed in the car's interior light, Brandon was on his phone, smiling. Messaging Claudia? Friends from the restaurant? How full his life. Be pleased for him, Nayan told himself. 'Shall I help you up the stairs?' Pyara seemed not to hear. He was still watching Brandon, or watching whatever recollection Brandon had sparked. So often Nayan found his father at the window lately. Waiting for Mum, Nayan continued to believe. As Brandon drove off, Pyara trailed the car, the withdrawing ruby lights.

'It was just Brandon, Dad,' Nayan said. 'You remember him. You loved his food.'

Pyara let the curtains close, extinguishing the fuzzy light on his face. 'Helen,' he said, after a moment's struggle.

It was the first time Nayan heard him acknowledge her; though, now he thought about it, hadn't Buddy mentioned . . . *You got yourself a rival for Helen, Ny. Perry couldn't stop with her name.* This was when Nayan arrived home after the debate, openly distressed, and Buddy tried to say something easy and cheering on his way out.

'Helen,' Pyara said again, this time raising his face to Nayan. He looked fearful, horribly confused, the cloud-less sky of his mind all black roiling crows.

305

'Yeah, that's right, that's Brandon's mum. Helen.'

Pyara flinched at the name; the birds pecking at him. 'She was in the car. Driving. Driving off.'

'She can drive, yes.' He must have seen her at some point. Hadn't she dropped him off home recently? So strange the things that lodge in his brain. He put his arm around Pyara's shoulders. 'Come on. Back to bed.'

'But she was there,' he said, shuffling forward with Nayan's help. Moving, being on the move, seemed to shift a piece of Pyara's mind into place. 'She was at the shop. Helen. Making the fire.'

Nayan halted, tilted his head towards his father. 'Say again?'

Pyara in bed, Nayan returned to the living room. Lamp off. Door closed. Lowering very slowly onto the armchair. He breathed. He tried not to think it could be true. But she'd refused to be his father's carer, hadn't she, when she most needed work? And had she ever come into his house? Once, she had. Yes. Just the once. She'd stood for so long in front of Veer's photo. And then she'd left in the night. Before Dad saw her? No. Yes. It couldn't be real. When did she leave town? The same year. But why get involved with him, then? Why sleep with him? He's not thinking straight. Is he? And round and down his mind went, all the night long, the hours pitiless and his thoughts, oh his thoughts, swinging between the wolves and the dogs.

The sun wasn't yet up and Helen let him inside, asking if everything was all right. Did she know in that instant the charade was over? Is that what explained the grim thrill when she'd opened the door to his unshaven, unslept face? For so long she'd been waiting for the guillotine, for the blade to fall. Encouraging it, really. And now look at her: the flickering skin, as though excitement stormed beneath. She wanted to be found out. We know this. That's why she went with you, Nayan. Well: not long now, Helen. Not long now.

'Where's Brandon?'

'At Claudia's. Is he not picking up?' She scouted about for her phone. 'He said he was going round to yours last night?'

'It's not him I want.'

She stopped, looked at him. Up shot her defences. 'Right. Well, what is it I can do for you?'

He said nothing at first. He walked around the room, around her, and she tracked him with her gaze, her feet still. Only when he entered the kitchen, behind her, did she turn her body.

'What's going on, Nayan?'

Facing the window; his back to her. He could see her in the glass, riddled through the darkness. 'Why did you leave town?'

'First tell me what's going on. Is Brandon okay?'

'It doesn't work like that. First you answer my question.'

'I refuse to be bullied.'

'Oh, you do, do you?' he said, giving a joyless little laugh as he turned to her. From his pocket, he presented the original photograph of his mother and Veer. 'You spent ages staring at this. What were you thinking?' She glanced at the image, glanced away. '*Look* at it.'

She did, with an impatient sigh that inflamed him.

'Fuck you.'

'What do you want?' She was shaking; trying hard not to. 'Get to your question.'

'Which one? Why did you come back here? Why did you get with me? Why won't you ever come into my house?' A pause. 'Do you even think about my son?'

Neither spoke, until Helen did. 'I'll say it again: if there's something you want to ask me, then please – go ahead and ask me. I'm ready.'

'Don't misunderstand,' Nayan said to me. 'It wasn't Helen. She didn't cause the fire.'

But it was Helen. There was no doubt. She'd confessed, to the landlord, to Mal. For a moment I assumed she'd not come clean. Then, Nayan's furtive sideways check told me all I needed to know: she had confessed to him, too, and now he was protecting her.

'Dad's not reliable, obviously. He confused her with someone else. Her mother.'

'Her mother?' My voice echoed in the Monsal valley and fellow walkers looked over. The trail, in spite of the early start, was busy.

'She was one of the women my dad knocked about with. The junkie. They had a tiff and she threw a lit fag through the letterbox. Sent the whole place up. Dad knew. He knew everything. Always did.'

'Right.'

He was looking straight ahead, to a brightness on the horizon, a tiny, faraway, flashing light, the way to Veer. He just needed to get there. 'The mother's dead, Dad's a mess – can't do anything about them. But there's no need for anyone to think Helen was involved. It wasn't her.' Lies. Oh, Nayan.

———

Stepping out of Helen's house, his entire body felt benumbed, as though existence had become a denial of feeling, of emotion. The photo was still in his hand. Somehow he got to the bottom of the drive. He turned round. Helen was standing in the doorway, arms limp at her side, her face silent, empty, weightless. Nayan drove home, climbed the stairs. He stood in Veer's old room for a long time and then went into his own, laid down flat on his bed. The ceiling was white. Level. Without dimension or shape. Nothing held meaning. Nothing connected. Minutes passed. Years. Maybe centuries. His chest contracted with pain. He exhaled, and as his breath rushed out, it hauled up a few tears, balanced on his eyelids. He swatted them away, sat up. He kicked open the door to Pyara's room. He could feel how fierce his eyes looked, how deranged he must appear to his father, scrabbling for a shield, for the duvet. Nayan threw him against the wall; then onto the floor.

'You knew! You knew all along!' Nayan covered his own face with his arm, his elbow. 'You've always known what happened to them.'

He screamed, yanked Pyara up by the collar. He

couldn't think of anything else to say other than to repeat: 'You knew.'

This is what kept circling his mind, sitting on his bedroom floor, shoulder to the wall: his son's life had merited no compassion, no guilt on her part at all. While he and Deepti were left to scatter Veer's ashes into a sorry river one cool, September morning, Helen ran away, washed herself clean, and stepped easily on to the next event in her life. She'd told him the story of her time in London. The death of his son had meant so little to her. She even stood by and watched while Nayan took *her* son under his wing. Got him a car. His dream job. And she just stood by and watched. All the time knowing what she'd taken from him. He felt cheated, hoodwinked, his love mocked. When would Veer ever get his first car? His dream job? His girlfriend? It was as if Helen had stolen these dreams from Veer and given them to Brandon. Had tricked Nayan into giving them to Brandon. Veer had been killed several times over. How could *her* son be benefiting from the life she'd stolen from his. How could that be fair? How could it? He wanted to destroy them both.

Choking down rage, he found a Facebook post about Brandon's sacking at the school; copied and pasted the link into an empty email. Who could he forward it to? The restaurant, yes, of course. Local groups, too. All he had to do was press send. His finger poised, he began to see what would happen. The boy would lose his job. So what? How did that even compare? But he wouldn't only lose his job. He'd hide in his bedroom, afraid and suicidal. Nayan thought of Brandon's face. Of Veer's. Of Brandon's.

He didn't press send. He managed to wrench back from his fury and three days later he drove to Helen's and told her to leave town. She didn't protest.

'Pack your bags. Go away. Both of you. I never want to see you again.'

Perched on the settee's armrest, she nodded. 'I'll tell Brandon something.'

'I can't keep seeing you around town. I won't cope.'

'Yes.'

'Tell him the truth. That's the only way you'll get him to go with you.'

'Yes. Thank you. We'll go. I promise we'll go.'

He thought of his own mother; how he'd never managed to escape with her. 'Just go.'

From Helen's he drove to his childhood road and sat outside their shop's old corner. The door to the shop had been here. The ambulance parked just there. He had texts from Lisa-Marie that he'd left unread. And from Megha: *Just checking in. R said you're still ignoring his messages? Take care x.* That was from yesterday. He looked at the small garden, freshly mown, the space where Veer had lain. *Can I come round?*

Parked outside Megha's, he was as surprised as anyone to find himself there. But she'd said, hadn't she, that if he ever needed anything . . . So what did he need?

311

Showing him indoors, barefoot, she removed some papers from a chair – *Sure! I'm WFH. I'll pop the kettle on for a 'brew'* – then returned from the kitchen and put the mugs of coffee on a table by the fireplace. A child's table, made of red plastic.

'I keep buying bits of furniture,' she said. 'You not going to sit?'

For a long time he didn't speak, didn't sit either. And then: 'It's just a tough time. I'm sorry, I don't know what I'm doing here. I should go.'

'Stay, please. It *is* a tough time. Stay. Sit. Please.' Then: 'Has something happened?'

'I'm sorry. I don't know why I'm here,' he said again. 'I was such a shit to you. And you're being so kind. I'm sorry.'

'Work's been hellish,' she said. 'It's understandable you'd want to talk to someone. I'm always here.' She smiled. 'I'm not some monster. Just privileged. Allow a small difference.'

He smiled, too, but the effort of it triggered a sharper, sadder emotion that he needed to get away from. 'I should go.'

'*Has* something happened? Maybe I can come over tomorrow and check you're okay?'

But he was already in the corridor, fighting the door-latch.

'Let me?' she said, and his hands stilled, his shoulders fell.

'I just can't believe . . .' he began. 'Did my son's life mean nothing?'

'Of course it meant something. It meant everything. Who says it meant nothing?'

'The ones who killed him. It meant nothing to them.'

She made a desperate face, wondering if this was the right time to deliver difficult truths. She decided it was. 'That's the way the world is, Nayan. It's what I've been trying to tell you. The death of someone who isn't white means nothing to them. And it means nothing to them because in their eyes we're not fully human. In their eyes, our lives, our daughters' lives, our *sons'* lives, are worthless. And they always will be. This fight will never end.' She shrugged, only stating facts, but tears stood in her eyes. 'Tell me about him,' she said.

Nayan shook his head, but still: 'He was all my effort. All my strain. He was my son. My brightest star.'

It was that word – effort – that was hardest to bear: the effort of life, the work of it. Crying, Megha said, 'Do you feel him around you?'

He closed his eyes. 'If I'm out in the rain, the wind. In a storm. A big blue sky.'

Lisa-Marie rang and said Claudia couldn't get hold of Brandon – his phone was dead, he hadn't turned up to work. Was he with Nayan? she asked.

By then, Nayan already knew they'd gone. When he came down the stairs early that morning, the keys to Helen's house lay posted through his letterbox. For several weeks, he imagined them – mother and son – leaving in the middle of the night; until, buying a couple of frozen ready-meals, Margot at the post office said she'd not seen hide nor hair of that woman he sometimes *associated* with.

'Which woman?'

Margot frowned, because Nayan was being obtuse. 'The one whose stare could turn milk. Last I saw her was ages ago. Dawn. I was still opening up and in she swooped, for cigarettes. In an agitated kind of mood. Son shivering outside in the cold. He had a huge holdall, like they were going somewhere. He looked ever so upset.'

'And you've never seen her again?' I asked Nayan.

'No.'

'What about the house?'

'Sonia sorted it. She's the lawyer.'

It made a crooked kind of sense that he'd lie about Helen's role in the fire. Maybe he felt she'd been punished enough: banished, her son in freefall. Or maybe it is both simpler and more complicated than even that, and he loves her still. Spoiled hearts, indeed.

I'd learned so much on that final walk with Nayan and it was hard to credit that months hadn't passed, that it was still morning when he finished; or, better to say, when he'd told as much of his doctored version as he was willing to. Our heads were bowed, our hands behind our backs, under rucksacks, and we'd gone beyond the point from which most walkers return. The trail, an old railroad long paved over, curved round, hugging a rockface covered in lichen. Such intricate patterns the lichen made, little complex threadbare blankets.

We continued around the overhang, the grey jut of it like an elbow in my face, but as the crags drew back the scene suddenly, unexpectedly, opened onto vast measures of sunlit hills, one on top of the other. I felt awed and said something to that effect.

Nayan chuckled through his nose. 'It's such a white people activity. Hiking.'

'You seem pretty good at it.'

'Know thy enemy,' he said, tapping his nose. 'Destroy them from the inside.'

I gestured ahead. 'Shall we go on?'

He stayed put, hands stuffed in pockets, face lifted to the sun. His eyes were closed. Springtime warmth spotted his smiling face. He didn't say anything. I knew then that, as far as he was concerned, our regular walks, our long conversations, were over. He'd told me his story. I'd listened. He had no more use for me.

'What do you say?' I asked anyway.

'I say I'm done.' He was still basking, a leopard atop his rock. 'You're not one of us.'

He was so unforgiving in his judgement, so certain of his limits. I wondered if somewhere beyond all that green country, beyond thoughts of what was particular, what universal, there was a small meadow where people might simply meet, and see each other, and connect. Maybe this is what hurt the most; that I thought we had forged a connection. I said this to Nayan; he gave a single, low laugh.

'Does it ever get embarrassing, peddling that sentimental liberalism? Hoping your tears will put out the fire?' He opened his eyes. 'We're done. We're really, truly done.'

On the drive back, I asked him if he'd always blamed my parents, my mum; if he'd always known.

'Not until you got in touch. That's when I remembered who they were. I could never quite picture them before.' We braked at a school crossing; kids on their lunch break. 'And then I wanted you to know what your folks allowed. You're so high and mighty, Mr Writer. Maybe not so much now, eh?'

He dropped me off on the pavement with not even a bye. Inside, Mum and Dad's cases piled against the wall, each box labelled in Mum's hand, with its Indian-English gestures, the hoop-eared r's and pregnant s's. I felt an urge to laugh: moving into a bungalow! Such an ordinary, English, prosaic happening – it seemed ludicrous that it was an event in my life, sitting alongside Nayan's plight. Mum came downstairs holding the basil plant she coveted: 'You'll only kill it.' Dad, she said, had gone on ahead, was already unloading the first batch of boxes.

'His mum wanted to leave,' I began. 'You stopped her.'

I saw the guilt descend, a weight that forced her gaze down, to the floor. 'I had a feeling he . . . He must hate me so much.'

'He's probably good cause to hate a lot of things.'

Mum didn't tell me right then – she was strung out with the move – but when I pushed her the next day she explained that Muneet, Nayan's mother, had rung one afternoon. She said her bags were packed. That she couldn't, wouldn't, suffer it any more. She was taking the kids and leaving him. ('He'd come home the night

316

before worse than ever,' Mum said. 'All drunk and smelling of other women.' 'What did you do?' 'We went to her. I remember very clearly putting down the phone, taking my chunni from the back of the chair, and running out to your dad in my slippers. I remember the sound of my slippers very clearly.')

'I wanted you to hear it from me,' Muneet said, letting my mum in through the side entrance because she'd closed the shop. 'I don't want anyone thinking I've gone off with anyone else. I don't want anyone talking ill of me or my children. Tell people the truth, won't you? I can rely on you to do that?'

A battered tan suitcase of soft leather, creased as if marbled, its handle beribboned, stood by the kitchen table. It reminded Mum powerfully of India, of being a young girl waiting to board the UK-bound plane. At the doorway, the children looked on, kiddy backpacks looped in their hands. Nayan, not more than twelve, placed a reassuring arm around Sonia. He seemed determined to meet this challenge. Feeling sorry for them, Dad handed Nayan the Derby County scarf from around his neck.

'This isn't right,' he said. 'You should sit down with elders and sort it out.'

'I've had years of this, bhaji. Years.'

'Where's Pyara gone? He should know. You can't just take his kids. What kind of woman are you? Where's—'

Mum ushered Dad out the door, told him to wait in the car, he was making matters worse. Then she turned to Muneet. 'Think first. Where will you go? What will you do?' These commonplaces were all she could marshal.

She was still in shock. Who'd heard of a respectable girl from India, married with children, a Sikh no less, walking out in this way? On some level, Mum felt sure, Muneet was blackening all of Sikh womanhood.

'There's a refuge. We can stay there for a bit and then I'll work something out.'

'And what if you don't?' Mum asked gently. 'What will become of these children?'

'They'll be better without him,' Muneet said. 'We'll all be stronger without him.'

Mum did not understand this. 'So who will marry your daughter?' she asked. 'You'll never be able to show your face back home. How will your parents cope? I only want you to think it all through first, sister.'

Turning away, Muneet willed herself not to submit, not now, not when she was so close. 'We'll work it out. You don't understand. He's killing me.'

Overcome with pity, Mum knelt in front of Nayan and Sonia and peppered them with kisses. 'Poor things.' Sonia began crying. 'No, no,' Mum said, brushing the tears away with the end of her chunni. 'Everything's going to be fine. Don't you worry. You want to go back to your room and play? Yes?' Sonia nodded. Mum looked round, to Muneet. 'She can go back to her room? That's all she wants.'

Muneet stared at the tiled wall, fighting Mum's words, fighting them all, until an inward buckling forced down her head.

'I was so wrong, Sajjan,' Mum said, and let out a short, stifled cry.

'You didn't kill her, Mum. Or her grandchild. The fact she called you in the first place – sounds like she half-wanted to be talked out of it.'

'That poor little boy.' Mum covered her eyes. 'I'll never forget when I heard. The sun was up and I was at the chest freezer putting the magazines into the newspapers. I was thinking how you used to sit on the freezer watching me mop. Do you remember? And I was annoyed because your father should have prepared the papers already. And then he came and said that customers were talking about a fire at Pyara's and Muneet's shop. That they'd found bodies. When he said that I thought my heart had stopped. I was standing there still in my party clothes and it really felt like my heart had stopped.'

'I don't really remember. You never said much about it.'

Mum nodded, not listening. 'I felt guilty. For weeks I didn't know what to do with myself. I just kept taking food to Pyara. Praying for them. My mind wouldn't settle. I went for walks and got lost. I kept losing the shop money. Every day the float was wrong. I felt so guilty. I thought I was helping her, making her see sense. But there was no sense at all.' Another short, stifled cry.

———

Some months later, on a Saturday, I drove to The Beeches and waited in line at the desk. It was visiting hours and the place was overrun, the queue six deep. Still, efficiency triumphed, and soon enough I gave my name to the receptionist. When she couldn't find my details, I pulled the mask away from my mouth and explained that I'd made an appointment only the previous day.

'That'll be why, then,' she said crisply, tapping once more on the mouse, her eyes roving the monitor. A plastic screen separated us. *Hands. Face. Space.* 'You'll be on the non-regulars' list.'

I obeyed her directions, along sunnily wallpapered corridors, hand-sanitiser at every turn, and came to the Woodland Wing, and then Room 818. Two doors down a TV blared – some bushy-tailed cooking quiz entertaining residents in the communal lounge. I knocked once, cranked the handle and looked inside, stepped inside. Pyara, as the receptionist predicted, was sitting in the corner armchair ('Won't ever move, that one'), head hanging low and an oxygen tank intermittently beeping on the floor beside him. I stood by the bed, mere feet from him, and slipped my mask down so it hung like a hammock for my chin.

'Hi, Pyara. I'm a friend of Nayan's.' Nothing. He didn't stir. 'My name's Sajjan Dhanoa. We had Pine Lane Stores. Around the same time you had your shop. You knew my dad. Dhanoa,' I said again, with stress, and he raised his eyes, only his eyes. He didn't seem to like what he saw: his breathing shortened, shrilled, and it took him several panicked attempts to dock his hand onto the arm-rest, onto the ventilation mask, and then successfully fix it to his mouth. Becalmed, his gaze fell again to his lap and he forgot all about me.

Earlier that month, helping my dad rake leaves in their garden, I'd asked him why he'd never mentioned he was out with Pyara on the night of the fire – Dad's hand shot up, as if to silence me, hit me; as if, ever since that evening, he'd been alert to this moment. He didn't ask, so there was no need for me to explain that for half a year now I'd been running things over in my mind, seeing holes in the tapestry, asking Mum why she'd been at the party all night, what stopped Dad from picking her up; hadn't Pyara been waiting for a friend? Dad tried to move past, saying he'd left his gloves in the kitchen, and why the hell hadn't I called BT yet? By then, of course, his face had given so much away. I held him by the arm. 'Tell me, Dad. Please.'

He didn't know much, he said, though it became clear that, apart from raddled Pyara, Dad was the only one who knew everything. He knew, for instance, that when he left Mum at the party, she assumed he was heading back home; instead, he picked up Pyara from his shop, and from there they hit the pubs with Helen's mother. She and Pyara were over a year into their affair – a torrid, volatile entanglement – and once the pubs closed, they fetched up at her place, still drinking. ('Squalid,' Dad said to me, in Punjabi. 'Squalid, disgusting hovel. No place to bring up children. I hated being there.')

The night went on, the laughs ran dry, and Helen's mother needed to score. She was clutching her stomach, then the phone.

'He won't answer,' she cried. 'How can I score if he won't fucking answer?' She moved to the fridge, trembling in its light. The racks were empty save for a half-jar of jam.

'Let's go,' Dad said to Pyara, drunk and spread over the settee, his massive gold belt-buckle all askew. Dad lifted him – 'Up we get!' – and was carrying him to the door when Helen's mother charged and elbowed Pyara in the back.

'Fuckssake!' Pyara said, shocked into sobriety.

'Get me my booze. You skanked it all, you fuck.'

'Shit it out my arse, do I? We brought our fucking own.'

'Small-dicked shit.'

She went for his face, he for her neck. Dad cleaved them apart, said, 'Stop! Stop now!'

From the doorway, came a loud, fake cough – Helen: not yet eighteen, blonde and uninterested, in baggy camo pants and a black T, her wrist fully decked with friend-ship bracelets. 'How about you do this another time? It's gone two. I'm tryna sleep.'

'Get to bed,' her mother spat, eyes on Pyara. 'I'm sort-ing this cunt out.'

'We're just leaving,' Dad said. Cowed by Helen's dis-dain, he tried to sound like the adult in the room. 'Ready, Pyara? You need to sleep it off.'

'What about my booze? I'll torch your place if you go without getting me my booze.'

'I'll bring you some in the morning,' Dad said.

'I won't make it to the morning!'

Pyara, who hadn't spoken since Helen appeared, said: 'Fine. Tell your daughter to stick her shoes on. I'll give it to her.'

'No. I'll come,' Helen's mother said.

'Will you heck as like. I don't want you near me. Because you, my dear, are most violent,' he added, as if arriving at an elusive diagnosis.

What thoughts must Helen's mother have been wrestling with? But she was clean out of options and found a grotty fiver tucked beneath the wallpaper lining of a kitchen cupboard. She waved it at Pyara as if to prove a point, or beg a concession, then screwed the note into Helen's palm. 'No hanging about,' she said. 'A bottle of voddie and back quick-smart or I'll tan your hide, I will.'

'It's two in the fucking morning,' Helen said again, but without fervour, and she was already shoving feet into unlaced trainers, grabbing a packet of fags. She was used to this, to heading out to the shops for booze, to events of this sort.

'Give her a bag to carry it in, won't you?' her mother said to Pyara, as though it were this that separated her from the riff-raff.

In the car, Pyara sung along to the radio, drumming the glove box. Dad was driving, hating every second of this, frightened of how depraved his friend could be. Through the rear-view mirror he saw Helen blowing cigarette smoke out the window. It was a warm August night.

'Like this?' Pyara asked, meaning the music.

'Don't bother trying,' Helen said. 'I have nothing to offer you but my contempt.'

Pyara laughed: 'No flies on you. Do you know my two? Nayan and Sonia?'

'Again: fuck. You.'

There wasn't a light on anywhere when Dad applied the handbrake, killed the engine.

'It's late,' Pyara said to Dad. 'You go.'

'It's fine. I'll drop her back.' He wasn't going to leave her alone with him.

'She can walk.'

'I said it's fine.'

While they argued, Helen climbed out of the car, extinguished her cigarette on the tarmac and lit a second. One more year of school and then I'm off, she thought, as he fiddled the key about in the lock. All three stood in the small shop, with its dark aisles and big chest freezers. Near the back, the spirits were sealed behind two steel shutters.

'Well, go on, then,' she said, when Pyara failed to move, when he was only standing there humming, the radio still in his mind. She threw the fiver at his feet.

'Take a bit more than that.'

'Oh, sod off.'

'Just give her what she's come for,' Dad said.

'A bottle of vod,' Helen said.

Pyara shook his head, once, his face all pained, as if denying her was a source of deep and lasting regret. 'You need to come upstairs with me.'

'Pyara,' Dad cautioned.

'Muneet's not here. No one is.' To Helen: 'Come on.'

'Like fuck I am.'

'It's nothing I'm pretty sure you've not done a thousand times.'

'You've gone crazy,' Dad said. He leaned over the counter, fishing his hand around. 'Are they here? Where are the keys, Pyara?'

'Stop being a twat. My mum can't cope.'

'Me and her both.'

Dad took the fiver from the floor and held it to Helen. 'It's better if you just go. He's not going to listen.'

She could feel tears stinging, but she wasn't going to let them see her cry. She slapped aside the money. 'I want what I've fucking come for!'

Furious ('Why couldn't she see the danger she was in?'), Dad bundled her towards the door and out.

She heard Pyara laugh as the door closed on its hinged spring, and got to the end of the forecourt before stopping, spitting, dragging a sleeve across her eyes. She was angry at so much: at her mother, at him, at her life. On top of everything, she'd stupidly spurned her mother's fiver. Coming back for it, the door was locked and there was no one around. 'Cunt,' she muttered. Then she flinched – she'd forgotten the cigarette was still in her hand, burning. A long tail of ash. She blew on her fingers, thoughts on thoughts. No one else was in. Something of her mother's words flitted through the air, a silver flash: *I'll torch the place.* Helen bent down, lifted the letterbox and flicked the lit stick onto the doormat. A parting shot, nothing more. A small token of her rage. Suddenly cold, her pulse astounded, she hurried away, trainers soundless on the pavement.

Inside, Dad was berating Pyara on the stairs when an

acrid smell drew them back to the shop floor. The door-mat, burning a black circle into itself. Pyara snickered, stamping it out.

'Was that her?' Dad asked.

'Nasty little bitch,' Pyara replied, but already the idea began to grip him. To be shot of this place. This shop, this life that was a noose around his neck, around his freedom. Was this a way out? And the money – what he could do with that money. He looked to Dad. 'That could have burned the place down. Maybe it should have.'

'You're drunk,' Dad said, taking a heavy second to understand what he was driving at.

'I'll say she did it.'

'Then it'll all come out. What you were . . . trying to do with her. You'd be the one in jail.'

'Then I'll say I don't know who did it.'

('We were always speaking of getting rid of the shops,' Dad said. 'They're so hard to make work. But not like this. I mean, we joked about it. Planned it sometimes. But jokingly. Over beers. Only ever as a joke, you understand? But he was serious.')

'I'm doing it, Dhanoa Sahib,' Pyara said. 'It's now or never. I'll see you right – we've always seen each other right.'

('I left. All I wanted was to get out of there. But he – we – honestly, we had no idea they were upstairs. No idea at all.')

My dad gone, Pyara returned to the doormat and found her squashed cigarette. He got another of the same brand, lit it. He ensured some flammable material was

326

close at hand – crisp boxes, plastic wrapping – and checked, too, that he had a way of escaping once the fire took hold.

('And then later you gave her money to go away, right? From the shop. Mum said the till wasn't adding up.')

Yes, a week after, Dad met Helen under a tree in Ringwood Park. She was on her way back from school, in her uniform, and she was terrified. He'd never before or since seen anyone so terrified. Her tears, her shaking, none of it would stop. She hadn't meant to, she cried. He said no one was in. He said so. You heard him. Dad advised her to leave. To start again somewhere new.

'Why?' she asked.

'You'll never get over it if you stay here.'

'No. Why are you helping me? Why hasn't anyone told the police?'

'No one's coming out of this well if we go to the police. There's enough damage done.' Dad offered her a sum of money – a few thousand – to help her, if she left and if she promised to forever keep his name out of this.

('Did she keep her promise? When you heard the story?' Dad asked. 'She did,' I said. I wasn't able to look at Dad's face. I don't know if I ever will. 'That she did.')

The morning after the fire, all of them with their slanted knowledge, their anguish. Nayan at the hospital, numb with culpability, leaning against the wall. A nurse holds Deepti's hand. Helen hears the news while making breakfast and begins to shudder. Pyara sits weeping into a cushion, biting it. Across the estate, in my parents' shop, my dad tells my mother that apparently there's been a fire at Pyara's, and that Muneet and Veer are dead. There is a strange note of bafflement in his voice which my mother, still wearing party clothes, doesn't hear in her shock. And there I am, too, sixteen, upstairs in bed. My parents' voices are muffled, some sort of upset; but I close my eyes to return to sleep, wondering when my life will start.

My visiting hour up, and Pyara hadn't shifted from his armchair, in the corner of that room.

'So. I spoke to your Sonia not long back,' I said. 'I got the number of the lawyer she dealt with about the house.' I brought up an email on my phone and showed it to Pyara. 'And he, the house lawyer – you keeping up? – he eventually gave me Helen's address. As was. She's moved around a fair few times since, so believe you me, Pyara, it's taken some doing, but – look: her current address. Where she's now living.'

I left him, alone, slumped, drool in his stubble and the tank still beeping, and then I drove, for hours, the radio off. Along motorways and through towns I'd never heard of. Over roundabouts, toll booths, and down long, darkening lanes. As the sun dipped and the air coloured with evening plenitude, I felt myself wanting to reject Nayan's words, getting angry with them, with his insistence that our isolation prevails. No, I wanted to shout. Distance need not be maintained; it could be bridged.

It was late, very dark, when I pulled up outside the quiet house. Helen's was the ground-floor flat, where the curtains were shut but a light shone. Behind the curtains, a shape, a shadow, sat on the sofa. I will tell Nayan the truth, too; but I owed it to her first. This woman I'd never met, of whom I'd never even seen a photo. Will she look how I've imagined? Behave how I've described? There she was, in that house, sitting in silence, on a sofa, thinking. No: she was watching the news from a chair. No: reading a book. No: asleep after a long day. I didn't know. I'd never known. I was always just trying to connect, and connect despite what must remain unresolved. Nayan was right on that score: we can't know everything. We mustn't know everything. To see the pit of Nayan's pain, of Helen's, would be unbearable. I stepped out of my car and knocked on the door. A pause, then the shadow stood up. I heard footsteps, my heart. Yes, I mustn't know everything, but must strive to; this much felt true, as the door unlatched and began to open.